Shadows of Montsegùr

Shadows

of

Montsegùr

a novel

J. Sowards

Summerhouse Books

Printed in U.S.A. First Printing October 2017

ISBN: 978-0-9993174-0-2
Ebook ISBN: 978-0-9993174-1-9

Library of Congress Cataloging-in-Publication Data
2017912861
Sowards, J., 1953—
        Shadows of Montsegur
        ISBN: 978-0-9993174-0-2
        1. French Inquisition 2. Historical Fiction
        3. Religious Historical Fiction 4. Medieval Romance

dedication

Religious freedom is a flighty thing—
an elusive butterfly guaranteed in constitutions and bills of rights.
But if each man does not write it upon his own heart,
if it is not ingrained in each culture,
or re-taught to each new generation, it is of naught.

Man fears the misunderstood.

This novel is dedicated
to all those throughout history
who were persecuted for religion's sake—
victims of the Inquisitions, the Holocaust,
today's religious terrorism,
my own pioneer ancestors . . .

May we stop repeating the darkest parts of history.

Occitan and Other Foreign Words & Phrases

Adieu-deman. — See you tomorrow.
adieussiatz — greeting: hello, goodbye
antchoubi — exclamation of surprise
bonjour — hello
Cachafuoc — Yule log
chevalier — French knight
domaisèla — unmarried woman, title
dòna — married woman, title
fifille — little girl
Je suis vraiment desolé. — I am so sorry.
ma chérie — my dear girl
ma petite — my little one
ma soeur — my sister of the church, a nun
maire — mother
mémé — grandmother
mercés — thank you
mon père — my father, priest
Monsen — Mister
Óc — yes
Polit nadal e bona annada. — Merry Christmas and
  Happy New Year.

troubadour — musician who sings music he composes
jongleur — musician who sings the troubadours' music
Albigensian, Good Men — names for the Cathars

The spelling of *Montsegùr* is historically Occitan. In
French, the accent is *Montségur*.

1

*On the road from Toulouse to Lavelanet
in the Ariège Region of Midi-Pyrénées, France.
December 1243*

The pounding hooves of fast-approaching horses echoed through the gently rolling hills. Andreva whirled in her saddle. Three riders were swiftly overtaking their small traveling party. All wore white robes under their black cloaks. *Inquisitors!* Shining silver crosses rose and fell against their chests with each lunge of their mounts.

Her gloved hand grasped the throat of her hooded cloak. She drew it tight across her chest to hide the wimple of the nun's habit she'd worn for almost a year. She revered these powerful, holy men of the Church. But even though their tireless work in the name of God and papacy made them worthy of adoration, Andreva had always tended to shrink in their presence.

What had brought these priests so far from Toulouse, unguarded by soldiers? Andreva directed her horse alongside her traveling guardians, a middle-aged couple from Lavelanet, Gerrard and Dianne de Fortaner, and their guide Pons to better hear any conversation that might ensue.

"Hail, Fathers!" Pons' words steamed and churned in the cold morning air.

"We are in a hurry." The leader of the priests scarcely

reined his horse as the others rode ahead, slowing a few yards up the trail.

Andreva leaned forward. The holy man had spoken in her native *Óc* tongue. Her mount, made nervous by the other horse's close, impatient prancing, jerked backwards. She let go of her cape to grasp the reigns and regain her balance.

"Sister!"

With her wimple revealed, her own cross gleamed in the light from the distant winter sun. Of course the priest had noticed. Andreva lowered her eyes and forced a polite smile. "Yes, Your Reverence."

"It is unusual to find a nun on the road so far from any nunnery. Why do you travel here?"

Andreva drew a calming breath. "I lived as a novice at St. Sernin in Toulouse, but my grandmother now asks my company." She raised her eyes to his face, but lowered them again under his obvious scrutiny. "I have permission to go to the village of Lavelanet to see her."

The sudden summons from her mother's younger brother filled her with joy. Andreva had longed to return to her ancestral home from the day she arrived at the convent upon her parents' deaths ten lonely months before. She anticipated the coming reunion with her grandmother and uncle, her only remaining relatives.

The priest seemed satisfied with her response. He turned to Pons and the Fortaners. "We are members of the Dominican Order, in search of a criminal—a Catalan named Garcia—a tall, dark troubadour perhaps thirty years in age. We suspect he is headed to le château Montsegùr."

Montsegùr! Lavelanet is on the road to Montsegùr. Andreva bit her lip. Though she had lived her eighteen years of life in Toulouse, her family had resided in the Ariège region for over two hundred years, and now she was going there to live with her grandmother.

Pons glanced back down the trail. "We have met few on the trail today. Only French regiments on their way to the château."

Andreva's lip pulsed at the pressure from her teeth. The French were worse than mere criminals. That morning, arrogant soldiers had galloped past, driving their small party off the road. The sight of their royal blue flag with its gaudy gold *fleur de lys* had repulsed her. In the twelve years that had passed since the French took over the County of Toulouse, they were first hated as conquerors and now resented as intruders.

The priest leaned nearer the guide. "If you do see this Garcia, report his whereabouts to the authorities of the Church as soon as possible. You shall know him by a scar." He ran his hand down the right side of his face, close to the hairline.

"We shall keep alert."

The priest spoke no farewell, but impelled his horse to a gallop to rejoin his brethren. Soon they disappeared over the next hill.

Andreva shivered against the cold, and at the thought of perils that lay in this area she loved so well. These valleys held the only paths to her grandmother's home, but were they safe to travel with French soldiers, and now criminals, on the loose? And what of the war waged by her beloved Church against these heretics gathering at Montsegùr? She pulled her cloak closed again. How would living so close to the war against the Albigensians—often referred to as the Good Men—affect her and her family?

"Let us hurry on. We have lost time." With the Fortaners already some way up the road, Pons spoke only to Andreva. "My little nun, we must keep moving if we are to arrive at Avignonet-Lauragais before sunset. With so many interruptions and your childish dallying, our journey to Lavelanet will take four days instead of three. Keep alert, and stop daydreaming." He waved his hand for her to follow as he rode ahead.

Humph! Daydreaming? So what if I am always the last?

Yet he spoke truth. Often the others had waited for her to catch up. She slouched deeper into her hooded cloak, frowned at his chiding, and urged her light-colored palfrey forward. Pons and the kind-hearted couple who accompanied her probably considered this journey a means to an end, but to Andreva it was the first freedom in many months! How could she ignore the beautiful frozen landscape? How not to pause to breathe in the crisp, invigorating country air? Compared to the putrid smells of the city, this was heavenly.

They continued southward on the road the priests had taken. Andreva's thighs burned, her tailbone ached, and her shoulders throbbed. She wished the village of her mother's childhood was not so far from Toulouse. How could she endure the saddle another two days?

Dianne de Fortaner slowed her horse to ride beside Andreva. "I dread staying the night in Avignonet-Lauragais." These were the first words Andreva had heard her say since they'd left the abbey that morning. "I have no real fondness for the Inquisition, but the thought of staying in a village in which priests were murdered in their sleep? It sickens me!"

"Yes. I, I remember." *Too well.* She thought back to that morning in late May—a mere year-and-a-half ago—when the count's messenger pounded on the door, bringing the urgent news of the massacre to her father. How cold the stone floor was beneath her bare feet as she crossed it in her nightgown to hide behind a pillar to listen.

"It is not good news, Commander."

Her mother, clad in a dressing robe, clung to her husband's arm.

"A massacre at Avignonet-Lauragais." The messenger stood at attention. "Pierre-Roger de Mirepoix and his army from Montsegùr came by night to the castle and killed three Inquisitors and their tribunals in their sleep."

Andreva's heart had nearly strangled at that moment. Throughout her girlhood, she would sneak into the courtyard and listen in awe to knights boast of their courageous deeds and valor in battle. But she'd never before heard of an attack on holy men. Had the world tumbled into turmoil? She sank to the floor, shivering from fear and the cold, and stayed hidden in the shadows until the messenger departed.

She believed the attack at Avignonet-Lauragais had ultimately sent her parents to their graves, and almost ruined her life. But now, she had a second chance at happiness—she would soon live with her grandmother!

Dianne broke into her thoughts. "I hope these clouds do

not snow on us today. The weather is miserable enough."

Andreva gazed over snow-covered hills. "I have yearned these four years to see Lavelanet again, its hazelnut trees and river—the green fields in the summer."

Dianne sniffed. "All you will see now are snow covered fields and mountain tops."

But to Andreva, anticipation was warmth itself. "Ah, yes. But I will be happy to be home with my grandmother!"

"It is too bad she is unwell."

Unwell? What could she mean? "My uncle told me only to come." Andreva released the reins with one hand to fumble with her mitten. A moment later she extracted the cherished summons from her uncle, addressed to the abbey in her name. "I have his letter here." She shook it open, though the effort was unnecessary since she could recite the brief message from memory. "'Please come straightway to Lavelanet to care for your grandmother. Your uncle, Bostel de Lumbert.'" She turned to Dianne with wide eyes. "See? It does not say she is ill."

Before the older woman could respond, her husband approached. "Is it too cold for you, Sister Andreva?" Gerrard de Fortaner, a handsome man whose pointed goatee seemed to elongate his slender nose, slowed his mount to a walk alongside the two women. "I have a wrap for your shoulders, if you find it so." He turned to untie a bundle from the back of his saddle.

Flustered by his attention, but surely cold, Andreva glanced at Dianne whose thick wool cloak appeared amply warm. The woman nodded her permission to take the blanket. Andreva turned back to Gerrard. "Thank you, *Monsen*. I am grateful."

Gerrard de Fortaner smiled and rode ahead to rejoin Pons.

Andreva placed the letter back into her mitten and wrapped the soft, lye-scented cloth around her shoulders. Its warmth cocooned her body and draped her upper legs. "Your husband is a gentleman."

Dianne's smile weakened as she looked after Gerrard. "He can be charming at times."

Andreva hid her freezing nose beneath the blanket as they rode on. To her, Gerrard de Fortaner was the epitome of a gentleman. His speech was more refined than most men in Toulouse, certainly more so than any soldier in her father's regiment, and he was impeccably groomed.

Pons turned in his saddle. "Come ladies! Do not lag behind."

Dianne urged her horse into a trot, and Andreva kept up with her. "How long have you been a nun?"

"Ten months now, but I am still a novice. I have yet to take my vows." The abbess' counsel, to continue to wear the habit and remember that there could be no greater joy than a life devoted to Christ, still rang in her ears. She glanced sideways at her companion. Should she confess that despite these words, she was anxious to find another dress to replace her nun's frock?

Dianne's smile was kind. "You seem an unlikely nun. Was it your parents' wishes?"

Andreva hesitated. In the abbey, any talk of oneself was forbidden. But here Dianne had asked and there were no stone-faced nuns to discourage the discussion. "I was once betrothed," Andreva's cheeks warmed at the small revelation, "to a knight in my father's regiment."

Zavie's jubilant smile returned to her mind, framed by his dark, shoulder-length locks and delightful dimples. Her ribcage pricked at the memory. "My father chose him for me. He was one of the best men in his regiment. I only spoke to him on a few occasions." Dianne still smiled. "I gave him my flowered hair wreath to take into battle. He was very handsome, sitting upon his horse in full armor." A lump grew in Andreva's throat and she turned away. "He never came back..."

She blinked at the tears. Her grief was not entirely for Zavie—she had scarcely known him—but also for her brave father, her dear mother...and...and all her unfulfilled dreams. She still resented Count Raymond for sending her to the abbey against her will when she had requested to go to her grandmother at Lavelanet. But her letter there went too long unanswered and the count assumed Margaurite de

Lumbert had died. Knowing her parents' devotion to the Church, he bequeathed her father's modest fortune—and her dowry—to the abbey for her keep, with the understanding that she would always have a home there as a nun. Months passed with no *communiqué* from her family, so Andreva had no choice but to confine her hopes for a husband and children to the almost literal coffin of the close convent walls.

Dianne's eyes held sympathy. "Your father did not arrange another husband for you?"

Andreva chuckled. "My father had no time to think of himself, let alone choose a husband for me. Count Raymond had lost the Battle of Taillebourg and had the wrath of King Louis on his head."

"But surely after your father returned..."

It was too much to explain. "My parents died from the fever last January. My uncle and grandmother in Lavelanet are all the family I have left."

"Ah."

They topped a gentle rise and a cluster of homes surrounding a small church came into view. The two women prodded their horses to catch up to their impatient guide.

As they entered the village, Andreva's breath rippled in a small gasp. Soldiers wearing the Crusader's red cross huddled around an open fire. Though they were French, their resemblance to her father's regiment brought new pangs of homesickness.

Pons reined in his horse beneath a large oak tree. "We shall eat our noon meal here, but we must be quick about it. We have already lost too much time." He looked at Andreva before he slid to the ground and led his horse to a water trough.

Andreva frowned, but guided her animal to follow his. The sight of the men in uniform caused her to twist the reins between her fingers until they throbbed.

"Wait inside the church to get out of the cold." Pons surveyed the buildings along the road. "I shall find accommodations." He hurried away with Fortaner following.

Fifille! Fifille! The memory of soldiers shouting her pet

name echoed in Andreva's ears and she was once again a young girl, leaping into her father's arms and being lifted onto his shoulders as she waved to his army. *Fifille, our mascot!* How often the words had marched through her memory in the abbey, as vivid as in life. How often she had fought to counter their invasion, and yet could not. Her eyes dampened with emotion as she rehearsed her father's love and devotion.

Andreva gingerly slipped to the ground as the horse leaned into the trough.

Dianne came to stand beside her. "Are you unwell?"

Andreva swiped at her damp cheek. "It is nothing. I have sat on this horse for too long." She rubbed her backside and struggled to find her legs again to follow Dianne up the path and into the stone church. "What village is this, Dòna?" Andreva looked around the room, breathing in the chapel's homey, musty odor.

"It is Montgiscard." Dianne took a seat on a bench near the door.

Andreva padded across the bare floor to the statue of the Madonna. The hands were in an attitude of prayer as Mary stared serenely forward. Andreva dropped to her knees. She pled silently for strength to move past her loss, and the grace to come upon reminders of her parents and past life without descending into sorrow. She implored the Divine Virgin to strengthen her will to move forward with faith, rather than look back with regret.

As Andreva finished her devotion, footsteps echoed through the chapel.

"*Dòna! Ma Soeur!*"

Andreva turned to see who had spoken.

A plump, grinning woman with a soiled linen towel draped over one arm motioned. "Come! Come to the inn! We will prepare your refreshments." She led them into a house that smelled of burning timber and roasting meat.

More soldiers—all strangers—sat at a table at one end of the large room. None glanced up.

Monsen Fortaner stood as Dianne and Andreva entered and made their way to his table adjacent the hearth.

Windows in the wall on both sides of the glowing fireplace further brightened the room.

"Make yourselves comfortable." The hostess hovered over them. "Your wait shall be only moments."

Gerrard de Fortaner remained on his feet as Andreva removed her hood, mittens, and cloak, carefully leaving her uncle's note in place. He sat only when she did.

The laughter from the soldiers' table quieted. Uneasy, Andreva straightened her wimple and fingered the pewter crucifix that hung around her neck.

Dianne, still standing, removed her fur-lined cloak and warmed her hands by the fire. She turned toward Andreva with an amused smile. "Even ruffians are reverent in the presence of a nun."

Andreva's cheeks burned. She could not turn to look at the men.

Dianne's smile faded. "Because you have lived in the abbey, it shall take you no time to get used to the quiet of Lavelanet. Nothing happens there." Perhaps she recognized the exaggerated boredom in her tone. "It's a charming little place, actually; so remote and untouched by the outside world." A small frown played at the corners of her mouth as she seemed to rethink her words once again. "At least it was until the French Army and the Inquisition arrived."

Gerrard nodded toward the soldiers. "Yes, they pass through Lavelanet almost weekly. The place has lost a bit of its pristine innocence, I fear, and many villagers have gone to seek safety at Montsegùr, and elsewhere."

"Montsegùr? But that would mean they are…" Andreva could not say the words aloud: *Good Men. Cathars.* All who lived in the County of Toulouse knew that in the last century this heretic religion had spread rapidly throughout the Languedoc, and now was the target of the Catholic Inquisition.

Dianne placed her dainty hand on her husband's arm and chuckled softly. "Our situation is not so bleak. The peasants still enjoy themselves during festivals to the point of rowdiness." She turned to Andreva. "You ought to attend one sometime." She looked over Andreva's habit. "Or are you...allowed?"

"Óc, Dòna." Andreva couldn't help but smile. Her recent plea to Blessed Mary was for help to look forward. Surely, she would accompany Uncle Bostel and her grandmother on such outings. "I would enjoy a village festival very much." In fact, she had dreamed of such festivals all her life.

Even in Toulouse, Andreva had seldom associated with villagers, aside from her own servants. Her mother feared the outside world and kept her daughter closed off from it. She scolded Andreva when she'd sneak out into the courtyard to visit with the soldiers. Andreva had resorted to sitting with her embroidery at a second story window to watch people come and go, carrying baskets, pushing their rickety carts, and leading all manner of farm animals. Often, they stopped to chat with one another at the well. To her delight, some were boisterous enough to be heard from her open window. In this way Andreva not only learned who was who, she followed who married whom, who fell sick, and who died. Still, she longed to be part of it all. Perhaps now, living in Lavelanet, she would no longer need to eavesdrop from windows to take part in village life.

Dianne at last settled on a stool and took one of Andreva's hands in her warmer ones. "Then you have a treat awaiting you! The next celebration is the Winter Festival in January." Her face clouded. "Well, we might still hold it, if anyone remains in the village then." Dianne's eyes met her husband's briefly.

Gerrard leaned closer to Andreva. "As I said before, the war being so close to the village has driven many away. For safety."

"I understand." *Do I understand?* How close was this war? Surely the fighting would not affect her family. Looking for trouble ahead was as bad as lingering upon it in the past. She concentrated instead upon memories of sitting in her grandmother's kitchen: its warmth and the seductive smells of bread baking and stew warming on the fire. She remembered a woman brimming with love and infectious cheer, singing jovially off-key. She was everything a young girl needed in a grandmother. The recollections caused the corners of Andreva's mouth to lift.

Not ones to stay subdued for long, the soldiers soon boomed with boisterous laughter. Andreva caught a few words.

"Le château Montsegùr!" One man held up his wine goblet.

Andreva didn't understand the French oath that followed, but the answering cheers made her skin crawl. She didn't relax until a few moments later when the soldiers stood and filed out to the street. A frigid wind whirled into the room at their passing. When the door banged shut after the last man, the room fell silent.

In another moment, a tall man approached their table, carrying cups, troughs, and knives. As he set a meat knife in front of Andreva, the exaggerated yellow cross sewn onto his sleeve nearly brushed her wimple. She caught her breath.

Heretic!—a repentant.

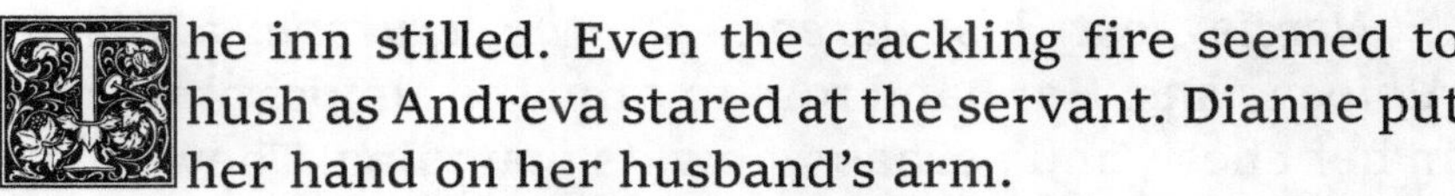

The inn stilled. Even the crackling fire seemed to hush as Andreva stared at the servant. Dianne put her hand on her husband's arm.

Fortaner's eyes rose from their servant's sleeve and the yellow heretic's cross it bore, to the man's drawn face. He jumped to his feet, and spoke in a hoarse whisper. "Narcis, my old friend! Why..."

Narcis turned away. He walked to the soldiers' now-deserted table, picked up a bottle of ale, and brought it back. As he poured the liquid into Dianne's cup, and then her own, Andreva could not remove her gaze from the yellow cross. Heretics who chose to denounce their false religion before Church authorities escaped extermination but must by mandate wear the cross, at least until they had proved themselves loyal.

Narcis avoided looking at Gerrard, who had sunk back into his seat. He glanced repeatedly at Andreva, as if each word spoken in the presence of a nun carried double weight. His Adam's apple bobbed as he swallowed. He leaned close to pour Gerrard's ale. "I *had* to denounce. My wife and children's safety mean everything to me!" His eyes met those of his friend's, then darted to Andreva and back to Gerrard. "The Inquisitors left my parents in their deplorable dungeon for weeks before burning them alive." He glared at Andreva. "Even upon my repentance, the Church claimed our home and lands, and confiscated our belongings."

Andreva shrank back in fear. Would this heretic take his anger out on her?

Fortaner leaned forward. "Watch your tone, Narcis. Soeur Andreva had nothing to do with this."

Narcis set the bottle on the table and left the room. Gerrard and Dianne exchanged glances, then fell into pensive silence.

Andreva looked from one to the other. Despite Gerrard's words, she felt the weight of her habit. She was not in her heart a representative of the Church, nor was she without sympathy for this heretic who had at least seen the error of his beliefs.

Narcis lost his parents in the crusade against the Albigensians. Her hand rose to calm the almost physical pain in her chest, and perhaps slow its pounding. They had much in common. She too had lost her parents to the Albigensian Crusade, if indirectly. The burden to carry out King Louis' orders to exterminate the Good Men had surely brought about her father's demise.

Andreva gazed toward the fire, seeing only her thoughts. *How would it be to wear a label so that all could see your shame?* The Good Men, she had heard, did not wear crucifixes, even abhorred them as a symbol of the barbaric cross upon which Jesus died. What more appropriate penalty, then, could the Inquisitors have chosen? Thank heaven Narcis had come to his senses and forsaken the heretics' evil teachings!

A stout man entered from the kitchen, dispelling dreariness with his smile and the large platter he carried, piled high with roasted chicken. He placed it on their table. The smell set Andreva's mouth to watering.

"Eat! Eat!" The man rubbed his chubby palms together. "Eat your fill. There is more in the kitchen." As the servant departed, Fortaner wasted no time sinking his knife into the chicken.

Dianne cut a more modest portion of meat and placed it on her trough. Looking kindly at Andreva, she cut a piece to serve to her. "My dear Andreva, I remember your mother, Sanche, before she..." Dianne's eyelids fluttered. "...married.

I had come to Lavelanet a year or two earlier, as a bride." She spared her husband not the slightest glance. "Sanche had your lovely coloring: blue-eyed and fair, with golden hair. Of course, I cannot see beneath your wimple, but I assume your hair is as golden as hers."

"Not as vibrant." Andreva had always wished for beautiful hair like her mother's, but her own waist-length tresses were a duller blonde. She sighed. Little would it matter if she returned to the abbey to take her vows. Nuns ceremoniously cut their hair to show humility and willingness to forsake the world.

Andreva sliced off a small piece of chicken, placed it in her mouth, and savored its rich flavor. *Mmm!* Convent food was usually filling, but rarely this savory.

"I am disappointed by the deterioration of Lavelanet," Dianne continued. "I hear it was once very charming, but now the village wall is mostly toppled, and the Count of Foix never rebuilt his summer home, Castelsarrasin, after Simon de Montfort destroyed it."

"I imagine the count's château was beautiful!" Andreva looked forward to viewing the village from atop the ruins, and longed to walk along the lazy Touyre River. "Please tell me, do the ducks still nest by the stream?"

"They do, but they have flown south for the winter."

"Of course. They will return in the spring." Would she still live in Lavelanet then? "My mother, upon the first blossom in the garden, always said, 'With spring comes new hope.' I have come to believe it. I hope to stay in the village forever!"

Still saddle sore, Andreva found it hard to walk as they left the inn. She feared to think how challenging the next two days might prove.

Pons stood waiting with the horses. "We must be on our way." He gestured to a monk who sat on a small horse nearby. "This is Friar David. He shall accompany us to Avignonet-Lauragais."

The newcomer appeared middle-aged, and was so large Andreva pitied his small mount. The man's tonsured, graying tresses were combed forward to hide, unsuccessfully, a large mole on his temple from which sprouted several black hairs. Despite the churchman's unappealing appearance, Andreva welcomed another traveler in their small group, and hoped that having a friar along would grant an even greater measure of God's protection.

The friar struggled to find comfort upon his mount. "I have fulfilled my stewardship here in Montgiscard."

Was Narcis his stewardship? Those who wore the yellow cross were accountable to the Church for several years. Out of love and a Christian desire to save the heretic's soul, the Church watched repentants closely lest they lapse. Had this friar come to give Narcis encouragement to continue his righteous path?

Pons peered up at the noon sun. "We should reach the village before sunset." His gaze fell upon Andreva. "If we have no more delays."

Andreva squirmed with guilt, but stepped forward when the guide motioned for her.

"This is Soeur Andreva from St. Sernin in Toulouse." Pons was at least respectful of her station, if not herself. He motioned toward the couple. "And this is Gerrard de Fortaner and his wife, whose home is in Lavelanet."

The friar studied the couple. "The village of weavers."

Dianne immediately turned toward her horse.

Pons helped her mount, and then assisted Andreva.

"Óc, weavers." Fortaner climbed onto his horse. "We have been in Toulouse trading the textiles of the villagers." His chest puffed in pride. "We return, fortunately, at the time Soeur Andreva needed companionship to Lavelanet."

The trail took them steadily uphill. They rode pleasantly for a time along a creek that flowed past bare orchards, dormant fields, and comely thatched cottages tightly shuttered against the cold. Nothing stirred but the smoke that billowed from each hearth's crude outlet. Andreva shivered in the heatless afternoon sun and missed the inn's blazing fire.

"You fall behind again, Soeur Andreva!" Pons' call pulled her from the landscape's bucolic spell. She hurried her horse forward.

Andreva concentrated on keeping up and shifting position

as often as possible to relieve her aching muscles, so she paid little attention to the men's conversation throughout the next hour.

The newcomer's loud voice broke her reverie. "The Good Men in le château Montsegùr will lose. They have somehow acquired a small militia of sympathetic knights to defend them, and yet what hope do they have to defeat the growing army that surrounds the mountain?"

"None." Fortaner inclined his head. "More regiments pass through Lavelanet almost daily. It is futile to fight King Louis' army, let alone the Church."

Dianne's jaw muscles tightened when she lifted her chin. Did she too feel uncomfortable with heretics gathered so near Lavelanet?

"The Good Men are known by many names." Friar David glanced over as if to assure himself that Andreva listened. "Albigensian, Christians—which they are anything but." He pulled a handkerchief from beneath his cape and blew his nose into it, and then used it to wipe his face. When he finished, he edged his horse a little nearer Andreva's. Clearly, he relished this opportunity to instruct and enlighten a novice. "Years ago, the Church sent Dominicans to convert them, but the Good Men would have none of it. They hold fast to their outlandish theology. Their *Perfecti*—those who have taken their *consolamentum,* or highest sacrament—claim to have secured their place in heaven. This consolamentum is often administered on a deathbed, and the recipient will then refrain from food to assure death comes quickly and without sin."

Andreva frowned. One could not hope for salvation without the sanction of priests from the Church.

Friar David sniveled into his handkerchief again. "Their bishops claim authority traceable back to Christ." He snorted. "Nonsense! God does not recognize heretical ordinations. Anyone who denounces the pope will be punished."

Dianne stayed silent no longer. "It is inhumane the way the Good Men are treated. The Inquisitors' methods are appalling. They use torture to force false confessions."

"Dòna!" Friar David's lips tightened. "A woman should not speak her thoughts openly. Show respect and hold your tongue."

Dianne's dainty nostrils flared, and she urged her horse ahead of the rest. Andreva's hands froze upon the reins. She glanced at Fortaner, expecting him to defend or comfort his wife, but he did not glance her way.

Friar David turned again to Andreva. "These are the Last Days. It is the Church's God-given charge to eradicate all heresy. John the Apostle tells us in the Book of Revelation that after one thousand years, Satan shall be loosed from his prison to go forth to deceive the nations. The thousand years is long past. The Good Men's religion emerged as an entity about three hundred years ago, and has deceived too many. Can you not see? The Good Men and their religion *are* the Antichrist."

Andreva felt bile rise in her throat.

"Dominicans do not shed blood." The friar raised his chin. "As you know, only *burning* destroys sin and obliterates the possibility of Christian burial. That is why it is necessary, even after a heretic is long dead and buried, to exhume the body and burn what remains. A heretic should not lie in the tomb as would a sinless saint."

If only this man would stop talking! His lectures, while surely true, grew more unbearable by the moment. Still, Andreva stayed with the men, not daring to drop behind for fear of Pons' wrath, nor catch up to Dianne and show disrespect to the friar while he was speaking. Ten months in the abbey had taught her to be quiet and courteous in the presence of a man of God.

Friar David became more animated. "They are dualists, these heretics, believing in a god of good and a god of bad." He held up one hand. "Their good god is god of all that is immaterial, such as light and men's souls." He held out the other hand though it still held the reins. "Their bad god is god of all material things—the world and everything in it. They do not believe in the Old Testament, for they say it was the evil god who cast Adam and Eve from the garden, who flooded the earth in the days of Noah, and punished the

Israelites." He looked at Andreva as if to gauge her reaction.

Unable to immediately decide what expression he sought, Andreva tried to appear as if in sober contemplation.

Friar David pulled closer still. "On the other hand, the New Testament teaches of the good god who taught of spiritual things such as love and living together peacefully." Friar David chuckled and lowered his voice as if revealing a secret. "And they are immoral, too."

Although Dianne rode several feet ahead, her ears must have been sharp because she huffed indignantly. Pons, who still led, acted as if he hadn't heard.

"Please, *mon père.*" Gerrard Fortaner's voice was apologetic. "We are in the presence of ladies, and one is a sister of the Church."

Andreva glanced at the friar. If only he would change the subject or, better yet, fall silent.

Friar David turned to Monsen Fortaner. "This god of bad contrives to capture souls and imprison them in human bodies through the process of," he whispered so loudly that even Pons could have heard him, "conception."

Andreva's cheeks burned in the chill as the friar's laughter danced off the hills and across the valley. Enough! She urged her horse into a brisk gallop to ride beside Pons.

Heretics. Montsegùr. What did a holy war between the Church and the Good Men mean to her? She held fast to her belief in the holy Catholic Church and gave no heed to heretical preaching. Even if she must live now in their midst, Andreva believed she could be confident in her integrity. Never would she dream of turning her back on the faith of her forefathers.

Andreva's paternal grandfather had ridden with Papal Legate Arnaud-Amaury in 1209, and been present in Béziers on the day of butchery that had begun the Albigensian eradication. When asked by the commanders of his legions how to distinguish between heretics to slay and Catholics to spare, their leader had ordered, "Kill them all! God will know His own." In the end, 20,000 people died that day—more Catholics than Cathars—in the name of God, law, and justice.

Her grandfather had recounted the story with fervor mixed with furtive tears while her mother left the room weeping. Whenever the crusade against the Albigensian heretics was mentioned in their home, her mother left the room, taking Andreva with her. When they heard that a burning of heretics would take place in their city, Sanche drew the drapes and forbade Andreva near them or the doors.

Her mother's careful shelter proved for naught once Andreva entered the abbey. Although few were the times she left its hallowed walls, one day a visiting Inquisitor mandated that the nunnery view the burning of the *heretiques* for the sisters' "education." For weeks after, Andreva could not sleep. Each time she closed her eyes and stilled her mind, images of the victims' horror appeared. Again and again she heard their piteous cries and smelled the burning of their flesh.

Oh, Mémé! Dragging her thoughts away from heretics, Andreva took a deep breath and studiously ignored the men with whom she rode. She brought up every memory she could of the lovely woman who awaited her—she of the jolly laugh and warm, welcoming arms. Andreva could not wait to be with Mémé and Marta, her maid, while they puttered between table and hearth, endlessly preparing good things to eat.

A light snow began to fall before they entered Avignonet-Lauragais. Andreva gazed upon the imposing castle as they passed. Uneasiness grew within her. Not two years had passed since three Inquisitors were murdered within those high walls. She thought again of that morning in late May when the count's messenger pounded on the door, bringing urgent news of the massacre to her father.

Her father had paced the floor upon the departure of the messenger, ranting about how this foolish act sabotaged any hope the Good Men might have had to live in peace.

Her mother's face grew whiter than her gown. "You know what this means! Count Raymond shall have to make good his promise to exterminate the Good Men." She clasped her husband's arm as if to save him from some great peril. "It means you must lead his army. It means—" Overcome, she at last fled the room in tears.

Andreva *didn't* know what it meant. She knew Count Raymond had thus far avoided the Albigensian Crusade, and that King Louis, pressured by the pope to rid his lands of the heretic religion, had demanded Count Raymond do the job. Surely now the order must be carried out, and by whom else but her father? For the first time in her life, war was no longer the glory of battles won in far off lands—it was the massacre of neighbors.

The dread was too much. Her father's health failed, and he succumbed to the fever that swept through the city the following winter. The same illness claimed her mother only weeks later, leaving Andreva alone in Toulouse.

So alone.

The traveling party arrived at the inn at nightfall. Grateful for the respite from sitting on a horse, Andreva slept solidly. In the morning, and without the friar, she, Pons, and the Fortaners continued on through the hills toward Lavelanet.

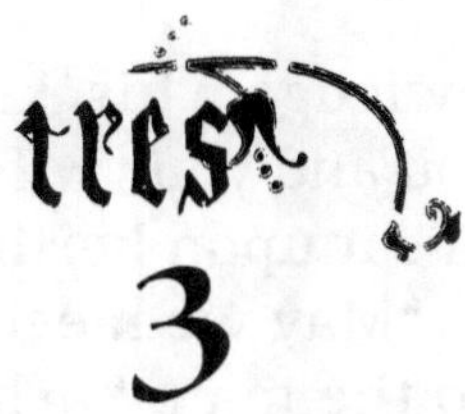

3

ndreva!" A towering, grinning man swung her off her horse and into a twirl. When at last he returned her to her own unsteady feet, he took a step back and regarded her from head to toe. "I had not anticipated seeing you as a nun."

Andreva laughed as she found her balance on the blessed Lavelanet soil. "But Uncle, I have not yet taken the vows. The sisters suggested I travel as a nun for safety." She straightened the bulky material of her habit as best she could. "Also, I own nothing but this and an identical one in my satchel."

"All the better." Bostel rubbed his square jaw and glanced toward the soldiers who loitered beneath a spreading oak on Lavelanet's commons. "The sisters gave wise counsel. These are perilous times."

"Because of the siege at Montsegùr?"

Bostel's gaze moved toward the mountains. "Exactly. The French soldiers give deference to very few." His eyes returned to her crucifix. "Perhaps they will respect a nun." He placed his rough hands fondly upon her shoulders and held her away as if to see her better. "Why, you are not the funny-faced little Andreva I remember from my visit to Toulouse last Christmas. How you have grown—and grown so pretty."

"It was two Christmases ago!" Two years since he had come to Toulouse and lavished her with attention. Yet she grinned, willing to forgive his neglect to bask in the warmth of the immediate ease between them. `

Gerrard de Fortaner stepped forward. "What a delightful niece you have. We owe her thanks for making our trip more pleasant."

Andreva acknowledged his kind words with a curtsy. "Many thanks to you and your wife, Monsen." She smiled up at Dianne who still sat upon her horse. "Farewell, Dòna."

Dianne nodded. "May we meet again."

Bostel bowed to the man. "I shall come to your home to finalize the arrangements we discussed."

Fortaner bowed. "Until then." Re-mounting, he and Dianne followed the always-hurried Pons, who now led Andreva's horse.

She looked around. "Where is Mémé?"

"Your grandméré awaits you at home." Bostel frowned as he picked up her small bag. "She has been bedridden too long, and is very weak." He frowned at Andreva's distress and brushed the tip of her nose. "But her pluck is strong. Be assured, she will keep you running all the day long."

"Bedridden?" Andreva's spirits plummeted. "Your letter did not reveal Mémé's ill health."

"I am sorry. I regret, too, that it took me so long to write. Matters...interceded. There has been much trouble here. To tell the truth, Maire and I knew your safety was more assured at the abbey." He took her elbow in his free hand and cast her a pleading look for understanding, and perhaps forgiveness. "I yearned to come to you when I heard of my sister's death, but I could not leave Maire, not in her failing condition, and not with...events as they are. It was a blessing to know the sisters took you in."

Andreva hid the pain of months of disappointment behind a forced smile. She felt only compassion now for her widowed uncle. He, too, had known great sorrow at the passing of his dear wife, Aimée. "At least now I know why Mémé never answered my letter. I do look forward to seeing her."

Two soldiers on horseback appeared to study Bostel as they passed. Her uncle stiffened almost imperceptibly, but turned his back to them and pulled Andreva forward. "We shall go to your mémé straightway. Come, let us hurry. As you remember, the house is just across the bridge."

But Andreva could not dismiss the soldiers as easily as he apparently had. She turned to look after the two men, who had stopped farther up the road to eye the passersby. "What are they doing?"

"They suspect everyone of anything." He released her elbow, offering his arm instead. "Act naturally."

Why would she act otherwise? Before Andreva could ask, he patted her hand. "Remember, these are risky times, but all will be well with you."

As they crossed the bridge, thoughts of the soldiers fled Andreva's mind in the sheer joy of the moment. She held tight to Bostel's arm and relished his nearness. "I am so happy to be in Lavelanet again!" Andreva breathed deeply of the mountain-scented air and gazed toward the snow-tipped peaks. "The landscape is beautiful. We have no mountains in Toulouse." She gazed up into her uncle's handsome face. "I so look forward to being with you and Mémé for Christmas and the Twelve Days."

To her dismay, Bostel fell silent and slowed. He seemed intent on an inspection of each stone house that lined the narrow street, most sharing common walls. Finally, he cleared his throat. "I must reveal the reason I sent for you." He stopped, set her bag on the ground, and turned Andreva to face him. "I am leaving Lavelanet."

The words took away her breath. "When?"

"As soon as you are settled. I asked you to come so that you might care for Maire in my absence." He squeezed her hands. "I regret that I took you from the comfort of the abbey."

"Oh, no! I wanted to come. I waited for your letter—for any word from Mémé—for so long. I would rather have come to you at once than to the abbey."

His smile conveyed an apology. "I trust you were treated

well."

"Óc." Andreva pushed away her hurt. "Of course. Now please tell me why you must leave. Where will you go?"

Bostel pulled Andreva out of the path of a cart that had just crossed the bridge. "Jaques Montré! My good friend."

The man reined the horse and tipped his straw hat to Andreva when Bostel introduced them. He was dark-haired and bearded, probably in his mid-twenties, with deep set, intriguing blue eyes. The heavy cloak he wore did not hide the well-developed muscles beneath it.

Finding herself staring, Andreva dropped her gaze.

"Bostel! What brings you out today?"

The stranger's voice was deep and soothing. She took another peek at him.

"Andreva, my niece, has come to care for my maire in my absence. She arrived this morning from the convent in Toulouse."

"*Bonjour,* Ma Soeur."

Andreva curtsied. "*Bon dia,* Monsen." Once again, she noticed his eyes—honest eyes.

"Ah, Bostel, will you be away long?"

"Óc, on business in Toulouse. It shall take two months, or longer. I will stay with a cousin."

Andreva shot him a questioning glance, which he ignored.

"Gerrard de Fortaner will manage my lands." Bostel scratched his strong jaw in thought. "My friend, could you also look in on Maire and Andreva from time to time?"

Jaques' eyes met Andreva's, sending unfamiliar prickles dancing down her spine. She lowered her lashes.

"I would be honored," Jaques said. "I return in a few days, and will visit then." He removed his hat. "Is that agreeable, Ma Soeur?"

"Óc." Her smile came easily.

"Until then." Jaques replaced his hat and urged his animal up the road.

As they walked on, Andreva stole a glance back at the handsome stranger.

Bostel took her hand. "You will get a better look when he comes to visit." He laughed heartily. "Remember, you are a nun."

Andreva stiffened. "I have not taken vows."

"Ah. Well, Jaques Montré is one of the best men I know. Any girl might be wise to give up the nunnery for such as he."

"Uncle! He is a stranger."

"Not to me. I would entrust him with my most valuable treasures." He patted her hand. "And he is one of the best farmers in all the valley."

"Farmer?" Andreva frowned.

"Yes. A *free* man from Gascony."

A *farmer*. Montré was of a lower class than a commander's daughter. Her lips pursed in thought. Her father had always said she would marry nobility. Perhaps the farmer was not as handsome as she first thought.

She removed her hand from Bostel's to again link her arm through his and lean into his side. "Uncle, I did not know you have family in Toulouse. A cousin of yours would be mine too, would he not? And I have been so alone in Toulouse all these months."

"He is a relative of my deceased wife." Bostel's eyes could not hide his concern as he looked down into hers. His next words were low, and earnest. "Andreva, you must, for your protection, tell everyone you encounter that I am visiting a cousin in Toulouse. Say I shall stay several weeks. It is for your safety."

She might have asked what he meant about "your protection" if "several weeks" had not brought such dismay. It was much too long a time. How would she and her grandmother manage?

Could he read her thoughts? "I have made arrangements with Monsen Fortaner to bring you housekeeping money each fortnight."

Hearing she would again see the pleasant gentleman and his genteel wife pleased her. Also, there would be the capable maid Marta upon whom to rely. She relaxed.

But Bostel had not finished his instruction. "Continue to wear your nun's frock. Make it known to everyone that you have lived at the abbey for a year, and are here only to care for Maire in my absence."

"But—"

He hushed her. "I could bear no harm to come to you. Trust me, Andreva. It is for your good."

She bit her lip. His directive made no sense. She raised her face to protest, but seeing the earnest expression he bore, held her tongue. Once he was gone, she could make her own decision about her dress. What difference would it make? But if it would worry him, he need not know. Andreva nodded.

Bostel was clearly relieved. "I know Jaques will visit when he can, and Raoul will come every other day. Depend on them in time of need."

"Who is Raoul?"

"A young man who lives next door. I have hired him to do the heavy labor." He smiled at last. "He is a budding troubadour, so humor him."

Andreva had scarcely heard her uncle's last words. She'd recognized the house that stood at the end of the road, somewhat apart from the others. Beige stone walls and a large wooden door—the same door she'd once found too heavy to budge—awakened recollections of previous visits. Its whitewashed second story gleamed in the sunlight under the clay-tiled roof. It was still, she saw, one of the finest in the village. She released Bostel's arm. He chuckled as he hurried to keep pace.

Moments later, Bostel pushed open the door. "Maire! Your lovely Andreva is here!"

Andreva stepped inside and felt as if she had come home. Across the large room, embers glowed in a fireplace beside a brick oven. Nearby, a cellar door hid the stairs she'd feared to descend as a child. A large cupboard stood next to its doorway, buckets, tubs, and baskets stacked beside it. Tapestries hung on two walls, and across the room, a wide staircase led to an upper bedroom.

Andreva ran her hand along the wooden table that filled half the room. It still bore the nick she had inflicted upon it years before, when wrestling with a knife and an artichoke. She traced the mark. "There is comfort knowing some things never change." But something was amiss. "Where is Marta?"

Bostel was slow to answer as he hung his hat upon a peg in the wall beside the door. "She passed away last summer, and Maire will not let me replace her."

"Andreva? Is that you?" The small voice came from the chamber room.

"Mémé!" Andreva hurried to an open door. Her eyes were slow to adjust to the dim room, lit only by slivers of sunlight filtered through seams in the shutters. Upon a canopy bed, a small form struggled to raise itself up beneath the coverings.

"Mémé!" Andreva flew to her side to embrace her.

Mémé cupped her granddaughter's face in her hands. Her teary, steel-gray eyes gazed into Andreva's own. "*Ma chérie!* You have come home!"

"Óc, Mémé. I would have come sooner if I'd known you wanted me—much sooner."

quatre
4

s evening fell, Andreva was still at Mémé's side, listening to her reminisce about her mother's youth, something of which Sanche had rarely spoken. Mémé's stories filled an aching void in Andreva's heart. She had come home at last.

Only Bostel's impending departure marred her happiness. He'd promised to stay two days to help her settle in, claiming that was all he could spare.

While Mémé slept the next morning, Bostel invited Andreva to accompany him to the marketplace. She wore the only dress she had, her nun's habit, with the convent cross of St. Sernin around her neck.

Andreva looked along the commons, surprised to see that so few tables now made up the market, compared to her previous visits.

Again, her uncle read her mind. "Many have left the village for Montsegùr. Lavelanet feels somewhat abandoned since the Inquisition now lurks in the Ariège."

Good Men lived in Lavelanet? Might she deal with them unawares? Intrigued, Andreva looked over the people who had come to trade. No one stood out as unusual. Andreva reassured herself that a good number of villagers remained, and she and Mémé would not be alone.

Bostel introduced her to the vendors who sold the many things she might need. Several were eager to sell their wares, but Bostel bought only loaves of bread.

"That is a lot of bread, Uncle." Andreva counted his eight loaves. "I had no idea you were so fond of it. How can we possibly eat that much before it is devoured by mold?"

After paying the vendor, Bostel handed two loaves to Andreva. "These are for you and Mémé. Follow me."

Andreva hurried to keep up as he led her down narrow streets to a rundown stone house. She regarded it critically. Its shutters needed repair, as did the roof. But the more she examined the dwelling, the more apparent it became that once it had been beautiful. The trim along the eaves was skillfully carved, and above the doorway, a small round window with its beautiful stained glass intact, glowed like a jewel in the morning sun.

"Bonjour!" Bostel pushed aside the cowhide that covered the doorway and entered.

Andreva timidly followed. Her eyes grew accustomed to the dim room, lit by the window and cracks in the ceiling. In the corner, a hearth of carved stone glowed with embers—another testament to the home's grander past.

Andreva gathered her cloak close, lest it disturb the dust clinging about.

Bostel kept up his good humor. "Good day, Dòna Gisèla, Dòna Jocelyne!"

A small form sat up in a bed and spoke in no more than a whisper. "You came!" Even in the near-dark, the wrinkled creature's eyes shone.

When another slight figure leaned forward in a nearby chair, Andreva jumped back in surprise. This woman was as frail as her companion. "Our prince has come! Bonjour, Bostel!"

"I brought my niece." Bostel motioned toward Andreva.

They struggled to see her better. "She is a nun." Jocelyn's face glowed in wonder.

Bostel seemed to expect her to speak for herself. "I, I am a novice, but have come to stay with my grandmother while Uncle—"

"And I brought bread for the two loveliest ladies in

Lavelanet!" He set two loaves on the table. Andreva's eyes widened at Bostel's interruption.

"You brighten our day with your flattery!" Jocelyne let out a girlish giggle. "Mercés, Bostel."

He gently removed the ragged blanket that covered Gisèla, went to a second bed in the corner for its blanket, and handed both to Andreva. "Would you kindly take these outside and shake the dust from them?"

Andreva frowned, but did as she was asked. She held the rags far from her clean wimple and stepped into the sunshine, grateful to be back outside. With care, she shook Gisèla's blanket, noting that its ragged edges and multiple holes still held the woman's warmth. Lint floated on the breeze, as did Bostel's cheery voice from inside, chasing away, it seemed, the tenant gloom. After shaking out the second blanket and finding it in no better condition, Andreva folded both and went back inside.

Jocelyne beamed at her. "Mercés, ma petite!"

Andreva forced a smile.

Bostel took Gisèla's hands in his. "I regret to tell you ladies that I am going away for a time. I will pray for you in my absence." He turned and extended one arm to take Jocelyne's hand also. "You have been a bright spot in my weeks. I will miss you both."

Gisèla's wrinkled hand trembled in his. "Away? Are you going to...?" Tears formed in her sunken eyes.

"Yes." He winked. "To Toulouse on business." He squeezed Jocelyn's hand then released it to pat Gisèla's. "You have no reason to worry."

A distant look filled Jocelyne's face as her gaze left Bostel and moved toward the fire. When her eyes returned to his, they glistened. "Go with God's blessing. He will watch over you."

Andreva pitied these old women who were so clearly alone and impoverished. When her uncle left, who would bring them bread?

Gisèla lay back. Bostel spread one blanket over her and laid the other carefully on Jocelyne's bed. "Goodbye, ladies. May God keep you in His care."

Andreva followed Bostel out to the lane, grateful to feel the sun on her face, but disturbed by what she had seen. Her uncle started down the road and she hurried to keep up. "Have these women no family to care for them?"

"Only one another. They are at the mercy of the villagers."

Andreva followed Bostel to the side of the blacksmith's shop where a tiny shack leaned against the sturdier building. "Dòna Felipa!" Bostel pulled aside the dingy gauze covering. He squatted and placed a loaf of bread upon a pile of blankets that lay just behind it.

A voice came from beneath the rags. "You are good to remember me. God bless you, kind son!"

Roaches scampered up the boards as if they'd heard a dinner bell. Andreva winced and stepped away. She listened to Bostel explain to the woman that he would not return for a month, if not longer. She pitied her when she heard the disappointed whimper that followed.

Back on the street, Bostel explained. "Peter the blacksmith allows Felipa to live behind his shop. He is a charitable man, and brings her food from time to time. She is ill, and I believe it is by Peter's goodwill she is kept alive."

Andreva pulled her cloak closer, grateful for its soft warmth and pleasant scent. What kind of life must it be to live beneath boards and heaps of rags, dependent upon the generosity of others?

Variations of these scenes played out three times more, until Bostel had no more loaves. Andreva had grown weary of witnessing dire poverty. She found no joy in disturbing rats and awakening hibernating roaches, nor in holding her breath to avoid smelling putrid stenches. Relieved when they finally started homeward for their noon meal, she looked up at her uncle. "What will these women do without you?"

Bostel looped her arm in his. "I do worry about them."

"Are you their only benefactor?"

"Perhaps. But I hope not." He paused and turned to look into her eyes. "The Book of James says pure religion is to visit the fatherless and widows in their afflictions." He touched her nose as if brushing away a breadcrumb. "And to keep ourselves unspotted from the world." A smile spread across his face and he resumed the stroll home.

Lost in thought, Andreva did not move. In the abbey, she had promised to live a benevolent life, but then rarely left its walls to serve. The nuns' goodwill had consisted primarily of praying for mankind and sewing for the poor. Caring for Mémé was one thing, but did she have charity enough to also visit the poverty-stricken—*alone*?

"Are you coming?"

She looked up to see Bostel several steps ahead, holding out his hand to her. "All shall be well. Remember, Andreva, we are God's eyes and hands. He has no others but ours."

Andreva caught up, took his hand, and they walked home in silence. Back at the house, her grandmother still slept. Andreva removed her cloak.

Bostel motioned for her to join him at the table. "Gerrard de Fortaner shall bring your allowance in a few days. Our family rents out land that brings profit each month. This includes fields my wife inherited. Fortaner is her cousin, and has agreed to manage them in my absence." Bostel took a few coins from a pouch and offered them.

It was a moment before Andreva thought to extend her hand. When he dropped the money into it she stared, sorting out what he had said.

Bostel smiled. "Have you never seen currency before?"

"I have, but…" She squeezed the coins and tried to muster courage to do what he asked. *Why is he so determined to leave?*

"Use the money to hire help if you need it. Buy the necessaries for mending and housekeeping—and of course vegetables and bread. You may buy other foods to which you are accustomed, but do not prepare meat, cheese, or eggs for Mémé."

"But why?"

"It is her personal preference." He took back the coins and returned them to the purse while Andreva tucked Mémé's strange dietary restrictions into her memory. "Questions you may have about housekeeping, Mémé will answer." He met her gaze and held it. "I have included allowance to purchase loaves for the widows, if you desire to serve them."

Andreva let his last words pass almost without note and chewed her bottom lip at her more immediate concern. She knew almost nothing about cooking or running a house. She had done some sewing and much embroidery in her eighteen years, but had received little instruction in other chores needed to maintain a home. At the abbey, she'd been assigned to sweep and mop the refectory. Perhaps the floors, at least, would not suffer.

She wrung her hands in desperation. "Please don't leave us! We need you—and the widows will miss you, too."

"Oh, ma chérie." Bostel drew her up into his arms. "I am so sorry, but I must go. You have Raoul and Jaques to help you. And the chapel is nearby. Friar Tomàs is a good man and will aid you when you need him." He chuckled and stepped away. "Though I doubt he shall speak kindly of me, for I have brought him too many questions that he answers with," he mimicked a slow, deep voice, "'It is not ours to know the mysteries of God.'"

"Except..." What to point out first? Sighing in dismay, Andreva gestured toward the pot of vegetable stew that hung over the fire. Surely, he had noted her sorry attempt to help in its preparation. "I lack skills in cooking. We could starve. Please do not leave us."

He kissed her forehead. "Your grandméré can instruct you, even from her bed, if you ask."

Andreva sank onto the kitchen stool. No matter what she argued, she could not change his mind.

The next morning, it took all her courage not to cry and plead with Bostel to stay. She watched in silence as he tied a bag onto his mule. She wished to throw her arms about him to hold him with her forever. In her heartache, she barely noticed the cold morning breeze that danced about as if attempting to lift her from her misery. When her uncle was ready to leave, she glumly followed him back into the house and to her grandmother's room.

Mémé turned her tear-stained face toward him.

Bostel knelt beside her bed. "Goodbye, Maire. May you come to a good end."

Andreva lurched forward. What did he mean? Did he not

expect his maire to live until he returned? Andreva opened her mouth to protest, but her grandmother spoke first.

"And you, as well." Mémé stroked her son's cheek. "I shall forever pray in your behalf. May God's protection be with you."

Andreva closed her mouth. Had Mémé understood what "a good end" meant?

Bostel kissed Mémé and paused with his hands still clasping hers. Pain clouded her eyes when at last he rose and stepped away. The woman let his fingers slip from hers.

In the kitchen, Bostel gathered his cloak and a final small bag. He looked around as if to memorize every detail of the home, then turned to Andreva. "Use anything you like. The upstairs chamber is now yours, as is my wife's clothing in the wardrobe."

Memories of the beautiful Aimée, who'd died giving birth to a stillborn baby boy, fluttered in Andreva's memory. She touched her drab, formless frock, and the idea of shedding it for one of her aunt's dresses lightened her mood slightly.

He touched the sleeve of her habit. "But again, I suggest you not replace your convent apparel too soon. You will find being a nun advantageous. Remember, my dear, these are dangerous times."

"I am not one of the Good Men. What could happen?"

He studied her eyes. "More than you can imagine." Bostel brushed the tip of her nose, and his manner turned playful. "The authorities suspect everyone—even young girls."

"Oh, Uncle!" She leaned into him to invite his comforting arm around her shoulder as they walked together out to the mule. If he thought her a child, as his teasing suggested, why would he entrust her with Mémé's care? "Promise me you shall return."

"If I do not—" Bostel held her close. "I pray that someday you will understand." Before Andreva could respond, her uncle climbed onto the mule and saluted. "I hope in some better day we shall be together."

Gloom closed around her as the mule carried Bostel up the road. Overcome by panic, Andreva ran out into the road, wishing to call her uncle back. When he was out of sight, she turned toward the house and sank to her knees, overwhelmed by responsibility, loneliness, and dread.

Over the rooftops, the church tower glistening in the sunlight caught her eye. She could go to the chapel to pray for strength—and for Bostel. Prayer had always been the balm that calmed her anger and stilled her fears. She could slip away for a few minutes while Mémé slept. Her grandmother would not miss her.

Andreva went inside to retrieve her veil. She reached toward the peg where it hung, but froze when she heard Mémé's muffled sobs.

5

"Mémé?" Andreva paused in the chamber doorway. No answer. The weeping stopped. She walked to the bed. "Mémé, are you all right?" She lifted the bottle of ale, half-filled a cup, and held it out for Mémé to take. "Shall I bring a morsel to eat?"

"Nothing now." Mémé kept her face half-buried in the pillow. "I want to sleep." Andreva returned the cup to the table. Mémé closed her puffy eyes and a tear escaped, lingering as a puddle of sadness before it was absorbed into the white linen.

Andreva touched her shoulder. "While you sleep, if you do not mind, I shall go to market and also to the chapel to light a candle for Uncle Bostel."

"Óc, go. Pray for us all." Mémé wiped her tears. "But take caution with whom you speak. There are...suspicious eyes all around."

"I shall, Mémé."

Andreva kissed the woman's cheek and left the room. She paused with her hand on her cloak and shuddered. How could she and her grandmother fare alone? Did her uncle realize how many hearts he'd saddened with his departure? How could he be so thoughtless? She lifted her chin. They must manage, and she must stay strong and cheerful for Mémé.

Andreva put on the cloak, and raised the hood. She grabbed the purse her uncle had given her. Bostel's coins jingled and she froze. He hadn't left them destitute. He had provided for their welfare by storing food and arranging an allowance. They would make do until he returned.

Andreva took an empty basket from a peg on the wall. She paused to listen for Mémé before opening the door; only quiet. She stepped out and closed the door securely before she turned to face the frigid morning air.

We shall manage. As Andreva walked, she was overcome by a strange sense of independence. She had scarcely ever left the convent, even in the company of nuns. Earlier, while living with her parents, she was not allowed to venture alone into the marketplace. But now here she was, walking along a village street.

Just ahead, soldiers had gathered to watch two chevaliers on horseback engage in jousting practice on the town's commons. Several men shouted advice, and others heckled.

The chevaliers charged. One man's hit hurled the other to the ground. "Get up and try once more, you rogue!" The victor pulled his horse around. "With enough practice, you might someday become skilled."

"Careful who you call a rogue!" The downed man stood, brushed himself off, then remounted.

"This is your last chance today," a soldier shouted. "Keep your eye on the grand guard! Hold your lance steady! We don't have time for boys to play at being men. We need to get to Montsegùr!"

Other soldiers hurled their rude comments and choice names toward the loser.

Just before Andreva turned away, a soldier stepped back and heedlessly knocked down a peasant woman. The contents of her basket were strewn across the ground.

"I beg your pardon." The apology was mocking. The soldier ignored the woman to rejoin his comrades.

Andreva hurried to assist her to her feet. Together they gathered the spilt goods—a block of cheese, a loaf of bread, and a few vegetables and fruits.

"Mercés, Ma Soeur." The woman stood, glanced over her shoulder toward the soldier, and knit her ample eyebrows. "They take over Lavelanet as if it is their own. Drunk with the excitement of pending victory at Montsegùr, they are blind to anyone in their way." The woman straightened her scarf and hurried on.

Montsegùr. Andreva made a hurried sign of the cross. The château seemed to be on everyone's mind. How close was it to Lavelanet? Would the war it stirred come any closer than the soldiers loitering in the village?

She continued on to the church, but stopped briefly at the door to watch the two jousters. On contact, the unfortunate man who had been bested again whirled in his saddle and tumbled to the ground. Applause, and some tittering, drifted on the cold breeze.

Andreva slipped inside the narthex and inhaled a familiar musty odor. She gazed over the chapel. This humble edifice contrasted greatly with the grandeur of St. Sernin. Despite its lack of ornamentation, she felt the peace of coming home as she moved across the stone floor, her echoing footsteps announcing her presence.

Glazed eyes stared down at her—the fixed gaze of a kindly saint from centuries past, standing mute against the wall. The central figure in the church was the large crucifix at the front of the cross-shaped chapel, backed by sunlit, stained glass windows. The head of the Christ rested upon his chest, eyes closed, an eternal tear upon his cheek.

Andreva made the sign of the cross, then stepped into the right transept and approached the altar. There she lit two candles, one for Mémé and another for Bostel. Kneeling at the feet of a carved image of the Virgin Mary, she raised her eyes briefly to admire the woman's serene face.

Andreva uttered the prayer she had known almost from infancy, while in her heart she begged for Bostel's safety and Mémé's recovery. Andreva's throat tightened and tears threatened to escape. How her life had changed over the last year! Her parents had died, she'd been sent, friendless and alone, to the solitude of the abbey, and then at last beckoned to Lavelanet by her uncle, only to be abandoned by him two days later.

She looked up at Mary. "Please, let me stay with Mémé. Bring Bostel home safe. And please do not allow me to go back to the abbey. Ever."

She wiped away the tears before they could dampen her cloak, and rose to her feet.

A priest wearing a large crucifix on a chain around his neck, stood but a few feet away. He seemed surprised as she pulled back the hood. "Ma Soeur! I am sorry if I startled you. I am Father Tomàs. You are a stranger to Lavelanet." He paused as if to consider. "Are you here with the Inquisitors at le château Montsegùr?"

"No!" She made the sign of the cross. "Mon père, I am the granddaughter of Margaurite de Lumbert. She is not well, and I have come to Lavelanet to stay with her in my uncle's absence."

One eyebrow lifted over his clear blue eyes. "Bostel de Lumbert. He is away?"

"Óc."

The eyebrow went higher.

"Where has he gone?"

Andreva stood. Her hands had grown clammy. "He is traveling to Toulouse to take care of matters of family business and will return in a few weeks."

Andreva's fear deepened with the wrinkles on the priest's brow. Nevertheless, his kindly tone didn't change. "Your uncle is a heretic, a lost soul who will burn in hell. I would sooner believe he has gone to Montsegùr."

Andreva almost choked. "I beg your pardon? No! You are wrong. My uncle is a good Christian."

The man smiled. "My daughter, because you wear the attire of the Church, I assume you are among the believers."

Andreva opened her mouth but words to counter the stinging accusation against her uncle, did not come quickly. She cleared her throat. "I am. I have lived as a novice at the Basilica of St. Sernin for the last ten months."

"The saints be praised." His delight showed in his eyes. "The monks who founded this parish also came from the Basilica of St. Sernin. They had hoped to influence the heretics for good, but alas, heretics are stubborn, and blind to the true light of Christ." He smiled kindly. "If I can assist you or your grandmother in your uncle's absence, you have only to ask."

Sensing their conversation was at an end, Andreva curtsied. "Mercés, mon père." As she walked back toward the entry, the priest departed through a side door. Before leaving the church, she closed her eyes and allowed the quiet to envelop her.

Should she believe the priest? No, she'd seen for herself that her uncle had a good heart and Christian ethics. Surely the father had misjudged him. Hadn't Bostel told her as much? Andreva bowed her head. *Bostel is not a heretic and he would not have lied to me.*

She left a coin in the offering box before walking from solitude into the sunlight.

A few soldiers still lingered on the commons, warming themselves by a fire. Two matted trails in the grass were the only evidence of the morning's jousting practice. Andreva waited for a cart to pass before crossing the road to the market.

Wanting to hurry home, Andreva scanned the vendors' tables. With Christmas only days away, she hoped to gather foods for an adequate celebration for her and Mémé, while remembering her grandmother's strange restrictions. Perhaps a miracle would happen to make her a good cook overnight.

She stopped at a table displaying cheese and bread. Bostel had introduced the vendor the day before. "Good day to you, Monsen."

"Please, call me Perrin!" The vendor's voice boomed. He chuckled, and his large belly shook. "The weather is nippy today." His head jerked toward the huddle of soldiers before he smoothed his beard and lowered his voice. "Hedges have eyes, and walls ears."

"Oh? And who listens?"

"They do."

Andreva glanced at the soldiers.

"The Inquisitors suspect we are all Good Men. They have commissioned that lot to apprehend anyone who reveals himself."

"Do they find many?"

"Some. But most have gathered at le château Montsegùr."

Perrin raised a beefy hand to his forehead in chagrin. "Sorry, Sister. Of course, you are sympathetic to the Inquisition."

"I am neither a hedge nor a wall." She smiled. "My sympathies are for my grandmother only." She glanced over her shoulder. "What do the soldiers say?"

"They boast that victory at Montsegùr is imminent. The army has camped at the base of the mountain for months, but now mercenaries climb its cliffs as we speak, determined to attack."

"Do the soldiers only boast?"

"I know not." He rearranged his cheeses. "Did Bostel leave as planned this morning?"

She looked up in surprise, but remembered her uncle had shared his plans the day before.

"Óc."

Perrin clicked his tongue. His boom returned. "I saw you come from the chapel, Sister."

"It is a peaceful place. I have lived at the Basilica of St. Sernin for almost a year. Since leaving, I have missed my daily devotional."

"Ah! The magnificent St. Sernin in Toulouse. A beauteous place. I visited there once as a lad." The vendor's eyes crinkled at the corners. "And how is your grandmother today?"

"No better. My uncle did not leave without breaking hearts."

The twinkle in his eyes vanished. Perrin clicked his tongue again, in pity.

Andreva chose two small cuts of cheese, remembering Bostel's warning not to serve any to Mémé. She added butter to her basket and preserves to serve with the bread. Even she could spread butter and cut cheese.

Perrin tamed his voice once again to a whisper. "There have been no casualties reported at Montsegùr as of yet." He looked southeastward toward the mountains. "Even though the distance is near eight Roman miles, you can see the Good Men's fortress on clear days, particularly in the morning." He walked a few paces from his table, then squinted and pointed. "There. You can barely see it on the pog."

She followed. "Pog?"

"The type of hill upon which it sits; very steep on all

sides."

Through the valley, and despite the haze of smoke from the morning's cooking and heating fires, the outline of a high, steep hill against the background of the Pyrénées became visible. Walls rose from the pog's plateau.

"Mercés, Monsen Perrin. I see it." Andreva glanced back toward the chapel. Did the vendor, like the priest, presume Bostel had gone to Montsegùr instead of Toulouse?

She looped her arm through the handle of the basket. Other people's suspicions didn't matter. She trusted her uncle had told the truth.

She bid Perrin farewell. "*Polit nadal!*" she said, wishing him a happy Christmas.

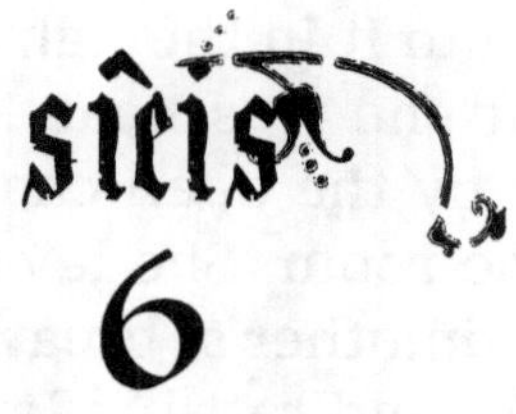

6

ndreva carried a candle up the stairs. She and Mémé had shared a bed the night before, but her grandmother had slept restlessly.

With Bostel gone, the upper chamber was now hers. Andreva stepped inside the room and held up her light. Next to the entry, crossed swords hung over a small, well-used fireplace. Had Bostel, or some ancestor, once used these swords in battle—perhaps in the service of one of the Counts of Toulouse? Next to them, a glass-paned window overlooked the garden below, and opposite it, stood the bed beneath another window that faced the street. A large wardrobe took up the remaining wall, casting its shadows in the flickering light. She set the candle on a small table beneath the window.

The wind howled through the eaves, rattling the panes, and seeping through indiscernible cracks. In the chilly draft, the candle's flame created ghostly moving shadows. A shuffle sounded behind her and Andreva whirled toward the wardrobe, but saw no one.

The hair upon the nape of her neck rose and her knees weakened. Frozen in place, Andreva's heart pounded. She took a step toward the bed, grabbed its straw mattress, and yanked it toward the stairway. Invisible, eerie intruders were at her heels with every descending step. She slipped once, but caught her balance. At the bottom of the stairs, pausing only to catch her breath, she dared to look back. No one followed.

She listened, but heard nothing besides the howling of the wind and the thumping in her chest.

Silly girl. Afraid of your own shadow. Nevertheless, she'd not return at night to the upper room until she'd become more accustomed to it in the light of day.

Safe now that she was near Mémé, Andreva made her bed on the floor by the open chamber doorway. The fire's glow softly lit the room. She lay awake, listening to every sound—her grandmother's breathing, an owl hooting in the distance, the wind rattling latched shutters, and a cart rolling, stopping, then continuing up the road.

Thud! Thud!

She turned over to look toward the front door, reminding herself she had barred it earlier. Her blood raced, waiting for the next blow. Her eyes moved to the only other door, the one leading out to the garden. Had she latched it after dumping the evening's dishwater?

Thud! Thud! Thud!

Andreva sat up and stared at the door. Who would come to a dark house at this hour of the night? Who but goblins? She rose and slipped on her shoes. Going silently to the door, she rested her hand on the latch.

Her throat went dry. "Who is it?"

"It is I, Raoul. I live next door." The voice from outside was masculine, but youthful. "I saw the candle in the upstairs window and hoped you were still awake."

"I am now." She looked up the stairs and remembered she had left the lighted candlestick on the table. She must remember to see to it. Andreva opened the door. "With all the racket, no doubt Mémé is awake, as well."

A hooded young man in his mid-teens stood on the step, wrapped in a blanket. His covering rose unnaturally above his shoulders. Andreva had seen a hunchback before, but never one so young.

"Do not be afraid." He grinned. "Monsen Bostel asked me to look in on you. I promised him I would as soon as I returned to the village."

She motioned him inside. "We are doing quite well." He came in and she closed the door.

Raoul shivered. "There was a commotion at Dònas Jocelyne's and Gisèla's house. The wind toppled a candle, lighting the table linen. Hugo the cobbler lives next door and heard their screams. He was able to put out the flames before they spread."

"Oh! Were the sisters harmed?" Andreva looked up the stairs toward the candle she had left on the table.

"They are unharmed and safe now. I was happening by, and stayed a few minutes to help calm their nerves." His eyes held a gleam of boyish pride.

"Blessed are you—the bringer of peace." Andreva smiled. His late-night visit might prove a blessing, after all. "Would you mind going upstairs? I left a candle on the table. Would you bring it down to me?" She looked over the lump on his back. "Or can you?"

"I'd be happy to." He dropped his blanket to the floor.

"It is a lute!" He wasn't a hunchback at all!

"Óc. I have been at Castle Roquefixade playing with the troubadours." His smile widened. "It was a grand time!"

"But I heard Count Raymond took possession of the castle."

"Ah, yes, but the tenants still enjoy a party." He slid the instrument to the floor before bounding up the stairs, two steps at a time. He returned in a moment with the candlestick.

"Mercés. It is a blessing you saw the flame. Mémé and I could have been in the same danger as Jocelyne and Gisèla!" His lopsided grin made her giggle. "Do you mind if I ask how old you are, Raoul?"

He broadened the grin. "Fifteen—almost sixteen. May I ask your age?"

"Eighteen." She noted that she stood an inch or two taller. "Uncle Bostel speaks highly of you."

His beardless cheeks turned rosy. "Monsen Bostel speaks highly of everyone. He is a good friend." He looked toward his lute. "I hope someday to be a great musician. I shall play for you soon."

"I would like that." Music would be a welcome diversion from the quiet of Mémé's home.

Raoul set the candle on the table. "Come. I want you to see something." He grabbed her arm and the door latch at the same time.

"What?" Andreva pulled away, laughing in disbelief. "I am not dressed to go outside, and it is freezing out there." Was this boy mad? Who would go willingly out into this cold and wind?

"Grab your wrap." He retrieved his blanket and lute and opened the door. "Come see the lights of Montsegùr."

Montsegùr? Andreva took her cloak from the hook and slipped it around her shoulders. She glanced toward her grandmother's chamber and decided she would be fine alone for a moment or two. After closing the door, she followed Raoul into the street. He dragged her to a point where trees would not block their view. There, they stared up at a star-filled sky, brilliantly lighting the world despite the moonless night.

He motioned toward the mountains. "It is unusual to see the soldiers' campfires on Montsegùr. But the wind has cleared the air."

Andreva barely made out lights flickering in the distance.

Raoul said, "One of the troubadours told me of ruins near Jerusalem called Masada—it's an ancient fortress on top of a flat-topped mountain. For years, rebel Jews hid there to escape the Romans." When he saw he had Andreva's attention, he continued. "The Romans gathered at the bottom of the cliffs and the Jews looked down at them. Then the Romans heaped up dirt and built a ramp up to the fortress. They used a battering ram to break down the door, only to find that all the people, except a few women and children, had ended their own lives by the sword."

"And that reminds you of Montsegùr."

"Yes, my lady." He looked over to her. "Hopefully, the Good Men do not end their own lives before the siege ends."

She paused a moment. "Perhaps they shall not die by the sword, but if the Inquisitors have their way, they will burn at the stake." Which would be worse, death at one's own hand or being burned alive?

"My troubadour friend—the one who told me about the siege at Masada—has been up to Montsegùr. He says the Good Men have their own village: full water cisterns, a metal forge for weapons and armor with an ample wood supply to fire it, and plenty of food."

She looked again toward the lights. "Everyone's thoughts are on the fortress."

"Why not?" He shivered against the cold. "We all await the outcome. And it is the only thing happening around here—besides little old ladies almost burning down their house." He chuckled.

"How did your troubadour friend get up the cliffs to Montsegùr without being seen?"

"There are caves all over the pog where he could hide on his way up." He still stared at the lights. "Can you imagine being in the château, looking down at those fires every night, knowing each represents numerous knights and soldiers who have sworn to stay until you surrender? Just like the Jews peering down at the Romans."

Andreva blinked in wonder, and shivered. She pulled the hood over her head. "It is an ominous thought, like standing upon a perch while being circled by hungry wolves."

"These wolves hope to catch the mangy dogs cowering on the mountain." He winked.

Andreva bit back a witty reply. With whom did she side in this war? She took a resolute breath. The Church, of course.

"Did Monsen Bostel leave today?" Raoul shivered again. "I wanted to say goodbye but..."

"Óc." She tried to read his expression. What did the boy know about Bostel's whereabouts? She put the question out of her mind. It would do no good to second-guess everyone's meanings, nor try to read their thoughts. She turned back toward the house. "Thank you for your concern about Mémé and me."

He walked beside her. "I will not be able to come for a few days."

"No?" She liked this boy's energy and suspected she would enjoy his company, if only he would stay in the village.

"I am committed to work up in the valley. The army will be bringing in food and supplies. They need the road repaired to accommodate their carts."

"We will fare the best we can then, but do not stay away too long." She yawned and reached for the door latch. "Now hurry home out of this wind."

ndreva answered a knock at the door. She hoped it was Raoul, at last returned from his work on the road, but it was not. Rather it was the farmer with the intriguing eyes—the good friend of Bostel's from the bridge. She tried to remember his name. Jaques, was it?

He held up two fish on a string. No longer seated in a cart, he stood taller than she'd expected. And he stared. "Soeur Andreva?"

Her hand flew to her hair. It hung freely over her shoulders, held back from her face by a woven band. She glanced at the nun's veil hanging on the wall and realized at once the source of his confusion. "Yes. Monsen Montré! Come in." She gave a short curtsy and opened the door wider, unable to control her smile. He was as handsome as she remembered.

He stepped inside. "I went fishing this morning. Had to break the ice." He held up the fish and grinned. "I brought you trout for your fast-days before Christmas."

The Church did not restrict fish on fast-days that excluded other meats. But what about her grandmother? Would she eat fish?

"Mercés." Andreva hoped she looked appreciative as she scrutinized the scaled creatures. She liked cooked trout, but raw fish made her squeamish.

"How is your grandmother feeling today?"

She looked back up at the man. "Mémé still has no strength. I had planned for us to feast on bread and preserves."

"These fine fellows will give her strength." Jaques handed her the line of fish. "Bread and jam does not sound like much."

She held the fish away from her dress. "Oh, Monsen! But how do I prepare them?"

Amusement danced in Jaques' eyes. "First, you clean them."

"Clean? You mean wash?"

He chuckled. "You have never cleaned a fish?" The smile on his handsome face broadened. He had strong cheekbones, framed perfectly by dark hair that fell to an excellent jaw line.

"I admit it." Andreva looked away to ease her discomfort. "My maire had a cook, so I know nothing about cleaning fish, or much about cooking at all." She forced a little laugh, embarrassed by her confession.

He pulled off his hat, hung it on a wall hook, and took back the line. "Then I shall show you."

She sighed in relief and closed the door. Hopefully, no one had seen him come in. After all, he was only a farmer.

Andreva found a bowl and knife. Jaques unhooked the first fish from the line and took the knife. He used it to point. "You start here." The blade slid easily lengthwise along the belly of the fish and in seconds the intestines fell into the bowl. He sliced the next.

Andreva peered down at the fish innards. The smell caused her nose to wrinkle.

"And then you scrape off the scales with the edge of the blade." Andreva became nauseated at the sound. "Before you fry, dust them with flour. You will know they are cooked sufficiently when their eyes bulge."

Bulging eyes? Andreva's stomach lurched. She threw her hand over her mouth, but could not suppress a gag. She opened the garden door and gulped deep breaths of cold air until the repulsive sensation passed.

Jaques chuckled. "It is unfortunate you have a sensitive

disposition." He scraped the knife clean on the edge of the bowl. "I shall bury these innards in your garden. It will nourish your soil and fertilize your vegetables come spring."

She moved out of the way as Jaques carried the bowl outside. Andreva put a bucket of water and bar of soap on the table. When Jaques returned, she offered it to wash his hands. When he had done so, she held out a linen towel.

"You are kind." He dried his hands. Each smile, Andreva observed, caused his eyes to twinkle. Jaques took his cloak from the peg and pulled it on, and reached for his cap. "I hope your grandmother feels better soon."

"Mercés." He was leaving so soon? How could she make him stay a moment longer? His company had soothed her lonely soul and his smile brightened her spirits.

He placed the cap on his head. "You may be uncomfortable with common ways and domestic work now. With time, you shall adjust."

There was a teasing note in his voice at which Andreva stiffened. How dare a farmer tease a woman of higher status? A farmer and a tease—reason enough to dislike this man. No matter that he was handsome, and she welcomed his smile, he was a mere plow-pusher and a peasant.

Andreva raised her chin. "I have tried my best, for Mémé's sake, since Uncle Bostel left." She hoped he heard the edge in her voice.

Obviously, he had. His countenance turned somber. He opened the door and walked out to his horse. Despite her annoyance at the tease, Andreva followed.

Jaques looked off toward the mountains. "I have a clear view of Montsegùr from my fields. I hear the king's men are building a trebuchet halfway up the mountain. It will soon be only a matter of how far their machine can hurl the stones."

"The army has been at Montsegùr for months. Why have they not yet attacked?"

"Well, first—" He paused as two soldiers rode by. "Until a few months ago, many of the soldiers were locals, raised among the Good Men. Many had relatives who were Good

Men, so they did not want to attack. Most were from Count Raymond's army."

No! My father's regiment? This was what her father had feared. Had he lived, the count would have required him to lead his army against the Good Men, his own countrymen!

"Each week, King Louis sends more troops." Jaques motioned after the soldiers. "The pope insists upon the Cathars' extermination, but it is next to impossible for the army to climb the pog to attack. Can you imagine scaling those cliffs in mail armor and gauntlets, carrying swords?"

"I see what you mean."

More soldiers rode by. One took a long look at Jaques as if determining if he should be questioned on the spot.

"They suspect everyone." He remained silent until the soldiers had passed. "We are guilty until proven innocent. Bostel and the Good Men were wise to leave the village when they did."

Andreva managed to rein in her surprise and hold back any reaction. He had mentioned Bostel in the same breath as the Good Men! Did this farmer also suspect that Bostel had gone to Montsegùr? She had personally heard Bostel tell Jaques he was going to Toulouse. Her hand rose to the cross around her neck. "I shall say a prayer for those poor people in the fortress."

"What about those who pray in behalf of the army?" He mounted his horse and the teasing glint in his eye returned. "Perhaps we all should pray for everyone to go home and forget the whole matter." He turned his horse and trotted down the road.

Why would he say such a thing? He spoke his opinions too freely. Did he not accept the precept of the Crusades—that only believers in the Church were fit to live—nor fear the wrath of the Inquisitors who punished anyone who believed differently? Perhaps not.

She took a step forward as he rode away. "Mercés for the fish!" She returned to the house and pushed the door closed against the turbulent cold wind that had rushed in and twirled around the room.

Andreva went to Mémé's chamber and found her sleeping. She returned to the kitchen, and stared glumly at the two lumps of trout upon the table.

Flour and fry.

She found a pan, breathed in, sighed long, and dove into the task before her with all the gusto of a dead fish.

uerh 8

The morning after Jaques' visit, Andreva put on Mémé's apron, lit a candle, and descended into the cellar. She held up the candlestick and scanned the shelves and barrels. There were apples, cucumbers, carrots, and artichokes—none fresh but still usable—alongside jars of ale, raisins, spices, nuts, and various herbs. With time, and through trial and error, she would learn to use it all. She found a sack of flour and took it upstairs to the table.

Andreva measured the flour and added water according to directions her grandmother had given her earlier that morning. She found a large spoon and attacked the mixture, perhaps a little too vigorously, for flour puffed into the air and covered her apron.

Andreva moaned in dismay and tried again. Finally, she tossed the spoon aside to mix with her hands. The dough oozed between her fingers.

"Bonjorn!" The call came from outside the door. Andreva hurried to remove the apron and clean her hands. When she opened the door, Raoul stood upon the step, grinning like an old friend.

"Good morning." Andreva motioned him inside.

He pushed back the hood of a tunic that hung halfway to his stocking-covered knees. His boyish smile was as delightful as his auburn hair, cut straight across his forehead, but hanging to his shoulders in wild curls at the sides and back.

He glanced her over and his forehead puckered. "Monsen Bostel told me you are a nun."

She looked down. She wore her convent frock, but the wimple and veil still hung on the wall, and she had contained her hair with one of her grandmother's nettings. "Yes. I am...a novice."

"Raoul looked over the mess of dough. "What are you baking today?" "

"I have never made bread and thought I should learn." Andreva poked the flattened mass. "Pray tell, do you know the secret to making a good loaf?"

"No, but your grandmother is one of the best bread makers around. Ask her."

"All she told me was the portion of flour to water." Andreva sighed. Mémé had been too tired to say more.

"Did she mention yeast or barm?"

"What is that?"

"It makes bread..." He shrugged. "You know, bread."

"No." She didn't know. She moaned. "She must have forgotten that detail."

"Then, Soeur Andreva, you have my best wishes with the bread." He bowed. "And I am at your service in any other matters of need."

Andreva smiled at his formality, and found his enthusiasm refreshing.

Raoul chuckled and looked around the room. "What chores do you have for me, pray tell, my fair *lady*."

He mocked her inexperience but Andreva let it pass. She tried to think of a task. "There is a fireplace upstairs that needs its ashes carried out. You may use this shovel." She picked up a well-worn scoop from its place beside the stone hearth.

Raoul grinned. "I shall take care of it promptly." He took the scoop and an empty ash bucket, and headed up the stairs. The sound of scraping echoed through the house. Andreva feared the noise would awaken her grandmother. She peeked in on her, and found the woman sleeping heavily.

Someone else knocked at the door. Andreva went to answer it.

Gerrard de Fortaner's eyes traveled from her head to her feet and back to her face. "Domaisèla Andreva, I presume, and not Ma Soeur. It is good to see you looking so well."

Andreva touched the snood covering her hair, and couldn't help but smile. "Forgive me. It is easier to work around the house without the veil." The cold overpowered the meager heat from the fire. She invited him in and closed the door. "Did not Dòna Dianne come with you?"

"No. She is busy with the servants and housework."

"Then I am disappointed. I look forward to seeing her again."

His smile emphasized his handsomeness. "I have come to check on your welfare and bring your allowance." He stepped closer. "The sum seems on the meager side."

She felt discomfited by his nearness and newly-intimate air. "My uncle left but a few days ago. We have not required the allowance yet. And we have few needs aside from food and candles. You should not worry."

The man advanced another step. "Yes. The simple life is charming." He sniffed. "If you like living as a peasant."

Peasant? Mémé's house was one of the finest in the village.

He grinned and took her hand in both of his, creating a cold cocoon.

She stared at his hand as iciness crept up her arm. What was happening? Fortaner had acted so gentlemanly on their journey from Toulouse. Should she protest his advances? Were they advances? Perhaps she was wrong. It would not do to offend a man who did her uncle, and herself, a favor.

He took a step closer. "Now, we could make… arrangements—"

Raoul came down the stairs carrying the bucket of ashes. He stopped on the bottom step and stared at the scene. Fortaner looked up, and Andreva used this distraction to pull her hand away.

Fortaner glanced from Raoul to Andreva, and to the door of Mémé's bedroom. He raised an eyebrow. "I see you have made arrangements."

Raoul looked from one to the other, clearly wondering what he had missed. He walked across the room and set the bucket by the garden door.

Andreva took a step back. "My uncle hired Raoul to help me."

Fortaner bowed and handed her a gray pouch. "Here are your finances for the month, and it includes a little extra for your Christmas celebration." He straightened and peered down his nose at Raoul.

She thanked Fortaner and led him to the door while Raoul stayed where he was.

Fortaner stepped outside and bowed his farewell.

"*Bon dia*, Monsen," she said. Andreva closed the door and rubbed her forehead. Had she imagined untoward actions where none had been intended? Certainly, this morning he had seemed different from the man he had been on their journey.

"Monsen Fortaner did not mean well." Raoul regarded Andreva questioningly. "He seems to know you...intimately."

Looking for something to do while she unruffled her thoughts, Andreva returned to the dough. She forced a calmness she didn't feel as she kneaded. "We are acquainted. I spent three days traveling from Toulouse with Monsen Fortaner and his wife. Uncle Bostel left him in charge of our finances."

Raoul went to her side and touched her arm. "I heard what the man said. I do not believe his 'arrangement' was of an honorable nature."

She took a deep breath. "He probably wants me to take in his laundry or something."

"Fortaner has sufficient domestic help. My sister Elodie works for the man." Raoul plucked at her sleeve. "It was a proposition."

His choice of words made her cringe. "Then be sure you are here when he comes." Their eyes met for a long moment before she composed herself. "I am sure it was a misunderstanding, and he is a man of honor."

Worry still in his eyes, Raoul nevertheless nodded. He motioned toward the bucket. "The ashes will make efficient soap. Do not throw them out."

"Soap?" Andreva laughed, but felt grateful the conversation had changed. "Why should I go to the trouble? Take the ashes out and dump them in the privy. I can buy soap from the vendor in the marketplace."

"You can buy bread there as well, so why go to the trouble to learn?"

He made a good point. "Baking bread is basic to good homemaking. I have to start somewhere."

Raoul picked up the bucket. "Your grandmother used to bake bread and make candles. She is a wealth of knowledge—if you can get it out of that exhausted mind of hers." He took the bucket to the garden door. "I shall be back immediately, if not sooner." His smile returned, relieving the tension of the moment like a warm blanket on a blustery winter day.

She turned back to her task, but worry nagged her. She tried to dismiss it. If Fortaner was the gentleman she believed him to be, surely he would not again bring up "the arrangement."

Andreva focused instead on Raoul's protectiveness and smiled. Already, he was much like a brother. She didn't have a sibling. Her mother had never told Andreva why she was an only child, but seemed as discouraged about it as her questioning daughter.

She pushed the dough into a loaf of sorts, and set it aside. Perhaps it would miraculously rise.

Raoul returned, humming. He placed the empty bucket by the fire and plunked himself onto a stool. "Someday I shall leave Lavelanet and go to the city to play music with real troubadours."

Andreva looked up from washing the table. "The city is a dangerous place, it's crowded and full of beggars. Lavelanet is a peaceful village surrounded by beauty. Why would you want to leave? You can be a troubadour in Lavelanet, can you not?"

Raoul's thoughts often came with grand gestures. "I long for adventure, to see new places and things, to perform with the best musicians. I fear if I stay here, I will be a menial laborer the rest of my life."

"Working with your hands is an honest occupation."

"And entertaining people is not?"

"Well, yes, it is, but…" Andreva glanced at the lifeless bread dough. "I have lived in the city and prefer the country.

I hope never to leave Lavelanet. Oh, I will miss watching the regiments ride by on decorated chargers, and the pomp of royalty, yet there is peace within a village that you will not find in Toulouse."

He stood. "If you want to see regiments, wait beside the highway. Soldiers pass daily with all the pomp and ceremony one could ever desire."

She chuckled at his exaggeration.

He bowed. "Adieu-deman, Andreva. I am off to sweep the blacksmith's shop. I realize we may never see eye-to-eye on the subject of village life, so I will refrain from arguing."

After Raoul left, and discouraged that the dough might never rise, Andreva marched into Mémé's bedchamber. Her grandmother snorted as she awoke and rolled over. "Mémé, you must tell me how to make bread. The dough will not rise, and I fear the worst—that I may never learn."

"One does not 'tell' how to make bread." Mémé barely lifted her head to see Andreva. "One must show it." She lay back with a heavy sigh. "And I am in no condition to show anyone today." She lifted a hand a few inches. "Go next door to Colet, Raoul's maire." Mémé waved her fingers toward the neighboring house as if she could see it. "She will give you barm with which to start."

"But Raoul said you—"

"Go." Mémé relaxed and closed her eyes. "Colet will show you."

Andreva slumped in defeat. "Rest then while I am away." *What a silly thing to say. Resting is all Mémé ever does.*

Andreva bundled up in her cloak, grabbed a cup, and went next door. Chickens squawked, scattering in all directions as she entered the small yard. Her nose told her something wonderful was baking. She stopped before a shuttered window. "Dòna Colet!" Andreva stomped her feet to loosen mud from her shoes.

A broad-faced woman, with welcoming green eyes, opened the door. "What is it?" A few auburn curls had escaped the cloth tied around her head. Andreva saw from whom Raoul had inherited his hair.

"Bonjour. I am Andreva. My grandmother, Margaurite de

Lumbert, sent me for barm to start bread. Might you have a bit to spare?" She held up the cup.

"I do." Colet glanced at the graying sky. "Hurry inside, child."

"Mercés, Dòna." Andreva stepped onto the stone floor and closed the door behind her. A fire crackled in a pit in the middle of the room, and the smoke swayed its way to an opening in the ceiling. Andreva welcomed the heat.

Two boys and a girl gazed up at her in wonder. The older boy sat on a stool and used a hook to weave a rug. A smaller girl knelt at Colet's feet, scrubbing a large cooking pot. The youngest boy played next to her with a set of crudely-cut wood blocks. The children's cherubic faces greeted her with smiles.

"Such adorable children."

"Yes, these are the three youngest." She motioned for the youngsters to continue working. "Elodie, my oldest, is a maid for Dianne de Fortaner, and Raoul does work wherever he can find it. I hope he works hard for you."

"He does, so far. This is only his first day. I am thankful Uncle Bostel hired him before he left for Toulouse."

Colet took the cup. "I will get the barm." She turned to a cupboard, and in a moment handed Andreva the filled cup.

"Dòna Colet?" Andreva paused, looking at the goo and feeling embarrassed. "Could you tell me how to use the barm?"

A smile lit Colet's eyes. "Of course." She took the cup back from Andreva. "Come." Colet lifted a linen sack onto the table and measured flour from it into a bowl. "Your grandmother is the best bread maker around. Too bad she is ill."

"Óc. It is hard to see her lay in bed each day." Andreva watched Colet add water to the flour in the bowl, and then a scoop of the barm.

"Margaurite was the best cook and weaver." Colet worked the dough with her fingers. "All the older widows of the village are extraordinary, being as they had to carry on for so many years without husbands. They were the hunters, tanners, farmers."

The massacre led by Simon Montfort. Her mother had told her the story. So many men in Lavelanet had died that day.

"I have seen your grandmother throw three butcher knives into a tree twenty paces away, one after another, without missing—dead center." She pushed the bowl toward Andreva. "If she wanted to, that woman could cut off the tip of your nose without harming the nostrils—and at an impressive distance." Colet pointed to the bowl. "Now you knead."

"I had no idea my grandmother was so skilled." Andreva dug her hands into the dough and immediately detected the contrast between this and her own disaster.

Colet grinned. "Skill comes of practice."

A fortnight had passed since Bostel's departure, and Christmas was yet two days away. Morning dawned bright and clear. Andreva tied Mémé's apron, now clean, over her frock and set about her morning chores of fetching water, building up the fire, and scrubbing the stone floor.

Mémé had not taken even a nibble of Jaques' trout. Andreva had fried it all, eaten what she could, and buried the last of it in the garden. A pounding sounded at the door. What if it was Monsen Fortaner? Andreva flinched. She peered through a crack in the shutters. Three men in white gowns and black capes stood upon the step.

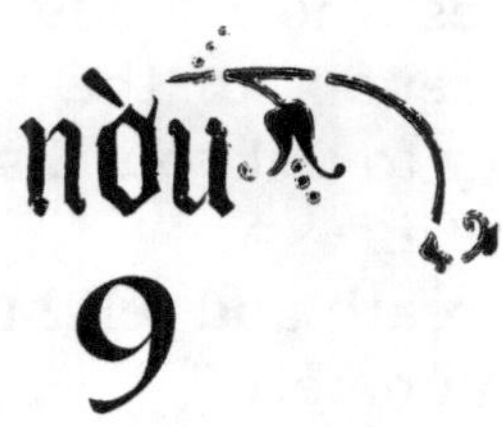

9

ndreva hurried to pull on the nun's headdress, and took a deep breath, before she opened the door.

A Dominican priest stood before her. At once she recognized his somber eyes and face framed by dark tonsured hair. It was the man who had overtaken them on the road from Toulouse.

His brow rose in surprise at her attire, but he showed no sign he recognized her from their previous brief meeting. Two priests stood behind him, neither of whom was Father Tomàs from the village. Perhaps they were his companions from the road.

"I am Father Stefe of the Inquisitors. These men are my council." The priest inclined his head. "Ma Soeur, who might you be?"

She nodded to each. "I am Soeur Andreva, and have come from St. Sernin to care for my grandmother, Margaurite de Lumbert."

"Ah. We seek Bostel de Lumbert. Is he here?"

She gripped the door frame. What would Inquisitors want with her uncle? She searched their faces for clues. "He is not, Your Reverence. He went to Toulouse on a family matter." That was exactly what Bostel had told her. She prayed it was also the truth.

Father Stefe turned to whisper a few words to the priests

behind him, and then turned back to Andreva. "And when do you expect him to return?"

"Not soon, mon père." Her hand went to her throat. "He said his business would take a few weeks."

A glint flashed in his eyes, but no smile crossed his thin lips. "I have witnesses who say Bostel de Lumbert rode with Pierre-Roger de Mirepoix to the massacre at Avignonet-Lauragais. I am sorry to tell you, Sister, that your uncle is a murderer and a heretic."

She caught her breath and felt her stomach sicken. "You must be mistaken, mon père."

"Perhaps. But I think not, and must speak with him." The priest continued to stare as if by so doing he would cause her to reveal more.

She somehow remained upright and composed herself. "Then inquire after him in Toulouse."

His eyes did not lower, but Andreva refused to flinch. "Mercés, Ma Soeur. God bless you." He and his companions turned and left, their white gowns billowing around them like a fog.

Andreva closed the door and sank against it. How could she not believe the word of a holy man? But how could she doubt her beloved uncle? Murderer? Heretic? Darkness seemed to spread over the room and fill her soul. She felt as if she might suffocate. She pulled the veil from her head, made the sign of the cross, and sat on a stool. To "speak" with an Inquisitor often meant interrogation. Interrogation often meant torture. It was impossible to prove one's innocence within the current mindset of the Inquisition.

But...had her uncle taken part in that awful deed that horrific action that started the decline of her father's health, and led eventually to his death? No, no, no! Until now, a mob of faceless men had committed the massacre. She refused to attach her uncle's face to the crime.

Even if Bostel was among the Good Men now, he had a charitable heart. Look at the way he cared for the widows. Yes, he is a good Christian. She must believe her uncle had kept his word and gone to Toulouse. But if he had not...*No!* Inquisitors often coerced confessions, true or not, from their captives. Perhaps some poor heretic had been tortured into implicating her uncle in a crime he did not commit.

Her grandmother had dozed off again. Andreva gazed upon her peaceful face. How she had longed to live with her! Loneliness had been her constant companion in the abbey, but here she was...still alone, and feeling very much abandoned.

She pushed away the lingering doubt. "Uncle Bostel, please hurry home." She believed in him. She needed to believe him. He and Mémé were all she had left. She leaned against the door frame. "Get well, Mémé."

Early Christmas Eve morning, Andreva remembered the holly she had seen growing along the path to the river. She took a knife and hurried down the road. Rich green shrubs grew everywhere, their berries a bright, glossy red. She cut several branches and clusters, gathered them into her apron, and turned back toward home, happy with her find. In past years, she had often watched the servants arrange wreaths for Christmas. She hoped she could duplicate that beauty.

"Bonjorn!" A young woman raised an arm in greeting just as Andreva reached the house. She extended a bundle of cloth. "I am Elodie. My maire sent this to you for your Christmas supper."

Andreva opened the door. "Come in before the wind takes over the house!" The girl followed her inside and closed the door. Andreva emptied the clippings from her apron onto the table. "Your maire?" Andreva took the bundle and pulled back the cloth. "Mincemeat pie!"

"Óc, Colet." She lowered her voice as if sharing a secret. "She added more nuts and left out the meat, knowing Dòna Margaurite's restrictions."

"How thoughtful of her." Andreva breathed in the wonderful spicy scent, and her mouth watered.

"Raoul is my younger brother. I believe you know him, too." The girl pushed aside a lock of auburn hair. "He has told me about you." She smiled mischievously. "I think he is smitten."

"Impossible." Andreva placed the pie on the table. Her face grew warm and she didn't want Elodie to see her blush. She returned the cloth. "Raoul is a fine young man, but he is like a younger brother to me." She invited Elodie to sit with her at the table while she began work on the wreath.

Elodie seemed to choose her words carefully. "Raoul tells me you lived with the nuns, but have not yet taken vows. Will you return to the abbey?"

"I hope to stay here with my family." Grateful for someone to listen, Andreva told Elodie how she'd lost her parents and been sent to the convent against her wishes. She motioned down at her dress, a sprig of holly still in hand. "Uncle Bostel told me I would be safer if I continued to wear the habit. So, until he returns, I shall do so each time I leave the house."

"He gave good advice. You should heed it...at least until the trouble has passed."

"The siege at Montsegùr?"

Elodie nodded.

Andreva bit her lip. Would Elodie imply, as had the priest, the vendor, and the Inquisitors, that Bostel had gone to Montsegùr?

Elodie folded the cloth and draped it over her arm. "Those poor people. There are well over two hundred of them in the fortress—men, women, and children—all living together, and their number increases daily."

"That is many." Andreva tucked a sprig into place.

"The Good Men are pacifists, so they refuse to fight. But they have hired almost 150 defenders, including Knights Templar and mercenaries."

"Impressive." Andreva added a cluster of berries and kept her face carefully placid. If Uncle Bostel had participated in the massacre at Avignonet-Lauragais, might he be one of those defenders? Her fingers trembled. The possibility of his betrayal hurt too fiercely to bear. She must change the subject before she broke into tears in front of this girl. "Do y-you—" Andreva searched her mind for anything else to discuss. "Do you enjoy working for Dianne de Fortaner?"

Elodie leaned against the table. "It is good work and I

am grateful for it. She has taken leave to visit her daughter in Narbonne for the Twelve Days and sent me home in her absence. It is good being with my family. Well, most of my family. Our father is dead."

Andreva looked up in surprise. His death had been recent? "Your youngest brother is no more than three years old."

Elodie pursed her lips and nodded. "It has been almost three years, but it seems much longer. My father was put to death for...heresy."

"Hush! Heresy?" Andreva hoped Mémé slept soundly. She lowered her voice. "Was he one of the Good Men?"

Elodie's brows knit. "He never joined, but he sympathized, not with what they believe, but with the notion that a man has a right to think for himself. He often said God created us capable of making our own choices, and that the Church has taken this right away."

That is *heretical thinking*. Andreva suspected mankind would cease to survive if they were no longer told how to think and behave by God's representatives.

"They kept him in prison at Carcassonne for several weeks." Elodie's lip quivered. "Then they burned him with Cathar bishops and other heretics." She lowered her eyes. "When I think of the torture he must have endured..." She straightened. "No wonder the last of the Good Men and their families have banded together at the château for protection."

"Oh, Elodie, I am so sorry about your father." Andreva scooted her stool closer and placed a hand on the girl's shoulder. She could relate to the pain of losing a parent. "How has your mother managed with all her small children?"

"We work, Raoul and I. Maire weaves. Sometimes we go to bed hungry, but none of us have starved. Monsen Bostel paid Raoul before he left the village, and the money has helped so much."

Andreva laughed. "Be assured, I will see that Raoul earns his wages." She looked at the pie and felt a twinge of guilt at being the recipient of such a gift from someone so destitute. The treat's freshly-baked aroma filled the kitchen and, mixed with the holly, gave the room the scent of Christmas.

"Bonjour to all in the house!" The male voice just outside the front door sounded merry.

Elodie jumped. "It is Raoul!" She hurried to wipe her tears. "I can't let him see me blubbering like a baby."

Andreva opened the door. Raoul grinned. His lute was strapped to his back. "Elodie." He stepped inside. "Will you stay with Dòna de Lumbert while Andreva accompanies me on an errand?"

Andreva smiled in surprise. A refreshing diversion was just what she needed. Elodie agreed and Raoul wasted no time in taking Andreva's arm and pulling her toward the door.

She grabbed her cloak on the way out. "My grandmother is sleeping and should not awaken until we return. Mercés, Elodie!"

Raoul had left a small handcart filled with baked goods and fire logs out on the street. He pulled it along as they headed up the road. The weather was warmer than it had been for days, and Andreva lifted her face, welcoming the bright rays of sun.

They went first to the house of Gisèla and Jocelyne, the elderly women Bostel had taken Andreva to visit the day before he left. The exterior wall of their home showed signs of the smoke damage from within, and a new shutter hung in place. Andreva stared at the house and hoped she'd not have to enter its dreariness.

Raoul stood close to the window, and called cheerfully. *"Joyeux Noël! Polit nadal!"*

"Come in!"

He held aside the animal skins that covered the entry. Andreva hesitated, but moved forward when he motioned for her to enter. She grimaced as she ducked through. Raoul followed. The smell of smoke from the unfortunate fire lingered in the air. As Andreva's eyes adjusted, the dim light revealed a blackened space under the window where once the table had stood. The thought of the women's fear and, worse, what might have happened, made the damaged plaster a distressing sight.

"We came to sing a song of Noel, and my maire sent a mincemeat pie to wish you a happy Christmas." Raoul handed Jocelyne the treat. "And a log for your fire, albeit a meager one."

"Mercés! Thank you!" Jocelyne's toothless smile was as beautiful as forget-me-not blossoms in spring.

Andreva took in a sharp breath. She had not expected such joy to transform the woman's countenance. How was it possible in a situation this stark and dismal?

Andreva gazed around in dismay while Raoul laid the log on the dying coals. He removed the lute from his back, pulled a stool close to the aged women, and began to play. Andreva recognized the tune as one she had long loved to sing at Christmastime.

> *I arose one early morning when the dawn*
> *Was putting its white mantel on.*
>
> *Let's sing Christmas, Christmas, Christmas,*
> *Let's sing Christmas again.*

Jocelyne's face glowed with delight. Andreva could not restrain herself from singing along.

> *I took my cloak, my hood, and my small mule*
> *And my short, warm coat made of violet wool.*
>
> *Let's sing Christmas, Christmas, Christmas...*

After each verse, Jocelyne and Gisèla joined in the chorus. "*Let's sing Christmas, Christmas, Christmas...*"

> *Then I found young William, the small shepherd.*
> *He said, "I can hear the song of a bird.*
>
> *Let's sing Christmas, Christmas, Christmas...*
>
> *It is not the nightingale that sings so nice,*
> *But a beautiful angel from Paradise.*

Let's sing Christmas, Christmas, Christmas...

Tonight, in Bethlehem, a manger stall
Holds a Child God, who is born for all"

Let's sing Christmas, Christmas, Christmas . . .

As they sang the last chorus, Andreva watched Raoul. She was awed at how simple he made this charitable act appear.

She thought of her uncle's weekly gift of bread. How had she forgotten Bostel's wishes? It stung to recognize that, overwhelmed as she was by her own worries, it had never crossed her mind to bring bread or Christmas cheer to these widows.

When the song finished, they clapped and laughed together. Andreva's heart was full. Despite the dust on the floor, she knelt beside Gisèla to give her a hug.

Gisèla cooed. "Thank you, dear children, for bringing cheer into our home." She placed her hand on Andreva's cheek.

"Now, tell me, my ladies," Raoul said, "what good things has life bestowed since last I saw you?"

"Since the fire?" Jocelyne glanced toward Gisèla. "We have been blessed with good friends who have come to our aid to make our home livable again."

Livable? Andreva's eyes strayed to the cobwebs dangling from the sagging ceiling, dust gathered on the humble furnishings, and sunlight peeking through cracks in rotting woodwork. Their home was a step above Felipa's lean-to, but was no place Andreva would want to live.

Gisèla told of other blessings, such as a stray dog that sat guard at the door through the night, giving them comfort. Her soft voice sounded truly thankful for each small wonder.

While Raoul continued to make conversation with the sisters, Andreva quietly took the bed coverings outside to shake out as Bostel had instructed on their last visit. She then spread them again over the beds.

The humble hovel seemed cheerier as Andreva and Raoul

left. He led her next to the blacksmith's shop, having to pass grim-faced soldiers, waiting while their horses were shod. Raoul and Andreva skirted the men, but overheard their conversation.

"Let us end this siege quickly." The man's deep frown matched his deep voice. "I want to be home with my wife before Epiphany."

"I say, let us climb that mountain and throw torches into the fortress." The soldier scratched beneath his beard. "We'll burn out those worthless heretics!"

A third man put his fist into his grimy palm. "Gah! The Inquisition will take the privilege of doing that deed themselves. Only it will be a heretics' pyre." He let out a ghastly chortle.

Andreva shivered and moved closer to Raoul.

Raoul took her arm, urging her to walk faster. "It is Christmas Eve, after all. A time of goodwill. Can we not forget war for a time?"

At the back of the shop, Felipa's lean-to was silent. Too silent. Had the poor woman passed away?

Raoul called Felipa's name, and a feeble hand pushed aside the blanket.

Andreva released the breath she'd held too long.

Hollow eyes peered out of the crude dwelling. "Who is it?"

"We have brought you mincemeat pie and a song of Christmas cheer."

Felipa took the pie Raoul offered and tucked in under her blankets. Raoul pulled out his lute and began to sing.

"Christmas, Christmas, Christmas." Andreva sang along with the chorus. She turned her head at voices that joined in behind them. It was the soldiers from the blacksmith's shop, singing along, their stern faces softened by the music and words.

When the song ended, the man who had laughed cynically dropped to one knee and, teary eyed, started another carol in a clear tenor voice:

Shepherds, bring your flocks in tonight

> *Run quickly in the greatest haste.*
> *Adore the Child so full of grace*
> *Sent down to us from Heaven so bright.*
> *Let us go now full of vim,*
> *Dancing five steps in front of Him!*

When he finished, Felipa reached for his hand. "Thank you." He took her gnarled hand in his and smiled. "Joyeux Noël! Polit nadal." He stood, and the soldiers each repeated the sentiment before they returned to the blacksmith's shop.

Andreva stood beside Raoul and watched the soldiers go. She was amazed at the change the tender moment had wrought in them.

But as soon as Raoul and Andreva bid farewell to Felipa, the voice of the soloist boomed through the wall. "What do you mean my horse is not yet shod? If it were not for inept tradesmen like you, we would have won this war by now!"

Andreva felt sorry for the blacksmith, but also for the soldiers who had too-briefly enjoyed the peace of Christmas.

To avoid the soldiers, Raoul took Andreva another way to Ponrada's house, and then on to visit the other widows. Each he cheered with a song, and gifted with a yule log and mincemeat pie.

After she'd returned home, Andreva sat on the edge of her grandmother's bed. "We visited the women to whom Bostel took bread. It is hard to see them so poor and alone, especially at Christmas."

"Each of them is a friend." Mémé's eyes held a faraway look. "Long ago, we were of different statuses—my husband the landowner, they the tenants—but status faded away when we each lost a husband in battle on the same day. We mourned together and raised our children together." She focused on Andreva. "And now look at us—we are alone, old, and in failing health. I wish I could take each by the hand and lift her from her sickbed. But, alas, I am as they. I cannot leave my house."

"Tell me about that battle—about how you lost Grandfather."

Mémé looked into Andreva's eyes for several moments. "It is Christmas. I will tell you another time. Let us talk of happy things. I know what I would like—for you to sing to me."

For the next while, Andreva sang every Christmas song she knew. Sometimes Mémé sang along, and then added a few Andreva had not heard. Long after sunset, they still sat together, eating bread and fruit.

Mémé reached for Andreva's hand. "Before you came, I hoped to die. I prayed God would take my soul to Him. But now you are here, and your goodness has brought joy back into my home. You have given me reason to live."

"Oh, Mémé!" Andreva's eyes filled with tears at the encouragement. "We will get you well. After my parents died and I received no word from you, I too prayed God would take me." She returned her grandmother's gentle squeeze. "And now we have each other. Let us thank Him that we both live."

Mémé smiled, but it was only seconds before she became drowsy.

Andreva stood and added another log to the fire. "I would like to go to the chapel for Communion."

"Then go. I shall be fine." Mémé yawned. "Do not worry, I promise not to dance in the street while you are gone."

"Mémé! For shame!" She could not stifle a giggle at the vision of her grandmother skipping joyfully under the stars.

The corners of Mémé eyes crinkled at her own wit. "It is blessed Christmas Eve, but I am confined to this bed. You must allow me a little teasing fun." She chuckled.

"And I shall light a candle for you."

Mémé motioned Andreva close. "The Lord hears our prayers wherever we are. Remember this: You need not pray in chapels nor light candles to receive His attention. God knows you well, and He will judge you by your heart. You cannot escape His watchful eye."

The words sounded odd coming from the devoted Catholic Andreva believed Mémé to be. "Yes. I will remember."

The chapel was full, as she'd expected for Communion on Christmas Eve. Soldiers knelt on the stone floor alongside villagers. She looked from one to the other. Did not the townspeople feel as she did that their privacy had been invaded tonight, along with their village?

She hesitated before slipping off her cloak, and took time to admire a crèche at the back of the chapel that portrayed shepherds, wise men, and the Holy Family.

Father Tomàs finished reading from the Book of Luke, and then a small choir of priests sang. Andreva moved to the front of the chapel and knelt to await her turn as Father Tomàs administered the bread and wine.

After she'd received Communion, Andreva stood. The room held a chill, so she donned her cloak before she walked to the statue of Mother Mary. There she knelt and looked up to admire the image. Mary's blue robe, carved expertly in wood, draped softly over a white gown. Her halo seemed to glow as her kind eyes looked down upon Andreva.

Andreva removed her mittens and lit two candles, one for Mémé despite her parting message, and another for Uncle Bostel. Knowing she should not leave Mémé too long, Andreva pulled the hood over her bowed head. A sense of peace came over her. She uttered a prayer in Mémé's behalf. "And please, send Uncle Bostel home to me." A lump grew in her throat. "Forgive him."

At last she rose. Father Stefe towered over her, his dark eyes critical. She curtsied in greeting, but a chill of fear quivered through her. She wanted only to leave.

Andreva turned and hurried toward the door. With her head bent, the hood obscured her vision. She bumped into a hard body, dropping her mittens. "Pardon me." She dived for the mittens, but a man's hand beat her to them. Andreva stood and looked up into the man's face—a strong, familiar face with clear blue eyes and a firm chin. "Good evening, Jaques Montré!"

he chapel hushed as worshipers glanced toward Andreva and Jaques.

"I beg your pardon, domaisèla." Jaques handed the mittens to Andreva with a smile of recognition.

Heat came into her face and she lowered her lashes. "Mercés, Monsen. Happy Christmas." She curtsied and headed toward the door.

Jaques reached for her arm and held it gently. "Please, stay."

Heads turned again. Embarrassed, Andreva held a finger to her lips and the worshipers turned back to their prayers. She motioned Jaques toward the exit. Together they stepped out into the cold.

"Polit nadal." Jaques smiled again as he wrapped his wool scarf around his neck.

"Mercés." She looked up into his eyes. The loneliness she saw there jabbed her heart. Alone on Christmas? "Jaques, have you no family?"

His weak smile answered before he spoke. "I do, in Gascony. My brother is a priest in Lanpoix. And you? Do you have family elsewhere?"

"No. Only my grandmother and uncle."

"With Bostel away, that is not many." The tease of a smile returned the glint to his eyes. He pulled her aside to allow another couple to enter the chapel. "I hope you enjoyed the trout."

"I did." She did not disclose that Mémé didn't touched the fish, nor that she had buried the last of it. Doing so would seem ungrateful if not wasteful. She looked at Jaques and considered him. No one should spend Christmas alone, but would it be wise to invite him to join Mémé and her for dinner on Christmas Day? Associating socially with a peasant might prove embarrassing. And perhaps she was wrong. Perhaps he would celebrate with friends. "You will not be alone on the morrow?"

Jaques shrugged. "My dog Lonell and I shall spend the day beside the fire."

"Oh? Where is your farm?"

"To the west." He looked that direction. "I do not own the land, of course. It belongs to Bostel."

Bostel? His answer hit like a blast of frigid wind. Jaques was not only a farmer, but also her uncle's tenant. Despite his good looks and the attraction she felt to him—rather *because* of it—she'd best respect their social stations.

She ought to bid him farewell and be done with their conversation. But Bostel had spoken highly of Jaques. Wouldn't her uncle want her to show kindness to his good friend on Christmas? She had failed the widows, could she perhaps do penance with a charitable act now?

Andreva bit her lower lip a moment. "You should not celebrate alone on Christmas Day. Come by Mémé's house in the afternoon for a slice of mincemeat pie. Colet sent one over with Elodie today and there is plenty to share." The words had tumbled out, but she could not retract the invitation now.

He smiled and she held her breath. Would he decline as society would expect him to, and save her possible embarrassment?

"Mercés, Soeur Andreva. I shall come."

She released her breath and smiled. "Mémé and I will look forward to seeing you, then."

Jaques said goodbye and walked back inside the chapel.

Andreva headed toward home, and the farther she walked, the more she regretted the invitation. True, she had chosen to be charitable, but having the farmer socially in their home might prove awkward. But she enjoyed the farmer's company, so perhaps his visit would play out fairly. *After all, it is Christmas.*

With that settled, she allowed her mind to dwell on his conversation, his uplifting smile, his gorgeous— *Stop now!* Noblewomen did not marry peasants. Nothing could come from an infatuation between people so clearly mismatched. Surely Jaques knew that, too.

When she arrived home, she found Mémé snoring lightly in her bed. The fire in the chamber had died down to a glow. Andreva removed her veil and changed into a nightdress. After putting another log on the fire, she made her own bed near the hearth.

The fire burned strong. Andreva stared into the flames. *Tomorrow, will I regret more deeply inviting Jaques to share our pie? It is only a pie...not even dinner...nor forever.* She turned her back to the flames. Still, it had been unwise to extend even a small invitation.

When Andreva closed her eyes, she pictured his. The loneliness she had seen there haunted her. Andreva knew loneliness only too well. Its darkness had engulfed her for the last year, its oppression lifting only when she walked out of the abbey.

Mémé moaned and stirred in the bed. Andreva arose and went to her. "What do you need, Mémé?"

"You are home." Her grandmother opened her eyes.

"I only stayed to take Communion." Andreva sat on the bed. "Are you in pain?"

"It is only my muscles aching from lying here these many weeks."

"Then let me rub them for you."

Mémé turned her back and Andreva began massaging her shoulders. "I am sorry you are not with your parents for Christmas. You miss them."

"Óc." The log still blazed brightly. Andreva looked up as it crackled.

Mémé sighed as the rubbing gave relief. "Tell me of your last Christmas with them."

Andreva continued working her grandmother's muscles.

"Well..." She had to dig in her memory. Since coming to live with her grandmother, she had not dwelt as much on the past. "Our entire household ate a hearty meal of venison and wassail together—our maids and gardeners at the table with us. It was a jolly time. Father hired a minstrel to sing songs of the Nativity. It seems he sang for hours, but it was over much too soon!" She smiled at the memory. "Later, Mother, Father and I attended Mass. I remember kneeling between them for Communion." A sob caught in her throat. "None of us suspected it would be our last together." She lowered her head.

Mémé turned to face her. Pleading tinted her voice. "Do not stop, ma chérie. Go on, tell more."

Andreva wiped at an escaping tear, and tried to remember. "At bedtime, I left my shoes by the hearth, and in the morning they held colorful hair ribbons." Her parents had been truly generous. "We held another celebration that day with friends, with a banquet again laid out, and..." Her words faltered with tears.

Mémé patted her hand. "I am sorry to press you. You need not tell me more."

Andreva wiped her face dry and smiled. "No, Mémé. It feels good to talk of them again."

"Then I am here to listen."

Andreva drew in a deep breath. "I remember that when the fever took Father, the Twelfth Day candles were still burning. He lasted not two days. Maire followed less than a month later. My maid stayed with me another few days before Count Raymond decided I should go to the abbey." She did not mention the letter she had written to Mémé and Bostel that received no reply. Somehow it didn't matter any longer.

Mémé lay back on the pillow, closed her eyes, and sighed. "Did you light a candle for Bostel at the chapel tonight?"

"Yes, Mémé." She stood and took care as she straightened the covers around the woman. When her grandmother said no more, Andreva settled into the chair to watch the flames.

Uncle Bostel. How would he celebrate this Christmas? At midnight Mass in a fine cathedral in Toulouse, or crowded within the walls of Montsegùr? Andreva placed her hand over an almost physical pain in her chest, a deep ache caused by the mere possibility of his deceit.

Soon Mémé's breathing became steady. Andreva continued to watch the ever-changing fire. Life was like the leaping flames. Its circumstances changed shape so quickly—one moment dancing, and then in seconds, if death desired, its embers dwindling to nothing. She would take one day at a time.

She opened her eyes. Morning's blue haze filtered through the shutters. *Christmas morning!*

Andreva bolted upright and glanced at her shoes. Empty, of course. She felt a pang for childhood lost. After dressing, she slipped the shoes onto her feet, and then arranged bread and preserves on a tray before turning her attention to heating water for Mémé's bath. While she waited for it to warm, she glanced up the staircase toward the empty upstairs chamber. "No matter where you are, Uncle, I wish you a happy Christmas."

Recalling Jaques' smile caused the corners of her mouth to lift and her heart to flutter. Last night's fretting seemed unimportant now in the morning's bright sunlight.

She picked up the tray. She would have a peasant over for pie on Christmas Day. *A peasant whose voice is deep and musical.* What was a mere hour spent with a man who worked with his hands? *Strong hands, strong shoulders.* After all, he had agreed to look in on their welfare. *He is kind, thoughtful.* She caught herself sighing, and had to laugh. *Silly romantic girl!*

Mémé awakened. Andreva brought the tray, placed it on the foot of the bed, and helped her grandmother to the chamber pot. "It is Christmas morning. We are expecting a visitor this afternoon and must get you presentable." Andreva plumped the pillows and straightened the bedding, dreading Mémé's reaction.

"A visitor?" Mémé raised her head and blinked. "Who is

coming?"

Andreva pulled the nightgown off over Mémé's head. "Jaques Montré. I invited him to share the mincemeat pie Colet sent."

"I do not want anyone to come today."

It was the protest Andreva expected. She tossed the gown aside, removed a linen cloth from the warm water, and washed Mémé's back. "I saw him at the chapel last night. He is all alone today, so I invited him. Bostel would want us to. Do you not agree? No one should be alone on Christmas Day."

Mémé's face showed no sign of agreement. "I hardly know the man. I cannot sit at the table, and it is improper for a man to come in to a woman's bedroom."

"Then he shall sit outside the door." She handed the washrag to Mémé to finish the routine, and then opened the wardrobe to remove a beautifully embroidered nightdress and bonnet. Andreva helped Mémé dress and get back into bed. She straightened her bonnet and arranged the sheets around her. "You look lovely for any visitors today."

Mémé's stern face appeared unconvinced.

Andreva settled on the bed and moved the tray between them. She had hardly taken a bite when they heard a commotion outside the door, children's chatter accompanying it.

"Who could that be?" Andreva stood and went to the chamber entrance as banging echoed throughout the house. She hurried to the door and opened it.

Andreva laughed when Raoul's younger brother entered, carrying the lute, followed by Colet's two smaller children, bouncing with excitement. One carried a plucked chicken, and the other a pine wreath. Next came Raoul and a friend, carrying a large log on their shoulders.

"John and I have brought you a little something for your fire. Where shall we place it?" Raoul had a wide grin on his face.

"*Cachafuoc*! A Yule log!" Andreva clapped her hands. She pointed to the hearth in the large room. "No, no! Take it to Mémé's chamber. It will warm her and lighten her spirits."

The young men obeyed. After directing the children to leave the chicken on the table, Andreva herded them into the bedroom.

Mémé pulled the sheet to her chin and yelped. "There are men in my chamber!" Andreva and the children giggled. Even Mémé's eyes danced with merriment.

The log stood tall, even on its side. Raoul rolled it toward the back of the fireplace so it would burn safely. Andreva helped Colet's youngest son crawl up to sit at Mémé's side, and in the long-standing Occitan tradition—the youngest and oldest together—in unison, they chanted:

> **Light up Yule log, delight us**
> **Give us the joy to be here next year.**
> **And if we are not as numerous, let us not be less!**

The children clapped with glee. Raoul played the lute while his younger sister danced, and the others clapped along.

At the end of the song, Raoul's sister placed the pine wreath atop the log, and the wreath took flame. The younger brother squealed, "Make a wish!" They all closed their eyes. Andreva searched for the wish of her heart and found it: that Uncle Bostel would soon return.

Raoul turned to Mémé. "This log should last many days, hopefully until the Feast of Epiphany."

Mémé's eyes glowed, and her spirits were higher than Andreva had ever witnessed. "We will enjoy it to its last ember. Mercés, Master Raoul."

He blushed at the generous title. The children gathered close. *"Polit nadal e bona annada!"* The smallest girl, who had danced, crawled up on Mémé's bed and planted a kiss on her cheek.

"Joyeux Noël." Tears glistened in Mémé's eyes.

As fast as they'd entered, the visitors left. Snow flurries played on the breeze as Andreva stood at the open doorway and waved goodbye, grateful for their generosity and good cheer this Christmas morn. She wanted to call them back, but settled for enjoying the song and laughter that echoed along the street, even after the children were out of her view.

Andreva returned to the quiet of the chamber room. A smile still lingered on Mémé's lips as her eyes feasted on the flames from the large log. They held a melancholy glaze, as if her thoughts were of sweet memories. She sighed. "Blessed Christmas has come again."

Andreva sat on the bed and began to eat. Her home-baked bread was dense and hard to chew. "Oh, Mémé, you must teach me to bake and to cook. Everything I make is like leather to chew."

"You will learn with experience like everyone else, my dear." Mémé nibbled a crust.

"In the meantime, we shall suffer through many tasteless dishes." Andreva's moan set Mémé to giggling.

The rest of the morning passed slowly, almost too slowly for Andreva to bear. After her noon dinner of boiled chicken and more bread, she peeked out the shutters. The farmer was not on the road.

He will not come early. She closed the shutters, walked to the window in Mémé's room, and looked out. *I know perfectly well he will not come early.* She returned to the great room. Even though she'd already cleaned the floor several times, she grabbed the broom and swept imaginary dust toward the door, opened it, and finished the task, only to search once more for Jaques. *Why doesn't he come?*

After dusting the bedchamber and kitchen, she arranged the stools, and better positioned the holly and berry wreath on the mantel. Finally, she sat on a chair beside Mémé and fidgeted while she watched the fire.

Mémé frowned. "Your young man will come."

Andreva huffed. "He is not my young man."

"You flutter so around the house that I cannot rest." She turned over. "There are several bags under the bed. One of them is an apron with unfinished embroidery. Let it occupy your hands if not your mind."

Andreva found the bag. She returned to the chair and pulled out a white apron with a needle and floss still tucked carefully into its flowered pattern. With each stitch, Andreva listened to the noises on the street. Would the knock ever come?

Mémé dozed, propped up by pillows. She appeared angelic and ready for visitors.

Andreva looked down at the three flowers she had stitched. Beside Mémé's, they looked wilted. "I am only nervous because Jaques is coming."

Mémé grunted her disapproval.

And she was right. Andreva would not make this mistake again. She would never again invite him over. And when he came today—or after today to check on their welfare— she would not look into his eyes, or allow him to make her smile. She would definitely *not* lose her heart to him...at least no more than she might have already.

Finally, after she had stitched several flowers in a finished row, she heard a knock.

Onze

11

Andreva flung the door open to find Jaques Montré standing on the stoop. His hair was combed neatly, his beard trimmed, and he wore flawless stockings and a tunic of a fine weave. Even his tattered cloak had been replaced with one of good wool.

He bowed. "I hope your grandmother is feeling better today." His smile sent tingles dancing down her spine.

"She is in good spirits." Andreva invited him in and shut the door. She took his cloak, but her fingers fumbled when she went to hang it on a peg, and it slipped to the floor. He picked it up. She laughed nervously as she took it and tried again. Success. She then turned to serve the mincemeat pie, but could not keep her fingers from trembling. Somehow, she moved it onto pewter plates without making too much of a mess.

"We shall eat with Mémé. Please bring the stool." Now her knees trembled. She could barely walk and juggle three plates at the same time. "Being the gentleman you are, you will sit on this side of the door." She tried again to clarify her request. "As you know, it is improper to enter a lady's chamber—you not being family, or clergy, and..." She stopped herself before adding *only a farmer*.

Jaques carried the stool to the door and set it in place while Andreva served her grandmother. Returning to the doorway, she extended the plate with his treat. He accepted it and balanced it carefully while taking a seat. At last he peered into the room. "Bon nadal, Dòna de Lumbert!"

Mémé pulled the sheet higher. "I return the sentiment to you, young Montré." She sniffed and avoided looking in the farmer's direction.

They ate in an awkward silence. Andreva chided herself for inviting him. Clearly, this had been a poor idea. The deliciously moist pie became hard to swallow. The yule log crackled and popped, but its warmth barely reached the doorway.

Jaques' brawny legs were too long to comfortably straddle the stool, and kept him off balance. His slice of pie crumbled, and bits fell to the floor. With a mumbled apology, he bent to retrieve the fallen crumbs.

"Leave it be." Andreva smiled. "I will sweep it later."

"But…"

"No harm that a broom cannot fix."

"Both of you sit still."

Andreva straightened in surprise at her grandmother's order.

Mémé looked at Jaques. "I remember the first time I saw you, young Montré. It was at the village festival—the last I felt able to attend. Of course, villagers are suspicious of newcomers, but your reception was something more. The young girls' eyes could not help but wander to you." She chuckled.

Jaques choked on his mincemeat while Andreva fought a smile.

Mémé sighed and seemed to leave the present. "Many a couple has fallen in love at the festival." She closed her eyes briefly. "I was betrothed to Gilbert de Lumbert at a very young age. His family descends from the Counts of Foix. We both lived in Lavelanet, so it was at the Spring Festival that our parents arranged for our betrothal to be made public. Gilbert wore a fine woven tunic and a cap to which he had attached a long feather." She chuckled again.

Andreva listened closely as Mémé continued. "He told me he'd stolen the feather from a pheasant that very morning so as to be dressed appropriately for our meeting." She placed a hand over her heart. "I fell in love that day, and have loved him ever since. He died courageously, but much too young, leaving me a widow with two children yet to raise."

Jaques inclined his head in a gesture of honor. "My sympathy, Dòna. To have raised a son as fine as Monsen Bostel clearly reflects your strong character."

Mémé blinked in surprise. "Thank you, Jaques." Her eyes moistened, and she relaxed into the pillow with a smile on her lips.

Andreva, too, was pleasantly surprised by Jaques' genteel reply. Who was this farmer in fine clothing who could ease an old woman's burden by his thoughtful words?

Soon Mémé's breathing rattled in a slight snore. Andreva took her grandmother's plate and pulled the coverlet around her before leaving the room and beckoning Jaques to return his stool to the table.

She set the plates aside. "Care for another slice of mincemeat?"

"Yes. Please." He accepted with a boyish grin that made her smile.

She bid him sit back down and handed him a slice larger than the first. "Tell me. Do you enjoy your work?"

"I like it very much." His mouth twitched into a smile. "You have spent little time on a farm. Am I right?"

"No time, actually. Tell me about your life here." She sat across the table from him to listen.

Jaques chewed the bite of pie and swallowed. "A farmer must work from sunup to sundown. He feeds his animals and milks his cows, morning and night, without fail. He must till the land, plant, hoe, and then harvest his crop when it is ripe. He gives part to the lord who owns his land, a tenth to the Church, and a measure into storage for his own support. He sells the surplus, and if there is money left over after paying his rent, he buys bread, butter, and cheese—if he cannot make those things himself—and perhaps clothing to wear." He took another bite.

Andreva glanced at his fine-woven tunic and wool stockings. He must have had a prosperous year to buy the excellent garments he wore today.

Jaques looked toward the fire as if recalling a memory. The flames reflected in his eyes. "If his lord or king requires it, he will take up the sword in battle."

"Have you gone to battle?" Andreva tried to imagine Jaques wielding a blade, but the image turned to Bostel, a sword at his side, riding to Avignonet-Lauragais. Could Jaques tell her the truth about that incident?

"Nothing I have to brag about." Jaques' glance was brief.

Because of the sad look in his eyes, she abandoned the topic of war, nor did she ask about the massacre. But still, his humility was commendable. Most men were quick to expound on even the smallest act of bravery in battle. Had something happened to make him reluctant to talk? She returned to the first subject. "What you tell me about farming, it requires then a goodly amount of labor."

"It does." He focused again on her. "It brings great satisfaction to watch clods turn under the blade of the plow, knowing the seeds are tucked away in the sun-warmed earth. Nothing is sweeter than the smell of freshly turned soil, nothing more heartening than watching the rain seep in to help the plants sprout and grow. Nothing is as gratifying as taking part in it all with my own two hands."

"You have broader shoulders than any man I have met." The thought had boldly tumbled out in words! Heat rushed up Andreva's neck, burning her cheeks and ears.

His eyes gleamed and he brushed the last of the crumbs from his beard. "I shall take that as a compliment."

Andreva opened her mouth, but only a croak escaped.

Mercifully, he politely returned to the subject. "But I am also thankful for the winter season and the time it gives me to rest from growing crops. Because I must plow my fields the day after Epiphany, I confess I shall enjoy the days before—and feel a bit lazy."

"In that case, may the Twelve Days never end." She feigned a pout. *Oh, no! I am flirting with a farmer!* What demon had possessed her to turn so bold? Did Colet's pie possess magical powers to make her say forward things?

Jaques' dark blue eyes studied her face as if deliberating her meaning. "You toy with my affections, domaisèla, which can only come to naught."

Andreva pursed her lips. If only the hasty words could be taken back. As handsome as the farmer was, she should not encourage him.

"Forgive me, Monsen." She stood, walked to the hearth, and busied herself with the fire until she regained her composure. "I look forward to the Winter Festival. When is it?"

"Two weeks from Friday. Pray tell, have you been to a festival in Lavelanet?"

"No, only in Toulouse at the castle courtyard. What do Lavelanetiens do to amuse themselves at festivals?"

"Well," he traced the nick in the table with his finger, "people come from all over the countryside—farmers and villagers alike. In the morning, there is a jousting tournament. There are plenty of knights at the château to fill the roster this year."

"Yes? Do you enjoy watching the tournaments?"

A shadow clouded his eyes. "No. I shall care for my animals during those hours."

She had not expected that response. The jousts were definitely the most appealing part of festivals. "Then you will come when you can?" *Oh, no!* The question sounded eager and, once again, encouraging.

"Óc, I shall come. I would not miss it. There shall be tables filled with all the food you can eat. In the afternoon, troubadours will sing, jesters and jugglers will entertain, and villagers will dance and play jolly games in the churchyard. Hope for good weather." He paused. "Are you allowed to come? Are you still...uh, a nun?"

A nun? She had almost forgotten! Her eyes moved to the veil and wimple hanging on their peg. Should she remind him she had not taken vows? Perhaps not. "You are right. And I cannot leave Mémé."

"I can stay alone an hour or two!" Mémé called from the next room.

Andreva threw her hand over her gaping mouth and looked upon Jaques' bemused face. "Watch what you say. Mémé may not be well, but she hears all she wishes."

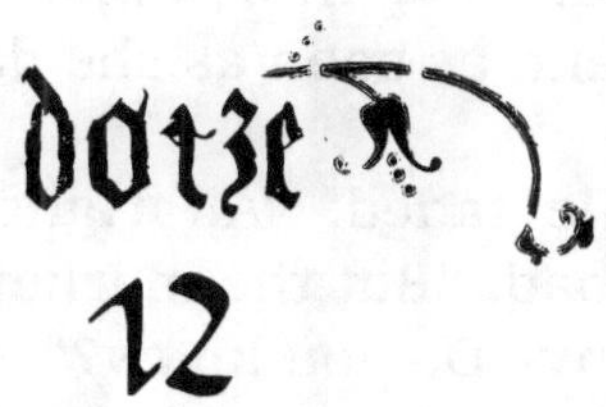

12

December passed in a windstorm, but the first week of January calmly crept by.

The sun had set hours ago, but sleep would not come. Andreva tossed on her straw mattress. Finally, she left her bed, went to the window and opened a shutter only enough to glimpse the waning moon's winter radiance. Jaques Montré had occupied her thoughts since Christmas Day. His eyes, his voice, his...lips often flashed through her memory. Had he felt ill at ease around her? He had accused her of toying with his affections. A smile formed as she admitted to herself he had been right.

A glow in the mountains caught her eye. This could not be the flame of the soldiers' distant campfires. She opened the shutter, despite the cold, for a better view. Judging by the size of the flickering light, there must be a huge fire on the mountainside. She watched until the glow diminished. Had a campfire burned out of control? Had the soldiers set a bonfire against the cold? There was a third option she did not want to consider—that there had been an attack upon Montsegùr by night. Uncle Bostel! Was he there? Was he all right?

✦

"Andreva!" A girl's voice called from outside the door early the next morning. The hinges on the window shutters squeaked as Andreva pushed them open. Morning light rushed into the room, but the air was much too chill to allow her to think the sunny day pleasant.

Elodie stood bundled in a cloak. "I am going to market. Come along."

Andreva moaned with disappointment. "Mémé has not yet awakened, and as soon as she does, she will call for the chamber pot."

Elodie's smile faded. "All right, I will go alone." She peered up the road. "But the market is full of soldiers."

"Why so many? Do you know?"

"Perhaps it is their shopping day." Elodie's effort to be cheerful failed. "You know how I feel about Crusaders." The girl bit her lip and started away.

Andreva closed the shutters. She took a log from the woodpile and placed it on the kitchen fire. As she watched it catch flame, she wondered about the lights she had seen during the night.

An urgent-sounding knock came at the door. Andreva froze. Judging by the firmness of purpose, it was not Elodie returning. Jaques Montré had never knocked so loudly, and certainly it was not Raoul either. She stepped cautiously toward the door.

Mémé called from the bedroom, "Andreva! Who is making that racket?"

Andreva turned and went into the chamber. She pulled the blanket around her grandmother's shoulders. "I do not know, but I shall return soon to attend to you."

The chamber door creaked as she closed it behind her. She headed across the room and donned her veil, leaving the wimple. She peered through the shutters. It was a man, but who, she could not tell as he was turned away. Her hand rested on the latch as the knock sounded again. She slowly released the latch and pulled the door open a few inches. "Monsen Fortaner." Remembering his last visit, she did not widen the gap.

"Ma Soeur." His eyes glanced over her attire. "I have brought the allowance your uncle wished you to have. Has he returned?"

"He has not. We have received no word from him."

"Is your grandmother sleeping?" He looked past her at the closed chamber door.

She wished for Raoul's presence. "No." She avoided his eyes. "She is awake, but is not ready to receive visitors." Andreva glanced over her shoulder, regretting that she had closed the door to Mémé's room. She looked back to Fortaner and forced herself to smile. "I assumed you had gone to Narbonne with your wife."

"My wife took leave without me." Fortaner smiled and placed his hand on the door. "May I come in?"

She pushed the door closed another inch. "I fear not, Monsen. Forgive me but—" The man's foot slid forward, preventing the door from closing any farther. Andreva's stomach lurched. "Please, my lord, I must attend to my duties. My grandmother—"

He forced her to step backward as he pressed the door open. "You grow prettier each time I see you, domaisèla. Even while disguised as a nun."

The fears she had harbored since his last visit returned. "I wear no disguise." *It is my protection!* She kept her lashes lowered, and silently, but fervently, prayed for help. *Saint Agnes, holy child, all purity, keep me undefiled.*

He reached for a lock of Andreva's hair not hidden beneath the veil, and slid his finger down her cheek to lift her chin.

Andreva cringed.

His eyes reflected his lust. "Hair of gold and eyes the color of the sky."

"Monsen!" She moved away. "Tell me, how was sweet Dianne before she left for Narbonne?"

Fortaner lifted a groomed eyebrow. "She was fine. It is a holiday for me as well when she travels." His eyes held a famished look.

Andreva's glance darted around the room. The broom stood inches away. She would grab it if the man took another step.

He kicked the door closed with a bang. A line appeared between his brows. "It is bad luck to leave open a door.

Besides the cold, it invites the entrance of evil spirits."

"At times evil spirits enter uninvited." Andreva grasped the broom and held the straw end between them. "The allowance, please, Monsen. And then you must leave."

"Andreva?" Her grandmother called from the bedchamber.

Andreva tightened her grip on her improvised weapon though her hands trembled.

"Answer." Fortaner rested a fist on his hip and amusement danced in his eyes.

She swallowed. "Y-yes, Mémé?"

"Who is here?"

She saw her knuckles grow white. "It is Monsen Fortaner. He brought our allowance and is asking after Uncle Bostel."

"Thank him and politely ask him to speak to you from without the door. A man should not be in the home of two unmarried women."

Andreva dared to look up to the man's face. "You heard my grandmother's wishes. You have had your fun teasing me. Now, please leave."

He threw back his head and chortled, showing rotting teeth. He caught his breath. "Jaques Montré is not a man? I doubt he is a eunuch." He laughed bitterly.

Horrified, Andreva's jaw dropped. How did Fortaner know Jaques had been there? Did he spy upon her?

"Put the broom down. I will not harm you." He pulled a coin pouch from his vest and tossed it onto the table. "You could live much better than this meager way your uncle left you if—"

She recoiled and lifted the broomstick.

Still he raised his hand to touch her. "Shall we discuss... an arrangement?"

Her veil slipped as she whirled out of reach. "Sir!" She straightened it. "I am a sister of the convent at St. Sernin. I beg your respect!"

At that moment, the door opened and Raoul entered with a dark-haired man at his back. Raoul looked from Andreva to Fortaner. His jaw flexed and his fists clenched. His companion stood close, skepticism on his face. "I assume you are leaving, Monsen Fortaner." Raoul's body was so tense the hem of his tunic trembled.

Fortaner calmly straightened his vest. "What have we here? The neighborhood rubbish. I could have you arrested for forced entry."

"Try," Raoul's friend hissed. He picked up a stool.

Andreva feared he would throw it at Fortaner. She reached out. "No!"

Raoul took the stool from his friend and stood it in its place. "I have been a neighbor and workman for Monsen Bostel most of my life. He considers me family."

Fortaner scowled, but moved to the door. "You will regret this intrusion, young Raoul." He turned to Andreva. "I shall return in two weeks."

Raoul bolted the door as soon as Fortaner stepped out.

"Andreva!" Mémé called again. "Pray, tell what is happening?"

"Monsen Fortaner has gone." Andreva hurried to the chamber door and opened it. "Raoul has arrived with a friend."

"I heard Fortaner. I had thought better of him." Mémé rose up on her elbow. "I am surprised at the roguish character that has emerged from his façade of nobility. Bostel should never have trusted him." Mémé clenched her fist. "If Gerrard Fortaner comes here again, I will leap from my bed to defend you." The look of determination in her eyes told Andreva she meant what she said. "You have my solemn promise."

Mémé's pledge, while heartwarming, gave Andreva little comfort. Her grandmother struggled to sit up in her bed, never could she leap from it. Nor did Andreva trust her own success if forced to face Fortaner alone again.

Andreva left the chamber to find Raoul and the stranger waiting at the table. Raoul gestured toward the man. "Andreva, this is Garcia, the troubadour friend I told you about."

Garcia? The name was somehow familiar. Andreva studied the man. He appeared to be years older than Raoul. A scar ran down his face close to his ear. Her breath caught in her throat as she remembered meeting the priest on the road to Avignonet-Lauragais and his warning about a dangerous man they sought. "Bonjour, Garcia." Her eyes did not leave his face. "Thank you for coming to my defense." She curtsied briefly, but kept her distance. "Are you from Lavelanet?"

"No." Garcia's smile filled his round face. "I am an adventurer, and have come to explore the Pyrénées."

"I have never met an explorer. Your accent tells me you have traveled far. Where are you from?"

Garcia opened his mouth to speak, but Raoul interrupted. "We watched Fortaner pound on your door. I do not trust the man."

Garcia added, "Have you recovered from your fright?"

"Óc. I shall be fine." Andreva straightened her veil. "I thank you for your help, and God bless you." She made the sign of the cross.

The two men made the sign also, and said, "Keep your door bolted," almost in unison.

Raoul took her hand. "I cannot save you from every intruder who comes." A minute later, and with Andreva's promise to be more careful, Raoul and his friend left.

She watched from the window. If this was the same Garcia Father Stefe sought, and she was certain he was, what should she do? Reason told her to report him immediately to the Inquisitor, but that did not feel right. He did not seem dangerous or evil—and he had come to her rescue.

Andreva grabbed a pail and headed toward the door to retrieve water for Mémé's morning routine, but had second thoughts. What if Fortaner still lurked in the shadows? Fetching water could wait. She set the pail down. She needed her uncle's protection. She was unsafe with Fortaner coming to the house and now possibly a dangerous man in the village. Could she write to Bostel and convince him to return sooner? She would send letters to Toulouse and... to Montsegùr, begging him to return. She wanted her family, what was left of it, to stay together.

Andreva turned toward the cupboards, intending to find parchment, but hesitated. *Would a letter, if intercepted by the wrong person, incriminate him?*

A light knock came at the door. *Oh, dread!* Had that awful man returned? Or perhaps it was Elodie.

Andreva went soundlessly to the window. To her delight, Jaques Montré stood on the stoop. She searched the street. Was Fortaner there somewhere, hiding in the shadows? Seeing no one, she released the latch. "Jaques, what a pleasant surprise!"

Jaques stood before her, a reserved smile on his face. Leather lacing held together the vest he wore over a tunic. He also wore knee-high sheepskin boots. "I thought you could use a few eggs." He handed her a basket.

She smiled, placed her hand over her dancing heartbeat, and peered into the basket. "Mercés, Monsen."

He held up a plucked, headless chicken. "And a hen for your pot."

Alarm replaced pleasure. "Do I have to clean it?"

Jaques' eyes twinkled as he handed it to her. "I have done it for you. It is to thank you for sharing your excellent mincemeat pie on Christmas Day."

"But I thank you for sharing it with us." She heard loud voices and peered outside to see French soldiers gathered around the well.

"Their spirits are at their highest today since taking over the barbican on Montsegùr during the night."

"The barbican?"

"The lookout on the lowest point of the plateau, the eastern tip of the pog. They burned it down and killed two guards in the process."

Andreva gasped. *The glow on the mountainside.* "Who were the unfortunate?" Her throat tightened. Had her uncle been one of those poor guards?

"As of now, no one has been named."

"I saw the fire from my window," she said. Surely, even if he were there, her uncle was safe. She prayed for him daily, lit candles, and even wished upon the Yule log for his return.

"I regret being the bearer of ill news, but it is the talk of the village." Jaques turned to leave. "I hope to see you at the festival in two weeks."

"But, Monsen," Her heart seemed to drop in her chest. "Will it be two weeks before I—*we* see you again?"

He appeared to mull over her words. "I will try to stop by before then, if you would like."

"Óc, I...we would like that very much." Had her honest response sounded too eager? Would she ever feel at ease conversing with this man? Andreva held up the plucked fowl. "How can I thank you for your kindness?"

He pulled off his straw hat. "Do not mind. But..."

"Yes?"

"If the next time you make apple fritters you save me a bit, I would be grateful. It is my favorite."

"The next time? Oh, Jaques!" Andreva laughed. "I regret it, but I have never made fritters. Actually, I never had to cook before coming to Lavelanet." Would he think ill of her now that she'd admitted her shortcomings?

His grin widened with amusement. She was glad when he didn't laugh outright. "Forgive me for asking, domaisèla." Returning the hat to his head, he turned toward the street.

"Mercés!" she called to him after he'd climbed onto his cart and started up the road. "Please come again soon!"

When he was out of sight, she hummed a happy tune as she found a pot in which to cook the bird. Andreva giggled. If it gave Jaques Montré a reason to return, she would learn to make fritters.

"Andreva," Mémé called from the bedroom. "Please help me to the chamber pot!"

Andreva dropped the chicken into the kettle and hurried to help her grandmother get settled. When she was as comfortable as possible, Andreva sat on the bed and, though she tried, could not hide her pleasure. "Mémé, please tell me how to make apple fritters!"

treize

13

ave you told me all the ingredients?" Andreva teased after Mémé explained how to make fritters.

"My dear, I am not sure. It has been many years since I tried my hand at fritters." Mémé sighed. "I cannot tell you more."

"But someday you may be gone. Who will answer all my questions then? Who will teach me to cook, and tell me the family stories?"

Mémé turned her head to look at Andreva. "What stories do you wish to hear, child?"

Andreva cleared her throat. "Well, Maire told me Grandfather died when she was a little girl. You have mentioned his death, but never told me the whole story. Will you talk about it with me now, or is it still too painful?"

Mémé thought a moment. "I have been a widow for thirty-two years. I have lived so much of life since then, and the pain has eased." She squeezed Andreva's hand. "Gilbert died in the year of our Lord, one thousand two hundred and twelve."

"So long ago."

"Óc. It is time you knew. Help me sit up, ma chérie, and I shall tell you."

Andreva helped Mémé to sit up against the pillows, and settled beside her on the bed.

Mémé took her hand. "It happened early in the war

against the Albigensians. An army led by Simon de Montfort—a horrible and heartless man—marched through the Languedoc, giving battle to every village, conquering in the name of King Philip and Pope Innocent III. When they came to Lavelanet, they gave no warning, but rode in, wielding their swords. Gilbert hid the children and me in the cellar behind the brine barrel, and grabbed his sword to join the other men in defense of the village."

Andreva tightened her squeeze on Mémé's hand. This story could not have a happy ending.

"The children and I trembled, afraid to cry or make a peep, and waited in the dark for his return. After the commotion ceased and the sound of pounding horses' hooves faded into the distance, there was only silence. I left the children hidden—Bostel not even a year old—climbed the stairs, and peered out. I saw dead men in the streets, their wives weeping over them. I ran through the village, searching everywhere for my Gilbert."

"And you found him—"

"With a slash through his neck, lying on the commons, his sword still in hand."

Andreva looked away. "It must have been too horrible to bear."

"Horrible, indeed. Montfort's army murdered nearly every husband and father—and several of our women—that day. We were able to bind wounds and save the lives of a few men, but it was the mothers and children who buried the dead."

"How did you find the strength?"

Mémé's eyes turned misty. "We had to carry on. What choice did we have? As hard as it was, we harvested the year's crops, planted the next, and raised the babies—alone." She smoothed her hand over Andreva's. "Never underestimate what women, what *you*, can do."

Andreva took a deep breath. Would she have the strength to rise to meet such a challenge?

"Our men were killed in the name of God and France that day—" A sob escaped Mémé's throat. She let go of Andreva's hand and raised the sheet to cover her mouth.

"I am so sorry. I had no idea..." Andreva slid off the bed, onto her knees, and put her arms around Mémé while she cried.

At last Mémé dried her face. "Montfort did not fear a village of women and children, so he left us to fend for ourselves during the years Lavelanet was under his rule. Finally, with the Treaty of Paris, Raymond VII regained his father's lands, but we will always be subject to King Louis."

Mémé looked into Andreva's eyes. The lines on her face had deepened, making her appear even older than she was. "Now my husband and daughter are dead. I have but you and one son—and who knows his fate? The Crusade might claim all our lives before it is over."

"Hush! Do not talk that way, it will bring bad luck." Andreva made the sign of the cross. What did Mémé know of Bostel's activities? Had he told his mother something different than what he'd told her?

Mémé's blue eyes seemed unfocused as she stared up at the beams. "Bad luck brings itself. It is all around us. It waits behind closed doors." She blinked and moved her gaze to Andreva. Sadness filled her eyes. "What hope is there for the County of Toulouse? None. France has conquered us." She chuckled dryly. "Someday, your grandchildren will speak French instead of Occitan."

"Mémé, you are wrong." Andreva grabbed her grandmother's hand and held it to her heart. "Count Raymond will rise again. We will take back our freedom. We will—" She froze. Those were her father's words, a phrase he repeated often, at least until his defeat at Taillebourg. She had believed them, even when her world began to crumble.

"No." Mémé's weak smile vanished. "With France and the Inquisition in power, we will never know freedom again." She exhaled as if in surrender. "We are conquered. What can we do but live our lives and hope for a better future?" Mémé closed her eyes.

Andreva waited, but Mémé spoke no more. The discussion had taken all her limited energy. Andreva's spirits flagged with her grandmother's strength, leaving her melancholy.

She felt sad for her homeland, sad for Mémé's loss, and even sad for the loss of a grandfather she'd never known. After a few moments she rose, tucked the woven blanket around her grandmother, and went to the window.

She drew in a breath. "There are Crusaders on the commons." She latched the shutters. "I have never seen so many in Lavelanet."

Mémé turned onto her side and nestled deeper into the pillow and mattress. "I dreaded the coming of this day."

Andreva glanced back over her shoulder. Her grandmother appeared so small lying under the blanket. She waited until Mémé's breathing turned heavy then slipped from the room. Outside the door, she fell to her knees. The cold of the stone floor seeped through her skirt. Andreva turned her heart toward heaven, but no words came, only tears.

14

Happy that the day of the festival had arrived, Andreva went early to the marketplace, wearing her veil as usual. The villagers were in a jolly mood. All around, people were building tables and decorating them with ivy, tree bows, and strung berries. It was perfect festival weather: clear skies that promised a warmer afternoon than usual.

Fabric swags adorned the trees surrounding the commons—the commons where her grandfather and so many others had died. Andreva stared a long moment. Was today's merriment irreverent, considering the lives lost on this soil? She brushed away the notion. The tragedy had happened long ago. The villagers had put it behind them, as they must, and moved forward with their lives, as her grandmother had said.

On her return home, she met Raoul at the well and recognized her pails at his feet. "Thank you for drawing water for me."

He cranked up the well bucket. "I want you to know I have remained Catholic myself."

What a strange greeting! "As have I. You can see, I hope." She indicated her habit and veil. *What is he up to now?*

He glanced around as if looking for someone who listened. "But that does not mean I would not do something daring."

Andreva waited for whatever idea would follow the cryptic remark, but he was silent as he balanced the bucket on the rim of the well. She lowered her voice. "Are you saying you might go against the Church? That is very dangerous. Even you have warned me to be cautious."

Raoul's eyes brightened and he moved close. "Garcia has told me an astonishing story and I believe what he says. I have decided to help him."

"Garcia is wanted by the authorities." She gave him her most indignant look. "You keep company with a criminal, not a musician."

He looked truly surprised. "You know of his misfortune?" His eyes narrowed. "I beg to reason with you then. I believe he has done nothing wrong, and I think I should help him."

"Help him?" Andreva took the bucket and emptied the water into one of her pails. "Why do you tell me this?"

"I hoped you might want to assist because..." His eyes took in her veil but settled on her face. "...well, you seem to think for yourself."

She feigned offense. "It is unlawful to think for oneself."

"Especially for a female." He winked.

She turned away, pail in hand. She would not listen if he was going to be irritating.

"But of all the girls I know, you are the most capable." He followed.

"What about your sister Elodie? Why don't you ask her for help?"

"Ah. She has gone back to the Fortaners' manor. Dòna has returned."

Andreva turned and frowned. "I will miss her and shall pray for her safety." With Fortaner around, how could any maiden be safe? "And no risks for me. You know my time is taken up with caring for Mémé, and I stay as far away as possible from Inquisitors and Crusaders."

"The knights shall compete in the tournament. Will you ignore them?"

Andreva raised her chin. "I shall do my best."

"Then I insist upon being your escort to the festival. You will need protection. I shall come by your house and walk you to the square—with your promise that I may have the first dance—and several following."

Her mouth snapped shut. *What?* The possibility of being limited to Raoul's company was worrisome. It would only encourage the romantic notions Elodie had hinted he bore. Also, what about Jaques? *How best to discourage Raoul?* "You would dance with a novice?"

He lifted her chin. "Ah, Andreva, are you a nun, or a girl full of dreams, wearing a disguise?"

Fortaner flashed through her mind. He had also accused her of using the habit as a disguise. Andreva stepped out of reach, annoyed that Raoul would take such liberty to touch her. Her mouth settled into a hard line.

Raoul leaned close. "Perhaps it is time to forsake the wimple, Andreva. You have not taken vows, and you may never return to the abbey, at least not for a long time."

She stiffened. How dare he tell her what she knew, or assume what she might do?

He patted her shoulder, and her impatience deepened. "Well, think about it." Raoul turned and nodded politely to a woman who passed on the road. After she could no longer overhear, he turned back to Andreva. "I have written a song for you. I will come to escort you, and will play it with the troubadours at the festival. Please promise me the first dance."

In her mind, Jaques' manly smile replaced Raoul's boyish grin. Jaques had not offered to escort her, though she wished he had. Had he considered it, perhaps, and felt too shy to ask?

What am I thinking? Why would she wish to be seen with the farmer? Surely people would gossip. She glanced at Raoul. But to attend with a young, aspiring troubadour who worked for her family? No one would assume anything but friendship between them. Besides, Raoul had proved himself a faithful friend. She couldn't turn him down.

"I would be honored to walk to the festival with you. But I will wear my habit, I think, and I shall watch and not dance." She curtsied and headed toward her house.

"But you shall listen to my song! The one I wrote for you."

She turned to nod and then hurried on.

Oh, how she had looked forward to the village festival! And now she must go with Raoul. Her bottom lip pouted as she opened the door to Mémé's house.

Still, she was pleased and excited to go at all. This festival would most likely be less elaborate than those she'd seen near the château in Toulouse, but the freedom of it would be a brief respite from her daily duties and a welcome distraction from worry. She would not stay long, only the hour or two Mémé had urged—long enough to watch the tournament and enjoy the music of troubadours.

And, perhaps, there would be time enough to see again the handsome smile of Jaques Montré.

Raoul's question still bothered her after she returned home. Was she using the habit as a disguise? Not quite, but it was her protection, as Bostel had called it. She had no intention of returning to the abbey, so why continue?

She looked up the stairway to the room where Aimée's gowns still hung in the closet. Bostel's warning came back to her and she had hesitated. But...

Andreva drew a deep breath and climbed the first step. Then she paused. She must obey her uncle.

No! She gazed up the stairs. The time had come to think for herself. After taking the stairs in almost a run, Andreva stood in the doorway. Even in daylight, the room held the eerie air it had the evening she'd robbed it of its mattress and made her bed downstairs near Mémé.

From the doorway, Andreva first scrutinized the imposing wardrobe. Then, treading on dust and cobwebs, she crossed the room. She hesitated before the wardrobe's carved walnut doors. Did ghosts dwell therein? She made the sign of the cross before touching the door handle. The disused hinges whined at the invasion of privacy. A musty smell greeted her, but there were no spirits.

Several articles of clothing hung within on wooden pegs. A pair of linen slippers peeked out from beneath the gowns' hems.

Andreva took out a dress and held it up to her. Lovely. It might fit. Before entering the abbey, she had owned fine dresses, but never linen this soft or of a color so true to the sky.

She shook out the dust from the dress' folds and lay it carefully upon the bed frame. Then she slipped off her own frock and hung it on the wardrobe peg. Her hand shook a bit as she pulled Aimée's dress over her head. The square neck and shoulders fit perfectly, the bodice was not too loose, and the skirt followed her silhouette to the floor as if it had been tailored for her figure. She glanced toward the drab, unattractive convent frock that had concealed her curves as it had been designed. She would not miss it.

Venturing deeper into the wardrobe's treasures, Andreva discovered a gold brocade vest, a homespun linen chemise, and a leather vest. The last article upon the pegs was a brown dress with green embroidery. She longed to try each item on, but that must wait for another day. She took off her plain shoes and pulled on the slippers. Their leather soles crackled, as if being re-awakened from years of dormancy.

A colorful cluster of silk had fallen to the floor of the cabinet. Andreva picked it up to discover a hairnet with beads woven throughout. Surprise caught in her throat when she again moved aside the dresses and found a decorative metal circlet. She gathered her hair and pressed it into the hairnet. When she'd completed the task, she slipped on the circlet.

Andreva bounced down the stairs. "Mémé, look! I feel elegant!" She went in to her grandmother's room and twirled for her to see. "It is Tante Aimée's dress. Uncle Bostel offered it to me!"

Mémé struggled to her elbow to get a better look. "You are stunning, my dear, but perhaps a little too much hair is showing?"

Andreva touched the hairnet. "Oh Mémé, I am yet unmarried. Showing my hair is not improper."

"It is still daring." Mémé pulled herself up and carefully swung her legs over the edge of the bed to sit. "Now turn around and let me tie the laces."

Andreva stood with her back to Mémé and felt the dress tighten around her torso.

When she'd finished, Mémé lay back on the pillow. "You will be the most handsome damsel at the festival today."

"Oh, mercés! I feel beautiful." She smoothed her hands over the silky fabric and twirled again. She felt liberated.

"You will need a shawl. Take mine. It is on a hook in the wardrobe." Mémé pointed to the closet on the opposite wall.

Andreva found the shawl. "This shall do very well." She shook it out. "It is so elegant!" The natural black wool had gold threads woven throughout. She wrapped it loosely about her shoulders.

Ready and impatient, Andreva sat at her grandmother's side and tried to occupy herself by embroidering while she waited for Raoul. Her impatience grew. A cheer arose in the distance, evidence the tournament had begun. Andreva longed to be in the crowd. She put down the needlework and walked to the open doorway. "Where is Raoul?"

"He'll come. He has always been trustworthy."

"By the time he comes, the tournament will be over." Andreva went to the kitchen and returned with a tray of bread and nuts. She checked the pitcher to be sure her grandmother had plenty to drink. "This should tide you over while I'm gone. I shall not stay away but an hour—if Raoul ever comes."

Mémé did not react to the offering nor the complaint.

Andreva paced. Finally, she heard the long-awaited knock. She whirled toward the bed. "I am grateful you are feeling better, Mémé, I feel badly to leave—"

"Go!" Mémé shooed her away. "I will be thankful for the hour of peace without listening to you rant and watching you pace about."

Andreva hurried to open the door. A dark young man stood on the stoop.

His eyes widened when he saw her. "Good day, Ma..." His words trailed off as his gaze followed her silhouette down to the slippers.

Andreva studied him as well. The man wore a brown thigh-length tunic, tan leggings, and a black beret. A flute protruded from a leather pouch strapped over his shoulder. The scar that ran down the side of his face appeared more prominent than she had remembered.

"Monsen Garcia!"

quinze
15

arcia removed his hat and bowed. "Your friends thought me standing here would be a good joke." He replaced the hat.

Father Stefe's warning flashed through her mind. Should she beware of Garcia? She hesitated a moment. "It is good to see you again." She looked past him to Raoul and his friend John, holding their sides and chuckling. Andreva pursed her lips impatiently and ignored them. It was Raoul's fault she was missing the tournament.

Though the sun shone bright, a chill touched the air. Andreva wrapped the shawl around her shoulders, careful not to hide too much of the dress. She stepped out and closed the door behind her.

The two juveniles stopped laughing when they saw her. "Golden sunrise!" Raoul exclaimed under his breath.

"I thank you for coming to my rescue a few days ago, Garcia." She smiled and looked around. No one was within range to hear. "Raoul tells me you have a story to tell, one he claims to believe. Will you share it with me?"

Garcia smoothed his tunic. "Only if I must."

"Does it have to do with why Father Stefe seeks you?"

Garcia's Adam's apple jumped as he swallowed. "He is here...at the festival today?" Garcia's eyes widened when he looked up the road.

Andreva turned to Raoul and John. "You two look handsome today. Are you ready to sweep the village girls off their feet in a round or two of dance?"

John laughed nervously, but Raoul offered his arm. "Only with you, my friend." Raoul winked and flashed his biggest smile. "Remember, *I* am your escort."

She took his arm and looked at him in feigned innocence. "Then why did you send a man to do a boy's task?"

The confusion on Raoul's face was priceless, but she felt a twinge of guilt for teasing him. Still, how much of her precious time would she have to give exclusively to him?

Garcia silently left them before they arrived at the festival.

"Does no one guard Montsegùr today?" Raoul's voice was tinged with sarcasm. It appeared that every soldier and Crusader for miles about had turned out for the games, with the entire village—who was left in it—on hand to watch. He led Andreva to a place from which she could see the joust. A charge was about to begin.

Ignoring the horsemen, Andreva scanned the crowd for Jaques, but saw him nowhere. He must have stayed to care for his animals as he'd said.

The contenders rode to opposite ends of the worn path, and each turned his mount to face the other's. One jouster's shield was decorated with a fire-breathing dragon. The other's portrayed a hawk with spread wings and raised talons. The men posed majestically, their flawless armor gleaming in the sunlight.

Andreva's heart pounded with anticipation.

The impatient horses scraped their hooves in the dirt and blasted air through flared nostrils. The crowd hushed, a flag fell. Lances ready, the knights set their horses galloping forward with furious speed.

Clash!

Andreva held tight to Raoul's arm as the onlookers cheered. She watched breathlessly as both opponents reeled in their saddles, and was amazed when each man successfully clung to his mount and recovered his balance.

She joined in the cheers.

"Rematch!" The energy of the crowd intensified. "Rematch!"

Yes, again! Andreva stood on tiptoes to better see the knights circle their horses for the next charge. The cheers, the gleaming armor, the horses and excitement in the air all took her back to Toulouse. She reveled in the moment and craved more.

"Come." Raoul pulled Andreva from the crowd. "The tournament will soon end, and I want to sing my song for you before the dance begins."

"But I want..." The charge was about to begin, and she turned back to watch.

He tightened his grip and dragged her across the grassy field past food-filled tables and around children playing circle games. At their backs, the crowd cheered again. Andreva longed to know who had triumphed. He led her over to two young men seated beneath an oak tree. One strummed a dulcimer, and the other coaxed a haunting melody from the wooden shawm at his lips.

Raoul greeted them and picked up his lute from where it was propped against the tree. He held it to his ear as he plucked the strings to bring it into tune.

Andreva crossed her arms over her chest to control her impatience.

The shawm player lowered his instrument and gazed around. "Where is Garcia? He said he would join us on his flute."

Watching the match with everyone else! Andreva caught Raoul's warning glance and stayed quiet. If Garcia was wise, he had left the village.

The other man shrugged. "We cannot waste time. Let us begin. The crowd will be upon us in moments."

Raoul strummed a few strands of a melody. The other two joined on their instruments. He smiled bashfully, his voice light and airy as he sang:

Another holds the heart of the damsel of my eye.
Alas, her love is pledged to One greater than me.
I cannot hope her heart will change.
And I can only pray
That someday she shall come to clearly see—
That I love her.

Andreva felt her embarrassment rush to her cheeks. She forced a smile when Raoul's eyes sought hers.

I should sooner hope the stars would fall
Or the moon would lose its shine
Than to think she ever could be mine.
And to see her morning smile
Puts to shame the rose of spring.
Her voice and choice of words
Are lovelier than the melody of birds.

Andreva looked away when Raoul stole another glance and started the next verse. The beautiful melody and clearly heart-felt sentiments touched her, but also made her want to run away. Raoul was proclaiming his love, and she was not ready—would never be ready. She would have to say something when the song ended, but what? He did not have her heart in the way he wished, but she did care for him and could not be hurtful, especially before his friends. She glanced around, relieved that at least there was nobody but her and the other minstrels to hear his poetic declaration.

At the end, Raoul took a deep bow and added a little flip of his hand in true troubadour style.

Andreva clapped, but couldn't contain a nervous giggle as he came to her. "It is a beautiful song. I am impressed by your talent, and convinced you will someday be a troubadour of great renown." Her nervous chattering almost stuck in her dry throat.

He took her hand and kissed it, the look in his eye conveying his uncertainty at her response. "You are its inspiration, my beautiful Andreva."

"I—I..." *I don't know what to say to not encourage you.* Andreva pulled her hand away and glanced over at the two other men. "Thank you." Her voice shook. "Lovely." The other minstrels acknowledged her discomfiture with smiles.

The chatter and laughter from the crowd moving away from the tournament field signaled an end to the joust. Relieved by the distraction, Andreva turned to watch them come. The dance would soon start. More troubadours arrived with recorders, a zither, and another dulcimer. But there were no flutes—and no Garcia.

The older villagers gathered at the edges of activity to visit and watch, while the children moved a bit farther afield to continue their games of tag. The other young people paid little attention to Andreva as they gathered, happy and excited, to await the dancing. Soldiers came with them, still exhilarated by the tournament. Because of their numbers, there was an overabundance of men compared to young women.

Perrin the baker stepped forward to welcome all to the dance. "Weapons must be left beneath the oak." He pointed toward a tree that stood several yards away.

The soldiers grumbled as they released their belts holding knives and swords, and headed toward the tree. The music began immediately. It took little time for the girls to pair with village men, and soon about twenty couples circled the dance area.

The soldiers returned to find themselves partner-less and forced to watch from the sidelines. Andreva stayed close to the musicians and searched the crowd for someone she recognized—Elodie, Jaques, or perhaps John.

A sudden gust of chill wind whipped her skirt against her legs. Andreva pulled the shawl tighter and wished she had not been so foolish as to forgo her cloak so that Jaques might better see her beautiful dress.

"This is our dance."

She turned to Raoul who now stood at her side. "The troubadours are able to continue without you?"

He winked. "Long enough for me to dance with you, my lady." He bowed.

She had agreed to give him the first dance, so she must be pleasant, especially after he'd offered her that beautiful song.

He took her by the hand and they joined the other couples. He danced well and stepped on her toe only twice.

As they rounded the circle, Andreva's heartbeat quickened. Jaques stood by the way with a dark-haired girl at his side. He wore the linen tunic she'd seen at Christmas, and a hat adorned by a long, striped feather. Andreva raised her hand in greeting, but he didn't notice as he offered his arm to the girl and led her into the dance circle.

Was Jaques the girl's escort? Was she the reason he hadn't offered to escort Andreva? The young woman's smile was radiant, her green dress exquisite. No wonder he wanted to be with this girl. Andreva tried to dismiss the jealousy that flared up inside when the girl looked adoringly up at him, her delight in his attentions evident in her eyes.

Andreva could not help glancing at Jaques as the dance proceeded. During a right and left weave, their hands touched briefly, and their eyes met.

"May I have the next dance?" he asked in passing.

"What about your young lady?"

The line moved on. When she returned to Raoul, she saw Jaques across the circle and their eyes met again. He grinned. She couldn't help but smile.

Raoul looked over his shoulder. "*I* am your escort. Giving your attentions to any other man while dancing is poor etiquette."

She lowered her eyes obediently. Still, knowing Jaques wanted a dance made her grin. When the song ended, Andreva lost sight of him as the group moved from the dance area.

"Ah! The music begins again." Raoul took Andreva by the hand. "Before some soldier claims you, let us dance."

Andreva stood firm and looked around for Jaques. "But I promised..."

"Come." He chuckled. "The farmer seems smitten with Ermessen at present." Raoul pulled again.

Ermessen? That is her name? She searched again, but

found neither the girl nor Jaques, only soldiers with hope in their eyes. Before she took a step, a hand gripped her wrist. She looked up.

There stood Jaques peering down into Raoul's upturned face. "This is my dance with Andreva."

Raoul straightened to his full height. "There are other girls."

"Good. Then go ask one to dance." Jaques grinned at Andreva. "But I must agree that none are as pretty as your partner."

Andreva's cheeks warmed.

Raoul jutted out his chin and looked between Andreva and Jaques. "I am her escort." He moved to stand toe-to-toe with Jaques, but several inches in height separated him from facing off eye-to-eye with the farmer.

Jaques held to Andreva's arm as he peered down at the younger man. The feather flopped forward and hit Raoul in the eye. Andreva stifled a giggle.

Raoul scowled, pushed away the feather, and took a step back. "As you wish, old man, but you must promptly return her to me. And no dawdling."

Jaques didn't bother to thank Raoul. He led Andreva to fall in line with the other couples, mostly soldiers this round, dancing with village girls.

Andreva looked up at Jaques. "You should refrain from intimidating young men and complimenting women in public."

"He needed putting in his place." His smile brought the twinkle to his eye. "And why not compliment when the words are true?"

Andreva hid her smile. "Socrates said, 'Flattery is friendship in show, but not in fruit.'" Jaques glanced at her in surprise and she saw that her comment smarted. Would a farmer even recognize the name of a Greek philosopher?

The pattern of the dance separated them momentarily, giving Andreva time to regret chiding Jaques. Had he not gone out of his way to serve her and her grandmother in Bostel's absence? His gifts of food and time had not been offered "in show."

Soon he was at her side again. "I am sorry for my words, Jaques. I misspoke. Your kindness to Mémé and me is the best 'fruit.' Your loyalty to my uncle is commendable. I should not tease."

The song ended. The village men rushed in to move between the girls and the soldiers, whisking the girls off for the next dance.

Jaques did not return her to the side. "Will you give me another dance?"

"What about Raoul?" She saw him watching. "He asked for your word." A twinge of obligation and guilt made her take a step toward the young musician.

Jaques held to her elbow. "I never gave any such promise." He bowed and the feather bobbed.

Andreva couldn't help but snicker. "What an impressive feather. Did you steal it from a pheasant?"

He tipped his cap. "This very morning."

Andreva clapped with delight that he had remembered Mémé's story. "You dance as well as the lords at Count Raymond's festivals. Where did you learn?"

He took her hand to join the other couples in the promenade. "Any person with two good legs can dance."

She laughed. "No, not as noblemen do. Obviously, you have had training."

As soon as the song ended, the soldiers pushed their way among the dancers. A red-faced soldier yelled at a villager. "It is our turn to dance. Stop hoarding your maidens. We will do them no harm."

Andreva turned to see a soldier holding Ermessen by one arm while a villager held her other. His companion had raised a clenched fist to the villager's face. "Renaldo, we will show them who is in charge here."

Ermessen's frightened eyes pled for her release. Within seconds, Perrin ran to her, followed by others of the older villagers who had been standing on the fringes.

Perrin pulled Ermessen away from the two men and stepped in front of her. "Keep your filthy mercenary hands off our women!"

Jaques and the men of the village moved the girls together

and formed a protective circle around them. Renaldo glared from one villager to the next and then spat at Perrin. "You will be sorry for this." At his signal, his comrades, nearly half the crowd, stomped toward the oak tree to retrieve their weapons before heading across the jousting arena to their horses.

The villagers stood in stunned silence and watched them leave.

A few moments later, notes from a lute floated on the breeze. One by one the other instruments joined in. The dancers hesitantly fell back into position, but most men kept watch over their shoulders. Jaques took Andreva's hand and moved into the circle.

Andreva tried to put the unpleasant episode out of her mind. She positioned herself in front of Jaques and placed her left hand in his. *Step, point, walk-2-3-4, step, point, walk 2—* "Oh! I am so clumsy!"

"Do not be hard on yourself." Jaques brought her back into step. "We are all a bit out of rhythm after that confrontation."

Andreva concentrated and gained more confidence in her silent counting. "I did not see you at the jousting tournament. Even though soldiers are known to stir up trouble, the games are fun to watch."

Jaques didn't answer.

"Pray, tell. Why did you not come sooner?"

He led her in a slow outside turn in sync with the others. "The tournaments do not interest me."

The sound of horses' hooves pounded above the music. Andreva looked up and froze at the approach of the soldiers. The music ceased as the riders circled the startled dancers.

Renaldo shouted, "Lavelanet—you village of weavers!" He laughed. "You Good Men sympathizers! It is no use to resist. King Louis and Pope Innocent III will win this war, so deliver up the heretics you harbor among you!"

There are heretics among us? Andreva feared to move, to turn to Jaques, or to breathe. All about her, villagers stood paralyzed, fear or indignation on their faces. Several seconds passed during which the only sounds were a horse's neigh and the rising wind's rush through the barren tree branches.

Renaldo gave a whoop and the horsemen began to circle the dancers, holding high their swords and shields. Their leader shouted, "Le château Montsegùr will fall! God wills it!" Soon all the soldiers had taken up the words in a chant.

God wills it—the Crusaders' Oath—rang in Andreva's ears. Did God will it? Would God will so many people, perhaps even her uncle, to die?

She felt Jaques' arms around her, pulling her into the tightening circle. The earth seemed to rumble beneath them. Jaques held Andreva upright in the press. How acutely aware she was of his warmth and protection.

Renaldo reined his horse at Ermessen's side. Before anyone could react, he reached down and lifted her onto his saddle.

She screamed as he carried her off to join the circling riders. Her face filled with a panic shared by most of the villagers. Andreva could do nothing but watch in shock.

Jaques broke from the dancers and stepped forward. Other men followed his lead. From the sidelines, Perrin, Fortaner, and others joined them. They waved their arms, confusing the horses. Finally, the soldiers slowed the frightened animals. Jaques hurried to Ermessen. She slid from the saddle into his arms and buried her frightened face in his shoulder.

Renaldo's voice rang out. "Let this be a warning! The Inquisition will bear no resistance. Cooperate with the king's army and you will be left unharmed.

Jaques held Ermessen close as she trembled and sobbed.

The soldiers circled one more time before they rode out of the village and up the road toward Montsegùr.

Andreva could not stand and watch Jaques and Ermessen together. She turned away to find Raoul. *I do not begrudge Ermessen a moment of needed consolation, but why must Jaques be the one to offer it?* By the looks of things, they knew one another well. Andreva huffed. What did she care? He was merely a farmer who watched over her and Mémé as a duty to her uncle. She would never forgive herself for wearing this dress for him.

"Andreva!"

She knew Jaques' voice but did not turn.

"Are you leaving? Let me walk you home." He took hold of her arm.

His touch set her head spinning. "Óc, Mémé needs me. Go back to your friend." She kept walking and didn't look up for fear he'd see the fire in her eyes. "What is her name? Ermessen?"

He kept up with her. "She will recover. Her brother is with her now."

But surely Ermessen would rather have your arms around her! Andreva halted to survey the common. "Thank you for your offer, but I fear I have neglected my escort too long." Where was Raoul, anyway? He was no longer with the troubadours, but it appeared the dance had ended. The ordeal with the soldiers had spoiled the festive spirit.

Andreva turned back to Jaques but still didn't look him in the eye. "I thank you for your kind offer, and the dances." She curtsied, freed her arm from his grasp, and hurried away. If she didn't want him to follow, why did tears threaten—now of all times?

Gerrard de Fortaner stepped into her path. He wore a blue velvet tunic with beaded cuffs and knee-high boots. His smile looked much too sultry for a married man. "I had hoped to see you here today. A bit upsetting the way the Crusaders imposed themselves on the party, was it not? They act as if they rule Lavelanet." He pulled a pouch from his vest. "Your allowance, my dear."

Had he seen her tears? "Thank you, sir." She took the bag and curtsied but didn't smile. She would give him no encouragement. How fortunate that she would not have to face him in private this time. Turning without meeting his gaze or making further acknowledgment, she was certain he continued to stare as she headed across the field toward home.

Raoul stood on the edge of the commons. "I see you made your escape from the farmer."

Andreva's jaw tightened at his sarcasm. She clasped the pouch beneath her shawl and kept walking. "Monsen Montré is a fine dancer."

Raoul kept up. "Better than me? I thought I did well—never stepped on your toes even once."

She ignored his pout and the opportunity to point out he had stepped on her twice.

Three imposing figures, dressed in black capes atop white robes, stood near the bridge. As Andreva and Raoul approached, Father Stefe moved into their path and scrutinized Andreva from head to foot. "Have you heard from Bostel de Lumbert since last we spoke?"

Andreva curtsied. "No, Your Reverence."

The priest cocked his head and again looked over her dress. "Is this fitting attire for a nun?" He touched one of the sleeves.

Andreva stiffened. "There is nothing wrong with my dress, mon père. I have not taken vows, if that is what you mean."

"Nothing wrong with it in your eyes, perhaps. But it is vain for a novice of the Church to don such attire. For shame." He swept past her toward the commons, his consorts following.

Andreva's hand flew to her cheek. The Inquisitor's words stung like a slap to the face.

Raoul took her arm. They crossed the bridge before he spoke again. "Do not let the priest's words further ruin the day. You look beautiful in the dress."

"Mercés." She tried to smile.

"And I am honored to escort you home, even after you left me for Montré." He added an exasperated huff.

Still reeling from the priest's chastisement, Andreva didn't respond.

"Would you rather have Jaques Montré accompany you?"

"No." Could he not let it rest? "You misunderstand. I am upset at the way Father Stefe spoke to me."

"You should not have left your escort to watch from the sidelines."

It was as if Raoul had not heard her remark about the priest. Andreva gritted her teeth. *Why did you not play longer with the musicians?* Her head began to throb. "There were other girls at the festival. You could have danced with one of them."

"I have known those girls all my life," he pouted. "And they do not...dance as well as you."

Andreva stopped and turned to face him. "Raoul, thank you for the kind words. Thank you for escorting me today. And thank you for the song." She frowned at his eager smile. "I like you very much but—"

"But what? You think of me as a younger brother, do you not?"

She continued toward home, ready to end the conversation. How did she allow herself into this situation in the first place? "Well, yes. You are like a brother, and you are younger—by almost three years."

He stomped behind her. "Pray tell, do you think of Jaques Montré as an older brother?"

She pressed her lips together. Perhaps Jaques' smiling eyes and his touch made her want to nestle into him, but the vision of Ermessen in his arms made her bristle. Besides, she was far from ready to give her heart to a farmer. "I—I do think of him as an older brother. He has been kind to Mémé and me. That is all. There is no reason for you to be a wind-sucker, Raoul."

"Me? Jealous?" Raoul stopped short and his jaw dropped in shock. He laughed. "No, no. Now you have misunderstood."

Andreva could bear no more conversation. She marched toward the house before he could say another word. As she turned to close the door, she saw Raoul's feet still riveted to the spot where she had left him.

Andreva continued to go to the market daily, even though the war against Montsegùr was now waged literally in Lavelanet's backyard. The military rode or marched through the village regularly, and almost without exception stopped, looking for supplies.

Perrin's eyebrows rose when Andreva walked up to his table. "You are Soeur Andreva again, I see. The beautiful dress you wore to the festival—was it only a dream?"

She lowered her eyes but smiled. "I shall wear it just for you at the next festival." *Or for myself, but not for Jaques Montré!*

Perrin chuckled and waved his hand over his goods: one block of cheese and a dozen loaves of bread. "I have very little from which to choose today. The soldiers came early and bought most of what I had. I managed to conceal a bit for the villagers." He lowered his voice. "I heard the soldiers say they have completed the trebuchet. They use it to hurl large stones at the fortress. The rocks demolish a few walls and then they move the contraption up the mountain to destroy even more. It is said they have laid waste to all the dwellings without the fortress walls."

"That explains the rumblings I have heard." She bit her lip. Not only must they endure soldiers in the village, but now the noise of war would also become their daily companion.

Perrin shuddered. "It is a great show of determination, I say, to level the Good Men's homes on the terraces below the château." He made the sign of the cross while lifting his eyes toward heaven.

At that moment, another thud echoed through the hills. Andreva gripped her basket tighter, squeezed her eyes shut, and grimaced while imagining the devastation.

"And how much cheese would you like today?"

She opened her eyes. Perrin had spoken calmly, as if nothing had happened, but his face paled. Still shaken, she used her thumb and one finger to demonstrate the amount she wanted, and watched him cut the small chunk. She put the cheese in her basket along with eight loaves of bread.

The vendor smiled. "You have become your uncle."

She curtsied. "I take that as a compliment."

Ignoring how unnatural it felt to call upon people she hardly knew, Andreva pressed forward to Gisèla and Jocelyne's house. When she came close, she stopped in amazement. A new wooden door had replaced the animal skins at the entrance. She touched its solid, simple design and smiled.

"Gisèla! Jocelyne!" She knocked lightly before opening the door to peek inside.

A small voice came from within the darkness. "Come in!"

She stepped inside and closed the door behind her. "I am Andreva, Bostel de Lumbert's niece. I—"

"Óc!" the voice answered.

As Andreva's vision adjusted to the dim light, she saw Gisèla sit up in bed. Jocelyne occupied the same chair as before. Gisèla's eyes lit up in happiness. *"Polida neboda de Bostel, Andreva."* Beautiful niece. She reached out to Andreva for a hug.

Andreva placed her basket beside the door and with gladness, carefully returned the woman's embrace. Beneath skin as delicate as flower petals, Gisèla's bones protruded, sharp and distinct. Andreva next hugged Jocelyne. She too was frail.

Jocelyne kept a tight but shaky hold on Andreva's hand. "We have missed Bostel so much."

"Óc," Gisèla agreed. "His smile and cheer have long brightened our tiny home."

"I have missed him a great deal, too. Let us be thankful we still have each other." Andreva squeezed Jocelyne's hand. She gathered their blankets and took them outside to shake. Back inside, she straightened the women's bedding and took a few moments to sweep their floor.

She left the sisters two loaves of bread, and next called upon Felipa, Ponrada, and Trelise. Each visit proved uplifting and easier than the one before. After an hour in the village, Andreva headed home with the last two loaves.

At home, Andreva hung her veil upon the peg beside the door. Since the festival, she had donned the nun's smock and pulled her veil from the hook each day when she went to market. The priest's ridiculing words had struck deep, and reinforced Bostel's counsel that the garb would provide a measure of safety.

Mémé's health declined more each day, as did the amount of snow on the peaks surrounding Lavelanet. Andreva gave thanks each time her grandmother stood or took a step, though each was unsure and shaky. Mémé still ate her meals sitting up, and Andreva perched on the bed so they could share a platter. Mémé ate very little, and only picked at her food.

Mémé broke the silence one afternoon. "When I am gone, which may not be long hence, what will you do?"

Andreva bit her tongue in shock, and waited momentarily for the pain to subside. "Mémé, do not talk of such things."

"We must talk, Andreva. You must have a plan."

Mémé likely spoke the truth, but facing it was almost more than Andreva could bear. "I would like to stay in your house, if I may, and care for Uncle when he returns. I want to remain in Lavelanet."

Mémé's fingers touched the sleeve of the girl's frock. Love shone from her eyes. "You do not wish to return to the abbey?"

"No!" Ashamed for speaking sharply to her grandmother, she placed her hand over Mémé's. "Not if I do not have to. I would like to marry someday and have a family." She looked into her grandmother's eyes. "Is that a wicked desire?"

"Marriage is noble in itself." Mémé reached for her cup and raised it to her lips.

Andreva helped hold it steady. "Could you arrange a marriage for me? Perhaps you know a good man?"

Mémé shook her head. "I am in no condition nor position to arrange a match for you. Times are not as they were." She chuckled and broke off a piece of bread. "Besides, the only available man I have seen of late is Jaques Montré."

Andreva's first thought was to object. "My father expected me to marry nobility. He would not have considered a farmer an acceptable candidate."

Mémé scowled. "Our family has little wealth left to protect. And, sadly, your father is no longer with us to dictate his choice, nor provide a dowry." She sighed. "All I have left is this house and a few fields. After I die, it will go to Bostel. If you choose to marry, ma chérie, the dowry will be at Bostel's discretion."

Melancholy swept over her at the mention of Jaques. She'd had time to forgive his attentions to Ermessen at the festival, but had he forgiven the way she had spoken to him? Perhaps not. Days had passed with no sign of him in the village.

"In light of your situation, you may choose a husband for yourself." Mémé lifted a finger. "And, mind, you might never find another man as good as Jaques Montré."

She huffed in surprise. "You could barely tolerate him at Christmas."

"Óc, but he has proven his worthiness."

Her grandmother had essentially given Andreva permission to marry Jaques, but it brought no comfort. She had always felt secure knowing an authoritative male in her life would arrange an advantageous marriage for her. Andreva studied her hands in thought. When Uncle Bostel returned, could she not depend upon him to provide a dowry and a husband of status and nobility, as her father had wanted? Yes. She had to keep faith. She thought of Jaques' kind eyes and tingled, remembering the warmth of his touch. *If only the man were not a farmer.* Then she frowned. *And if only he wasn't interested in Ermessen.*

At the brink of twilight, Andreva locked the shutters, but paused to listen to the racket of horse hooves coming up the gravel highway. The sound of clanking metal confirmed it was a regiment, surely on its way to Montsegùr. She knew the sound well. When she'd heard it as a child, she would run to the balcony of her home in Toulouse to wave. Some soldiers made it their habit to watch for her and return her greeting.

As soon as the evening quieted again, there was a knock at the garden door. Andreva admitted Raoul with a scolding. "Why do you sneak around the back as would a thief?" Even though he had come to do chores each day, she had purposely not spoken to him more than needed. She had no desire to revisit his song with its intimate message. Now she sighed. She could not avoid him forever.

He ignored her question and snorted. "I expected to find you sitting with your feet up after all that dancing at the festival."

"Still jealous." Andreva groaned and went to cover the pot that held warm vegetables and broth from their supper.

"I have a small favor to ask of you."

She turned toward him with suspicion.

Raoul held up his palms. "It will not hurt. I promise." A mischievous glint shone in his eyes.

Although she suspected that whatever he wanted would bring trouble, she lit a candle and placed it on the table. "You must be cold. Sit, and I'll bring you a bowl of warm soup."

He thanked her and sat while she dipped from the cauldron. She set the bowl and a slice of bread on the table before him. Steam drifted up from the soup. "All right, I am ready to listen." She sat on a stool across the table from him. "But that does not mean I shall grant this favor. If I suspect mischief," she shook a finger, "I—"

Raoul stilled her hand and leaned forward. His laugh lines disappeared, and the candlelight lent a soft glow to his serious eyes. "I need you to go to the stonecutter and ask him to make a box yea big." He held his hands out about shoulder's width. "And so high." This measurement was about half the other.

Andreva raised an eyebrow. "A stone box?" She waited for him to explain. He put his hands on the table and stared at her as if expecting her to agree to his request. Tired of his game, she turned from his gaze. "Are you going to tell me more, or am I to guess at the rest?"

"What do you need to know?" He went back to eating.

Did this young man delight in testing her patience?

"Things such as for whom is this box to be crafted?"

"The purchaser wishes to remain anonymous," he mumbled with a mouth full of food. "I shall give you the money and you shall buy the box and bring it home. I will then come to take it off your hands. There. Simple."

Andreva glanced toward her grandmother's bedroom. "Why does this 'purchaser' not order it himself?"

"Because he cannot!"

"Keep your voice down, please." She stood and lowered her own voice to a whisper. "You talk in riddles, Raoul. And I want no part of anything I do not understand." She grabbed the broom and swept crumbs from around his chair, hoping the action would calm her nerves.

Raoul pushed aside the bowl, and stood. "But no one will suspect you."

"Of what?"

"Of..." he scratched his head and would not meet her eyes. "...heresy."

Her jaw dropped. "I refuse to take part in any heresy." She dragged the broom with greater force, as if to rearrange the stones set in the floor. "You would lure me into a conspiracy without even a hint of explanation?" She turned to face him, thoroughly annoyed. "Then my last request will be that they tie your hands to mine when they burn us at the stake."

"Ah, so romantic." Raoul winked.

Andreva scowled and turned back to her sweeping.

Raoul remained silent, watching. At last he walked to the door. "You are right. I will buy the box myself. Involving you in Garcia's plan is too dangerous, even for a girl who is not afraid to think for herself." He opened the garden door.

"Garcia's plan?" She turned to face him. "Then he is a heretic!" She should have guessed the Catalan was involved.

Raoul stepped outside. "*Au revoir.*" He closed the door.

Andreva felt betrayed. Uncle Bostel had hired Raoul to help her, but now he had asked her to put her life at risk—and for a heretic sought by the Inquisition. Her eyes lingered on the closed door. It made little sense. Why would Raoul involve himself with a man like Garcia when his own father had died by fire? If only for the sake of his mother and siblings, wouldn't he keep as far from such trouble as possible?

Rain fell for three days and Andreva grew restless at being cooped-up in the house. Raoul came daily to do chores, but she hardly spoke to him. Still she seethed that he'd put her life, and his own, in jeopardy. She avoided asking about Garcia's whereabouts. He hadn't returned since the festival.

Nor had Jaques.

Andreva slipped into the convent frock. It still held a hint of dampness from being laundered the night before. She grabbed the bucket to fetch water for her grandmother's bath.

"Andreva!" Mémé's words were hardly louder than a whisper.

Andreva set down the pail and hurried to the bedside. "Are you ready to arise?" She took hold of the covers.

"I have no strength," Mémé moaned.

Andreva put her hand to Mémé's forehead. "You have no fever. Here, let me help you to the commode." Sitting up proved laborious for Mémé. She grimaced as Andreva gently moved her legs to the side and lifted her from the bed. Once she had her grandmother situated on the chamber pot, and knowing she required time, Andreva said, "I will go now and fetch water for your morning wash."

Mémé hardly had strength to hold up her head, but she grunted in agreement.

Andreva placed a shawl around the woman's shoulders. Then she went to the hook by the door for her veil and cloak, grabbed the pail, and hurried out into the wet day.

Dark clouds hid both the sun and the distant château. Few villagers were out at this hour, especially in the dampness. She filled her pail.

As she headed back to her house, Father Stefe rode up to her on a horse. "Ma Soeur." His dark eyes seemed to bore into hers. "Do you know where the Catalan named Garcia lodges?"

She thought at once of Raoul and choked out an answer. "I know not, mon père. Is he a soldier?"

"He is not. He is a heretic."

Andreva tried to react as he would expect, widening her eyes and allowing her lips to open in surprise. The Inquisitor watched her, his jaw set. She forced herself to remain calm.

Father Stefe scanned the quiet houses. "If you meet the man, report to me. And tell him I wish to speak with him."

Andreva curtsied. "I will, mon père." She knew it was a lie. She had not thus far betrayed this man who had treated her only with kindness.

The priest raised one eyebrow. "Any word from your uncle?"

She wagged her head no. "I did not expect to hear from him before his return."

He cocked his eyebrow while he considered her reply. "I bid you farewell, Ma Soeur." He bore his heals into his horse and rode on.

Andreva let out a breath of relief and hurried back to the house.

Mémé sat where Andreva had left her. Andreva carefully poured a portion of the water into a warming kettle over the fire. "There is an Inquisitor in the village asking about Bostel."

There was apprehension in Mémé's voice when she replied. "And what did you tell him?"

"That I did not expect to hear from Uncle before he returned." With care, she pulled the nightdress off the woman, and wondered if now was the time to discuss

Father Stefe's previous accusations—that Bostel had been at the massacre at Avignonet-Lauragais. No, her grandmother didn't need that additional worry.

Mémé leaned forward and signaled that she was ready for her bath. "We must keep the windows closed and stay to ourselves today. Trouble is brewing. I feel it." She winced when Andreva put the warm wet rag to her back. "No good shall come of this day."

louds still dominated the sky at twilight when Raoul appeared at the garden door. Worry lined his brow. He leaned against the door frame. "I beg to ask of you another favor."

Andreva raised her chin. "I refused to do the first, so don't ask for a second. Besides, Uncle Bostel paid you to do favors for me." She jabbed him in the chest. "Not the other way around." She peered past him and caught her breath at the sight of a man standing in the garden, his face concealed within a deep hood. "Raoul, who is that person?" She grabbed the broom for protection.

He pulled the fellow into the house. Andreva moved out of his way, but gripped the broom tighter as Raoul shoved the door closed. "Garcia must hide here for the night. Please, Andreva."

"Garcia!" Her hands went suddenly lax and Andreva almost dropped the broom.

"We cannot expect him to sleep in the wilds when the weather is this bad."

Andreva stood firm. "He is a heretic, perhaps even a murderer."

"I...I am not a murderer." Garcia's dark face peeked out from beneath the hood.

"Are you one of the Good Men?"

"No." His brow creased. "I know not where else to go that they will not find me."

"Father Stefe asked me of your whereabouts this very morning. You are fortunate I did not know."

Garcia's face fell. He squatted near the fire to warm his hands. Andreva returned the broom to its place and stood beside him. "Garcia, do you realize Father Stefe is a Chief Inquisitor?"

"I do."

"What have you done to attract his attention?"

He did not rise, but instead spoke over his shoulder. "If I do not tell you, you can again say you know nothing."

Andreva's head began to hurt. "I am weary of all this secretiveness. You want my help, but tell me nothing." The two men stayed quiet. Andreva crossed her arms against her chest. "Monsen, I have been told you are a criminal, and you do not assure me otherwise. You cannot stay here. We are two single women and it is improper for..." Her words trailed off. Propriety seemed intangible in the face of heresy. She glared at Raoul.

Raoul motioned toward the small cellar door. "He can stay down there." His eyes moved to the stairway. "Or in your upstairs room."

Andreva shook her head. Her gaze moved to the Catalan. "Has this to do with the story you declined to share the other day?"

A silent communication passed between Garcia and Raoul, but neither spoke.

"Hold back," Andreva placed her fist on her hip, "and I will not offer you even the privy for a bed."

Raoul chuckled. "I told you she has a feisty spirit." He winked.

Andreva growled. "No more of this nonsense!"

Garcia stood, but his shoulders slumped. "Very well, then. I will tell you everything. But you must swear not to repeat it."

Andreva sighed. Had she triumphed, or lost all? If he were a heretic, knowing his story might cost her life. She motioned the men toward the stools and seated herself across from Garcia, next to Raoul.

"It is a long story." Garcia removed his cloak. He straddled the stool, but kept his satchel over his shoulder. "So that you will understand, I shall start at the beginning." He rubbed his neck as if the telling would be painful.

Though still daytime, the clouds had darkened the sun enough to cast the shuttered room into twilight. Andreva lit a candle against the gloom. Its light illuminated Garcia's face while he spoke. "My grandfather grew up in the Champagne region of France under the tutelage of the Knights Templar."

She held up her hand to stop his story. "But you are a Catalan."

"Hear me out." Garcia took a calming breath and rolled his shoulders. "As a Knight Templar, he traveled to the Holy Land. After one battle, my grandfather and part of his regiment chased the infidels into the desert. They lost track of them and ultimately became lost themselves. At last, climbing a high plateau in hopes of regaining their bearings, they found an ancient fortress—one he later learned was called Masada."

Masada. Raoul had spoken of it. She leaned forward as Garcia continued.

"The mountain was in the hills east of the Dead Sea. As the story goes, decades after Christ's death—when Romans still ruled the Holy Land—many Jews took their families up to this fortress, hoping to escape the war the Romans waged against them."

"It sounds similar to Montsegùr." Raoul said.

"The Romans spent weeks building a ramp of dirt to allow them to attack, but in the hours before they entered the fortress, the hundreds of men, women, and children within took their own lives rather than be slaughtered or made slaves at Roman hands."

Andreva considered the story solemnly. What was worse, taking one's own life, being murdered by soldiers, or burned at a stake?

Garcia continued his story. "My grandfather and his friends explored the ancient ruins, hoping to find treasures long hidden and forgotten."

"Did he find anything?"

"Only a scroll of papyrus, sealed within a vessel. When he moved a flat stone panel away from a wall, he found it tucked into a crevice. He unrolled it to find an ancient Hebrew text."

Garcia stopped speaking, but his expression conveyed there was more to the story.

"Go on. I'm listening." Andreva perched on the edge of the stool.

Garcia glanced at Raoul. "This next was his mistake. When he brought the curiosity back to Champagne, Grandfather showed it to a monk whom he had known all his life. The old fellow examined it and was astonished that it contained the blessing Jacob, also known as Israel in the Bible, gave to his grandsons—the sons of Joseph—before he died in Egypt."

"*Antchoubi*!" Raoul cursed in surprise.

Andreva hushed him. "Go on, Garcia."

"The monk asked Grandfather to leave the scroll with him so that he could write out a translation, which he did. When Grandfather returned a week later, the monk gave him the manuscript, but insisted on keeping the scroll, claiming all such artifacts rightfully belong to the Church. He said his superiors insisted Grandfather had no claim on it."

"That is true." Andreva returned Garcia's disapproving frown. "Is it not?"

"No. Now listen." He closed his eyes briefly and let out a long breath. "My grandfather was sick about losing the scroll, so he returned to the monastery the next day. He sneaked into the courtyard where the monks' robes hung to dry."

"And he stole one." Andreva guessed before Garcia disclosed it.

Raoul hooted. "A clever deed—dressing like a monk."

"A punishable sin," Andreva scolded.

Garcia ignored both comments. "Dressed as a monk, Grandfather easily walked into the monastery by way of the dormitory, and searched until he found the scroll in the abbot's private room."

"How fortunate," Raoul said.

"But a monk walked in right after Grandfather had slipped the scroll beneath the robe. He demanded to know what he was doing. Knowing there was no good reply, Grandfather spun around and knocked the man aside. He dashed out the door and through a group of friars gathered on the steps."

Raoul clapped his approval. Andreva stilled the boy's hands, uncomfortable that Garcia's grandfather had treated holy men with such disrespect. She failed to understand what was so important about the scroll to drive him to such extreme measures.

"He ran home," Garcia continued, "stuffed a few belongings into a satchel, jumped on his horse, and rode southward until he reached the sea."

"Incredible," Andreva breathed. "Where did he go?"

"The Straits of Gibraltar. There he kept the scroll and its contents a secret the rest of his life. He never returned to Champagne or the Knights Templar, but became a trader. Eventually he married and raised a family in Catalonia."

Andreva's curiosity persisted. "But why does Father Stefe seek you? Surely you do not have the scroll."

Garcia leaned closer. "But I do. When I was twelve years of age, Grandfather called me to his deathbed and charged me with the scroll's safekeeping." He lowered his head. "He should have chosen a more responsible steward."

"I still don't understand. How did the Church learn you have the scroll? Where is it now?"

Garcia rubbed his neck. "I became drunk one evening in the company of knights. I talked too much, and related this story to a man whom I considered a friend." He grimaced. "Alas, he showed his true colors and betrayed me." He pointed to his scar. "This is but one proof of his esteem."

"And this man went to the Church?"

"He told Father Stefe himself. This scroll is a relic not easily forgotten by Rome. The order for my grandfather's arrest remained in effect throughout his life and now bears my name. Therefore, I must hide. Father Stefe knows I am in the County of Foix."

"But why would you not want to give the scroll to the Church?"

Garcia's eyes narrowed. "Because they will destroy it. It is not in their favor."

Andreva rolled her eyes. "Stop speaking in riddles. Say what you mean."

"When I read the scroll's translation I knew why Grandfather had risked his life to keep it from the Church, and why I must now risk mine. The Church will either hide the scroll in its darkest vault, never to surface again, or they will make a show and burn it as heretical writing—and me along with it. Thus, the world will lose this treasure forever."

Andreva regarded him in disbelief. "The Church would not do that."

"Have they not declared there can be no more scripture or revelation? Do they not thereby dictate to God what He can and cannot do?"

"But never would they dismiss such a valuable artifact."

Garcia gazed into Andreva's face and grinned. "You are very naive, my friend. If you knew the atrocities the Crusaders and Inquisitors have committed in His name, you would doubt that these religious men whom you so admire ever knew that Jesus taught us to love one another."

She stiffened. "The actions of the Church are justified in the war against heathens, and I am well informed about the Crusades." She had known many kind friars who had been the epitome of Christian love. "And I know that no one is exempt from judgment. No one but the pope." Garcia raised an eyebrow, and she pitied him his skepticism. But she softened. "Tell me what is on the scroll that is so heretical."

Garcia leaned forward into the candlelight, perspiration glistening on his forehead. "Jacob prophesied that after Christ's death, men with self-serving intent—grievous wolves, he called them—will rise up to change the pure doctrines of Christ. As the Prophet Isaiah wrote, they will 'grind the face of the poor' to get gain." The flame flickered, releasing a ribbon of smoke that rose and dissipated. "These wolves are our current oppressors, setting themselves up as judges, declaring war upon the honest in heart, killing innocents—all in the name of God. They forbid a man to read the word of God for himself, and punish anyone who attempts to translate it into another language."

Andreva gazed at him wide-eyed. "But...what doctrines have these so-called oppressors changed?"

"The nature and personality of Deity, for one. Jacob said that God has a glorified body of flesh and bones; that He is a loving God who cares for His children, and that the Holy Ghost, the Messiah, and God the Father are three distinct beings."

A thrill danced across Andreva's scalp and down her spine, and she rubbed at the goose bumps rising on her arms. "But why would the Church..."

"Because His true nature as a loving God does not serve their purpose. They need for us to believe He is jealous and quick to punish. This way we live in fear and do only as the pope instructs."

Andreva looked at Raoul who was seemingly also moved. She rubbed her arms again, unable to decide what the burning but pleasant reaction meant. "It is hard to believe."

"It is. But I have dedicated my life to the inquiry and study of this doctrine and found that it was known and taught in the early Church. In the records of the first council at Nicene, the matter was argued contentiously. Only after weeks of debate did they agree to define God as an entity without body, parts, or passion."

Andreva closed her eyes. *How can this be?* Could the Church be wrong about such basic theology?

"The prophecy upon the scroll goes on to promise a happier day and a restitution of all things, including the understanding of the Godhead's nature. God will raise up men and women who will prepare the world for the Messiah's Second Coming. Jacob promises his children that they will one day hold the word of God in their own hands and read it in their own languages. And when the Messiah comes at last, oppression will be defeated, and all shall live in harmony with Christ as our King."

"But the Church instructs us to look forward to Christ's coming."

Garcia blinked and sat up straight. "With fear and

trembling! Can you not see the rift?" He reached for her hand. "We are fed only a form of doctrine—one that allows us to be preyed upon. Do you not recognize these grievous wolves? Is it not obvious?"

She removed her hand from his and searched her mind for an intelligent defense of that which she had always believed. "The Inquisition will tell you that it is the Good Men who are the wolves."

"No, no, no! The wolves are the clerics of the Church whose intent is to control the people, and thereby lift themselves up for the glory of the world. That includes the Inquisitors."

He looked into her eyes as if begging her to accept his story as truth.

Andreva had no doubt Garcia believed his own words. She had little doubt he was a good man at heart. Still, Father Stefe's hard eyes seemed to stare out at her from the corner shadows. She shook the vision away. Despite the differences between these men, she could not believe God had allowed His Church to become corrupt.

Garcia turned to Raoul. "So, instead of allowing the words of Jacob to speak for themselves, the clerics will get rid of the scroll and ignore the prophecy, lest it should in any way introduce opposition to their power."

Raoul clearly agreed. "But destroying the written word could not change prophecy."

Garcia smiled at his friend. "True."

Andreva stood. She had listened to his heretical reasoning long enough. Surely, Mémé would not approve of such conversation in her home. She raised a palm to her throbbing head. She would think on this more, but only when it hurt less. "Is this scroll with you now?"

Garcia put his hand on the satchel. "Yes, but I can no longer carry its burden. I have proven myself incapable of honoring the charge my grandfather gave me." He nodded toward the door. "After hearing of the fortress at Montsegùr and the caves upon which it is built, I came here to find a suitable hiding place. It is time I return the record to God's hands."

ndreva glanced over at her grandmother each time she stirred. Mémé's mind seemed as restless in sleep as Andreva's was fully awake.

She had returned her straw mattress to the bedstead in the upper chamber where Garcia now slept. Though she lay next to her grandmother, sleep eluded her as she listened to every noise in the house and garden. She had not been able to send Garcia away in the storm, but her complicity in his heretical plan haunted her. When she had explained to Mémé why Garcia was staying in the room above, her grandmother grumbled under her breath until she fell asleep.

But it was not only fear of discovery that kept Andreva awake. She still smarted from Garcia's accusations against the Church. Catholicism was all she knew, all she had ever known. It was as much a part of her as breathing. Her father had seen to her education—she knew the doctrine and had memorized aspirations and the Apostles' Creed. Her mother had seen to her faith, by precept and, especially, example. At the thought of her mother, Andreva felt the pains of homesickness. Her throat tightened, and tears puddled at the corners of her eyes and rolled across her cheeks onto the pillow.

Fear that Garcia could be discovered in her home lay like a heavy stone in the pit of her stomach. What would her parents think—they who had devoted every breath of their lives to the Church—if they knew she harbored a heretic? They had given her so much, and this was her thanks, to allow a heretic to sleep in Mémé's home? Her grandmother was not only Andreva's link to her mother, she was all she had left of her family. She turned over in the bed as if turning away from the possibilities.

Mémé's white cap peeked out from under the covers, and by the way she stirred, Andreva suspected she was also awake. "Mémé?"

"Óc." Mémé remained on her side, facing the fire.

"May we talk?"

"About the stranger upstairs?" Mémé grunted her disapproval.

Andreva felt her grandmother's resentment. "No, not about Garcia. Will you tell me more about my maire?"

Mémé turned onto her back. "Sanche? What is it you want to know?"

Her mother had been gone for a year now, but still it was hard to think of her without tears. "My maid—when I lived in Toulouse—told me in whispers one day that my parents had run away to be married. Is it true?"

"Not exactly." Mémé sighed long. "When your mother was a maiden, a young knight in Count Raymond's regiment came to our village. His name was René de Béringer—"

"My father." Hearing his name spoken again warmed her heart.

"Óc. Sanche fell in love the moment she saw him."

Andreva smiled. "He was handsome, he was."

"I was relieved when the regiment left the area, hoping that would be the end of her infatuation."

"Why would you object?" To her, her parents were a perfect match.

"She was so young, and I feared if she married the soldier, he would take her far away from me. I did not want to lose her. But after René left, Sanche suffered a broken heart. Some weeks later, he returned. They begged me to allow them to marry and, reluctantly, I agreed."

"So, they did not go in secret." Andreva was relieved for her mother's salvaged reputation.

"But it was with heavy heart I met them at the church. All through the ceremony, I cried. Then René put her on his horse and they rode away together. No pomp, no flowers, no wedding dinner. At least I was there to give my consent to... my only daughter."

Hearing the hurt in Mémé's voice, Andreva rested her head on her grandmother's shoulder. "They loved each other very much." Andreva had always felt secure in that knowledge. She recalled the tears in her mother's eyes each time her father led out his regiment, and the tender look in her father's eyes upon seeing her mother when he returned. "The maid told me Maire did not come back to you for a year. Is that true?" Andreva looked at her grandmother, but the room was too dark to see her expression.

"Óc, it was not until you were born." Mémé paused. "Something happens to a woman at the birth of her first child. She needs her own mother and yearns to connect to her somehow."

"And so, she returned." Andreva smiled. It must have been a wonderful reunion.

"I remember the day." There was sadness in her voice. "René brought her. She walked into the house with shining eyes and handed me a small bundle. I unwrapped the blanket to find you—a rosy baby girl sleeping so peacefully. It was a day of joy. Sanche and I laughed...and cried."

Andreva placed her hand over her heart and treasured up her grandmother's tender words. A lump rose in her throat. "And being the good Christian woman you are, you forgave her for leaving."

"I forgave her," Mémé sniffled, "though there was no longer anything to forgive. During the lonely year she was gone, I had reminded myself that I once loved as she. Though my marriage was arranged, I would have run away with Gilbert, had it been necessary."

"Now my parents are both gone. While in the abbey, I pled with God to take me too, and not leave me alone in the world." The lump in her throat made it hard to continue.

During those months, she could not understand why God had answered her prayer with life—life in the abbey, life as a novice—until Bostel sent for her.

"At least," Mémé patted Andreva's hand, "we have each other now...for a time." She kissed her forehead. "I thank you for coming to me, ma chérie. Mercés."

"There is no place I would rather be."

Mémé rolled back onto her side and, in a few minutes, breathed deeply in sleep.

Andreva fought her tears no longer. Some minutes later, she at last fell asleep on a dampened pillow.

Andreva awoke to the rumble of war echoing through the valley. Although the noise had become a daily occurrence, she found it unnerving. She could not help but envision the destroyed walls of the fortress tumbling down the side of the pog while victims ran for their lives, some still wearing nightclothes.

She slipped out of bed and left the chamber without awakening Mémé. In the main room, Andreva looked toward the stairs as she listened for any movement from Garcia. Surely, he too had heard the noise.

The sooner he left, the better. Once he was on his way, she'd be able to breathe easier, and perhaps the Inquisition's pyre would no longer haunt her dreams.

Through the shutters, she saw the sun's rays barely peeking above the horizon. The clouds had moved on during the night. Andreva heard the chirping of a bird outside. She unlatched the door to breathe in the fresh air, and then carried out the night's wash water and dumped it on the street.

She stepped back into the house and listened. Still no sound from upstairs. She put a log on the fire, returned to her grandmother's room to dress, and then prepared bread for Mémé's breakfast, not caring to be quiet. She hoped to awaken Garcia and speed his departure before the village stirred. But she heard no movement from the room above.

"Andreva!"

Mémé. Andreva grabbed the tray and hurried into her room. She set aside the food and helped the woman sit up.

"Has the stranger gone?"

"I have heard no stirring."

"A man should not sleep in a house with unmarried women," Mémé grumbled. "It is not appropriate."

Andreva attempted to keep her voice calm. "I agree, but as I explained last night, he had no place to go and I could not put him out in the rain."

"Why could he not sleep at Raoul's house?"

Andreva grimaced. "You know Raoul's family crowds into a hovel." She helped her grandmother move to the side of the bed. "And, remember, the authorities seek the man. Raoul's mother has small children, and has seen trouble enough, as you said yourself."

Mémé let out a harsh breath. "Yet you would keep a criminal in my house."

"We have discussed this, Mémé. He is not a criminal. He has done no wrong. They have *labeled* him a heretic."

Mémé fell silent. Andreva helped her through her morning routine, grateful she'd stopped arguing. When her grandmother was back in bed, she pulled the covers over her and positioned the tray. "I hope you feel better today, Mémé."

"Óc. Now go see to the stranger and encourage him on his way."

"I will." Andreva left the room. She would tell Garcia he must find other housing. If someone learned she had allowed him stay even one night...*God forbid!*

She stepped over to the staircase and listened. "Monsen Garcia? Come, break your fast." No answer. "Monsen!" Only silence. She placed a fist on her hip and tapped her foot. Surely by now he had awakened.

There came a single knock before the unlatched front door swung open. A dark figure filled the frame. "Soeur Andreva!"

The voice seemed to penetrate her bones. "Father Stefe!" She stepped back in alarm, but quickly regained her composure and curtsied.

The man's powerful presence filled the room even before he entered it. His two comrades' long white robes brushed the floor as they followed. With the door opened, cold air filled the room, but more chilling was the judgmental gazes that swept around Andreva, toward Mémé's chamber, and up the stairs. "Where is Garcia?" Father Stefe demanded.

"I know not, mon père." Still stunned by their sudden appearance and uninvited entrance, she clasped her hands behind her back to hide their trembling.

The priest's voice was stern and belittling. "No? He was last seen with your neighbor, the would-be troubadour Raoul. I am told you and the young man are good friends."

Andreva could not force herself to move or speak. Father Stefe walked over to the cellar door and yanked it open. He motioned to his companions and the shorter one descended the steps.

Could Garcia have sneaked down when she was unaware?

The comrade returned immediately "No one is down there, Your Reverence."

Father Stefe's flashing eyes followed the wall to the bedchamber door. He walked over and peered in.

Andreva reached out to him in desperation. "My grandmother is resting. Please do not disturb her."

Though she had not touched him, the man recoiled in repulsion. He then disappeared into the bedchamber.

Andreva hurried to the doorway in time to see him lift the comforter and hear Mémé complain. "What is the meaning of this?"

Andreva gasped. "Mon père! Please!"

Father Stefe dropped the covers, and Andreva hurried to comfort her grandmother. "They search for a man, Mémé." Andreva gave her a hushing glance. "We must cooperate."

Grasping hands, they watched Father Stefe open the wardrobe and brush aside the clothing. When he left the room, Andreva followed.

He looked down at her with eyes of flint. "Domaisèla. People hide heretics in strange places. Of course, when they are found, it means certain death to the one who has harbored them." His eyes moved to the stairway. One of the priests had already climbed halfway up the stairs. Andreva's knees weakened, and she grasped the table edge for support.

Seeing, Father Stefe smiled with satisfaction.

She lowered her face and waited, her heart banging in her ears. Footsteps descended the stairs. There had been no shouts, no sound of a scuffle. She looked up.

"No one is upstairs, Your Reverence, though someone may have slept in the bed."

Andreva's jaw tightened as Father Stefe's piercing gaze fell upon her face. "And who slept there?"

"It is my bed, Father." She held his stare despite her lie.

The Inquisitor smiled. Did he know? Andreva lowered her eyes again and felt the blood drain from her face. She locked her knees so she would not collapse in their presence, but her legs trembled within her skirts.

At last, the men returned to the still-open door. Father Stefe turned. "Pardon the interruption." His eyes seemed to darken. "I will have the man Garcia. Remember, Ma Soeur, it is against the laws of the Church to aid a heretic."

She managed to nod.

The men filed out of the room, not bothering to close the door. She watched them stride toward the village center. Father Stefe's determined gait reaffirmed that he would stop at nothing to find Garcia.

Andreva closed the door, latched it, and sank back against it, willing her strength to return. *Raoul!* She clenched her fist in frustration. *Look what you have brought upon me— upon us—and your family!* His name was now linked to Garcia's in Father Stefe's mind. The Inquisitor would not treat him lightly.

"Andreva!" She went to the chamber room door. "Hush, Mémé, while I investigate. I shall return promptly."

Andreva went to the table and fixed her gaze upon the stairs. Not daring to call out Garcia's name, she waited several moments before starting up the stairs. *One, two, three, four...* Counting might calm her until she could peer into the room. At the doorway, she whispered toward the empty bed, "Garcia, are you here?"

Andreva stared at the closed wardrobe. It was large

enough to hide a man, but surely the priest had looked inside. She walked over and hesitated, holding her breath as she opened the door.

Empty, except for Aimée's dresses.

She glanced around the room. How had Garcia disappeared? The blanket she had lent him lay draped over the foot of the bed. Her gaze went to the shutters. The man had left by the window, she was sure of it. After the rain, the ground would provide a soft landing. Were there telltale footprints? She reached to open the shutter, but thought better of it. What if the priests still watched the house?

Andreva descended the stairs, her chest pounding. As quietly as possible, she stepped out the garden door and crossed the small yard. The brush and trees hid her from the street. She looked to the window of the upstairs chamber. Halfway up the side of the house was a ledge onto which a person could lower himself without much difficulty. From there, the drop to the ground would be little problem. Her gaze fell to the damp soil at her feet. Two boot prints. The evidence.

With her pulse still hammering, Andreva glanced around, but saw no one. She smoothed over the prints with her foot to make them disappear.

Andreva went back into the house and directly to her grandmother. Mémé looked up in concern. "The priests have gone." Andreva stroked her hand soothingly across Mémé's shoulder.

"And what of the man upstairs? Did they take him?"

"No. He is gone, too. I never saw him."

Mémé closed her eyes. "We must be careful. Lock the doors and we will keep to ourselves."

Andreva returned to the kitchen and stirred the pot. She dipped broth into a mug, and sat with it in her hands, too uneasy to sip it. She listened to every whine of the breeze and rattle of the shutters, lost in thought.

A thump came from the bedroom, followed by a mournful cry. "Andreva—"

Mémé! She hurried to the door and found her grandmother in a twisted heap on the floor, her legs splayed awkwardly beneath her. "Mémé! Why did you get up without calling for me?"

Mémé moaned. Andreva tried to straighten the woman's legs with little success. She knew she could not lift her back into the bed alone. She grabbed a pillow and placed it under Mémé's head and covered her with a blanket. "I shall go for Raoul. Try to relax. We will return shortly."

"No!" Mémé grasped Andreva's arm, her eyes squinted in pain. "Stay by my side. Let me rest here a moment."

"But Mémé, I cannot leave you on this cold floor." Andreva panicked. "The stones will rob the heat from your bones and surely you will die."

Mémé placed her cool hand on Andreva's cheek. "Then you—you lift me into bed. I will die there."

"No one will die in this house!"

Could she not at least call for Raoul? He could easily lift her grandmother. But before she could again protest, she met the woman's frightened eyes. The look there caused her to change her plan, but strengthen her resolve. She put her hands beneath Mémé to help her to sit. Mémé winced in pain and fell against her. Andreva breathed deeply. It took all her strength to raise the woman, but after much effort she got her into bed.

"Oh, Grandmother, I am sorry this happened." Andreva wiped her brow and fought back a sob. "Please let me go now for a physician."

"No!" Mémé closed her eyes. "There is no physician. Wait out the day. I will feel better. You will see."

ndreva invited Colet to sit at the table. The older woman removed a few small pouches from an apron pocket and placed them on the table. "Raoul told me Margaurite fell."

Andreva had sent the young man away without letting him in, still upset with him for putting her and Mémé in danger. "He wasted no time spreading the news. He left here only minutes ago."

"I brought a few herbs that may help her heal." As she explained each one, she pushed it in front of Andreva, and explained which ones should be used together. "Steep them into tea."

"I will. Mercés." Andreva stood and moved the kettle of water over the fire.

"And, Andreva, any time you need help, come for me. I know what it is like to be alone. I can imagine how hard it is for you and Margaurite."

Gratitude swept over Andreva as she sat back down. "You have helped me so much. I never think of you as alone with your big family, but of course you are." She hesitated. "Elodie told me how your husband died. I was sorry to hear it."

Colet lowered her eyes and brushed crumbs from the table into her hand. "After a long interrogation and much torture, he was burned to death." The words were matter-of-fact, but her eyes now mirrored the horror she had endured. She rose, crossed to open the garden door, and tossed out the crumbs. Then she stood, staring at nothing.

Andreva allowed her time to overcome the wave of fresh grief at the memories, but there was something she must know. When Colet turned back to her, Andreva said softly, "But Elodie told me he was not one of the Good Men."

Colet returned to her stool at the table. "No one would mistake us for Good Men. It is not their way to marry or have large families." Their eyes met and Andreva appreciated the emotional effort it cost Colet to help her understand. "No, my husband was too outspoken about his beliefs that God gave man the ability to choose for himself, that choice is part of God's plan, and that the Church had taken those God-given rights away. The Inquisition answers no question, bears no opposition. At the first indication of even the mildest dissent, they stomp out the one making noise."

"I am so sorry."

"As am I. But do not pity me, child. I still have my children. They are, as the Church teaches, a blessing to me. As you are a blessing to Margaurite." Colet stood and gathered her shawl around her to leave.

Andreva reached out to stop her. "Speaking of children." Andreva settled back on her stool. "Bostel's wife Aimée died in childbirth. He hardly speaks of it."

Colet leaned forward and lowered her voice. "The Good Men believe that children—*that giving birth*—is evil."

"Yes, I have heard the doctrine." Andreva's voice dropped to a whisper. "The Good Men believe that when a man dies, his spirit goes into another body. The human body is a creation of their evil god."

"It is true. So when Aimée died, and because of his belief in the heretic doctrine, Bostel blamed the child." Colet looked up the stairs as if the uncle still lived there. "Bostel had a very hard time after his beloved died, and he has never given his heart to another woman."

Andreva stared at Colet for several moments. This was the first acknowledgment that Bostel was one of the Good Men. Andreva bowed her head and took a deep breath. "Do others in the village know Bostel is...?" She couldn't bring herself to say the words.

"Óc. Many villagers are Good Men. Most went early to Montsegùr. Bostel remained to watch over those who could not make the journey up the mountain. At last, he could delay no longer." Colet glanced toward the shuttered windows as if even her near-whisper was a danger to them both. "We do not speak openly about who is of the Good Men and who is not. In times of great fear, neighbor can turn against neighbor. It has happened."

Father Stefe... Andreva blinked back the tears warming her eyes. "Is it true Bostel went with Pierre-Roger de Mirepoix to Avignonet-Lauragais? Was he part of that horrible massacre?" Despite her best effort, the tears spilt onto her cheeks.

Colet circled the table to place her hand on Andreva's shoulder. A long moment passed before she spoke. "It is true."

"No!" Andreva dropped her head into her hands and sobbed. "Why would he—"

"Put yourself in the Good Men's place for a moment. The Inquisitors had tortured and burned so many of them, thousands of their family, friends, and countrymen. The Good Men bore the senseless cruelty as best and as long as they could, but finally took action to protect themselves and others. Truly, can you blame them?"

Andreva could not decide. Though her mind agreed, her very center throbbed in pain.

Colet massaged her shoulder in sympathy and she bent to speak into the younger woman's ear. "Forgive him. He, and the others, felt it must be done."

Forgive murder—an unpardonable sin? Bostel would never know what impact that deadly deed had had on her father, driving him and her mother to their graves.

Colet squeezed Andreva's shoulder in farewell. "I will return if you need me."

Andreva remained on the stool and watched the woman leave before leaning on the table and burying her face in her arms. Her fears had been confirmed. Bostel was a heretic.

Resentment swelled within her. The uncle she loved had killed holy men. He would go to hell for his actions, if not his beliefs. How could he have forsaken his family and the true faith?

Another thought struck. What if Mémé died too? Andreva would be left alone. She looked up and glanced around the room. Oh, how she loved this house she now called home! She would stay as long as circumstances allowed. Fortaner would probably try to exert jurisdiction over her, but she would stand up to him. She must.

Andreva dried her face and stood to make the tea. *I must be strong, not only for myself, but for Mémé, too.* She took a deep breath and lifted her chin.

Raoul reappeared before sunset.

Upon seeing him at the door, Andreva shoved it closed. "I refused you entrance this morning, so do not think I will let you in now," she called through the door, "you...you traitor!"

His voice was desperate and low. "I am sorry Father Stefe came and searched your home. But listen, we must speak. Please, let me in. Our troubles have worsened."

"You mean *your* troubles. I am no longer part of any scheme."

"Please."

Something in his voice made Andreva take a deep breath and open the door a crack. Still, she moved her foot to block it from opening farther if he pushed.

Raoul peered in at her with worried eyes. "King Louis has strengthened his troops. Six thousand are now on the highway. We must work quickly."

"I refuse to help you anymore." Andreva clutched the door handle. "The Inquisitors know Garcia is your friend."

"Óc" His voice was contrite. "They searched our house as well. Please. Let me in and we will talk." He looked over his shoulder. "What if someone watches? No doubt they will wonder."

Andreva bit her lip. She edged open the door to look up and down the street, hoping there were no Inquisitor spies.

"Come in, but don't think I will help you further."

Raoul stepped in and took off his cap. "I have not seen Garcia in too long, and I am worried."

"I think you help him merely to outwit the Inquisition," she said with disgust. She closed the door and bolted it.

"Hush!" The stool screeched against the stone floor as he pulled it from its place and sat. He spoke barely above a whisper. "Please, Andreva, reconsider going to the stonecutter. Garcia will return, I know it. And he will need the box to preserve the scroll when he buries it."

"No!" She stomped her foot. "I want no part in this."

"Who would suspect you—a sweet little nun?" His brown eyes pled.

"That is ridiculous." She grabbed the broom, wishing to sweep him and his heresy out with the dust to the rubbish heap. "I am already under suspicion for being your friend."

"Father Stefe and his spies watch every turn I make, or I would go myself. Please? Tell the stonecutter you need a box in which to hide family treasures. With all the soldiers passing through, it is a likely story, is it not?"

It was. And Raoul had come to her rescue twice when she'd faced Gerrard Fortaner. She owed him, yes, but must the repayment involve heresy? "The Inquisitors will watch me too." Andreva glanced toward the veil she hadn't worn for several days. "And I am Catholic, not a heretic."

"Do not think of it as going against the Church. Think of it only as a favor for a friend—or a favor to mankind if we help to save the scroll."

"How do we know this scroll is real? Have you seen it?"

Raoul sheepishly shook his head no.

"And if we did see it, how would we know it is not a forgery or trickery?" She replaced the broom and crossed her arms, awaiting his answer.

"What has Garcia gained in making himself a target for the Inquisition? Besides, I know he speaks the truth." He tapped his chest. "I know it here."

Andreva rubbed her arms, remembering the tingles she'd felt when Garcia told his story. Nevertheless, she turned away from Raoul and his ill logic. He brought only trouble to her door.

He stood and reached for her elbow to pull her back to face him. "Come, Andreva. Please help me."

Could she ignore the earnest pleading in his eyes? She rubbed her hands over her face, wondering what it was that bade her consider the mad request. Yes, he and his family had been kind and come to her aid, but she did not owe her life to mere kindness. And yet something—she knew not what—prompted her to agree.

She paced in thought. "Oh, fie on you, Raoul!" Andreva slapped both hands on the table, moaning in surrender. "If we are discovered, give me your word we burn together!"

He threw his hands in the air. "You are obsessed with burning."

"It was your father who died in the flames. You should be the one obsessed." Andreva stomped to the stew pot, lifted the lid, and stirred it out of habit. The familiar chore was calming. She replaced the cover and turned to the young man. "Listen, Raoul." She took a deep breath. "No one is exempt from the Inquisition's scrutiny. When I lived in the abbey, most nuns were afraid to speak any thought out loud, and so they murmured nothing but memorized prayers. We were subjected firsthand to the burning of heretics—those poor people tied to poles...and the flaming pyre." She shuddered at the lingering visions. "I'll never forget the horror on their faces as the flames engulfed them, nor the smell of burning hair and flesh." She dropped her head and drew a ragged breath to relieve the tightening of her chest.

Raoul put his arm around her shoulder. "The Inquisition has been very successful in scaring everyone away from independent thought."

She leaned into him as he enfolded her. It had been a long time since she had felt consoling arms around her. She relaxed, and tears came.

His lips brushed her cheek.

Andreva stiffened. She moved away and used her apron to wipe a tear. "Mercés," she said firmly. "You are as good to me as a brother."

He planted a fist on his hip. "A brother? Always putting me in my place."

Andreva smiled.

He heaved a sigh and reached into his pouch. "Garcia will return. He left this to pay for the box."

The coins clinked as he placed them on the table.

"I will think on it." She picked up the money and put it on the mantle.

ndreva slipped into the humble chapel. She glanced up at the vaulted ceiling before she walked across the large room to the statue of the Virgin Mary. Andreva fell to her knees and chanted words she'd memorized long before.

"Mother Mary, Mother of our Lord..."

When finished, she paused to seek inspiration, a sign, or any reason to change her mind about helping Raoul and Garcia. None came.

She stood and lit two candles. Palms pressed together, she touched her fingers to her lips. Footsteps echoed from a room off the transept to her left. Not wishing to encounter anyone, Andreva hurried out to the road and walked on toward the village gate.

Raoul had promised to stay close to the house and keep an eye on Mémé while Andreva did his errand. His errand. She huffed, reprimanding herself for her involvement in the scheme, especially now when her grandmother most needed her.

The sky had darkened and there was a cold drizzle of rain. She dodged puddles as she left the safety of the village and hurried up the road, following the directions Raoul had given her. To her relief, the small shack at the edge of the stone quarry soon came into view. A soft yellow light emanated through the open doorway. Just outside, a horse waited, laden with seemingly empty leather bags.

Andreva heard heated voices as she made her way between stacks of cut stones and past the horse to peek into the shop. The stonecutter held a mallet in one hand and a chisel in the other. Nearby, a knight waited. They stopped speaking and the soldier made the sign of the cross when Andreva entered. The stonecutter nodded, but continued his work, tapping the chisel against a large stone on a worktable.

At last he turned her direction and lifted one bushy eyebrow. "Ma Soeur, how may I help you?"

Andreva glanced toward the knight and back to the cutter. She hesitated. "I n-need a box. One of stone."

The stonecutter glanced around the shop. "How big do you require it to be? And its use?"

The dark-haired chevalier interrupted. "I will return for the stones for the trebuchet." His brow furrowed. "Two balls a week is a pathetic effort. Your incompetence in meeting the directive of your king is distressing. Or is it that you are a Cathar sympathizer?" He strode to the door. "I shall return with a cart to carry the many balls you have made before the end of the week."

An accusation by this knight could lead to action by the Inquisitors. Andreva watched the stonecutter to gauge his reaction.

The cutter continued tapping but did not look up. "Óc, Sir Wilhem."

The chevalier frowned and exited the shop to his mount. Through the doorway, Andreva watched him, with his several empty bags, gallop up the road in the direction of Montsegùr. She turned back to the stonecutter.

He stood frozen as if listening to the sound of the horse's hooves to assure himself they grew fainter. His eyes held defiance, and when the sound sowas gone, he jerked his head as if to dismiss the episode. "Now, Ma Soeur." He put down his chisel and straightened. "Is this order for the Church?"

Andreva took a deep breath. "No. I am Andreva of the family of Lumbert in Lavelanet. I have recently arrived in the village to care for my grandmother."

"Ah!" The man's eyes lit. "I know her well. I am sorry she is not in good health."

"Mercés, Monsen." She held out her hands, trying not to tremble. "The box needs to be about this long." She mimicked Raoul's dimensions as best she could. "And this wide and this deep. We wish to secure a few family keepsakes. For safety, you understand."

He nodded. "I have nothing of the sort on hand, but can provide it." He quoted a price. "Come back in a few days—at the end of the week."

"So soon? I thank you, but..." She hesitated. "I do not wish to cause you any difficulty with the officer who demanded balls for his trebuchet."

The mason picked up his tools. His gray eyes darkened. "I will make them," he grumbled, giving the chisel a whack. "They are not your worry. Ladies first. Always."

The sky turned even darker as Andreva made her way home. She had given her name at the quarry, and now worried that would further link her grandmother to the heresy Raoul and Garcia planned. Andreva glanced toward the open chapel and looked around the marketplace as she passed.

No glimpse of Jaques.

When she returned to the house, she removed the veil and looked in on her grandmother. Colet's herbs had given Mémé very little relief from the pain. Andreva stood by the bed. "Permit me to bring help," she pled.

Mémé moaned. "It is time I die."

Andreva straightened the blankets. "Please do not die very soon." The words barely escaped the lump in her throat. She leaned closer and forced a smile. "The weather is too poor for a burial. That would bring as much joy as a rainy-day outing. And I dread the long Mass it would require." Her attempt at jolliness faltered and the next words came out in more of a sob. "Besides, I cannot lose you!"

Only then did Mémé smile.

Throughout the next day, Mémé grew weaker. She seemed to have no will to live. Andreva saw the pain on her face deepen at each distant rumbling of the trebuchet. Did she know her only son had made his way up the mount to cast his lot with the Good Men?

Andreva grew more discouraged each passing hour. "Mémé, I beg you, let me bring someone who can help you get well."

"There is no one, and your nagging tires me." She closed her eyes. "I need only to rest." She fell silent.

Close to tears, Andreva dropped to her knees beside the bed. Her resolve to be courageous had crumbled hours before. "Stay well for me, Mémé. Please do not leave me alone."

Please, do not leave me alone! Without Mémé and Bostel, she had no family. No real friends. No one. The fear of abandonment consumed her thoughts and twisted inside her.

The rattle of a cart coming up the road drew Andreva to the bedchamber window. "Jaques has returned!"

Mémé didn't open her eyes. "Then go be cordial to the man."

Andreva wiped at her tears as hope filled her. She hurried to the kitchen. A flurry of nerves danced in her stomach. She glanced toward the nun's veil, but left it where it was and instead smoothed her braid and donned her grandmother's linen scarf. The apron she wore was presentable enough. She stood at the door with her breath caught in her throat while she waited for his knock. Almost before it came she pulled open the door. Her genuine smile was her first in days.

The farmer, dressed in his usual work clothes, held a full basket. Seeing her smile, a grin spread across his face. "I thought you and your Mémé might enjoy these vegetables." He held out the basket.

"Oh! Please come in." Andreva took Jaques' arm and pulled him into the house. He tugged off his hat as her words tumbled out. "Mémé has fared badly for almost a week. She fell and has yet to recover, and I am worried for her." She closed the door and took the basket. "These will give her strength, I'm sure." She emptied the contents onto the table, placed the basket near the door, and then stood between it and Jaques to discourage him from picking it up and leaving immediately.

"I am sorry to hear it. What can I do to help?"

His presence lifted her spirit—his smile warmed her. Finally, they were together again. "She accepts no help." His mere presence was balm to her. "Mémé claims there are no physicians to fetch."

Jaques held his hat in one hand and rubbed his beard thoughtfully with the other. "Only midwives."

Andreva was desperate for him to stay. "Please sit. Mémé will rest while we visit." She offered another smile—and a stool. "I...I had hoped you would visit sooner..." Her voice trailed off, realizing how telling her words were. She still felt the hurt that had come from seeing him with Ermessen.

He sat with a twinkle in his eye. "I have wanted to come, but other matters have kept me busy." He turned his hat in his hands.

What matters? Ermessen? She took the hat and hung it on a wall hook. She bit her lip and silently prayed to know what to say next. "Tell me...um...my Uncle Bostel...I have missed him so much. How well do you know him?" She regretted her choice of subject at once, realizing he might have heard rumors about Bostel's involvement with the Good Men.

After his initial surprise, Jaques squinted as if calculating the impact of his answer.

Andreva admired his strong jaw, the line of his nose, and the curve of his lips.

"I know him well," Jaques began. "He is my landlord and also my friend. We have discussed religion...life...politics."

"Pray, tell." She stilled the trembling of her hands with effort. Would he too mention the Good Men?

"Well." He shifted on the stool. "He has helped me on occasion with my crops, when an emergency arose. A year ago, last fall, there was threat of an early snow. Bostel came to thresh rye at my side. We finished just as dark clouds rolled in. Bostel is one of few who have come to my rescue. I will always be indebted to him."

"Of course, he wanted you to be able to pay your rent." She meant her comment lightheartedly.

Jaques didn't laugh. "It was more than that. Bostel is an extraordinary Christian. He is goodhearted, honest—"

"Yes, it is impressive," she agreed. "A landowner coming to the aid of a tenant is...uncommon. But—"

Jaques frowned. "You see wrong in it?"

"Wrong? No. I—I am only saying that I am impressed by my uncle's good Christian nature."

Jaques' frown remained, causing Andreva uneasiness. He sat silent a moment and glanced toward his hat near the door. "Domaisèla. I understand you were raised in royal fashion—"

"A commander is hardly royal." Andreva bristled. "Are you insinuating that I don't understand your circumstances or my uncle's actions—that I am spoiled?"

At that he smiled, but rubbed his face as if to wipe away his smirk. The amusement in his eyes betrayed him. "I am sure...well, a girl of your age not knowing how to cook—"

"I thank you kindly for your assessment." Andreva jumped to her feet and the stool tumbled to the floor behind her. Her cheeks burned with embarrassment. "Mémé and I have survived these several weeks on my limited abilities to run a house. I hope never to return to the abbey, so I am trying my best to learn domestic ways. I do not need your criticism."

Jaques stood and stared at her in confusion. "Forgive me. I did not mean to offend." He took his hat from its perch and hesitated. "I will return to look in on you in a few days."

"Do not bother. Mémé and I are doing adequately on our own." Immediately she regretted her words. Of course she wanted him to return. *Cursed foolish pride!*

"But you told me she..." He motioned toward the bedchamber. His bewildered eyes avoided hers as he opened the front door, took the basket, and walked out. He turned for a curt bow in farewell. "Give my regards to your grandmother."

Stunned at his sudden departure and dismayed by the conversation gone awry that had caused it, Andreva closed the door and righted the stool before sinking onto it. She had waited many days in hopeful anticipation for Jaques to visit. Why had she reacted with such arrogance when he pointed out the simple fact that she was domestically inept?

Perhaps only because it was true. Bostel had placed too much trust in her abilities. He should never have left Mémé in her care. Her grandmother's health had not improved, in fact it had declined.

Mémé coughed and Andreva went to the bedroom. The covers hid the woman's face. Andreva gently pulled back the blanket. "Mémé?"

Mémé coughed again. Andreva touched her skin and felt relief. No fever. "I will bring you tea."

Mémé made no objection, so Andreva went to the cook fire and dipped a cup from the cauldron of medicinal tea. From a second pot, she took a small piece of chicken, hoping Mémé would eat the meat and receive the strength it could give her.

Andreva re-entered the chamber, carrying the tray. "Jaques Montré brought fresh vegetables. We shall eat well on the morrow."

"We always eat well," Mémé whispered. "God is good to us."

"Sit up and drink the tea." Andreva helped her into position and placed the pillows behind her head and back. The woman tried to hold the cup, but her hands shook too violently. With Andreva's help, she took a sip.

When Mémé spoke, her voice sounded stronger. "The farmer's attentions to us are generous."

"He told me of Uncle Bostel's kindnesses toward him in past seasons," Andreva stated flatly as she offered another sip, causing Mémé to cough again. When she calmed, Andreva added, "The farmer only returns the favor."

Mémé gazed at her. "Something is wrong. What has happened between you two?"

Andreva did not reply.

"Well, with time, young love has a way of working itself out."

"Love? I am not in love with the farmer!" Andreva spit the label. "He thinks too highly of himself—for a peasant." Guilt swept through her. Denying her love for Jaques did nothing to ease her pain.

A distant boom echoed through the valley and both women flinched. When silence returned, Andreva offered Mémé another sip of the tea. The woman emptied the cup, but left the piece of chicken.

"Will this siege never end?" Andreva wondered aloud.

Mémé wiped her mouth, lay back onto her pillow, and sighed. "Not until the last flicker of the Good Men's burning bones dies out, ma chérie."

The stonecutter loaded the box into the small pull-cart Andreva had borrowed from Raoul. Not only did the tight-fitting lid meet the specified measurements, it held a beautiful motif of a hazelnut tree bearing the letter L.

"For Lumbert," he explained. "I hope Dòna de Lumbert approves of the cutting."

"It is beautiful. She will much appreciate the personalization. I will put our treasures into it as soon as I return home." She ran her hand over the carving. "And, kind sir, if we wish to seal the box for many years to preserve its contents from water what do you suggest we use?"

He raised his brows. "A mortar?"

"Precisely."

"If you seal it, you will have to chisel it open." He wagged his head. "Hard work."

Andreva smiled to indicate her understanding.

He shrugged and went back into his shop. After a moment, he returned with a small pouch. "Mix this powder with a bit of water to make the cement. Cover the rim of the box completely and place the lid upon it. It will serve your purpose.

She thanked him and dropped coins into his hand.

He seemed pleased. "Mercés!"

Andreva turned to leave, but paused when the knight

she'd encountered there earlier rode up with two soldiers in a horse-drawn cart. "My old man! How many balls are ready for the king's trebuchet?" he demanded before dismounting. Turning to Andreva, he made the sign of the cross in greeting.

She returned it and stepped back towards the wall to get out of his way.

"Three, sir."

"Three? A measly three?" He roared, "You imbecile!"

Trepidation filled Andreva as she retreated into the shadows.

The stonecutter remained calm. "I have had other orders to complete. You are fortunate to get three."

The knight, who stood much taller than the stonecutter, grabbed the front of the shorter man's tunic. "We are at war, do you understand? And if you want to avoid being strung up yourself, you will have ten stones cut by sunrise." He hurled the man to the ground, joined the others on the cart, and rode away.

"Monsen!" Andreva rushed to the fallen man's side. She took his arm and helped him stand. "Are you injured?"

He brushed debris from his torn stockings and spoke in a low tone. "Many of the Good Men at le château Montsegùr are my friends, my neighbors of Lavelanet. I resent being forced to aid their enemy." He limped back into his shop without a farewell. "I am sorry."

Ten trebuchet balls seemed an unreasonable number to expect in a day, but there was nothing she could do to help him, and she needed to get back to Mémé.

Andreva tucked the pouch under her belt and pulled the cart down the road. As she entered the village, the wheels squealed as if to blab her secrets to all. Curious faces peeked out windows. She was too conspicuous in her habit and veil.

"Andreva!" She turned to find Elodie hurrying to join her. "How fortunate to meet you. I am upset and need someone to help calm me." The girl's cheeks were mottled from tears.

"Whatever is wrong?"

"Oooh!" Elodie groaned and wiped her face as they continued toward home. "Monsen Fortaner dismissed me.

He said he could not employ a silly girl who had an impudent brother."

"No!" Andreva's fist tightened. "Monsen told Raoul he would pay for standing up to him in my defense." She fumed. "So, this is Fortaner's revenge."

Elodie halted. Her eyes grew round. "I know nothing of this."

"Twice Raoul has come to my rescue when the man tried to take advantage of me. Under his handsome looks, Monsen Fortaner has an evil heart."

Elodie pursed her lips and walked on.

"What is it?" Andreva tugged the cart, trying to catch up.

The girl turned and leaned close. "Please tell no one, but one day when Dianne was in the garden and I was making up beds, Monsen forced me into a corner and kissed me. His hands were everywhere. I fought him, and Dianne heard my screams. When she came inside, I knew by her expression that he had treated previous maids with similar disrespect. She was thereafter always careful to know where I was at all times. She never left me alone to give him opportunity."

"You poor girl! It must be some relief to not return."

"But for the pay. I regret telling my maire of my lost position. She depends upon my small support." Elodie bowed her head. "Dianne is leaving on a trip, back to her daughter's in Narbonne. I prepared her clothing, so I expected some days without employment, but then Monsen Fortaner told me not to return—ever. Hopefully I can find work in the fields when the crops are ready." The girls continued on to Mémé's door.

Raoul came from within the house. He squatted by the cart to examine the box. "These carvings are much too beautiful to bury," he declared in awe. He looked up at his sister. "Why are you home, Elodie?"

Elodie gave Andreva a cautionary glance. "Uh...Dòna Dianne is leaving again for Narbonne on an extended visit, so I am needed no further." She gave a quick curtsy and hurried on to her house, but not before Andreva saw the tears return to her eyes.

Raoul watched her leave. "This will disappoint Maire."

"Perhaps Elodie will find other employment while Dianne is away." Andreva thought she might hire her to cook or sew occasionally. Her allowance had been generous, and she had put several coins aside.

"She is fortunate to work for the Fortaners. There is no other employment for a girl in Lavelanet except weaving and selling handmade wares, for which she hasn't the disposition. Or harvesting the fields come summer." Raoul ran his hand over the carvings again.

Andreva gazed down at the box. "A pity he spent the time making it so beautiful, is it not? The stonecutter believed the box was for my grandmother, so he carved the hazelnut tree of Lavelanet for her." She remembered with a shudder the wrath he had incurred from the knight for his thoughtfulness to her.

Raoul lifted the sturdy lid and looked inside. "This should be plenty big. Garcia's whole satchel could fit in here."

He handed the cover to Andreva, picked up the box with both hands, and lugged it indoors. She followed him to Mémé's room where they planned to keep it out of sight until Garcia's return. He gently placed it just inside the door without awakening Mémé, and then followed Andreva back to the kitchen.

"I must find a treasure to put into the box immediately." Andreva glanced around.

Raoul's brow knitted. "You have me wondering."

"I told the stonecutter it will hold family treasures. If I should chance upon him, I want to know I kept my word. I wish not to be guilty of lying to a man who treated me with kindness."

She walked around the room and then to the cupboard. She moved a stool over to stand upon, and sorted through the odds and ends. Behind some chipped crockery, she found a small doll. "A poupée!" Andreva held up the doll with delight and dusted it gently to remove years of dust. The cloth head and body were one piece. Its small face had eyes and a nose sewn in black thread, and a mouth stitched in red. Its creator had sewn pieces of green cloth together for a tunic and tied a braided string belt around the waist.

"This will do." She stepped from the stool.

"A poupée?" Raoul asked.

Andreva carried the doll into her grandmother's room without reply.

"You are back," Mémé said from the bed. She scarcely opened her eyes.

Andreva took the doll to her. "I need a family treasure to keep in this stone box while it is at our home, and I chose this." She held up the doll.

Mémé turned over and looked toward the box without comment. She took the little doll to examine it. A weak smile came to her lips. "It belonged to your maire. I made it for Sanche when she was just a babe." She handed it back. "It is now yours, ma chérie, if you wish."

"Mine?" Andreva examined the doll, trying to imagine her mother playing with it as a child. Had she kissed the funny little face and snuggled it when she needed comfort? Did her childish fingers tie the belt of twine over and over? She smoothed the stitched mouth with one finger and thought of her mother's sweet smile with a twinge of longing.

Andreva put her hand over Mémé's. "Mercés. That is so kind of you." She straightened the doll's dress and laid it in the base of the stone container.

Returning to the kitchen, she found Raoul sitting on a stool, warming himself beside the fire.

"A poupée." He snickered, staring into the flames. "I supposed you meant real treasure such as gold or gems."

Andreva sat next to him, still melancholy. "It belonged to my maire when she was a girl."

"Oh." Raoul considered her more seriously. "Then it is a treasure. You lost her, what, a year ago?"

"Yes." The flames in the hearth danced as Andreva recalled a little doll of her own that she had loved dearly. It had coarse thread for hair, but more exquisite than its coif was the doll's dress. Her mother had fashioned it from a remnant of brocade.

When Andreva's parents died, she took the doll with a few other belongings in a small basket to the abbey. There she had shared a room with other women, but after the candles had been extinguished, she would take the doll from the basket beneath her bed and hold it for comfort. One night she had particularly missed her mother. Overcome by self-pity, she had reached beneath the bed, but the doll was missing from the basket. Her last tangible memory of her mother had been stolen from her forever.

"A silver denier for your thoughts?"

Andreva returned her attention to the present. "Ha!" She scrunched up her nose. "As if you had a coin."

"Did you desert me to dream of Jaques Montré?"

"No." The hair on the back of her neck bristled with annoyance. She stood, found the broom, and swept a few dangling cobwebs from the corner. "I was thinking of the doll. Boys may not understand about poupées. I am sure my maire loved that funny little thing."

After another moment of watching the flames, Raoul stretched. "I shall go move the cart to its proper place, but will return shortly." He pulled on his mittens. "Poupée. Ha!" He smirked before he closed the door.

The invigorating scent of afternoon rain had breezed through the open door and Andreva stopped to enjoy it. The squeak of the cart faded away as she set aside the broom and prepared a tray of nuts, bread, and boiled parsnip for her grandmother.

"Mémé," she said softly at the chamber door. "Would you care to eat?"

Mémé tossed on her pillow. "Do not take me!"

Andreva set the tray aside and put her hand on her grandmother's forehead. Thankfully, there was still no fever. "Who would take you?"

The woman opened her eyes and blinked a few times. When Andreva caught her gaze, Mémé sighed with relief. "It was simply a bad dream."

"Caused by the turnips we ate last night, no doubt. They were a bit strong." Andreva helped Mémé sit up. Mémé did not appear humored. "I am glad you feel better, Mémé. I worry about you."

With an unsteady hand, Mémé took a nut from the tray. "You are what keeps me alive. But I regret that I am a burden. You are young and should not be tied down to an old woman like me."

"If Uncle had not summoned me here, I would yet be an inmate at the abbey. Please know I would much rather be here with you. Now we need only to get you well."

Two weeks passed, and the stone box caught Andreva's eye each time she entered Mémé's room. No word had come from Garcia. No letter had come from Bostel, and Jaques had yet to return. Perhaps none of them would ever come again. Andreva grieved. She often breathed deeply to ease her pain, and it was then she most longed to hear the rattle of Jaques' cart or his knock at the door.

Fortaner had once again brought the allowance, but Raoul was there helping Andreva scrub the stone floors. The man had not come into the house, and Andreva said a silent prayer of thanks for protection.

One frosty morning when Raoul finished bringing water from the well, he shoved the door closed and stole a peek out the window. "The Inquisitors are back in the village. Their faces cause me—"

"They have nothing to do with us." Andreva walked over and bolted the door. "So, do not speak of them."

Raoul dropped onto a stool at the table. "They are asking who of the Good Men are left in the village."

When his eyes met Andreva's she saw the fear within them. A cold chill passed over her skin.

"They go from door to door, searching for written gospels, especially ones translated into vulgar languages." He made a face. "Meaning our language—Óc."

She sat next to him. "It is illegal for anyone to own a Bible."

Andreva glanced around the room, her eyes settling at the top of the cupboard where she had found the doll. She had not found even one book in the house.

Raoul continued, "And yet the Good Men continue to copy the verses and keep them in their homes. And wherever the soldiers find them, the people are dragged away and imprisoned. They will be burned as heretics."

"Here in Lavelanet?" Uneasy, Andreva carried a stool to the cupboard to make one more search.

Raoul followed. "What is worse is that the soldiers' spirits are high. They are in the streets, swearing oaths to take Montsegùr by the end of the week. We have no time to lose."

"We?" Andreva looked down from the stool. "No, no! Whatever you have planned, leave me out of it."

"The army has blocked all communication into the fortress, and here the stone box waits." He motioned toward the bedchamber.

"What does the box have to do with the fortress?" Finding only dishes in the cupboard, she closed its doors, and stood on tiptoes to make sure there were no pages among the clutter on the cupboard's top. "Has Garcia gone to the château? He said he was not one of the Good Men."

"It is true. I don't know where he is, but that is my best guess. He had planned to take the stone box with him, but had to flee the Inquisition." Raoul offered his hand to help Andreva step from the stool. "I must find him and will leave today."

Was he mad? "Why put yourself in danger with the Good Men when you do not even know Garcia is there? Wait for his return."

"I will stay out of sight." He hit his fist on the table. "I have made up my mind, so do not think to talk me out of going."

How senseless it sounded, but Andreva knew Raoul could not be persuaded. "Then you will take the box with you." She moved toward her grandmother's room.

Raoul grabbed her arm. "I cannot take it. Do you not understand? I must go in secret. The Inquisitors know of my father's sympathy toward the Good Men. They know that I befriended Garcia. No one must see me climb the mountain." He let go of her arm and fingered a piece of pewter that hung from a chain around his neck. "My cross might as well be sewn onto my shirt—yellow in color and two hands high—

the Cathar's punishment. The priests watch me with cynical eyes, waiting for me to slip and confess by my actions that I am also sympathetic to the Good Men."

Andreva thought at once of the mousy repentant who had served them in the tavern at Montgiscard. "Then stay away from Montsegùr. I do not understand why you would take such a risk."

The cross fell against his chest when Raoul took her shoulders in his hands. "Before I leave, I will arrange for someone to bring the box to Montsegùr. When I have found Garcia and the scroll, together we will find a place there to bury it."

Andreva's jaw dropped. "You risk your life for nothing!"

"For nothing? My dear friend, we bury the scroll to keep it safe from the Inquisition's destroying power."

"You sound like Garcia." She stepped away. Both men's stubbornness baffled her. Why would anyone knowingly commit such heresy?

Before she could again beg him to reconsider he said, "Bar your doors and close your shutters. This day is no friend to anyone in Lavelanet." Their eyes met and she saw his apprehension return. Still, he pulled her to him and gave her a quick kiss on the cheek. Without a goodbye, he rushed out the door.

Andreva touched the spot he had kissed, and smiled. Surely it was the influence of the troubadours' music that had turned him into a romantic. She loved him as a good friend. Making the sign of the cross, she pled toward heaven. "Please watch over my dear brother."

In moments, Andreva heard voices from outside. She peeked out the door to see soldiers swarm down the street like locusts, stopping at every door. Pulling on the nun's headdress, she braced herself for the knock. Her muscles tensed and she prayed she had missed nothing, and had nothing to fear.

When the knock came, she opened the door to a young man who wore a cloak with a large red cross on its shoulder. "Ma Soeur!" After his initial surprise, he bowed, and then peered into the room. "We have come to search the house."

The two soldiers who accompanied him also greeted her with signs of the cross and a polite, "Ma Soeur."

She returned their greetings with a curtsy. "We have nothing illegal here. We are strong in our Catholic faith and loyal to the pope." She began to close the door.

"Of course." The soldier put out his hand to keep the door open. "We are sorry, but our orders are to search all premises."

The three pushed forward. Andreva stepped back and started to protest, but knew it would do no good. One man headed up the stairs, another searched the cupboard and then descended into the cellar.

Andreva nervously bit a fingernail. Had her uncle left evidence anywhere she had not thought to look? Might there be a gospel tucked away somewhere?

The third invader walked toward the bedchamber. Andreva slipped past him to hurry to her grandmother's bedside.

Mémé's eyes widened. "What is happening?"

"Hush." Andreva knelt at her side and took her grandmother in her arms. They held to one another while the soldier searched the wardrobe.

He approached the bed without an apology, and even though Mémé lay there with fear in her eyes, he lifted the foot of the straw mattress to investigate beneath, and then under the head. He dropped to his knees and briefly sifted through the few bags beneath. He removed the lid of the stone box, pushed the doll aside, and finding nothing else, replaced the lid and walked out.

Andreva quietly explained why the men were there. When she returned to the kitchen, the soldiers had gone.

Bolting the door no longer held much reassurance of security. She released a heavy sigh. Intruders had invaded her privacy twice now by searching her home without her permission. With Raoul gone, Mémé ill, and soldiers taking over the village, she felt angry and vulnerable.

What would the Inquisitors require next?

vint·e·un

illed with apprehension, Andreva headed toward the marketplace, a basket on her arm. She'd expected to see Inquisitors and Crusaders still occupying the village. To her surprise, she saw only merchants, shoppers, and a group of villagers gathered near the oak tree.

She stopped at the cheese vendor's table. "What, pray tell, is happening?" It felt good to smile again after too many days of worry.

The vendor beamed. "After nine long months, Pierre-Roger de Mirepoix, the leader of the Good Men's forces at Montsegùr, has come to an agreement with the French commander. All who will deny the Good Men's religion may leave the fortress safely. They have until the sixteenth of March to recant and depart. That is more than a fortnight."

"This is good news." Would Bostel soon come home? Andreva's pulse quickened as she tried to make out the outline of Montsegùr's buildings through the morning haze that engulfed the pog. A few of the buildings perched upon the top reflected glints of sunlight.

Andreva paid for eight loaves of bread and a bit of cheese. She bid the vendor farewell and hurried toward the group that had gathered by the tree. Because she had kept so much to herself since coming to Lavelanet, she had no names to put with their familiar faces.

"I do not believe they will abjure," said an older woman wrapped in a gray shawl.

"They are strong people, a stubborn lot, and will hold firm to the conviction that God will rescue them."

"Even as the flames engulf them?" a second woman countered. She held up a crooked finger. "God has not saved the others."

A stout man looked toward the pog. "I am glad to hear they have surrendered. The war will be over and the Crusaders can leave the Languedoc."

"It is not as easy as that for the Good Men," another man pointed out. "For many, it is a choice between life without conscience, and death. The Church has promised to pardon them if they abjure."

"Ha!" the first woman said. "You cannot trust the Inquisitors to keep their word." She spat into the dirt. "They will dog each man, woman, and child the rest of their lives, waiting for one incriminating act or word."

Andreva felt the skin on her back crawl.

The stout man started away with a grumble. "I know not what they may choose. I, for one, would come home."

Yes, home! Bostel might now come home! Raoul and Garcia were safe! They were not Good Men, so there was no reason for them to stay at the fortress.

She rushed up the street and delivered the bread and news to the widows. Afterwards, she hurried home to tell Mémé.

But Mémé shook her head in dismay. "Bostel will not renounce."

There. Mémé had finally confirmed what Andreva had known but did not wish to believe—Bostel was one of the Good Men. Her knees buckled, and she lowered herself onto the bed. "But Grandmother, I still hope he will choose to come home."

Mémé smiled, but her eyes held sadness. "Then hold to your hope, ma chérie."

Andreva waited through the long days, hoping the dawn of each would bring the return of Bostel, Raoul, or even Garcia. She was desperate to learn what was happening at the fortress, but nobody in the village seemed to know more than she.

Hints of an early spring brought cheerfulness to the valley despite the imminent arrival of Montsegùr's deadline, and the horrific deaths it might bring. A few brave birds had returned and Andreva enjoyed their lively chirping in the tree outside the back door. The first buds appeared on the hazelnut trees. A few random blades of grass peeked through the lingering snow, soft as the hair of a newborn baby.

Jaques finally came. Andreva opened the door and anxiously chewed her lip as she watched him climb from his cart. When he saw her, she curtsied in greeting. He held up a chicken—cleaned and plucked—but did not return her smile.

"I cannot stay. Have you heard the news from Montsegùr?" He handed her the chicken and took a step back toward his cart.

"About the truce? Yes, very good news! I hope Uncle Bostel will—" She stopped herself and blushed furiously. Never had Jaques indicated he knew her uncle's whereabouts.

His eyes showed no surprise as he tipped his cap. "I must leave. Good day." He pulled himself up to the cart seat.

Please! Do not leave! she wanted to call to him, but stood silently, watching him urge his animal toward the village. He never glanced back. She hung her head and heaved a sigh of disappointment. What a mess she had made of things!

Back in the house, Andreva drove a long skewer through the bird to roast it over the fire. Her mind replayed Jaques' previous assessment. He was right, she could barely cook, housework was a challenge, and her nursing skills had proved lacking. Poor Mémé!

Tears blurred the flames of the fire as she turned the bird and vowed that if she saw Jaques again, she would... would what? Apologize for her upbringing?

Andreva pulled over a stool upon which to sit. Honesty

about herself and her feelings for Jaques had come more easily since their confrontation. No matter his status, no matter that he was her family's tenant, she loved him.

When the bird turned a golden brown with its meat hanging from the bones, she sliced a chunk of the breast and put it on the tray along with a meat knife. She also took bread, jam, and herb broth in case Mémé still refused to eat the meat.

She perched on the bed and set the tray between them. The chicken was juicy and tender. Andreva took a bite and closed her eyes to enjoy its flavor. She had finally cooked a chicken properly.

Mémé declined to taste the meat. She sipped the broth and nibbled the bread, resting between bites. As they ate, the sun hung barely above the horizon and shone directly through the bedroom window.

The latch on the front door rattled. Andreva knew she had bolted it. "Who would try to enter?"

Mémé's eyes widened. Andreva's hand hovered a moment over the knife on the platter. Maybe Raoul had returned! Leaving the knife, she wiped her hands on her apron and went to the door. The lever jiggled again.

"Andreva?" It was Fortaner. Under no circumstance would she have that man in her house without Raoul present. She took hold of the broom and approached the door, determined to stand up to him.

She leaned close to the door to speak through it. "Why do you attempt to enter uninvited?"

"I am sorry to alarm you. I have brought news about Montsegùr that will be of interest. Let me in!"

Andreva regretted leaving the knife behind. "That does not explain why you attempt to open our door without permission."

"Forgive me, I did not think." His voice was forceful, but calm. "I am only anxious to tell you the news. Please, let me in."

"We have heard of the treaty already, thank you. Now please leave."

The latch rattled. "My news is not about the treaty."

"What could Montsegùr have to do with me? Why would I want to hear your news?"

"Bostel is at the château." His voice lowered. "He is badly wounded."

Andreva gasped at the stinging words. "You must be mistaken. My uncle is in Toulouse." True or not, she would not reveal what she knew to this man, no matter what he said.

"I have been there," Fortaner insisted. "I have seen his mortal wounds with mine own eyes."

Against her better judgment, Andreva released the latch and opened the door a mere inch, using her foot as a doorstop. "Is he hurt badly?"

"He is. Let me take you to him."

"No!" Even if she was reading into his countenance a deviousness that was not there, allowing this man to drive her anywhere could only mean trouble. She pushed the door closed, but before she could latch it, Fortaner forced it open.

He rushed in, toppling her to the floor, and causing her to drop the broom. He bolted the door behind him.

She recoiled when he held out his hands to help her up. She rose to her feet unaided.

"Accept my apologies. I knew you would wish to hear what I have to relate."

She backed toward Mémé's bedroom. "I think you lie, Monsen. What business could you have had at Montsegùr when it is yet under siege?"

His eyes darkened. "I am one of them." He towered over her. "Now, to the other reason I am here, I spoke of an arrangement, and I am still willing to bargain."

She lifted her chin despite her fear. "But I am not."

"Even the Good Men are not against a little...recreation. To us, it is not a sin. We live as we wish, knowing the consolamentum will save us in the end. It is much like your Catholic deathbed repentance."

Andreva looked from the front door toward the one to the garden. "You are a horrid man. I want nothing to do with you!" She straightened her spine. "How is your lovely wife today, Monsen? Surely Dianne misses you."

 J. Sowards

Fortaner scowled and scooped Andreva into his arms. He held her firmly no matter how hard she fought, and carried her toward the stairs.

"Let me go, you monster!" She screamed and hit him repeatedly with her fists.

His grip only tightened. "Relax, my lady. You will not win, so you might as well enjoy." He took the first stair.

Realizing her struggle was for naught, she forced herself to relax, nuzzled close, and bit him hard on the jaw.

He cried out in surprise and pain. She fell to the floor as a string of obscenities flowed from the man's mouth. His hand touched his wound. "Why, you wench!" He backhanded her across her face.

With her hipbone and face throbbing, Andreva scrambled to her feet, stepping on the hem of her dress. The sound of it ripping unnerved her. She grabbed a stool and held it as a shield. "I will report you. I will proclaim your filthiness."

He held his hand to his wounded jaw. "No one will believe you, not after I tell them Dòna de Lumbert is a Cathar and that I came here to confront her. He glanced up the stairs. "But I will not tell, if you—"

Andreva's lungs constricted. "You monstrous liar!"

He grasped the leg of the stool and yanked it from her. Then he grasped and twisted her wrist, and dragged her again toward the stairs.

"I will not!" Andreva screamed, struggling to free herself.

Fortaner slowed, but did not release his grip. "All right. If you prefer, I will take care of matters right here." With one hand, he released his belt and tossed it aside. His foul lips pressed against hers, banging her head against the wall.

Andreva clenched her teeth.

"Fortaner!"

He whirled toward the voice. Paralyzed with fear, Andreva could hardly breathe.

Mémé stood in the chamber doorway, one hand raised above her shoulder.

"Well." Fortaner loosened his grip on Andreva enough for her to pull marginally away. "Margaurite de Lumbert, you want to join us."

Mémé reacted swiftly. Steel flickered across the room. Fortaner gasped. His hand flew to the knife squarely embedded in his chest, blood oozing from the wound onto his shirt. His eyes widened in horror and he fell to his knees. His free hand balanced against the floor before he rolled onto his back and breathed out a long, wheezing groan.

Andreva sank to her knees beside Fortaner. His vacant gaze stared at nothing. "Mémé!" she cried in panic. "He is dead!"

vint‑e‑tres
23

émé slid to the floor. Her eyes rolled back and her lids closed.

"Mémé!" Andreva crawled to her grandmother and pulled the woman's head against her shoulder. "Do not leave me now!" She patted her cheek. Mémé's eyes fluttered, but she gave no response other than a reflexive, throaty gurgle.

"Mémé, what do I do?" Tears flooded her eyes as she gazed in horror at the corpse on the floor. "He is dead! Fortaner is dead!" She held Mémé and sobbed.

What would happen to them? Would they be arrested for Fortaner's death? Would the authorities believe her story—that Mémé had acted in her defense? They would be shunned, maybe imprisoned, or even executed.

Andreva swallowed her sobs. No matter the consequence, she couldn't leave her grandmother on the floor, nor the dead man in her home.

"Mémé," she finally managed, "I will get you back into bed. Help me if you can." Placing her grandmother's arm around her shoulder and her own arm around Mémé's waist, Andreva struggled to stand and drag the older woman back onto the bed. Though her hands shook violently, she managed to situate Mémé on the pillows and pull the covers up to her grandmother's chin.

Andreva knelt and listened to the woman's ragged

breathing. "Mémé, oh, Mémé!" Tears distorted her vision of the dear woman's face. "Sleep, Mémé. Rest until I return." She crossed herself and uttered a plea for safety, then rose to her feet.

Andreva's hands continued to shake so badly that she could hardly pull on the nun's wimple and veil. She grabbed her cloak before glancing once more at the crumpled corpse. Andreva covered her mouth to try to keep from gagging. She stepped outside.

The setting sun's red glow barely lingered along the horizon as Andreva looked up and down the street. A soft light poured from the window of Colet's house, but Raoul was gone and she could not bring his already-suffering family into the matter.

Andreva passed the commons and hurried into the empty chapel. A door opened in the right transept and the priest stepped out.

"Father Tomàs!" Andreva ran to him and fell to her knees. "Mon père, I need help. A man lies dead on the floor of my grandmother's house. Please, tell me what to do!"

The father moved closer. "Who is the man?"

She could no longer look into his eyes. "Gerrard de Fortaner, mon père." She wrung her hands.

He motioned for her to stand. "Take me to him."

Relief swept over her. Her training to trust the Church in time of need had not failed her. She stood, but before they reached the doors that led to the street, the priest paused and opened a side door. Andreva held her breath. Father Tomàs mumbled a few words she could not decipher. She dreaded that he might be speaking to Father Stefe. The stern Inquisitor would see no justification and show no tolerance.

But it was a large man dressed in a monk's robe who came from the room. Andreva peered up into his unfamiliar face and released her breath with relief.

"Come." Father Tomàs took hold of her arm and hurried her out of the chapel and along the road. The large man followed.

The sun had set, coloring the landscape in the muted bluegrays of twilight as the three moved along the road toward the house. An owl hooted from a distant tree. Andreva unlocked the door and pushed it open. Fortaner's body lay unmoved on the floor, his blood pooling between the stones.

Andreva left the men and hurried to Mémé who still lay unconscious. Andreva lit a candle and returned to the doorway between the rooms.

Father Tomàs stood over the corpse. "Remove the knife and take him away."

The other man took hold, yanked the meat knife free, and laid it on the table. He hoisted Fortaner's body over his shoulder and carried it out. Andreva turned away from the pool of blood on the floor.

"Now, Sister Andreva," Father Tomàs said calmly, "tell me what transpired here."

Andreva moved over to a stool and sank down onto it as her tears returned. "Oh, mon père! Monsen Fortaner has made unwelcome advances since my uncle left, and offered me 'arrangements' for protection and money. I have denied him and avoided being alone in his presence. But today he pushed his way into our home. He forced himself on me—raving how the Good Men have no proper rules of conduct. We struggled." She could not stifle the sob. "He would have taken my honor if not for..."

"For what?" the priest said in even tones.

Mémé coughed, followed by a cry. Andreva stood to go to her. "My grandmother needs me. A moment please."

As she passed the friar, he took hold of her arm. "Who put the knife into Monsen Fortaner?"

Andreva opened her mouth, but only a small sound escaped. Looking into his eyes, it seemed unwise to confess for her grandmother. A sense of foreboding washed over her. She would reveal no more. She had to protect Mémé at all costs. Andreva lowered her eyes. "I—I did, mon père."

"You?" The friar glanced over her shoulder toward Mémé's chamber. "You then have excellent aim—particularly in a struggle." He raised an eyebrow. "As good as your grandmother's, I would say." He released Andreva and walked to the open chamber's doorway.

Andreva followed him. "Mon père, Mémé is not well.

Please, let a dying woman leave this world in peace. Give her some assurance of heaven." She took hold of his hand and sank to her knees. "Please!"

The friar looked down at her. The love and understanding in his eyes gave her hope.

He patted her hand. "Give me a few moments alone with Dòna de Lumbert. Afterward, you and I will discuss the matter further."

Andreva let his hand slip from hers. She stood and stepped back as he closed the door. She returned to the stool and sat, staring into the darkness.

The cool night seemed suffocating and sinister. All around, the shadows whispered their predictions of doom. Andreva shuddered. Would the priest and others in the village believe she had acted in self-defense? Would they question whether attempted rape merited death?

The tears had dried. No sob escaped her throat. She could only sit listless and stare. In time, she must see to the bloodstains, but not yet. Even the broom in the corner—long her comfort in times of duress—did not beckon.

The fire in the hearth had died to embers. Andreva finally regained enough presence of mind to know she shivered, not only from fright, but from the cold.

With motion born of habit, she rose to pull a stick from the woodpile and place it upon the coals. When it flamed, she lit another candle against the gloom.

The sound of the door opening, and Father Tomàs' footsteps, caused her to look up. He glanced at the blood drying on the floor and walked around it.

His voice broke the cold silence like a gust of warm wind. "Dòna de Lumbert has told me all that happened." He picked up Fortaner's belt from the floor, and lowered himself onto a stool. The flicker of candlelight deepened the worry lines in his face. "Say nothing of this to anyone until I have brought it before the council." His voice did not rise above a whisper. "The man received his just reward at last." He looped the belt in his hand and took a deep breath, releasing it slowly. "God will judge him." He rubbed his eyes. "I will go to Dòna de Fortaner now, and...I will see to everything...else."

Andreva opened her mouth, but found it difficult to speak of Fortaner's sweet wife. "Dianne is in Narbonne."

He lifted his eyes. "How unfortunate."

Tears that had held off since the priest entered Mémé's room now brimmed over her lashes. Andreva raised her hand to her cheek.

"May God bless you for your bravery." Father Tomàs stood. "And may He allow Dòna de Lumbert to die in peace. I have administered last rights and forgiven her sins." His voice grew huskier. "And I applauded her for ending the life of a scoundrel, but never reveal that to anyone."

Andreva cried. "I don't want her to die. I want her to live, to get well, to laugh again."

"We all must die." The friar lay a comforting hand on her shoulder. "She will go to a better place than this unforgiving, wretched world in which we live. And she has done the world one last charitable deed." He closed his eyes and made the sign of the cross.

When he looked up, the kindness in his eyes took Andreva by surprise. She felt inexpressibly grateful that she and Mémé were not alone in this tragedy.

He walked to the door. "Remember, speak no word about this to anyone until you hear from me." He opened it and stepped out into the cold evening.

After looking in on her sleeping grandmother, Andreva removed her veil, gathered up her skirts, and cleaned the floor, her tears mixing with the wash water. She wished she could awaken from the living nightmare that engulfed her.

Finished at last, she made her bed and lay upon it in the dark, grateful for Father Tomàs' compassion. She closed her eyes, but could not sleep. What would tomorrow bring? Would the kindly priest keep the secret? She relived Fortaner's terrifying advances and shrank from recurring feelings of helplessness. She saw again the glint of steel, the body on the floor, the stain of blood slowly filling the gaps between the stones.

The next day, drawing water at the well, Andreva overheard two village women conversing. "Gerrard de Fortaner was killed last night."

Andreva froze with her hand on the rope. Her heart pounded so loud in her ears she feared she would not hear the reply.

"Who killed him?"

Andreva drew up her bucket with shaking hands.

"I know not," the first said. "He was found on the road early this morning."

"And with his wife away. How awful for Dianne." The woman clicked her tongue.

Andreva tensed as she waited for one or the other to say more.

"I would not doubt but it was a soldier that did the deed. None of us are safe. Yesterday, Fortaner. And who will they take tomorrow?"

The second woman grabbed her friend's arm. "We shall no more venture out alone. Warn your husband and keep your children at your knee."

Andreva took her bucket and ducked her head as she left the well and hurried back to the house. She closed the door and leaned against it. Father Tomàs had kept his word!

Still, he would go before the council where the truth might yet come out. Andreva bolted the door and closed the shutters. She ached for Uncle Bostel to return to protect her, for the siege at Montsegùr to cease and the Crusaders and Inquisitors to leave Lavelanet forever.

She looked in on her sleeping grandmother, and the stone box caught her eye. It had sat in the same spot now for several days since no one had come for it. Where was Raoul? Where was the Catalan?

And what trouble would next come knocking at the door?

Gloom hung over the house for days following the awful night of Fortaner's death. Father Tomàs had not visited again, and to Andreva's relief, no one had pounded on the door shouting accusations.

Andreva opened the shutters early to invite the rising sun to cheer her heavy heart. She breathed deeply of the fresh spring air, noting it had been nearly two weeks since the declaration of the treaty, and still Uncle Bostel had not come home. As far as she had heard, only a few Good Men had denounced their faith, and none had yet returned to the village.

She so much wanted to believe that Fortaner had lied, and to everyone's surprise, Bostel would come riding home from Toulouse as he had promised.

Andreva placed one of the apple fritters she had made onto a tray, hoping Mémé would feel like eating. She added a small cup of broth and took it into her bedchamber. "Good morning." She tried to sound as cheerful as possible under the lingering cloud of despair. "I hope you feel better today."

"I am ready for the commode." The words were labored.

Andreva placed the tray on the table and helped her grandmother stand. Mémé grimaced and sat with a thud on the stool.

"I am so grateful, Mémé, that you are recovering..." *from that horrible night.*

Andreva heard the rattle of a cart coming up the road, and peeked through the chamber's narrow window to the street. "Monsen Montré is here."

"Be polite to him!" Mémé scolded. Then she sighed, exhausted. "He is a good man, not a scoundrel as was Fortaner."

Surprised by this first mention of the man since the incident, Andreva said nothing. She draped a shawl around Mémé's shoulders. "I will greet him."

Jaques had pulled the cart up to the door before Andreva opened it. She stepped from the stoop to greet him. He climbed from the seat but did not return her smile, and pulled off his hat. The wind flapped his knee-length cloak. "Good morning, Andreva." The look in his eyes hinted he was still guarded toward her.

"Good morning. I learned to make apple fritters in the hope you would visit. They are freshly made. Please, come in."

He looked past her into the house but didn't move. Instead, Jaques pulled a paper from his hat and handed it to Andreva. "This came today from Montsegùr."

She unfolded it and studied the script. She had been taught to read in childhood, and she'd had many opportunities to study at the convent, but this looping, artistic hand was hard to decipher.

All is ready. Bring the box in the morning. I shall meet you near the first house on the road below the pog.

"You have read this?" She didn't meet his eye, knowing most farmers lacked opportunity to learn to read.

"Yes. It came last night. I must hurry."

Andreva frowned and turned the paper over. Then the light dawned. "This was not written to me? You are the one Raoul asked to take the stone box?"

Jaques took back the note. "Lead me to it quickly. I must reach Montsegùr and return before my animals need tending."

Why had Raoul chosen Jaques? Was it for revenge?

"Montsegùr is a dangerous place." Andreva sorted through her thoughts. "Are you sure you should go?"

Jaques took a slow breath. "Before Raoul left, he asked me to bring the box when he sent for it. I must keep my promise."

Her heart dropped in her chest. "No! What if someone sees you, or something goes wrong? Is there no one else who could do the task? Someone who—"

"Who has no family to risk?" He grabbed her arm. "Who but me? I promised Raoul." He released her. "There is a truce in place, and I am Catholic. I have nothing to fear."

"But the treaty will end on the morrow. Who knows if the soldiers will—" Exasperation overcame her. Must he put himself in danger just when she knew she loved him? "Bah on chivalry and honor!" Seeing his jaw flex, she stepped back in surrender. "Come inside."

Jaques pulled off his patched mittens and tossed them onto the cart's bench. Upon entering the house, he glanced around as if expecting to see the box in plain sight.

"You must leave right away?"

"Óc."

Remembering where she'd left Mémé, she went to the chamber room door. "Please wait here while I help my grandmother into bed." Andreva went into the room to find Mémé slumped over in sleep.

Andreva gently awakened her. "Jaques is here to take the box away. Let me assist you back into bed." She helped her grandmother stand.

Mémé glanced wistfully toward the object. "I will miss it. Sometimes I lay here and study its beautiful design."

With Mémé settled, Andreva tried without luck to lift the box. "Jaques!" she called to him. "Please come."

He peeked around the door and seemed relieved to see Mémé covered in bed. "Bonjorn, Dòna de Lumbert. You are looking elegant today." He bowed.

Despite her weakened state, Mémé smiled and her eyes twinkled. "And your presence brightens our gloomy home."

"It never seems gloomy to me," he said with a boyishly

handsome grin.

Andreva chuckled, amazed at the ease with which Jaques could coax a smile out of Mémé. She should encourage him to visit daily if only for that.

Jaques stooped and picked up the box. He led her through the larger room and back outside where he placed the box in the back of the cart next to a shovel, centering its weight. At the top of the cart, near the seat, was a sword in its sheath.

"A sword?" she asked.

"For protection, if need be."

"I hope you know how to use it." Certainly a knife or saber would have been the weapon of choice for most farmers.

"I do." He wiped his brow with the back of his hand.

She sensed she had caused his defenses to rise, and quickly added, "Tell Raoul that the cement powder with which to seal the lid is in a pouch inside the box. It must be mixed with a little water."

"I will. Pray he and his friend are there to meet me, for I cannot leave my livestock untended for too long." He moved to climb up onto the cart.

Andreva stepped forward and touched his arm. "Jaques, I would lose hope if something happened to you."

He studied her expression. A chuckle rumbled in his chest. "You, the daughter of the count's top commander, raised in wealth—you worry about this poor farmer?"

Andreva lowered her head. "I...I am sorry for my words of the past." She looked up into his eyes. "Please, I consider you with the utmost respect." She meant her words.

"That is hard to believe. I am reminded of your upbringing each time we speak."

Andreva swallowed the knot growing in her throat. She peered down the empty village street and knew she would go with him if it were possible to leave Mémé. She could not bear for him to go alone. "Please, wait. Let me at least send a loaf of bread and the apple fritters with you."

A smile crossed his lips. "You are generous." He followed her into the house where she wrapped a loaf and the fritters in a cloth.

"Will you take the main road?" Andreva did not hand

him the bread—not just yet—in hopes of keeping him a few moments longer. When he looked down at her she bit her lip, wishing for some small tenderness from him in parting. She searched his eyes.

"The road is the only path I know." His voice was low. Jaques stood close, his face only inches away. His gaze dropped to her lips, sending the temptation flitting through her mind to rise on tiptoes until their lips met.

"Then go with God's protection," she whispered. She stretched taller, hoping, and gripped his arm to feel again the muscles that flexed beneath his shirt.

"I shall travel with care. Pray for this poor servant." His lips barely brushed hers.

Tingles rushed through her, leaving her longing for more.

"Andreva!" Mémé's voice shook.

Andreva jumped and turned toward the open chamber door. "Yes, Mémé?"

"Come!"

She pressed a palm to Jaques' face and smiled apologetically. "Please, wait."

"I will." A smile turned up the corners of the lips she had almost kissed moments before.

"You must go with that young man." Mémé rose onto one elbow and her eyes flashed with a spirit Andreva hadn't seen in days.

"But, Mémé," Andreva said in amazement, "you have no idea where he goes."

She grasped Andreva's hand. "Monsen Fortaner spoke the truth. Bostel is at Montsegùr. Go to him and bind his wounds. There is a bag of linen strips that I keep for such a purpose under the bed. Find them."

Andreva knelt and retrieved the linen bag with its strips of cloth.

"Take Colet's herbs for healing. And, if Bostel is well enough, bring him home to me." Mémé leaned back on the pillow, her brow creased with worry. "If he will come."

Andreva stared at the bandages. *Mémé fears being left alone as do I?* She dropped to her knees beside the bed. "I cannot go with Jaques! I promised to *never* leave you. Never!"

She reached for her grandmother's hand. Mémé would live only so long as Andreva could hold on to her.

"You must go." Mémé patted Andreva's hand then pulled away. "It is God's errand. I have heard you and Raoul talk. Also, I believe you are in love with that young farmer. Go. Help him." A faint smile crossed the dear woman's face.

"I do love him." Andreva looked into Mémé's eyes. "But my bond to you is greater."

"I promise to live until you kneel again at my bedside. Now, go retrieve Elodie. She can stay with me until you return."

Andreva nodded, dazed and thrilled at the change of plans. She gathered up the healing herbs and, finding a satchel, stuffed them into it with the linen strips. Only then did she return to Jaques. "I am going with you!"

His mouth opened in surprise. He followed her out the door. "You cannot. Moments ago, you told me of the dangers—and I know that your grandmother is not well."

Leaving him to stare after her, Andreva put the bag into the cart, and ran the several yards to Colet's small home. "Bonjorn in the house!" She pounded on the door.

In a moment, Colet emerged, wiping her hands on her apron. "Andreva! Why do you hurry so?"

"Is Elodie here? Could she sit with Mémé?" She peered into the house. The smaller children sat up in their beds, yawning and rubbing their eyes.

Elodie appeared, still in a nightdress, with wonder on her face. "Where are you going?"

Andreva stood speechless. She would not share knowledge that could put Colet and her family in danger.

Colet drew in her breath. "Montsegùr!" She pulled Andreva into the house and closed the door. "There is only trouble there. The truce ends on the morrow!"

"Pray, Colet," Andreva whispered. "Raoul is there already."

Colet's eyes clouded. She signaled Elodie. "You must help Andreva. Go stay the day with Donà de Lumbert." Elodie went into the bedroom to dress, and Colet turned back to Andreva. Worry lined her face. "Please bring Raoul home with you. I admire his adventurous spirit, but…I cannot lose him too."

Andreva gave her a hug. "I promise to do my best."

When Elodie was ready, the two girls hurried out into the cold morning. Jaques had turned the cart around on the road; Andreva's wrapped bread and pastries lay on the seat beside him.

The girls went into Mémé's house where Andreva began to instruct Elodie.

"Do not worry about Margaurite and me," Elodie interrupted. "We will lock the door and keep to ourselves. May God's protection go with you."

"How blessed I am for your friendship." Andreva hugged her. She grabbed another loaf of bread and the blanket from her bedding, thinking she would need the extra warmth against the wind. On the way out the door, she took the veil and wimple from their hook. Who knew what the day might bring?

But then she had a paralyzing thought. She turned, crossed the room, and motioned for Elodie to come to her. Andreva searched her friend's face. "Who will care for Mémé if I never return? Who knows what danger we face?"

Understanding shone in Elodie's eyes. "Do not think of it. Go in full faith that you will return. Fear not. I will care for your grandmother as my own."

Andreva needed one last goodbye—in case Death's reaper did not see the importance behind Mémé's promise, or lest he decided to take Andreva instead. "Mémé, I am leaving now," she said at the bedside, fighting back tears. "Elodie is here."

Mémé peered from beneath the covers. "Promise to return safely to me, ma chérie. *Adieussiatz.*"

Andreva turned on the cart seat to stare back at the house until it slipped from her view. Mémé had to stay well. If she grew worse—or died—in her absence, Andreva would never forgive herself.

As they drove over the bridge, she listened to the rushing river and remembered her idyllic dream of leisurely walks along its banks. How different her life had turned out from the one she had hoped for three months ago.

The quiet village seemed almost deserted now. Smoke billowed from a few homes, but the marketplace stood empty. She turned to look over her shoulder, even though she knew her home was no longer in view.

"Elodie will give her the best of care," Jaques said, as if hearing Andreva's thoughts. "Now, tell me why you decided to come with me."

She looked up to see his tender smile. He was a handsome man—thick lashes, a finely-shaped nose, and full lips... lips that she had kissed, almost. The memory sent tingles through her. Perhaps he might stop the cart and try the kiss again. She could hope.

But he had asked a question. Andreva gathered her thoughts. It was too late to keep secrets and he deserved to know the truth. "My uncle is within the fortress of Montsegùr."

His eyebrows lifted. "He is? How did you learn this?"

Jaques had not known? Suddenly, her resentment of Bostel for lying to her lessened. "My grandmother told me." She did not want to bring Fortaner's name into the matter. "My uncle may be injured, and I hope to bring him home with us." Andreva waited uneasily for Jaques' reply.

His long pause became awkward. "You need to understand that I must deliver the box and return to my farm right away. As it is, I will be late in caring for my animals, so I have no time to climb the pog to retrieve Bostel." He turned toward her. "And why do you believe he would come?"

She shrugged. "Why would he choose death?"

"You do not know your uncle well." He looked back at the road. "Bostel is a man of honor, a man of principles. The Good Men would rather burn at the stake than give in to the Inquisition and abjure. If he is one of them, I would expect him to be no different."

"I will give him the choice." Andreva raised her chin. "But I do not expect you to retrieve my uncle. I will go myself."

"It is a hard trail."

She fell silent as they followed the river through the valley. Andreva hoped Jaques was wrong and Bostel would be sensible and return home. She knew the farmer was also a man of principle. Surely he would wait for her to see to her uncle, or even help carry Bostel if he was too injured to walk. It would work out somehow. It had to.

Snow clung to crevices and lay in sparse patches upon the peaks that towered around them. Pushing up from the lingering ice, trees with tiny buds sprouting from their branches promised the return of spring. Andreva wondered if spring would bring her new hope; hope for Mémé's recovery, Bostel's return, and—she glanced at Jaques— perhaps to become the bride of a handsome farmer.

Andreva looked up the road as a cluster of houses came into view. The streets stood empty. "What is this village?"

"Villeneuve-de-Olmes. Many of the residents are Cathar, which explains the silence."

Had they all gone to the fortress? Andreva looked toward the mountains, but Montsegùr was blocked from her view by trees and hills. They rode on, leaving the village—a ghostly reminder of pending doom. The Inquisition never failed to follow through on its threats and punishments.

A chilly wind caused Andreva to unfold the blanket and spread it over their knees for warmth.

Jaques glanced her way. "You have aroused my curiosity. How did your grandmother hear that your uncle is injured at Montsegùr?"

"She..." Andreva could not meet his eyes. How could she lie to him? But then, how could she tell him about Fortaner's awful advances and horrific death at Mémé's hand?

He repeated the question.

"I will tell you the truth. I heard about my uncle, not Mémé." She pursed her lips.

"You—" He took hold of her arm. "From whom?" Andreva's heartbeat hammered, and she lowered her eyes, hating to speak the monster's name. "Gerrard de Fortaner."

Jaques let go. "And how did you hear this from a dead man?"

Andreva scooted toward the edge of the cart, as if the few additional inches of space between them would act as a barrier. "He told me the day he died. I—I met him in the village and he said he had just returned from Montsegùr."

"Why, Andreva, do I sense you are lying? There is more to this story, isn't there? You can trust me."

Could she trust him with this? It was not uncommon for women to be held accountable for men's aggression toward them. She pretended to watch the scenery.

He slowed the horse and turned her gently to face him. "Look at me." He touched her chin and lifted her face, but she averted her eyes. "You know how the man died, am I right?"

Andreva resented the insistence in his voice. She pulled free. "Monsen Montré, I do not wish to tell what I know. It is better left unsaid, so that no one is in danger."

"Danger?" Jaques stopped the cart. He turned toward her in the seat. "I wish that whatever burden you carry, you would not endure alone. Have I eased your burden in caring for your grandmother since Bostel left, if only a bit?"

She finally looked into his eyes. "Of course. Your

dedication in serving my uncle is much appreciated."

"You assumed my visits were only to return Bostel's kindness?" He faced forward again and jiggled the reins. The horse began to move. "It was all for you."

"For me?" *Me?* Andreva could hardly believe what she heard. She closed her eyes and allowed the elation to wash over her. An uncontrollable smile crept across her face. They rode in silence another minute. She wanted to trust Jaques. She *could* trust him, she assured herself.

At last she turned toward him. "I—I will tell you the truth about Fortaner." Her happiness fled at the thought of the gruesome event. She took a deep breath. "Monsen Fortaner forced his way into our home. His intentions were not honorable. We struggled. He died by the blade of a meat knife." She turned away as tears came. "Not by a thief on the road."

"In Dòna de Lumbert's house?"

Andreva lowered her head and studied her hands.

"It was you?"

She shook her head. "No. Mémé." It was a whisper. Andreva looked up and when she spoke, her lip quivered violently. "She protected me from that horrid man. After the deed, I fetched Friar Tomàs. He came right away. He knows all that happened." She hid her face in her hands, fearing she would sob. At least now he knew.

Jaques stopped the cart. "It is hard to believe a man like Fortaner would do such a thing."

She whirled to face him. "You do not believe me? This was not the first time he had tried to seduce me," she cried. "You must believe. I told you only because I trust you!" She stood, wanting to run back to Lavelanet and the safety of Mémé's house.

Jaques pulled her back onto the seat. "I believe you. I meant only that Fortaner was not what he seemed." He took her in his arms, but she stiffened at his touch. "It was a terrible thing to endure. I wish I had been there to defend you from the villain and save Dòna from the task."

Andreva sniffled. "You don't...blame me for his death?"

"Certainly not. The blame lies with Fortaner. I am sorry

you and your grandmother had to deal with him alone."

She sank into his embrace, feeling safe for the first time since her parents' death.

Jaques held her marginally away to look into her face and gently wiped a tear from her cheek. "Andreva, my little nun, I love you."

Andreva's joy swelled within her chest. Tears filled her eyes again. "I love you, too."

He rescued a strand of hair that had escaped her braid. "Even though I am a farmer?"

"Yes." She laughed through her tears. "No matter if you are a farmer or a king."

Jaques kissed her forehead and held her for several moments. She raised her face to his and he kissed her—a sweet promise of devotion.

With his arm still around her, he urged the horse forward again. The path led between steep hills, the château not yet in view. Andreva leaned into Jaques, enjoying their new closeness, and watched the mountaintops at each turn, hoping to glimpse the fortress.

Jaques reined the horse and his hand went for the sword in the cart bed. He stood, balancing on the foot board. Metal scraped metal as he drew the weapon from its sheath.

"What is wrong?" Andreva looked behind but saw no one. Ahead, was only a tree, laying across the road, it's branches fanning in a wide arc. Clearly it would need to be moved for them to pass, but a sword would be of no use.

Jaques waved his free hand. "Hush!" He scrutinized the hillside, and then the ravine. "This is an unlikely place for a tree to fall," he whispered.

Andreva gazed upward. Jaques was right. The hill above was covered in shrubbery, not trees.

A movement came from the creek. Andreva's whole body rang with alarm. She pushed the bread and pie beneath her skirt on the bench, and froze as two scruffy men climbed up the bank to the road. Their dirty clothing and rough hands and faces reminded her of the beggars on the streets of Toulouse, but the sinister gleam in their eyes told her they were no beggars.

The men drew their swords. Jaques' muscles flexed as he braced himself. Andreva could barely breathe.

"Your lives you may keep, but give us your valuables." The shorter man held his blade toward them.

The other ragged man had a perpetual squint from a missing eye. "We want only to collect what you have of worth and then to send you on your way." He smiled, showing large, rotting teeth.

Andreva pulled the blanket to her chin as her mind raced to remember what they had: the box, rags, the shovel. She didn't dare glance to where she'd hidden the food.

Jaques tossed the sheath aside and jumped from the cart to face the men. Andreva froze in terror.

The thieves' eyes widened, but they held their ground. "We want no trouble from you." The one-eyed man snarled. His sword flashed in the sunlight.

"We have nothing of worth." Jaques readied his blade. "Now let us pass."

Andreva glanced from him to the robbers, her heartbeat rapid in her chest.

The man signaled toward the cart. The one-eyed man circled Jaques until he could reach the satchel, which he emptied into the cart bed. Andreva scooted away from the man who now stood only inches from her. Jaques stepped backward until he again had both men in his view.

"Nothing here. Not even food," the robber declared, sifting through the contents. "The Good Men always bring food." He held up the nun's wimple and glanced at Andreva. "Hey, Patricio!" he yelled to his companion. "She is a nun."

Hoping the men at least held some respect for the Church, Andreva took courage and lifted her chin. She should have worn the wimple and veil while traveling. How many times had the sisters at the abbey and her uncle assured her of its ability to provide safety?

"Leave her alone!" Jaques warned.

Patricio crossed himself with his free hand, his tone mocked her. "Ma Soeur, your presence is a blessing."

Andreva's confidence waned. She didn't dare move, afraid of what the men would do next, but she hated to see the sacred veil defiled by the filthy hands of the thief.

"A pretty little nun traveling alone with a peasant?" Patricio cackled. His eyes never left Jaques. "Very cozy."

Andreva lowered her chin and pursed her lips at the implication.

"That's enough!" Jaques ordered. Beads of sweat had formed on his furrowed brow.

The one-eyed man tossed aside the cloth. A few foul words followed as he ran his hand over the stone box. "Hey, Patricio, perhaps we could sell this vessel. It must be worth many denier."

"Take it." The man tried to lift the box while holding a sword, but had no success. He let loose another expletive that made Andreva wince. The man squinted his one eye at her and came closer.

Do not touch me! If only she had a club, she would hit him if he dared.

"Leave her alone!" Jaques warned, glancing between the two thieves.

The one-eyed man ignored him to further scrutinize Andreva. His lusty smile reminded her of Fortaner's. She shrank away from him, but he pulled the hood from her head. "My little nun is a beautiful blonde." She cringed at the touch of his hand on her braid.

Jaques reacted fast. His sword caught the hilt of the man's weapon and knocked it to the ground.

The startled man froze at first, then backed away with fear in his eye. At last he looked from his friend to Jaques to his own sword in the dirt, and took off running down the bank.

The remaining man snarled and held his stance.

Jaques walked over, picked up the abandoned sword from the ground, and tossed it into the bed of the cart.

The man lunged.

"Jaques!" Andreva screamed in terror.

Jaques deflected the blow. The intruder staggered forward with a backswing that Jaques easily blocked again. The commotion spooked the horse and it took several steps backward. Andreva found the reins, hoping to be in control if the animal panicked, and allowed it to back the cart away from the fight.

Blade against blade, Jaques battled with as much skill as Andreva had witnessed from any of her father's trained swordsmen. But the other man fought like a madman, snarling with fire in his eyes.

Andreva turned to reach for the sword in the cart.

Grunt!

She looked up. Jaques stood with his back to her, blocking her view of the aggressor. Andreva held her breath, waiting. Seconds passed. Neither man moved. Had Jaques been stabbed? She gripped the reins tighter, stifling a scream.

Jaques jerked back his sword and stepped aside. Patricio gasped. Pain gripped his face as his eyes met Andreva's briefly before rolling back into his head. He fell, the impact forcing the wind out of his chest with a final humph.

All was still for one ghastly moment.

Andreva stumbled off the cart and ran to Jaques. She threw her arms around him. "Are you hurt?"

Panting and sweat-covered, he raised his elbow to examine a wound that oozed bright red blood onto his shirt. "I am fine." He managed to put his good arm around her. She fell into his embrace for several moments, but he did not hold her long enough to fully calm her terror.

He looked down at the body, and with his foot, turned it over. "He is dead."

Andreva turned away. "Thank heaven and all the saints it was not you!"

Jaques slipped his arms around her again, still out of breath, and placed his cheek against her hair. They stood together only moments more before he kissed her forehead. "We must leave."

She tightened her grip, but his arms loosened. He walked over and tossed his bloody sword into the cart bed. She numbly watched him return to the body, grasp its feet, and drag it toward the side of the road. A stain of blood marked the spot where the man had fallen. At the bank, Jaques gave the corpse a shove to roll it down the ravine into the brush.

The image of Fortaner's pained expression just before

he died came back to Andreva's mind. She dropped her face into her hands to will it away.

Jaques' arms enfolded her. "I'm sorry you had to witness that." He looked down the road. "I do not doubt the renegade who escaped will return with more friends. We must not waste another moment."

Andreva helped Jaques drag the fallen tree far enough off the road to allow the cart to pass. Soon they resumed their journey. Breathing deeply, Andreva fought back tears and a bad case of jitters, realizing how close Jaques had come to being killed.

She relived in her mind how Jaques had battled so valiantly. She broke the silence. "Jaques, you fought as capably as any trained swordsman. Where did you learn such skill?"

"From pushing a plow." The twinkle returned briefly to his eyes.

"Please." Her love swelled for this man she hardly knew. "Tell me the truth."

He stared ahead without answering. They rode in silence for several minutes. The path became steeper, but when it leveled out a stretch, Jaques brought the horse to a stop.

He stroked his beard in thought, took a deep breath, and finally turned to her. His smile held a hint of regret. "You are right. It is time I was honest with you, Andreva." He took her hand and gently kissed it. "I had no intention to mislead you nor to lie. I have not revealed my past to anyone, not even to Bostel, but realizing now that I love you, I believe the truth must be told."

Andreva caught her breath and too quickly pulled her hand from his. "I am honored that you would declare your feelings, yet..." Obviously, she hardly knew him, but she loved the man she thought she knew. She lowered her eyes. Could she handle whatever he had to tell her?

"You told me you could love a farmer." He gazed at her humbly.

Assured that she loved Jaques—enough to face danger with him, enough that his status no longer mattered—she took his hand again. "Yes, and I am ready to listen."

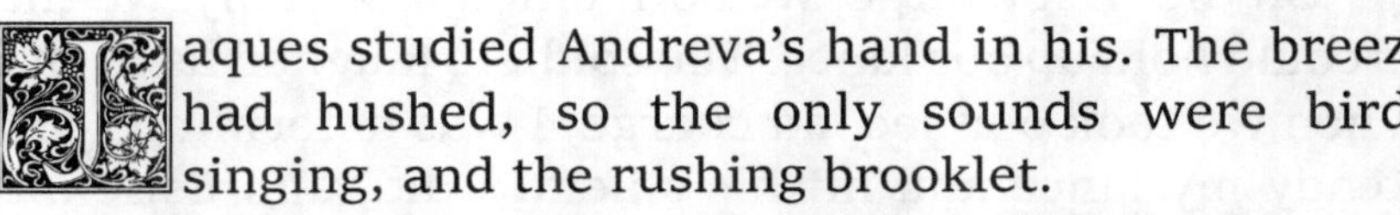

aques studied Andreva's hand in his. The breeze had hushed, so the only sounds were birds singing, and the rushing brooklet.

"I am from Lanfoix where my father is liege lord."

"Lanfoix!" Liege lord? *Taught to read. Skilled sword fighter.* A son of a noble was not the answer she had expected, but it did make sense. Most of it. "But why are you in Lavelanet?"

He kissed her hand and moved closer to her on the cart's bench. "Hear me out?" A breeze came up and rustled the leaves on the trees along the creek.

Andreva nodded and held her tongue, but her thoughts raced. "My father is a knight, as was his father before him, so you see, as the oldest son, I too was raised to become a knight." Jaques searched her face for understanding. "Likewise, my younger brother knew from childhood he was expected to enter the clergy."

"He is a priest in Lanfoix," Andreva remembered aloud, her head still spinning from his revelation. "But you—"

"Óc. I am a farmer." He smiled. "I will admit that growing up I was fascinated by the crops grown in my father's fields. I asked many questions of the peasants, and even pushed the plow when they allowed me to." He chuckled.

"So, you—"

He put a finger to her lips to hush her. "No, I was educated as a page and trained as a squire. Always at my side was my best friend, Estienne. His father served as blacksmith to mine. We were inseparable throughout my preparation to become a knight."

"Then how did you come to be a farmer?"

The twinkle left his eyes. "One day late in my training, some of the soldiers proposed that Estienne and I joust. They dressed us in helmets and gauntlets and provided us with shields and mounts. Neither Estienne nor I had been trained to joust seriously. It was all done in high spirits, and we thought we were the epitome of chivalry and knighthood."

Andreva did not smile at the weak jest. She knew he did not mean his story to entertain.

"On the first charge, we both failed miserably. Neither of us could hold up our lance. The soldiers laughed us to shame. When we took our second charge, I was determined to hold steady my lance and hit his shield. I did, and Estienne hit mine, but the force caused him to tumble. His foot caught in the stirrup and his mount startled and ran, dragging him." Jaques' voice caught. "We tried to stop the horse before he was trampled, but Estienne died shortly thereafter from his wounds." Placing his elbows on his knees, Jaques dropped his face into his hands.

Andreva smoothed her palm down his back. "I am so sorry," she whispered.

When he looked up, his eyes still held anguish. "I put the blame on myself. I could not work, could hardly eat. I could only grieve."

He sat up and raked his hand through his hair. "My parents understood. Being a compassionate man, my father arranged for me to journey to Foix to visit an elderly cousin." He gazed toward the mountains surrounding them. "Of course, he expected that when my heart healed I would return to training and become the knight I was meant to be."

"Yet you are here."

"Óc." Light began to replace distress in his eyes. "My cousin passed away shortly after I arrived. I was not yet ready to return home, so I came to Lavelanet where I met Bostel. In conversation at the tavern, I confessed my passion for making things grow." His mouth curved into a smile. "Bostel, being the person he is, set me up on his land with seed and a plow. I have been here since, enjoying the peaceful life of a farmer."

She placed her hand in his. He raised it to his lips for a kiss.

"Each season, my father requests my return. I know he is right, that I should honor my heritage. It is unheard of for a nobleman's son to turn farmer. I send back word that I will come after one more crop, one more harvest, one more year. Just one more. But when the year has passed, still I cannot take myself back."

"I would be sorry if you left Lavelanet."

With one finger beneath her chin, he lifted her face. "Andreva, I..." His lips brushed hers. The world spun. He kissed her once—warmth against the cold—and again with more feeling, sending wonderful tingles all through her. Their kisses blended with the music of the brook and merged with the vibrant beauty all around.

He held her close. "Andreva, Andreva, I have loved you since I first saw you dressed as a nun, so young and vulnerable. I have longed to take you in my arms and protect you. It is you who have imprisoned my heart."

"Jaques." She kissed his jaw and nestled against him, closing her eyes, knowing he was the man to whom she could devote her life. Her happiness seemed to tighten her throat as she tried to speak. "I love you, too, Jaques."

But suddenly he pushed her away. "Listen!"

Startled, Andreva sat up and heard the thud of footsteps approaching from behind. Her blood ran cold as he fumbled for the reins.

"It is he!" Andreva cried as the one-eyed thief who had attacked them drew abreast with two men at his side.

Jaques flicked the reins. "Get on!" he called to the horse. The animal took off with a jerk. Andreva held to Jaques to stay upright. "I did not expect that ruffian to chase us this far up the road." Jaques sat on the edge of the seat, urging the horse along the path's many ruts and curves at a speed that tore all thought from Andreva's mind. The stone box rattled its way to the end of the cart bed, the satchel with the bandage strips and her veil bouncing along with it.

After what seemed a sufficient distance, Andreva glanced behind them. "Surely they have given up their pursuit." She hoped he would slow the cart, for she worried that so much jostling would damage it. "We should be safe by now."

Jaques slowed the horse as they ascended another hill. At the top, le château Montsegùr came into view. Jaques stopped the cart.

Andreva gazed upward and took in her breath. The fortress stood majestically atop the pog, surrounded by a wide rubble of stones—all that remained of what had obviously been the former houses outside the fortress walls.

"The village is gone, demolished," Jaques muttered.

"Uncle Bostel!" The destruction was worse than she had imagined. Raoul? Garcia? Had they survived such devastation?

"Hopefully, the villagers had plenty of warning and managed to escape into the fortress." He urged the horse up the road.

Andreva's gaze dropped from the rubble atop the pog to the tents and catapults perched at several levels on the side of the mountain and at its base. She recalled the day Perrin, the vendor, had pointed out the steep, round-topped pog. The fortress upon it had seemed so small and far away, yet peaceful, with blue sky and fleecy clouds as its backdrop. But today, so much closer, it looked frightening and foreboding.

Jaques directed the horse past a line of empty carts. Soldiers sat in groups around campfires, their swords gleaming in the sunlight. Andreva expected a challenge at any moment, but the men watched the cart pass, showing only idle curiosity. Nearby, naked stone walls stood amidst blackened ruins and piles of rubbish. A partially charred hobbyhorse leaned forgotten against a tree, and a child's chemise hung from a branch, swaying in the breeze.

Jaques kept the horse moving until they came to the first house still standing. He stopped the cart. "This must be the place Raoul meant for us to meet." He shaded his eyes against the sky as he looked around. The door of the small hovel stood open, revealing its one empty room.

Shivering at the threat of impending death that hung heavily on the air, Andreva tightened her grip on Jaques' arm and spoke quietly. "Let us move farther from the soldiers." She feared they would be questioned, or mistaken for Good Men. "Please, let us move on."

He placed his gloved hand over hers. "There are soldiers everywhere. I have heard they number into the thousands. We will not be able to avoid them." Nevertheless, he again started the horse up the road.

They passed more tents and more soldiers. Andreva's anxiety increased. Why had she come? She gazed upward. The pog, with its steep slopes and cliffs, appeared impossible to climb. How could she get to her uncle? And, even though she had grown up around soldiers and loved many in her father's regiment, she felt unsafe around these men. Her fear, and the many poignant reminders that women and children had lived here before the devastation, made her once again long for the safety of Mémé's home.

The road ended. Jaques directed the horse into some trees and shrubs, out of sight of any tents. The horse immediately fell to cropping the grass. Andreva stretched her sore muscles, and breathed with relief.

They sat a few moments, watching the bushes move in the wind along the mountainside and listening for Raoul's approach. Andreva jumped when she heard neighing. An eerie chill crawled up her neck and she turned, only to see a fenced corral that held grazing horses. Too restless and worried to sit and wait, she gathered the scattered contents of her satchel.

Jaques' hand stilled hers. "What are you doing?"

"I—I must find Uncle Bostel. I hope Raoul comes soon." She stuffed the last strip of cloth into the bag. She was determined to leave, though she expected him to try to stop her. "Please wait for me to return. I promise to hurry." She gave him a peck on the cheek and climbed off the cart. She didn't know how she would get into the château, only that she must.

Jaques leaped from the seat and grabbed her arm. "Please, wait with me for Raoul. Perhaps he has word of Bostel. You cannot go up there alone."

She looked into his eyes. "I must, but I'll hurry." She moved toward the trees. Through their branches she saw a group of soldiers approaching on the road. Their tunics bore the cross of the Crusades. "Let us hide." Andreva tugged Jaques toward the brush.

But he stood firm. "They have seen us. If we run, we will seem suspicious and might be arrested. Stay calm and we will be safe."

Unsure, Andreva looked up the mountain again, and took a few more steps toward the trees.

A soldier called out. "Halt!"

"Bonjorn," Jaques answered.

Andreva froze in her steps. The soldier came closer. Andreva watched him gaze at the pewter crosses both she and Jaques wore around their necks. "What are you doing here?"

"We have come in hopes of bringing those who abjure and swear allegiance to the pope back to the villages."

A smirk filled the man's face. "Well, I'm sorry to say you will return with an empty cart." The soldier smoothed his beard as if to hide his skeptical smile. "There are over two hundred determined Perfecti on the mountain. They say they will not abjure, and will burn together—men, women—their guards, too. They are convinced heaven is their reward."

"No!" Andreva stepped forward. "All of them will stay?"

"Yes. Everyone who would abjure has done so and is gone. There were not many." The man pushed back his hood and scratched his head. "Let the rest burn, I say." He hurried to rejoin his comrades with the battle cry of the Crusades: *"Deus le volt!"*

'God wills it,'" Jaques repeated.

Sickened by the young soldier's callousness, Andreva watched the last straggler pass. She turned to Jaques. "What if Uncle Bostel is merely too injured to leave?"

Before he could reply, they both turned at the sound of someone coming down the hill. Andreva moved behind

Jaques and peered around him as a man dressed in a simple, brown tunic came into view.

"Garcia!" she called, relieved to see him.

"I have found you! Did you bring it?"

"We did." Jaques gestured toward the cart. "Where is Raoul?"

Garcia frowned. "My friend met with injury on the first day he arrived and could not accompany me. The last stone cast by the king's men caused a wall to fall, injuring his head."

Andreva gasped. "Is he all right? Can he travel?"

"Do not worry." He smiled ruefully. "Our friend has a very hard head and is on the mend."

Andreva stepped forward. "I must go to him. And tell me news of my Uncle Bostel. Is he also injured?"

Garcia placed his hands on Andreva's shoulders. "Monsen de Lumbert came close to death when a trebuchet ball flew over the castle wall. Several bones are broken and he suffers greatly."

Andreva stared up at the fortress in dread. Jaques put his arms around her. She leaned into him, feeling faint, and held tightly to his arm. No wonder her uncle had not returned. He could not. "You must take me to them."

"As soon as we have deposited the scroll." Garcia headed toward the stone box in the cart bed. "Come, there is no time to waste."

arcia and Jaques hefted the stone box from the cart and placed it on the ground. Garcia exhaled. "Whew! It is weighty."

"It is." Jaques unhitched his horse, and led it away to graze.

Andreva looked longingly up the mountain at the château. Garcia had agreed to take her to Bostel, but she hadn't counted on the time it would take to first hide his scroll. She stuffed the wrapped bread and fritters into the bag with the bandages and her veil.

Jaques returned. "Where shall we bury the box?"

Garcia motioned up the path. "There is a cave around the mount. Carrying it will be the challenge." He shaded his eyes. "See where the rocks jag out? It is just beyond there." He looked back into the cart. "Good. You brought a tool."

The men carried the box while Andreva brought the shovel and their satchels. She did not mention Bostel again, but hoped Jaques would go on to the fortress with her if it did not take them too long to hide the box. Soon she'd see Raoul again and embrace her uncle.

The path Garcia led them along followed the base of the mountain, out of the sight of any soldiers. He and Jaques set down the box and shook out their strained muscles. Andreva looked around for the cave.

"There are crevasses and secret passages throughout

these hills. We shall take our climb slow and easy."

Climb? We must yet walk farther? To keep from grumbling, she pursed her lips and readjusted her grip on the satchels and shovel.

Trees lined the path on its continual rise toward the jagged rocks Garcia had pointed out. As they climbed higher, tall trees gave way to scrub brush. Andreva basked in the beauty of white clouds and blue sky above the Pyrénées' skyline of snowcapped rock. Scrutinized by squirrels and deer, she breathed in crisp air invigorated by the scent of leafing trees. She watched hummingbirds and warblers, and marveled at the variety of other colorful birds and butterflies. All around, nature manifested the close of winter while trees and bushes announced the imminent arrival of spring.

They hiked to a spot where the side of the pog dropped steeply into the valley below. Andreva paused to take in the breathtaking view.

"We are here!" Garcia said and stopped before a trickle of snow melt tumbling down the mountain into a stream. The men carefully set down the box. Garcia cupped his hands to catch the water as it fell, brought it to his lips to drink, and then wiped his mouth, letting out an appreciative, "Ah!"

Andreva let the cumbersome satchels slip to the ground and joined the two men at the falls. The trickling water's frigid temperature was refreshing as she cupped the water to her mouth to moisten her dry throat. Revived, she looked around. "I see no cave."

"That is what makes it the perfect hiding place." Walking several feet from the water, Garcia took hold of a clump of bushes and dragged them away, revealing a hole barely large enough for a man to crawl through. He motioned for Jaques to push the box toward him, then dropped to his hands and knees and edged backwards into the hole. Reaching out, he took hold of the stone box and dragged it in while Jaques pushed.

Andreva gazed upward, amazed by the enormity of the pog. Ledges of rock hid the fortress from her view, and it would still be quite a climb to reach it. Thankfully, she wore the dress from the abbey. It afforded her plenty of room for needed maneuvers—she hoped. Her heavy cloak might present a challenge, but she would carry it if she must. She was prepared to do whatever it took to find her uncle. All that stood between them now were the steep cliffs soaring above her.

"Andreva, come!" Garcia's voice came from inside the cave.

Andreva left the shovel and satchels beside the trail and dropped to her knees. It took several moments for her eyes to adjust to the dimness as she gathered her skirt and followed the men into the cave. A heavy, musty smell of wet dirt greeted her. After a few feet, the tunnel opened, allowing her to stand. She stretched her muscles and brushed the wet gravel from her frock.

"Excellent!" Garcia exclaimed. His voice echoed through the small chamber and into rooms beyond. He rubbed his hands together and gazed upon the box. The dim light from a slit of a crevice many feet above their heads, revealed the approval on his face. "Help me remove the lid."

Jaques took one end and Garcia the other. They lifted it off and leaned it against the wall of the cave.

"What is this?" Garcia asked. He pulled out two objects. One was the bag of sealant, the other the doll. "A poupée?" Delighted to see the doll, Andreva took both items from him. "This belonged to my maire. I had forgotten I put it in there." She smoothed the brocade dress, and after a quick examination, tucked the doll into her belt. "And this pouch is mortar with which to seal the stone."

"We shall use it." Garcia ventured farther into the cave.

Suddenly, bats fluttered around them, their flapping wings startling Andreva. She covered her head and whimpered as the bats found their way deeper into the darkness.

"You do not like bats? Neither do I." Garcia let out a breath of relief. "But you must see this." He climbed a few steps and disappeared into the cave.

Andreva looked up at Jaques. Should they follow?

Garcia's voice echoed as if from a tunnel. "It is too dark to see well without a torch, but for years, the Good Men and

Women have brought their valuables here for safe keeping—their jewels and precious documents." He reappeared, carrying a wooden box. "They have vowed to live their lives in poverty, but sell the jewels from time to time for their minimal support, and to help the needy." He opened the box, revealing necklaces, bracelets, and several gold coins.

Amazed, Andreva touched an elegant white bracelet.

"Pearls. There is much more hidden in this cave. But I want you to see the best of all." He took the box with him and went back into the darkness. This time he brought with him a smaller box. From it, he ceremoniously removed a cup that appeared to be hewn from grayish stone. His eyes shone as he awaited Andreva's reaction.

Jaques grabbed it. "Why would anyone consider this a treasure?"

"It is far from ordinary." Garcia took it back, reverently. "It is said Our Lord drank from this cup at the Last Supper." Garcia held it out for Andreva to take.

It was cool and smooth to the touch. "A holy goblet?" In awe, she turned it over in her hands. "The Lord pressed His lips to its rim? How do you know this is the very one?"

"I do not. I am only told." Garcia took it back. "A Knight Templar entrusted it to one of the Good Men for safekeeping, saying he had taken it from Jerusalem." He held it to his chest. "And now it shall be joined by the scroll bearing the blessing of Jacob which my grandfather gave me to guard."

Andreva could not take her eyes off the cup. "But how—"

"The story goes that the man who provided the upper room for the Lord and His disciples on that evening of the Passover also provided his own cups for their use. This man waited upon their needs, and saw the Lord hold this vessel to His own lips and then pass it to His disciples. After that night, the man preserved the cup, as did his children after him, and so on, passing the relic and its story from generation to generation.

"When the knight visited in the home and shared a bottle with the descendant of this host, the man bragged about his ownership of the goblet. He held it for the knight to see, but did not allow him to touch it. After the braggart passed out from too much drink, the knight stole it, and brought it to the Languedoc."

Andreva frowned at Garcia. "That story sounds familiar. If it were not for the vice of drink—"

"Well, I—" Garcia fumbled for words. At last his embarrassed laugh echoed through the chambers. "You are correct."

Jaques looked at the goblet in awe. "We cannot leave so great a relic here in this miserable cave. It is something the whole world would revere."

"The whole world would fight over it." Garcia examined the natural flecks of the stone.

Andreva took it. "Please, let me keep the chalice." She held it close. "Think of the power it holds. Instead of burying it, we should give it to the Church."

"Rome is the last place the Good Men will see this treasure go." Garcia quickly reclaimed the artifact as if to protect it. "Objects do not hold power. To think they do is superstitious and detracts from God's true glory. It borders on idolatry." He slipped the goblet back into its box.

Andreva reached out her hand. "Of course it holds power. If the Lord Himself..."

Garcia went to the stone box and placed the goblet inside. "The cup belongs here with the scroll. In the Lord's due time, and if He chooses, it will be discovered." Garcia turned to Andreva. "If the goblet has purpose, let Deity decide what it is."

From his satchel, Garcia pulled out a crimson bag. "This is the document my grandfather gave me, and its translation." The papyrus crackled as he gently pulled a scroll from the bag. "See how fragile it is?" He unrolled it slightly for them to see the strange writing.

Andreva reverently ran her finger along the fragile paper. "This sacred scroll, the goblet, magnificent jewels— such extraordinary things gathered together in this small cavern."

"Yes, and there is more." Garcia went back into the darkness and returned with a wooden box that held loose papers. He added them to the stone box. "The Good Men want these documents preserved—genealogies, histories, the Gospels translation, and the Cathar doctrine." He placed his scroll back into its bag and nestled it on top of the others, then looked up at Andreva. "And now for the mortar."

She extended the pouch. "The stonecutter said to mix it with a few drops of water."

With his fingers, Garcia dug an indentation into the ground. He emptied the contents of the pouch into the hole and poured in a bit of water from the skin bag he carried, mixing with his finger. He scooped out the wet mortar and spread it amply around the rim of the box. Jaques helped him set the lid in place and Andreva examined the rim to make sure every inch had sealed.

Garcia smoothed the excess mortar from around the edges, then stood and rubbed his hands together to rid them of the residue. "Help me move the box deeper into the cave." He and Jaques carried it up the steps, then pushed it near the other treasures. Garcia brushed his palms together with finality and headed toward the entrance. "Now we are to close up the cave as best we can so it will not be found."

Outside, Andreva shaded her eyes from the bright sunlight. Jaques wasted no time finding the shovel and using it to move more dirt into the cave's opening. Garcia and Andreva added rocks, doing the best they could to completely conceal the cave's entrance.

Garcia moved the bush back into place, burying its roots in the soil. "It is done." He wiped his brow, breathed deeply, and turned to the vast valley that lay before them. "I am finished!" he shouted as if the mountains had ears to hear. He stretched his arms toward the sunlight. "I am free! For the first time in twelve years, I have no burden on my shoulder, no satchel to hide, and I run from no man." He shouted to the sky. "God, into Thy hands I give my burden to do with what Thou wilt!" He laughed in elation.

Jaques looked at Andreva and cocked a brow. "Perhaps he is touched in his head?"

"Óc!" Garcia shouted. "Perhaps it is woodness! I am touched. I am crazy!" He climbed a boulder and stretched his arms out again. Andreva's stomach tottered, fearing he would fall to his death. "I feel I could fly!" Garcia hollered to the world, and jumped.

She rushed to the ledge in panic, but when she peered over, there he stood only a few feet below, doing a joyful dance. Only when he was finally out of breath did he calm and allow Jaques to offer him a hand to climb up to the trail again.

"You gave us a scare." Jaques laughed nervously.

Andreva smiled too, but she could waste no more time. She felt a great urgency to find Bostel. "We share your joy, but Garcia, will you take me to my uncle now? Jaques must soon return home. There is no time to spare."

"Of course!" Garcia grabbed the shovel and sprinted down the path in the direction they had come.

Jaques raised his eyebrows at the Catalan's burst of energy, and glanced at Andreva, but followed.

A minute later Garcia called from up the path. "This is where our climb begins. Follow me."

Andreva arrived in time to see him pull a coil of rope from behind an outcropping, the other end of which was secured somewhere above their heads. He tugged on it to test its trustworthiness. "Here? We must climb?" She stared up in disbelief at cliffs that appeared too steep to scale.

Garcia began his climb.

Jaques studied the position of the sun. "I must get back to my livestock. My cows will start to bellow any moment."

"But Jaques...what about my uncle? I hoped to take him back with us in the cart."

"I am sorry, Andreva. I have duties. You would not want to be an engorged cow and—" He stopped and reddened. He took her hand and kissed it.

"Go find your uncle. I will leave the cart and take only the horse. On the morrow I shall return for you. Meet me at the cart before midmorning."

"Must I go alone?" Her shoulders slumped. "I wish your livestock did not take you from me."

He pulled her closer. "Remember, I love you. If I could, for you, I would stay."

She read the concern in his dark blue eyes. "All right. We will be waiting." Andreva held to him, reluctant to let him leave.

Jaques cupped her cheek in his hand. His tender touch sent tantalizing currents through her. "Garcia will watch after you. But promise me you will not stay the night inside the castle. Take your uncle to the empty house along the road. The fortress is not safe with the truce ending on the morrow."

"I promise." She lifted her face to his, longing for his kiss. "I wish you would stay." His lips met hers, soft, sweet, and honest. She wrapped her arms around him, returning the kiss willingly.

He released her and slipped away. Andreva opened her eyes and reached to pull him back—to kiss him again, to hold him forever—but caught only a glimpse of him sprinting down the path.

The sweetness of being in Jaques' arms passed moments after he disappeared into the brush. Andreva felt vulnerable upon his departure and wanted to go with him. Yet, the bag she carried reminded her why she had come to the pog. She raised her eyes to the limestone cliffs and rededicated herself to finding her uncle.

Garcia coached Andreva in how to use the rope to help drag herself up the first steep rock face. The trail then led behind large boulders where rough stairs chiseled into the stone made the climb more endurable. Still, the path seemed to lead straight up. She could hardly breathe from the exertion.

At the top, Garcia leaned over, hands on knees, and tried to catch his breath. He gave her an apologetic smile. "You are young and spry. I am twice your age."

"No." She panted. "This climb would be hard for anyone except mountain goats, I suppose, which we are not."

He chuckled, breathed deeply, and rested. Then, squinting toward a rock at least fifteen feet high, he headed up the trail toward it. "Look for the carved-out foot holes." He found another rope tucked discretely into a crevice. "Would you care to go first this time? I will do my chivalrous duty and catch you if you fall."

She frowned. How was she to climb ahead of him and preserve her modesty? "No, no. You go first," she told him.

"I will follow."

Garcia took hold of the rope and yanked it. "I hope it is secure."

"You hope?"

He laughed and used the rope and toe holds to climb several feet up the rock before looking back over his shoulder. "Coming?"

Andreva reached for the hem of her skirt at the back, pulled the fabric between her legs, and tucked it into the belt. Determined to keep up with Garcia, she took each step carefully. The soles of her shoes slipped from the first hole, so she pulled them and her stockings off and slipped them into the sling created by her skirt. Proceeding barefoot was easier; she balanced, holding to the rope and the rock, while managing to keep the bag's strap over her shoulder. She found the next foothold, and the next.

From atop the rock, Garcia took her under the arms, dragged her up, and steadied her on her feet. After a moment's rest, Andreva released her skirt, put on her stockings and shoes, and examined the rope burns on her palms. Making a fist, she willed them to heal.

Garcia led the way up a narrow trail that ran along the edge of a cliff. Andreva glanced down at the frightening drop, and dreaded their descent with Bostel later that day. How would they get an injured man down these cliffs? She put that worry out of her mind to concentrate on putting one foot in front of the other. There was no room here for a misstep.

The path led steadily upward until finally the enormity of the fortress walls stood before her.

"Oh, my!" she exclaimed. The stone wall seemed to rise all the way to the sky.

"The entrance is this way." Garcia motioned to the east.

Andreva followed him along the wall, around brush and over rocks. When they reached the corner of the fortress, more destruction came into view. A hearth stood without walls. One partition stood alone. Rock balls from the trebuchet were strewn among toppled bricks. Weaving among the debris, they came to a large oak tree with a thick trunk that grew very near the fortress wall.

"Here we are." Garcia stopped at the tree.

Andreva leaned against the trunk to rest in the shade and gasped at the spectacular view stretching out before her. *This is what an eagle sees as it soars!* Nestled in the valley to the northeast was Lavelanet with its winding river. To the south, the military camp perched motionless on the mountain's slope.

"Come. Let us hurry, or the soldiers may see us." Garcia motioned for her to follow.

He said this was the entrance? She looked around and saw no door. Garcia led her around the large trunk to a hidden stairway which led down into a dark, narrow tunnel.

Garcia cupped his hands around his mouth. "May you come to a good end!" he called into the tunnel.

Where had she heard the words before? Ah, yes! Bostel had said them to Mémé in parting. Was it some sort of Cathar watchword?

A face appeared from the darkness. "Hail, Garcia!" A tall, blond man came up the stairs and clasped wrists with him.

"Sicart!" Garcia indicated Andreva. "This is my friend from the village of Lavelanet. She has done us a great service. Our valuables are safely contained and concealed."

"Outstanding. Thank you, Andreva."

Looking into Sicart's sincere, green eyes, Andreva immediately felt she could trust him.

"Follow me." The man motioned for her and Garcia to follow. About twenty paces ahead were more stairs and, above them, sunlight.

"Please." She reached out to stop their guide before he led them up the stairs. "I have come to find my uncle, Bostel de Lumbert. Is he here?"

"He is. May we send him word that you have come?"

"Yes, please."

The man turned to Garcia. "Go ask her uncle if wants to see her. He is upstairs in the quarters."

Garcia agreed and ran up the stairs, his dark curls

bouncing against his shoulders.

The guard motioned for her to follow him out onto the square courtyard.

Even though she had heard that large numbers of Good Men and Women lived here, she hadn't expected to see so many people crowded together. A blacksmith hammered metal; women scrubbed laundry in washtubs; men and women sat together weaving baskets as children played a game of tag, all within the same limited space. Andreva watched in wonder that they prepared for the morrow as if it would be a day like any other.

She saw Garcia stop to talk briefly with an older, auburn-haired man in a dark-blue robe. The fellow looked over at Andreva. Garcia continued across the courtyard and disappeared through a door. Although few others took notice of Andreva, the older man left his small group to walk toward her.

"Welcome to the mountain of the Lord, Andreva." The man smiled. He stood much taller than she. "I am Bertrand. I understand you have come to visit Bostel."

"I have. I am his niece. I pray he is well enough to see me."

By the way he carried himself, and how the others looked to him, Andreva surmised that he was one of their leaders. He wore no cross and his countenance was totally different from Father Stefe's, more like the kind-hearted Father Tomàs. This man's face seemed to glow from within and his smile shone through his brown eyes.

"He fares well enough, but is badly wounded. Monsen de Lumbert is of fine character, one of the best of men." Bertrand had a comfortable, soothing voice.

"He is." Andreva fingered her cross.

"Andreva, are you not...one of us?"

She assumed he meant one of the Good Men. "I am not. I lived at the abbey of St. Sernin for ten months, but came by summons from my uncle to Lavelanet to care for my grandmother in his absence." She glanced around the courtyard. And then he had abandoned her to come to this crowded fortress.

"I also know and admire Margaurite de Lumbert."

He knew her grandmother? But didn't it make sense that if Bostel was one of the Good Men, he'd have perhaps introduced Bertrand to Mémé?

The older man seemed indifferent to Andreva's religious allegiance. "You are obviously an intelligent young woman, and any relative of Monsen Bostel is a friend of ours. Our beliefs are based on Christian love, unlike the Church's bloodthirsty papacy." Despite his surprising choice of words, Bertrand's voice held no animosity.

Andreva looked away from his gaze and scanned the guards standing atop the walls. "In Lavelanet, we wait anxiously to know if you will denounce, or die."

He placed her hand over his arm as they walked toward the doorway Garcia had entered. "We will not give in to pressure to denounce our faith. God will save us. Stay with us, Andreva, and learn our ways."

"God has not saved other Good Men before you—those living at Béziers, Minerve, Carcassonne... Why do you think He will save you?"

"There is more than one way to be saved." He turned to her with a serene smile. "If a miracle does not save us from the fire tomorrow, then it is God's will that we burn together."

Holding to this man's arm felt as comforting as if she were a child being led by a loving, protective father. She enjoyed the feel of his warm hand over hers as they walked around women and washtubs, and dodged children tossing a ball. Each person they passed made way and smiled, obviously in awe and respect for her escort.

A group of young women sat talking and embroidering. To Andreva's surprise, Ermessen was among them. She looked up briefly but her eyes showed no recognition when she saw Andreva. The girl looked as beautiful and radiant as she had at the festival.

When Bertrand and Andreva reached the doorway, Garcia bounded out, nearly knocking them down. "Oh, Bishop! Excuse me!" He turned to Andreva and his eyes gleamed. "Monsen de Lumbert is anxious to see you."

Bishop? She glanced at Bertrand. All the bishops she knew of lived in luxury and strutted around ceremoniously. She suspected they never consorted with common people, as this man was with her.

"Please take our honored guest to him." The bishop held out Andreva's hand for Garcia to take. "Make sure she is made comfortable and given refreshment."

Garcia took the offered hand to lead Andreva away.

She turned back. "Bishop! Thank you for your kindness."

He saluted. "I will see you again."

They climbed a narrow, circular stairway, and at the top, passed through rooms filled with people who were sick or wounded. They came to a smaller room that had a blazing fire in its center, the smoke escaping through an opening above. Two men sat on mats on the floor. Each had a bandaged leg.

Andreva choked back her welling emotions. "Uncle Bostel!" His wounded leg stretched out before him. His once neatly-trimmed goatee had grown into a full beard. She rushed to his side and threw her arms around his neck.

"Andreva!" Bostel returned her hug. "I have worried myself sick about you."

She kissed his jaw and noticed the gash on his forehead. Andreva examined it. "How were you wounded?"

He pointed to his wrapped leg. "A trebuchet ball and I collided. The guards gave plenty of warning, but for some reason, I still met it head-on." He pointed to his temple. "It knocked me down and damaged my leg. Double luck!"

"Bad luck." She retrieved a pillow that had slipped from behind his back and readjusted it so he could sit more comfortably propped against the wall.

"It is only the body, not my spirit, that suffers. My spirit is only the better for it." Bostel again adjusted the drifting pillow. "We are all divine sparks—angels who are imprisoned in a tunic of flesh."

"I have never considered life an imprisonment." Andreva looked up at Bostel. He was her uncle, but suddenly she realized there was a part of him she didn't know.

Garcia stepped closer. "That is what they teach here."

Bostel took both Andreva's hands in his own. "Tell me, how is Maire? Who is with her now?"

"Elodie tends to her." She glanced at Garcia, not wishing him to hear what she would say. "Thank you, Garcia, for bringing me to my uncle."

He looked surprised at the dismissal, but bowed and exited to the stairway.

She glanced at the other man in the room. He slept. Grateful for their privacy, Andreva found confidence to speak. "Mémé is not as well as when you saw her last. She sleeps most of the day and can hardly walk. I am thankful she still stands to move to the commode, for it is her only exercise." She lowered her voice and her lip quivered. "But Uncle, I have bad news."

He frowned. "About Maire?"

Not wanting to cry, she took a deep breath. "Several nights ago—"

A woman walked into the room, carrying a tray with two cups. She set it before Bostel and turned to leave. The woman looked familiar and Andreva stared a moment then jumped to her feet.

"Dianne de Fortaner!"

29

 ecognition dawned in Dianne's eyes. She glanced between Andreva and Bostel. "Andreva! I am surprised to see you here at Montsegùr."

"As I am you." Andreva's knees felt weak. "Monsen Fortaner told everyone you had gone to Narbonne to visit your daughter."

Dianne raised her hand to her necklace and fingered it nervously. "Well, yes. My husband wants me to say that is where I go so no one will suspect his wife is…a heretic."

"But have you not heard?" Andreva's hand flew over her mouth and the two women stared at one another for several moments.

Dianne's eyes filled with fear.

Bostel asked, "Heard what, Andreva? We do not keep secrets here."

She slowly lowered her hand. "Monsen is dead." It came out as a croak. Tears welled in her eyes as she recalled the horrible incident.

A smile of disbelief played on Dianne's mouth. "Dead?"

Bile rose to Andreva's throat and she swallowed with difficulty.

When Andreva could not speak, Dianne looked to Bostel. "How did it happen?"

He held up his hands. "This is the first I've heard."

Dianne fixed her stare on Andreva. "Pray, tell."

"He was...found stabbed...a fortnight ago." Would she burn in hell for holding back the story? She could not bring herself to tell his wife about his final moments. "Friar Tomàs had him buried in the churchyard."

Dianne never blinked. Tears filled her eyes. "I...I must go home. Immediately." She grasped her stomach and bent over, falling to her knees.

After a moment of helplessness, Andreva moved quietly to the woman and touched her shoulder. "Dòna."

Dianne jerked away, stood, and ran from the room. Her footsteps echoed in the stairwell.

Andreva forced her eyes to meet Bostel's, despite the guilt that swept over her.

"Where did he die? Does anyone know who stabbed him?"

She fell to her knees beside her uncle and buried her face in his chest, unable to control her grief.

Bostel soothed her by stroking her back. "What is it Andreva? Tell me."

Andreva lifted her head. "That man...Fortaner...came to the house and tried to... He tried to force himself on me. He tried to carry me up the stairs. He was determined, Uncle. Believe me!"

"Of course I believe you." He grasped her hand. "I thought I could leave you to his care." Bostel groaned. "Forgive me. I had no doubt I could trust him."

His words gave her courage to tell more. "He claimed to be one of the Good Men, and said that Cathars believe a little 'recreation' does no harm." She could not meet his eyes. "Is it true that your religion justifies a man forcing himself on a woman?"

"Of course not." He frowned. "Fortaner was not one of us. Father Bertrand could accept his skepticism, but not his tendency to stir up dissension. He finally asked him to leave the fortress. We are peaceful people who believe in brotherly love, never in abusing one another. Now go on, tell me the rest."

His reply was balm to her hurting heart. "Fortaner would not accept that I wanted nothing to do with him. I could not fight him off. Mémé heard the scuffle. Somehow, she gathered the strength to climb out of bed. She took the meat knife from our supper tray and threw it...right through his heart." Andreva grimaced and lowered her face.

Bostel stroked her hair as he whistled his awe. "The dear woman still has it in her." He lifted Andreva's chin. "And then what happened?"

Andreva swallowed, forcing herself to relate the rest of what she wanted only to forget. "Mémé confessed that evening to Father Tomàs. His man took away the body, and the next day they announced they had found Fortaner dead on the road." She looked again into Bostel's eyes. "That holy man keeps our secret."

"Father Tomàs is a good man." Bostel put his arm around her and pulled her closer. "A man who would act as Fortaner did does not deserve a good Christian wife like Dianne. Nor did he deserve to live. Carry no guilt for his death."

Still nestled against Bostel, Andreva wiped her tears. "Uncle, I've come to take you home. We need you." Another sob caught in her throat. "Mémé is dying."

After a long pause, Bostel loosened his hold on her. "I cannot return with you to Lavelanet. I said my goodbyes and must stay with the others. I have taken the oath—the consolamentum."

She looked up into his face. "What is this consola—?"

"It is the laying on of hands, the ultimate vow of the Good Men, a last reconciliation with God. It is our baptism, not by water, but by a total immersion of the Spirit. It is the cleansing of all sin."

"But why would this conso—, whatever it is, keep you from returning to your family?"

"It is the path to heaven. Tomorrow, if God does not save us from the fire, then I shall die and be saved in heaven with the best of men and women."

Looking into his eyes, Andreva saw the fervor with which he believed his words. Andreva left his arms to sit back. "But Mémé and I need you. Please come home. What good is it to give your life for naught when you are worth so much alive? Do you truly believe this...heresy?"

Sorrow clouded Bostel's eyes. "Catharism offers pure religion as Christ taught it. Perhaps we do not have all truth, but I cannot adhere to Catholicism. Although I will agree there are many good and honest clergy, the Church's greed for power and money has disfigured its pursuit of Christianity and poisoned its counsel and creeds. I believe the Good Men have the true line of authority from Christ himself. We practice goodwill to all men, just as He did." He set his jaw in thought, as if drawing his words from his inner soul. "I am ready to face whatever tomorrow brings."

Bostel moved his bandaged leg. "Not that I will be able to walk to the pyre. But the brethren have assured me they will carry me if need be." He took her hand. "Go home and care for Mémé. Her time is short. I pray that someday you, my beloved Andreva, will come to see that the Church has moved far from that which our Lord intended. I hope that you too will have strength to seek a better way."

The blood drained from her face. "I could never leave the Church, Uncle."

"Then stay true to your conscience. But whenever you think of me, remember: it is more important to choose eternal salvation than it is to choose merely to live."

His words confused her even more.

"It is time you learned the truth," Bostel continued. "Your maire, Sanche, was a *credente*—a believer of the Good Men's doctrine—who accepted Catholicism when she married your father. That is the only reason you do not now live in this fortress with us."

"Maire? I do not believe you." She pressed her hands to her burning cheeks as her eyes smarted with angry tears.

"Óc. She met a young soldier and was married in the Church. Maire was heartbroken. Sanche went to Toulouse and lived true to Catholicism after that."

Andreva's mind raced to put the pieces together. Her hope sank. "You could not mean Mémé...that she is..."

"Óc. She is highly respected as a teacher among us." He put his hands out to Andreva.

She ignored him, placing her own hands on her sickening stomach. She understood why her parents had kept such a shocking secret, but...

Andreva wanted to leave, to run away, perhaps to crawl back inside the cave and stay forever. Overwhelmed, her whole body drained of strength and she succumbed to her uncle's arms. She lay against his chest, trembling.

Bostel held her close. "I'm sorry I did not tell you about your heritage properly, Andreva. It should not have come out as it has at such a time as this. But, my dear, it is what it is."

After several moments, Andreva wiped her eyes and managed to stand. "Goodbye, Uncle," she whispered. "May God save you from a dreadful death." She made the sign of the cross and turned to leave, but then remembered the supplies in the bag.

She pulled out the fritters and extended them. "I am not yet an accomplished baker, but I made these."

"I am passing my last days in a fast."

Realizing he would not reconsider, she slipped the food back into the pouch. "Perhaps you can use these then. Mémé sent them." She pulled out the linen strips and herbs.

He took them and set the bundle on the floor. "Mercés."

It was impossible to return his loving smile. She turned toward the door, but did not look back. "Farewell. I will continue to pray for you."

"Please, Andreva. Do not leave angry."

Her head pounded from all she had learned. Before sobs betrayed her, she left the room, hurried down the stairs, and out to the courtyard.

"Andreva!" Garcia waved from across the yard. Raoul sat beside him, resting his bandaged head against a post. A sling supported his arm.

Andreva ran to him. "Raoul! I am so glad to see you are alive!" She dropped beside the young man to give him a hug.

Raoul touched his head. "Careful!"

Garcia chuckled. "Your friend met with a falling wall in the last attack. His head still throbs with pain."

Raoul squinted at her. "But I am happy to see you, Andreva."

"Oh, Raoul! Colet and Elodie will rejoice to have you

home. I promised them you would return with me."

He looked down. "Well, I... Did you find your uncle?"

Unsure why Raoul had ignored her comment, Andreva took his arm. "I did find him, and now we must go. Come, we must get down the mountain before darkness falls."

He looked away. "The bishop has told us to muster our courage and stay where we are. He promises that God will save us through our faithfulness."

Andreva was appalled. "You are not Cathar. Neither of you." She looked from Garcia to Raoul. What had happened to them? Had Raoul lost his senses in the accident? "How can you say such a thing? You cannot desert your family when your mother needs you. The children need you, too." She pulled his arm again but he didn't budge. "You cannot stay another night. The scroll is buried. The treaty ends on the morrow, so we must leave this place right now."

Both men avoided meeting her eyes. Rising frustration caused her head to throb. "I refuse to believe—"

"Come!" The bishop stood atop a boulder, his right hand raised to beckon all to move forward. Other priests in blue robes had joined him. "Gather around. We have many more who wish to take the consolamentum today.

trenta
30

en, women, and children paused whatever they were doing and gathered around the bishop. Raoul and Garcia leaned forward to listen to the man as well.

"Let us leave!" Andreva nudged Garcia. "There is no time to waste. We must get down the mountain before the sun sets." She took Raoul's good arm to help him up, but he gazed around her at the man in the blue robe. Andreva could not help but look over her shoulder.

Bertrand raised his hand to still the chatter. "The morrow marks the end of the treaty. By gathering here, we have fulfilled the prophecy that 'the house of the Lord shall be established in the top of the mountains'. You are from all walks of life, and have come here seeking safety and truth. I commend you for your courage.

"Only a few have chosen to denounce our faith before the Inquisitors and escape the death the morrow may bring. In the past, so-called repentants have been forced to wear the yellow cross of shame. Perhaps our friends will bear this disgrace the rest of their lives." He lowered his head. Silence fell over the crowd.

Andreva remembered the resentful repentant in the tavern at Montgiscard. He had chosen to wear a label of public humiliation to save his family and escape death by fire.

When Bertrand raised his face, his smile held sadness. "Blessed are you who have chosen to remain true to the faith. At sunrise, we shall leave the château and walk down the mountain to a place that those who have declared war on our religion have made ready for our deaths. We may all die, if God sees fit, but we should not be afraid. Death is not the end, but simply a passageway into another life."

There was a murmur from the congregation. He waited for them to silence. "Let us speak of spiritual things once more."

Andreva tugged on Raoul's arm. "Come with me." Again, he didn't budge. Andreva had promised Colet she'd bring him home, so he had to come. Then the bishop's words caught her attention and she turned back to listen.

"We do not believe in infant baptism, nor baptism at all. The true ordinance to which we cleave is the one spoken of in the New Testament—the laying on of hands. It is the consolamentum."

There was that odd word again. Despite herself, she was curious. Would they perform this rite in the courtyard? She looked around for a chapel, or any place that looked as if it had been set apart for sacred purposes, but saw none.

The bishop continued. "We reject the doctrine of transubstantiation, for it is superstition."

What? Andreva shook her head in disbelief.

A voice from the congregation asked, "Then what happens when a person dies who is not a Perfecti—or has not taken the consolamentum?" A hush came over the group. All eyes turned to Bertrand.

He raised his hand. "When a person who has not accepted the consolamentum dies, powers in the air swarm around and persecute his newly-released soul, and that soul then flees into the first lodging of clay it finds. This 'lodging' might be human or animal. His soul is thereby condemned to the cycle of rebirth, trapped in another physical body—" He interrupted himself to wait for the group to quiet. "Please! Listen so you will know truth. Unless in this new body he takes the consolamentum and becomes a Perfecti, the cycle repeats itself."

Andreva found it hard to breathe as an approving murmur passed through the group. She understood why this man was so compelling and had seemingly converted so many people. His explanation made salvation easy—as effortless as taking a vow immediately before death. Though she still appreciated the bishop's warm welcome and how good she had felt about him at first, anxiety now filled the pit of her stomach.

The bishop pulled a young woman up to stand at his side on the rock. When she faced the group, Andreva saw it was Ermessen, glowing with happiness.

Bertrand held Ermessen's hand above her head in victory. "When a Perfecti dies, her soul wins freedom from this world and returns to heaven, the immaterial realm of the Good God." He released her hand. "For members of the Elect, experiencing death is no more difficult than removing a dirty tunic." His hand swept through the air from Ermessen's shoulder to her feet, indicating the garment she wore.

"So that you understand the consolamentum, we will explain what will happen." Bertrand helped Ermessen step down as other men and women came to stand in front of the rock. They faced the crowd with an air of authority.

Bertrand continued. "It is simple for the honest in heart to become adopted sons and daughters of God. You who take the oath today shall kneel together before me and these other Perfecti." He motioned toward those with him. "We will recite The Lord's Prayer together, and then I will explain its meaning line by line. The next part is the Renunciation. Each of you will solemnly renounce the harlot church, their baptism and magical rites."

Andreva drew in a sharp breath at this heretical description of the Church.

"Next will come the spiritual baptism itself. The Parfaits," he waved his hand over those standing in front of him, "will lay their hands upon your head, and touch the Gospel of John to your brow." One of the women standing with Bertrand raised a book into the air.

Women performing rituals? It was a strange concept.

"Once that is done," Bertrand said, "you will commit to live the creed of a Parfait: pardon wrongdoers, love your enemies, pray for your accusers, turn the other cheek, and never judge nor condemn. You will answer, 'I have this will and determination. Pray God for me that He gives me His strength.'"

This last part, at least, sounded honorable to Andreva. *Should not we all strive for these virtues?*

"At that time, you will individually confess previous sins, after which we shall again place the Gospel and our hands upon your heads, and you will hear the words, 'Holy Father, welcome Thy servant in Thy justice and send upon him Thy grace and Thy Holy Spirit.' "We will again recite The Lord's Prayer and read from the beginning of the Book of John. We will end the ceremony with the holy kiss to welcome you into this elect rank."

He waited patiently for the group to settle again. "The consolamentum is usually given to credentes in the last days of their lives." Bertrand raised a hand again. "But, in light of what we may face tomorrow, I invite all who have not already received it—young and old—to take the consolamentum and save your souls, that we may all come to a good end and meet God in Heaven!"

The excitement level heightened as people clapped their hands and hugged each other. Many shouted, "Yes!"

Come to a good end! There they were again—the words Bostel had said to Mémé in parting. The meaning finally made sense. *A good end means being saved from a continual cycle of rebirth!* Andreva glanced around in astonishment.

Bertrand raised his hand to quiet the gathering once more. "But first, as you all know, Garcia has successfully buried the last of our valuables. God will protect these treasures until He brings them forth in His time and purpose."

An approving hum vibrated through the group.

"With our treasures, Garcia has buried a sacred scroll. The prophecy written thereon gives much hope for the future. It promises a better world to come. Garcia! Come forth and speak to us."

A hush came over the assembly as the eyes of young and

old turned toward the Catalan. Garcia stepped forward. Andreva listened with the others, anxious to see the reaction of the group when he revealed the true nature of God.

Garcia spoke loudly. "The scroll foretold of a widespread apostasy after the death of the Messiah, but also promised that in a later day God would establish all truth once again. The Messiah shall come a second time, not as a babe as He did in Bethlehem, but to reign in glory upon the earth. And in that day, man will gain freedom from his oppressors."

"The Inquisition is our oppressor!" a woman shouted from the crowd. "We will be saved!"

Bertrand waved his hand toward the Catalan. "Mercés, Garcia. We find hope in your message."

Garcia returned to Andreva. She tugged his tunic. "You did not tell them about God's body and passions."

He turned to her, eyes shining. His voice was low. "It would only cause an uproar. They will die on the morrow and will perhaps discover Him for themselves." Andreva looked over the group. Were any of these people capable of logical thought? Did they realize what "die on the morrow" meant?

Bertrand had paused a moment, but had a few final words. "Sadly, we may not overcome the oppressors of today, but our bravery in the morn may give others strength to stand against tyranny in generations to come. God will save us in heaven for our courage." He drew himself to his full height and shouted, "Who is ready to take the vows?"

Andreva was startled by the many hands that flew up around her. She looked to where Ermessen stood with her palm in the air. Andreva turned nervously to Raoul. His eyes were alert, but at least he had not raised his hand.

"We shall have a glorious ceremony this day." Bertrand gestured toward the east. "And at sunrise tomorrow, we will bravely leave Montsegùr, knowing we walk into God's hands. Let us pray for His intervention in our behalf. But remember, there is no need to fear. Even if we die in flames, we are saved!"

A man's voice rose from the group. "We will hold strong in our stand against the Inquisition, that those who live after us may look to our example!"

The throng raised one more cheer. Hope glowed in the faces around her, including Garcia's. Raoul's eyes shone as he tried to stand, but failed.

Andreva dropped to her knees beside him. "Raoul, no! Come home with me. How can you give your life so senselessly and leave your family destitute?" She glared toward Bertrand, who was bending to clasp the hands that reached up to him. "Please, Raoul. Do not allow this emotion to sweep you away. If you stay here, you will die!"

His smile faded and the glow in his eyes dimmed as he focused on her. "But he promises—"

"Do not let one charismatic man choose life or death for you." She took hold of his good arm. "I will help you down the mountain, and in the morning Jaques will come to take us home." She tried to help him stand, but Raoul's gaze had returned to the man preaching from the rock. "We must leave immediately. Montsegùr is not the place for us." She knew it in her heart.

The glow had returned to his eyes as he watched Bertrand.

"Garcia! Help me get Raoul to his feet."

Garcia turned. "Of course. I promised Jaques I would protect you." He picked up his satchel and water bag, and bent to lift his friend. "Andreva is right, Raoul. You should return home. Let me help you walk."

Raoul's compliance surprised her. He picked up the satchel at his feet and allowed Garcia to walk him toward the tunnel. On the way, he looked longingly over his shoulder at Bertrand who had begun to quote the Lord's Prayer.

Garcia held to Raoul's arm. "We will leave the way we came."

His willingness to go with them restored Andreva's courage. With Garcia's help and protection, she and Raoul had a better chance to make it down the mountain. When Jaques arrived in the morning, the four of them would ride away to safety.

As they began to descend the stairs into the tunnel, Raoul looked regretfully back toward the assembly and lost his balance.

Andreva steadied him. "Will you be all right?"

He lowered his head and nodded.

"Monsen Garcia!" Andreva turned toward the voice to see a woman standing in the shadows with a small child.

"May we leave with you?" The woman stepped forward and Andreva recognized Dianne de Fortaner. "I must return home to notify my daughter of my husband's death." Dianne smoothed the child's curly hair and awaited Garcia's reply.

"Come," he said. "We will manage together."

"Jaques Montré will come for us in the morning." Andreva motioned for them to follow. "There is room for all in his cart." There would have to be.

"Mercés!" Dianne lifted a bundle in one hand and took the little girl's hand in the other. "Come, Bruna." To Andreva she said, "Bruna is an orphan. I cannot leave her here to perish alone."

"I hope you are a good climber," Garcia said to the girl. Bruna confirmed that she was with a bounce of her curls.

The five slipped noiselessly through the tunnel. Outside, Andreva gazed down the cliffs and across the valley below. She remembered the climb, and despaired of getting Raoul and the child safely off the mountain. If only they could soar like eagles over the great expanse to Lavelanet.

Garcia rubbed his forehead. "We will never get Raoul down these rocks in his condition."

"There is an easier trail," Dianne said, "but we must pass the soldiers' camp."

"That I do not like." Garcia regarded his friend. "But it seems our best choice." Garcia took Raoul's arm and turned southward.

The path Dianne knew was much easier than scaling rocks. Andreva's spirits lifted until they came into view of the soldiers' camp, and her uneasiness returned. Garcia hesitated, surveying the mountain below for any route that could get them past the soldiers undetected.

"Wait a moment." Andreva pulled the veil and wimple from her satchel. "If we encounter guards, this might help."

Bruna's eyes widened at seeing Andreva transform into a nun. Andreva smiled to reassure her.

Dianne dug into her bag and drew out a handful of crosses. She pulled a wooden one free and hung it around Raoul's neck. "These were abandoned by some who joined the Good Men." She slipped a pewter cross over her own head. "I collected them, hoping my husband and I could sell them in Toulouse." She handed a leather thong holding an onyx cross to Garcia. "They might convince whoever stops us to let us pass." She found one for Bruna and knotted the cord to shorten its length.

Andreva fingered the cross she always wore. Then she took a deep breath and straightened her veil.

"Let us proceed." Garcia led, supporting Raoul as they descended the rugged path toward the soldiers' camp below.

Although they all tried to walk quietly, twigs snapped and gravel crunched beneath their shoes. The trail seemed to lead straight down, with only a few areas level enough to allow a normal gait. Andreva's calves ached with every step.

"Halt!" A soldier emerged from the shadows.

Andreva flinched as Garcia released his hold on Raoul and jerked his knife from its sheath.

ut your weapon away, man." The soldier held out his sword when Garcia didn't move. "Unless you want to battle."

Andreva huddled with Raoul and the others behind Garcia. The large man approached, his mail armor rattling. Bruna wrapped her arms around Andreva's leg and hid her face in her skirt.

Garcia straightened and returned the knife to its holder, but kept his hand on it, his stance defiant. "We want to pass. We are leaving the mountain."

The soldier's lip curled into a sneer. "You cannot leave without first denouncing your heretical religion before the authorities." His glare moved from Garcia to the rest of the group. When he saw Andreva he let out a gasp and froze. *"Fifille!"*

She looked closer at the man. "Vezias? Vezias of my father's regiment?" Her heart leaped with joy, and she pulled away from her friends and ran to him, a little girl once again, embracing a friend of her past. "What are you doing here?" She stood back and looked him over as her words tumbled out. "I thought this was a holy war."

"All wars are holy." He sheathed his sword. "Pope Innocent has mandated that King Louis exterminate the Cathars, so the king sent an ultimatum to Count Raymond to send his troops also or lose his position."

Andreva looked toward the tents below. "My father's men are here?" She stepped forward, thinking to go to them. Garcia grabbed hold of her arm.

"They are." Vezias glanced toward the fortress. "Fifille, you are one of the Good Men now? But you wear the garb of a nun."

"I am not of the Good Men. I have lived at St. Sernin since my parents' death." Andreva looked over the tents perched on the side of the hill, longing to catch a glimpse of the soldiers she knew. "Oh, Vezias, how I have missed the regiment."

"Then come." He extended a hand. "They will rejoice to see you again."

She turned to Garcia. Seeing his frown, she moved back to stand with the others. "I regret I have no time for such pleasure. My friends and I must reach the bottom of the trail before sunset." Bruna whimpered, and Andreva slipped her arm around the girl. "None of us are Good Men. I came to persuade my uncle to denounce and return home, but he refused. Now my friends and I depart. Please let us pass. We are of no consequence to the Crusade."

Vezias glanced at the crosses they wore. "Ah." He crouched before Bruna, who immediately hid her face in Andreva's skirt. "Do you want to go home?"

Bruna barely peeked at him and bobbed her head.

He stood and glanced over his shoulder. "You must go quickly, then. I will escort you as far as I can, lest anyone else detain and question you."

Vezias led the way down the trail. Carved steps in the rock made their descent easier. Garcia looped Raoul's arm around his shoulders, and took each step with caution.

They bypassed the tents. When Andreva had supposed they were a safe distance beyond the encampment, a man's voice shouted from behind. "Stop!"

She turned to see a robed man—an Inquisitor—come down the path after them. Something about his sharp cheekbones and stern demeanor sent chills down her spine.

"Who do we have here?" The priest's tone was demeaning. "Good Men who have come to their senses?" His hard eyes passed over each traveler. "And a *nun*?"

"They are not heretics, Father Petrus." Vezias ran nervous fingers over his black beard. "But visitors leaving the fortress. I have given them permission to pass."

"Oh? You know I must speak with all who leave." He squinted. "You place yourself above my authority?"

Vezias swallowed. "This is Soeur Andreva. Her father was René de Béringer, the man who before his death led my regiment in Toulouse. I know firsthand that she is devout, lately from the abbey, and of a solid Catholic upbringing. The others are her friends."

Andreva fingered the convent cross around her neck. "I am a sister at St. Sernin, Your Reverence. We came to persuade my uncle to return to his senses, but he is injured and wishes to remain in the château."

Father Petrus walked closer and looked down at Raoul. "And who are you?" Andreva's breath became shallow, waiting for his answer. *Please say the right thing so the priest will let us pass.*

"Raoul. I...live in Lavelanet." The young man could hardly hold up his head.

An eyebrow twitched on the priest's somber face. "Are not all Lavelanetiens Good Men sympathizers?" He took hold of the wooden cross on Raoul's chest and examined it. Letting it fall back, the judge folded his arms. "Are *you*?"

"I—I—"

Andreva was unable to stay silent. "He is Catholic also, and is but fifteen. A wall fell inside the château and he was badly injured. I am taking him to his maire for her to nurse back to health."

The eyebrow arched again before the Inquisitor's piercing eyes fell to Dianne. "And you?" His gaze moved to her pewter cross.

Please do not incriminate yourself! Andreva's fingernails dug into her palms.

The color drained from Dianne's face and her voice was only a whisper. "Dianne, Your Reverence." She gave a short curtsy.

Andreva added, "She is a dear friend who accompanied

me that I might not travel alone with these men."

The stern man turned to her and roared, "Are your friends incapable of speaking for themselves?"

Andreva stepped backward and curtsied. "Please, Your Reverence, I beg your forgiveness. We do not belong here and wish only to get down the mountain before sunset." *And I am trying to save these poor souls from tomorrow's death sentence.*

"And the quiet one?" Father Petrus stepped closer to Garcia and fingered the silk samit of his cloak. He pulled back the Catalan's hair to examine the scar that ran alongside his ear.

Garcia stared forward.

The man huffed. "I know who you are, Garcia of Catalan! You are the grandson of that thief and runaway, Henri of Champagne. You thought you could sneak by me?" With eyes flashing vengeance, he waved Vezias forward. "Seize this man! He harbors a long-sought, valuable relic."

Andreva froze as Vezias stepped forward and grabbed Garcia's arm. Garcia swung at Vezias, but the soldier knocked him to the ground, sending his water bag and satchel tumbling.

Andreva dropped to her knees at his side. "Are you all right?" She could not lose Garcia. She needed him desperately to get her and the others down the mountain.

"Get up!" Vezias demanded.

Garcia wiped his lip with the back of his hand and examined the blood. He grabbed his satchel and managed to pull himself to his feet. Andreva stood. Vezias forced Garcia's hands behind him.

Andreva could barely suppress a cry as she watched the conquered Catalan.

Father Petrus stepped closer and glared at Garcia. "Now will you give up the relic?"

Sweat ran down Garcia's temples, blood oozed from his lip, and the veins in his neck protruded. "I have nothing to give!"

The priest raised his arm as if to strike.

"No!" Andreva reached out to block him.

Father Petrus paused, his hand in the air, and frowned at Andreva. Instead of shrinking back, courage filled her and she raised her chin and returned his stare.

A sneer crossed the Inquisitor's face as he lowered his fist. "If your friend remains stubborn, he will die with the others in the morning."

"He is not one of the Good Men."

"He is a fugitive."

"I will never give you anything." Garcia spat.

The priest rolled his eyes with impatience. "Put him with the other prisoners."

Vezias gave Andreva an apologetic glance before he pulled Garcia's arm to lead him away.

But Garcia stood firm. When his eyes met Andreva's, he inclined his head toward the water bag still on the ground. "You will need it. Be brave."

Andreva looked at the bag. To get safely down the mountain, they'd need more than water. Her courage faded and her knees shook. Two women, a child, and a wounded man—their plight was precarious indeed.

Vezias led Garcia away into the foliage. "Garcia!" She lunged after him. Father Petrus caught her by the arm and his fingers dug deep. Terror mixed with pain and she surrendered.

The priest released his grip and stared down at Andreva. "I do not recall seeing you come up this path. I would have remembered a...nun."

She weighed her answer. "We—we did not know of this path, Your Reverence. We came up the other side of the mountain." She rubbed at the stinging in her arm.

"The other side?" He raised an eyebrow. "When?"

"Today, Your Reverence."

"With rats and mountain goats? Ha!" Father Petrus fluffed his beard and scrutinized the group before turning back to Andreva. "If you were not a nun, I would arrest you and your friends for further questioning, but what use would that be?" He gloated, "The end of the Good Men and their heretical religion is only a few hours from now." He waved his hand with disgust. "Be gone with you!" He whirled and walked away.

Dianne, who now supported Raoul, stared at Andreva in silence. Bruna ran forward to cling to Andreva's skirt and peer up at her with questioning eyes.

Andreva looked out over the valley. They had to keep moving—even without Garcia—if they were to meet Jaques in the morning. He would take them to safety. She forced a smile and smoothed the girl's hair. "Let us hurry. We have little time before dark."

Dianne took the lead as they started again down the trail, helping Raoul with every step.

Andreva glanced back over her shoulder. What more could she have done to help Garcia? No more. To have protested further would only have risked the lives of Dianne, Raoul, and the girl. At least they had been released. The Inquisitor could have detained them for little or no cause. That he had freed them was a miracle.

They took the narrow path cautiously, weaving through the thick growth. Descending one steep section, Raoul let his satchel fall to the ground and sunk to the dirt after it. "My head throbs!" He dropped his face between his hands, and moaned.

"Please, Raoul." Andreva knelt beside him. "We need to reach the road before sunset. Then you may rest. It is only a little farther."

He lifted his face and groaned again, his eyes despondent.

Andreva looked toward the disappearing sun, and then down the hillside. Her own endurance was growing fragile.

"Come, Raoul." Dianne aided him to his feet. "My dear! You are burning with fever!"

Andreva pressed her hand to his forehead. "This is not good." She opened Garcia's water bag. "Raoul, you must drink."

Andreva held the bag to Raoul's lips as he drank. Water ran down his chin and neck. He swallowed, closed his eyes and smiled. "Mercés."

With Raoul propped up between them, Dianne and Andreva started down the trail again, managing to keep him on his feet, with Bruna in the lead. They came to a clearing. What Andreva saw there alarmed her. Bundles of split wood had been placed in rings around several tall posts in the clearing's center. Nearby lay ropes, coiled and ready. It was a now-silent stage of torture, readied for the victims—and the torch. The sight triggered vivid memories.

No! Andreva fought off the visions of contorted faces, screams, and memory of the stench that had haunted her since that dreadful day of burning in open display on the streets of Toulouse.

Tomorrow the Good Men in the fortress would follow those unfortunate people's fate. She turned away from the scene, grateful Raoul was spared the sight since he could no longer hold up his head. Bruna, in her innocence, paid no attention to what she saw, but Dianne's eyes filled with tears.

"Let us hurry." Andreva averted her eyes and hastened her pace.

The four found the road as the sun slipped below the horizon. Andreva hoped the house she had seen earlier was still vacant. With the breeze picking up, they would need the shelter through the night.

"We are almost there," she assured Raoul. When he lifted his head, she saw that his complexion was sallow, and his skin damp with sweat.

The house came into view. Mercifully it appeared deserted. Just beyond it was Jaques' cart.

"Halt! Where are you going?" A soldier appeared as if from nowhere. His outstretched sword barred them from walking any farther. Then he saw Andreva, gasped, and made the sign of the cross. "Ma Soeur!"

Andreva indicated the house. "We hope this hovel is vacant so that we may stay the night within. We will leave in the morning. Please, sir. We have permission from the priest. We are not Cathar. We had only visited the château in hopes of bringing our loved ones home."

He glanced over his shoulder. "That house is filled with evil spirits, waiting to escort the heretics' souls to hell. I hear them wailing in the night."

A shudder went through Andreva. They must have shelter; Raoul needed a quiet place to rest. But a house possessed with evil spirits? Wailing? She listened, but heard only the wind.

"We will stay in the house." Dianne held up her hand to indicate Raoul and Bruna. "Surely the spirits will respect a nun and these innocents."

What courage the woman has! Sleeping with spirits was not Andreva's idea of a good night's rest, but it was the only available shelter.

The soldier stared wide-eyed at Dianne. "I shall set guards to watch through the night. No one may leave the area without my authorization. Promise you will speak to me again before you leave in the morning."

Dianne lowered her head. "We promise."

"Be on your way." He slid his sword into its sheath and stepped aside.

Andreva thanked the man, and the small party moved together toward the house. Wary of spirits, Andreva examined the shelter. Its shutters flapped in the wind and the open door hung crooked, but there was nothing otherwise unnatural about it.

They stopped cautiously in the doorway. Andreva peered into the dismal room that had a dirt floor, and was lit only by the twilight that filtered through the shutters and a few gaps among the eaves. It had one bare cot, a crude broom, and a fire pit, but no spirits. A mouse scampered across a rafter and escaped through an opening in the shingles.

Andreva took a deep breath and made the sign of the cross, praying the spirits would not manifest themselves. "Saint Benedict, please protect us through this night."

Dianne peered past her into the room. "I guess it is better than nothing at all."

They helped Raoul to the cot. Andreva brushed away the debris before they settled him upon it. He moaned gratefully and closed his eyes. Dianne set to work brushing away cobwebs. Andreva went out to gather wood for a fire, thankful for the lingering twilight.

After a fire was lit and the shutters closed, Dianne

attended to Raoul's wounds, cleaning them with water from the bag and Raoul's scarf.

Andreva opened her satchel to bring out bread for their meal and found the doll. She couldn't help but smile, and hold it close. Bruna's small, frightened face looked up from where she huddled near the fire, arms pulled inward for warmth. Andreva's compassion for the orphan swelled. She smoothed the doll's hair, straightened the dress, and knelt beside Bruna. "This belonged to my maire when she was little." She held it up for Bruna to see.

"Poupée!" Bruna's wide eyes lit with delight, but she did not reach for the doll.

Andreva feigned surprise and turned the doll to face her. "What did you say?" she asked the doll. She held it to her ear. "You want to be Bruna's friend?" She pretended to consider the possibility.

Bruna giggled and brushed aside the sandy curls framing her face.

Andreva spoke to the doll again. "I think that is a splendid idea. Dolls are for little girls, and Bruna needs a friend tonight." Andreva held the doll out to her.

The girl took it and gazed at it in wonder for several moments, examining its every detail.

After they had all bedded down, Andreva heard male voices outside. Had the guards been placed to keep them safe, or to make sure they did not leave? She glanced toward the closed door that had no latch. Either way, the presence of the guards gave her some peace.

How many of the Good Men and Women were finding peace enough to sleep on this moonless night? Were they on their knees praying for "a good end" as Bertrand had called it, or were their petitions perhaps for a miraculous delivery?

Her mother had believed in this strange religion before her marriage. Mémé had been a teacher among them. Of course, Bostel also believed. Why had they all kept their belief from her? She thought she had known her family, but they were, in many ways, strangers to her.

Despite all these thoughts churning in her head, Andreva's

exhausted body won out and she finally drifted off to sleep to the hooting of an owl and a symphony of night sounds underscored by the wind.

"Ohhhh!"

Andreva awakened with a jolt and listened. Were evil spirits restlessly awaiting the souls of the condemned Good Men? She heard the moan again. She shot up and looked around. The fire had died to embers.

"Ohhhh!" The sound came from Raoul, tossing on the cot.

Andreva went to him and pulled his cloak up around his shoulders. She touched his brow. It still burned with fever. "Raoul, I am here," she assured him.

He groaned again.

She found the kerchief, dampened it, and laid it across his forehead. "May that bring you some relief." She gave him a sip of water.

He calmed, and in moments, fell silent again.

Andreva added more wood to the fire before she lay back on her bed. Only the thin blanket she had brought separated her, Bruna, and Dianne from the dirt floor. Dianne's blanket covered her and Bruna, who still clung to the doll. Andreva pulled her wrap around her shoulders and tucked her feet underneath it, out of the cold.

It was not the wailing of spirits that kept her from falling back to sleep. She listened to the wind whistling through the eaves, a distant howl, and the scampering of mice. Andreva shrank further beneath her cloak in search of warmth.

Tomorrow. Fear for the Good Men gave way to thoughts of Jaques coming in the morning to take them home. She warmed at the memory of being held in his arms.

Morning could not come soon enough.

trenta • e • dos

Andreva awoke to the pounding of hundreds of footsteps and the accompanying clanking of metal armor. She went to the door. The guards were gone, but soldiers were everywhere. The expressions on their faces as they passed suggested that the Good Men's divine intervention—or else their doom—was close at hand.

Dianne had also awakened. She sat up and listened, dread on her face. "Today the treaty ends. If God does not save the Good Men, they will all burn together."

Andreva quailed at the thought of Bostel, Garcia, Ermessen, and the others in the château.

Bruna still slept. Her curls peeked from beneath the blanket. Raoul breathed unevenly.

Andreva crossed the room and knelt beside him. "Raoul, how do you fare?" He groaned and his eyelids fluttered. She placed a hand on his cheek. "You still burn with fever."

Dianne came to her side and unwrapped the bandage from his head. "We must wash his wound."

Andreva picked up the water bag. "It is empty."

"Go find a well. Hurry!" Dianne started to untie the knot in his sling.

Andreva jumped up and put on her headpiece before she went outside.

"Good morning, Ma Soeur!" a passing soldier called. Andreva heard excitement in his voice. At first, she was nonplussed. Did he not grasp the gravity of this morning? As she stood staring at the eagerness on the soldiers' faces, understanding washed over her. Few of these men were bloodthirsty. To most, this day marked the end—the last day of siege, of months away from their homes and families. To the Inquisitors, it marked the end of heresy and this part of the Church's duty. And to the Cathars, coming to their "good end"? Surely, she mused, "the end" held very different meanings this day.

The well stood across the road, and she went to it. The bucket made a splash when she dropped it into the darkness, and in a moment, she drew it up full. She filled the water bag and took it back to the house.

Thankful for Dianne's willingness to attend to Raoul, Andreva went back out, hoping to find yarrow to make a salve for his wounds, and early spring berries for their breakfast. As she entered the foliage at the side of the road, she heard singing coming from above. She stepped back onto the road and looked up toward the fortress. Though hard to see from a distance, it looked as though a line of people had begun to stretch down the mountainside from the château, singing as they made their way through the brush.

At the base of the mountain, a single trail of smoke rose above the trees, weaving a thin, gray pattern in the sky that looked to Andreva like beckoning fingers. She pressed her hand against her pounding chest.

"No!" she cried. "Not now, not yet!"

Dianne appeared in the doorway. "Why are you shouting? You will awaken Bruna."

Andreva pointed toward the top of the pog. "The Good Men are leaving the fortress. Have they all chosen to die?"

Dianne took a few steps into the road and turned to peer upward. The color left her face. She sank to her knees and clasped her hands beneath her chin. "Oh, God! Have mercy to save them! It is not too late! Please save them!"

The Good Men's hymn drifted down on the breeze. It was a melancholy chant to the Father for strength and deliverance. Rhythmic, resolute—the song had been a favorite of Andreva's since childhood:

Holy Father, save our souls...

Andreva recalled the clearing stacked with woodpiles and stakes she had seen yesterday, and imagined it now filling with the men, women, and children she had spent time with only hours before. She fought the urge to run up the mountain to find her uncle.

Dianne continued to pray between sobs. "Take them to heaven...their salvation make sure...Thou just God of the good spirits!"

Andreva looked upward again. A chevalier now stood at the entrance to the fortress, waving a flag. Was this the signal that all had departed?

Dianne stood. Her eyes swam with tears. "I should join them. Why should they die, and not I?" She started toward the mountain.

"No, don't go!" Andreva caught her arm. "Choose to live. Help me get Raoul back home." Dianne broke from her and ran up the path. "Dòna Dianne!" Andreva followed her up the hill. "Come back!" She couldn't allow her run to her death. "Dòna!"

A throng of soldiers covered the hillside. All were alert, awaiting the call of duty. Ahead, a small fire sent portents of death into the sky.

Several soldiers turned as Dianne approached. "Halt!" A soldier held out his sword to block her way.

"Let me pass!" She attempted to go around him. "Let me pass!" When another soldier moved to block her, Dianne sank to her knees and covered her face. Her shoulders heaved with her sobs.

Andreva caught up. "Please!" She looked up into the faces of the soldiers. "This woman is distraught over losing her friends. I will take her home now."

The soldiers parted as the priest who had detained them the night before approached. Father Petrus' gaze fell upon

Dianne's wrist. He lifted an eyebrow.

Andreva also looked down. A leather band bearing the Occitan cross—the symbol of the County of Toulouse, and therefore the only cross accepted by the Good Men—graced Dianne's delicate wrist.

"We shall leave." Andreva grasped Dianne's wrist, covering the symbol. She took hold of the woman's other arm to help her stand, but Dianne remained dead weight. "Please. We must return to Bruna and Raoul."

The priest held out his hand. "Ma Soeur." He smiled pleasantly. "Bring your friend. Come and watch."

"No." Repulsion rushed through her. "We must go home."

Father Petrus continued to extend his hand. "I want you to come." His smile disappeared. "I insist." He pushed Andreva aside and took Dianne by the arm, yanking her to her feet and dragging her into the mass of soldiers.

Fear surged through Andreva like lightning. What would the priest do? She stumbled over the hem of her skirt while trying to follow. Would he throw Dianne into the fire with the other Good Men? "Your Reverence!" She lifted her skirt and recovered her balance as she ran to catch up. "We leave behind a child and an injured man that we must..."

The priest marched far ahead now. She glanced back toward the house. Perhaps Bruna and Raoul would sleep. She could not desert Dianne in her present state of mind. Andreva wove her way through the horde of soldiers. Several made the sign of the cross as she hurried past and greeted her with, "Ma Soeur."

Andreva was short of breath by the time she caught up to Father Petrus. She followed as he dragged Dianne a few more yards up the mountain to higher ground that overlooked the gathering Good Men. Here, two more priests stood, wearing the black and white robes of the Inquisition. Father Petrus' smile tightened. "I want you to have a good view of your friends, all two hundred and more of them." He freed Dianne.

Andreva caught her, helping her to stay upright as the priest joined his comrades. Dianne rubbed the bruise on her arm from the Inquisitor's tight grip.

Below them, people crowded together, still singing the hymn and praising God. Children clung to their mothers, and mothers clutched their babies. Bishop Bertrand stood in the midst of his followers and sang out with his shoulders squared.

Then Andreva saw Garcia standing on higher ground, the prisoner of two soldiers. His face was bruised and swollen, and his wrists were tied behind him. Garcia raised his somber face and their eyes met.

Her body went weak. Just as so many who had tried to stand up to the Church, Garcia would be tormented into confessing where the scroll was hidden, or tortured to death.

Andreva looked again upon the Good Men, and recognized others she had seen inside the fortress the day before. Ermessen stood with eyes closed, clinging to another young woman. But Andreva could not find her uncle. Had his injuries kept him from being moved from the fortress? Her hopes soared. She scanned the line of people still descending the mountain. Soldiers stood along the path, commanding the Good Men to keep moving toward the clearing filled with wood and palisades.

Yet Bostel was nowhere to be seen. She imagined him still in his room, unable to stand and descend to his death. She would not go to him immediately, but when this horrible ordeal was over and she had Raoul home to his mother, she would return to find him.

Then the final stragglers came through the thicket and her breathing stopped. Two men carried another between them. The clearly injured man had his arms draped around the shoulders of the others. She watched closely, but could not see his face.

Finally, the man looked up. Andreva recognized his dark hair and large jaw. Uncle Bostel! Tears stung as she watched them carefully maneuver the rocky path. She held tighter to Dianne to keep herself from running to him.

The men carried Bostel into the circle and helped him to stand on his good leg. He looked out and saw Andreva. A smile spread across his face. He placed his hand over his heart, and raised it to her.

Andreva brought her trembling fingers to her lips and returned the acknowledgment, but could not hold back her tears.

When all the Good Men and their families were in the ring, the soldiers moved in. They shoved fagots of wood closer around them, creating an inescapable circle.

Father Petrus held up his hand for silence. "Pierre-Roger de Mirepoix! Bertrand Marty!" he called out. "This is your last opportunity to abjure."

Can the Good Men renounce even now? She looked to Bostel.

"We will not disown our faith!" The words came from a tall, husky man at the center of the huddle. "Do your murderous deed. God will receive our souls in heaven."

"Very well, Mirepoix. We will grant your wish, but I cannot promise you heaven." The Inquisitor chuckled and pointed a finger toward the bishop. "And you, Bertrand. Have you a last wish?"

Andreva held her breath, hoping he would call upon heaven for divine aid.

Bertrand straightened. "You may destroy our physical bodies, but not our souls. We are ready to meet our Maker."

Father Petrus laughed and gave a wave of his hand. Soldiers pulled glowing torches from the fire. In moments the woodpiles were ablaze.

Many of the doomed Good Men resumed singing, but others screamed in fear and pain. Distorted faces turned toward heaven, still pleading with God. The scorching heat overtook the spot where Andreva stood, and she pulled Dianne back. The smell of burning flesh was revolting. Even the soldiers moved as far back from the horror as they dared.

When Father Petrus turned his face to avoid the smoke, he saw Dianne and Andreva. "I almost forgot you ladies." He walked over to them and Andreva panicked when he took each by an arm. "Would you like to join your friends now? You lovers of heretics."

Andreva took in her breath, inhaling smoke, and choked on it. She coughed repeatedly as he yanked them toward the fire. He scowled and thrust Andreva to the ground.

The Inquisitor still held tight to Dianne as he pushed her forward. She screamed. He pulled her back and hissed in her ear. "Watching your friends die today will teach you to be loyal to the Church." He let go and she sank to her knees and sobbed.

When the priest returned to the other clergy, Andreva hurried to Dianne's side. "Come. We must leave!" She pulled Dianne up, hoping the men were absorbed with the carnage and would not notice them. In moments, they had slipped into the brush. A few yards down the mountain, Dianne burst into hysterics.

Andreva took her by the arm and shook her gently. "Quiet. The soldiers will hear."

Dianne's sobs soon softened to whimpers. They climbed over rocks and made their way through the brush to skirt the pyre and the press of soldiers.

Once off the mountain, they ran up the road toward the house. There were still no guards in sight. Before they reached the door, Dianne stumbled to her knees.

"Get up, Dòna." Andreva looked toward the cart. "Jaques will arrive soon."

Dianne refused to stand. She dropped her face in her hands, and wept.

Andreva went into the house and found Bruna still asleep in the blanket. She knelt beside Raoul and smoothed his damp hair away from his bandages. His brow still felt feverish. "Raoul...the burning of the Good Men..." Her lip quivered. "Your friends are no more!"

Raoul's eyelids fluttered and he gave her the weakest of smiles as he struggled to form his words. "History repeats itself ...Good people on a mountain...once again surrendering...to Rome."

Andreva understood. "You speak of Masada."

He closed his eyes. "Pray...for them," he mumbled. "Ask God...to save their souls."

Andreva buried her face in his cloak and sobbed. "I am thankful you came with me and that you are yet alive." He had to live! His family needed him and she would be heartbroken to lose her friend.

The distant sound of a horse galloping up the road sent Andreva to the door. "Jaques!" She ran to meet him as he jumped to the ground.

"You came!" Andreva fell into his embrace. "The Good Men are burning! Uncle Bostel..."

He kissed her forehead. "Thank Heaven you are safe. I feared I had lost you, my little nun." Jaques examined the sky, darkened by smoke. "Those unfortunate souls."

"Raoul is badly injured." She pulled him toward the house, passing Dianne who still knelt, crying. "Poor woman. Her friends are dead, her husband—"

"You have told her?"

"Only that he is dead." The smoke had reached them, causing her to cough. "We must be on our way while the soldiers' attention is diverted by events up on the mountain."

She went into the house. Jaques peered through the doorway, and then turned toward his horse and cart. "Give me time to hitch up the horse and we will leave." He took hold of the reins and led the animal away.

With desperation gnawing at her, Andreva awakened Bruna. The girl sat up, still clutching the doll. Bewilderment filled her eyes. "Bruna, come." Andreva helped her to stand. "We are leaving." She straightened the girl's dress and handed her a piece of the bread from her satchel. She gathered her own blanket and shook out Dianne's.

Jaques came into the house and knelt at Raoul's side. "Raoul." He touched the young man's shoulder and waited for him to open his eyes. "I shall take you now to Lavelanet. Can you endure the ride?"

Raoul nodded. With care, Jaques draped Raoul's arm around his shoulder, and scooped him into his arms as if he were a child. He carried him outside, with Bruna and Andreva following, and laid him in the cart's bed. Raoul moaned as he relaxed onto the wooden planks.

Grateful for Jaques' strength and touched by his tenderness, Andreva returned to the house and gathered the blankets and satchels. She glanced around the interior of the house and her heart swelled with gratitude. "Mercés." *A roof, a fire, a cot for a very sick man—all tender mercies.* She made the sign of the cross before joining Jaques at the cart.

"Is Dòna de Fortaner coming with us?" Jaques tested the connections of the harness.

"Óc, and Bruna, too."

The little girl stood close to Jaques, looking up at him with frightened eyes. He lifted her into the back of the cart next to Raoul. "Raoul is very sick. Will you watch over him?"

Bruna held up the doll. "And the poupée, too?"

Jaques smoothed her curls. "Yes, and the poupée."

Andreva smiled at the warm interaction between the two. Not often had she met a man who was gentle with children.

Dianne still knelt, praying, beside the house. Andreva hesitated before she touched her shoulder. "Dòna, it is time to leave." Dianne dropped her hands and blinked wet, swollen eyes. Andreva helped her stand. "We must go before the soldiers return. Hurry. I have your things. Raoul and Bruna are already in the cart."

Dianne rose slowly. She dried her face on her sleeve and followed Andreva.

Andreva rolled the blanket into a pillow as best she could, and placed it under Raoul's head. She lay his cloak over him and bundled him into it. "Try to rest."

He offered a feeble smile.

Once they were all in the cart—Jaques, Andreva, and Dianne on the seat, and Bruna and Raoul in the back—they started up the road. Jaques glanced toward the smoke-heavy sky. "Pray God will welcome them."

Andreva looked up, shocked. Did he also believe, as she had come to, that God's love and mercy might extend beyond the tenets of the Catholic Church, to encompass all the good in heart, believers and unbelievers alike? Could it be that one who did not profess to follow the pope might still be saved? Perhaps the Good Men would not go to hell for denying the pope and the Church. Her uncle had been an honest man, had studied the teachings of Christ, and lived as close as possible to his beliefs. Surely God did not force men as good as he to hell.

Andreva wanted to ask Jaques what he meant, but

hesitated with Dianne sitting next to them. She held to Jaques' arm and they rode in silence except for Dianne's sniffles and Raoul's groans.

"Halt!" A soldier stood in the middle of the road with his palm held high. "Stop in the name of King Louis and Pope Innocent!"

Andreva tensed. Jaques slapped the reins. "Get on!" he called, and the animal obeyed.

The soldier's eyes widened. He jumped out of the way only seconds before he would have been trampled. A string of obscenities followed them down the road.

Andreva's pulse raced. She tightened her grip on Jaques, and Dianne held to Andreva as he set the horse galloping. At a comfortable distance, Jaques slowed the cart.

When they came to the place where the thieves had attacked the day before, Jaques prodded the horse to move a little faster. Gooseflesh prickled on Andreva's neck and she shuddered, remembering how she had watched the corpse roll toward the creek. She looked back and forth at both slopes of the narrow road, ready to warn Jaques at every curve.

Dianne had calmed and Raoul now slept. Bruna sat with her hand gently on his shoulder—a child's instinct for tenderness amidst tragedy.

Once they were well down the valley, Andreva felt Jaques' bicep relax. "Did you have a chance to talk with your uncle?" he asked.

"I did. I begged him to come home with me, but he was convinced he would gain immortality and heaven, and was thus determined to stay." She remembered her uncle on the pyre and his gesture of farewell. Pain seized her heart. "Now he is...dead. They are all dead...but Garcia, and he is a prisoner of the Inquisition."

At her words, Dianne wailed. "I should have stayed! I should have died with them. I do not deserve to live!"

Andreva put an arm around her. "No. It is better that you live." She sensed her words gave little comfort to the woman. "Live for your daughter, and for Bruna. She will need someone to care for her."

Dianne gave a slight nod, and a smile touched her lips as she gazed at the little girl.

Andreva glanced back the way they had come. The midmorning sunlight illuminated the clouds of smoke spreading across the southwestern horizon.

They rode through Lavelanet's gates before noon. Raoul moaned restlessly and Andreva turned to look on him and Bruna. The girl had never cried nor complained the entire ride, but merely sat thoughtfully at his side.

The Fortaners' manor was the first house on the way. An open carriage blocked the front steps. Dianne stared at the buggy. "I wonder who is here."

Jaques climbed down from the cart to help her to the ground, and then lifted Bruna from out of the back. "Shall I accompany you inside?"

"No." Dianne gathered her meager belongings, and surveyed the upstairs windows. "We will be fine—I hope. I shall send for Father Tomàs if I need help." She looked toward the door.

Andreva stepped down and gave Dianne a hug. "Shall I send Elodie to you? She is attending to my grandmother in my absence."

Dianne smiled, though sadly. "If she desires to return, I could use her help."

"Mercés." Elodie would appreciate the employment, now that Dianne's house was safe.

Jaques waited until Dianne and Bruna were behind closed doors before heading the cart up the road toward Colet's dwelling.

"You are almost home," Andreva assured Raoul.

When Mémé's house came into view, Andreva sat up straighter, paralyzed by dread. Two men in black robes stood before the door.

trenta · e · tres
33

"Inquisitors!" Jaques directed the horse around another cart parked on the road. Several women sat in its bed. Andreva recognized the widow Gisèla at once. Confused, she searched the other terrified faces and found Jocelyne, Felipa, and Ponrada.

"What is happening?" The hair rose on the back of her neck. Why had these destitute women been gathered up like eggs in a basket? Her feet hit the ground before Jaques stopped the horse. She ran to the widows. "Why are you here?"

"The priests would tell you we are heretics, unfit to live." Felipa could barely hold up her head. "They want Margaurite, too!"

A jolt of foreboding went through Andreva. She spun to see a tall Dominican priest pound on their door. "Stop!" She ran toward him. "Mon père. I live here. What do you need?"

Father Stefe turned toward her with a scowl on his face. "We have come for Margaurite de Lumbert."

Andreva looked helplessly at the other man's grave face. "But she is not well. She is dying. Whatever do you need with her?"

His eyes held no concern. "No need to sweeten the bitter for you, my child. She is a heretic, and we will deal with her accordingly."

Andreva seethed. "Mémé is no heretic. Her heart is more

Christian than yours!" Thankful that Jaques had come to stand beside her, she leaned into him for support. She stared at the closed door, willing Elodie to keep the bolt in place.

The second priest pulled a parchment from his robe. "Margaurite de Lumbert is on this list of villagers who took the heretics' *consolamentum* on 26 September 1243."

"No! That is a lie!"

The priest's eyes moved toward the cart. "It is true, and her cohorts have yet to abjure."

Jaques took the paper and unfolded it. Together, he and Andreva looked down the list. *Ponrada, Gisèla, Jocelyne, Felipa—*

The list went on. Andreva's eyes stopped on *Margaurite de Lumbert.* She could not breathe. Her hands curled into fists.

Father Stefe stroked his beard. "It is fortunate Gerrard de Fortaner gave us this list before he died."

Fortaner? "The man was a liar!" Andreva's nails dug into her palms. She was ready to fight for her grandmother if she had to.

The official reached for the list, but Andreva swiped it away from him, crushing it in her hand. "All lies! Let these women go!"

Jaques' arm tightened around her. "Andreva—"

Father Stefe grabbed her wrist, squeezing it until the pain made her wince. She released the paper to him. "Now, open the door."

She pulled away from Jaques and stepped between the priests and the door. "You horrid people killed my uncle this morning at Montsegùr, but you will not take my grandmother from me as well."

"Young lady, you will burn for contempt." He grabbed her wrist to pull her toward the cart.

Jaques took hold of the priest's arm. "Please, Father, let her go."

Father Stefe glanced over his shoulder at Jaques and loosened his grip.

Andreva pulled from his hold. Though her head felt as if it would burst with fury, she spoke each word with deliberate calm. "I am a sister at the convent in Toulouse—" She heard the door's bolt slide, and in terror whirled toward it.

Jaques shouted, "No, Elodie! Lock the door!" He leaped to the step, but not before the shorter of the priests had forced his way inside the house. Father Stefe seized Andreva's arm again, compelling her to follow.

Elodie stood trembling, her eyes puffy. "I am sorry, Andreva. I do not want them to burn you."

"Elodie—" Andreva glanced toward the bedchamber as Father Stefe opened the door. "Leave her be!" Andreva pushed past the priest to her grandmother's side. Mémé lay lifeless in the bed.

Elodie whimpered. "She took a bad turn after you left, and has not awakened since."

"Mémé! Wake up! You promised to live until my return." The woman moaned. "She still lives! Thank the saints, she still lives!" Andreva gathered the frail body into her arms, but then Father Stefe grasped her shoulders and pulled her from her grandmother, forcing her against the wall.

"We have no time for sentiment." He turned to the bed, threw back the covers, and with one swoop lifted Mémé into his arms.

Andreva's heart jumped to her throat and she gagged on her protest. "But—"

"She will receive the heretic's reward." Father Stefe carried the unconscious woman, her limbs dangling, out of the house and into the sunlight. Mémé's jaw slackened when her head rolled back on a neck that could no longer support it.

Andreva shot a desperate glance toward Jaques. He hurried forward to block the priest's path and extended his arms. "Give her to me, Your Reverence! Please, allow an old woman to die in peace."

Father Stefe held tight and glared. "Peace? A heretic who has set herself against God and the Church deserves no peace. Now get out of my way or join these women at the pyre."

The threat stunned Andreva. She couldn't lose Mémé and Jaques. She had lost her parents and her beloved uncle. She had little real hope to save her grandmother—or to return her to health if she could save her. If she also lost the man she loved, she'd be left alone. She laid her hand on his arm. "Jaques, no."

He stepped aside, but continued to glare at Father Stefe. The priest shoved Mémé into the crowded cart with the others. He and his companion climbed up next to the driver, and the cart rolled away.

Andreva, Jaques, and Elodie stood together, watching Mémé's head bob uncontrollably against the rail with each bump and sway of the cart. Guilt swept through Andreva. Should she run after them? Her feet would not move. She felt instead as if she would crumple to the ground in exhaustion and despair.

"I must do something." She whimpered.

"We will not give up." Jaques took her hand and pulled her toward the cart. She followed numbly. "We shall follow and try again to persuade the priests to release your grandmother and the others." Jaques turned her to face him. "But care must be taken, Andreva. If we fight the Inquisitors too staunchly, they will view us as their enemy. Come, we must first take Raoul to his mother."

Andreva had briefly forgotten Raoul amidst the crisis. Weak and defeated, she must somehow find the strength to think, to keep going, to take him home, and make one more effort to save Mémé.

With Jaques' help, Andreva pulled herself onto the seat.

Elodie gazed into the cart's bed and cried out at the sight of her wounded brother.

"Run and prepare his bed, Elodie. We will take him there now."

Elodie entered the house before Jaques and Andreva could drive the short distance.

Jaques carried Raoul in while Andreva followed. "A wall at Montsegùr fell on him." She watched Colet begin immediately to unwrap the bandages from around Raoul's wounds. A wave of panic swept over her. "The Inquisitors have taken Mémé away. Jaques and I must hurry to find her and see what can be done." Tears rolled down her cheeks as she explained about the consolamentum list.

"Thank you for bringing Raoul home." Colet put aside the soiled bandages and gave Andreva a hug. "May God and the saints help you to save your grandmother."

Minutes later, Jaques and Andreva arrived at the church. The women still sat in the cart, weeping and clinging to one another. Seeing that Mémé's head still hung over the side, Andreva hurried to her and gently lifted it, hoping to give her comfort.

A priest emerged from the shadows. "Remove yourself!"

Andreva recognized him as one of Father Stefe's council. "Please, mon père, let me take these poor women to my home and care for them. They are harmless. Let them live."

"They will receive a fair trial. If we find they are heretical scum, however, they are not fit for life, and will receive their just reward. Now move away."

Andreva fell to her knees. "Please, let me take my grandmother home to die in her own bed. I beg of you."

A mocking smile crossed the man's bearded face. "You may beg, but she stays."

Andreva turned toward the echoing sound of an ax on wood. The too-familiar sight caused her to gag. Two men bundled wood in the field behind the churchyard. What little strength she had drained from her. She dropped her face into her hands and surrendered to tears.

Arms slipped around her shoulders, and she looked up. Jaques had dropped to his knees beside her. "How can I desert Mémé, Jaques? We must save her and these women. I will not leave." She meant it. No one could force her to leave before she had done all she could to save the widows.

"I am here. I will not leave you."

She looked into his determined eyes. "Thank you, Jaques." Embracing him, she put her cheek against his chest, grateful to know she did not face this trial alone, and drew courage from his strength.

Father Tomàs came from the church and went directly to them. "Let us speak, Sister Andreva."

Jaques stood and helped Andreva to rise. She looked at the priest through blurred vision. The possibility that he could save Mémé kindled hope.

"Come into the shade, my daughter." Father Tomàs led them to a bench beneath an oak tree where he and Jaques sat on each side of her. "I have known for some time about your family's sympathy to the Cathars. That is why your life at the abbey surprised me. But I did not know that Margaurite de Lumbert had taken the consolamentum until Father Stefe produced the list given to him by Fortaner."

"But Monsen Fortaner was deceitful," she insisted. "He could have invented that document."

He shook his head sadly. "Her life is out of our hands now. The best thing for you to do is to go home. You must not stay to see your grandmother perish."

"I will not leave." Sudden anger made civility difficult. "Why does this...atrocity...need to happen? They are harmless old women." She started to stand, but Jaques' arm tightened around her.

Father Tomàs' voice remained calm and compassionate. "What would happen to the Church if it allowed everyone within it to break away and declare their own religion? What would happen to the doctrines of Christ? They would cease to exist in their purity. The Church would crumble under such opposition. We must hold it together, even by force when necessary—even if it means the extermination of all dissenters."

Before Andreva could respond, Father Stefe came from the church, leading a procession of Inquisitors, priests, and a few of their servants. One of the priests had a large mole on his temple.

Friar David! The man on the road to Avignonet-Lauragais. She watched him, but his glance indicated he did not recognize her.

A servant let down the gate of the cart and helped each woman climb out around Mémé's still form. He lined them up beside the cart, facing the group of men. The women had difficulty standing, and held to the side of the cart.

Andreva left the bench to move closer, and Jaques followed. Father Stefe called upon Gisèla to stand forward.

The poor, hunched woman took a tentative step. "Gisèla de Gasquet, is it true you took the consolamentum of the Good Men on the 26th day of September in the Year of our Lord 1243?"

The woman straightened as much as her feeble frame allowed. Her voice was firm. "It is."

It is true? Sweet, gentle Gisèla? Andreva wanted to protest, but the other women did not appear surprised.

"And will you now denounce the false doctrine and pledge your allegiance to Pope Innocent III?"

Gisèla lifted her chin. "I will not."

The men in robes glanced at their leader. Father Stefe raised an eyebrow. "This is your last opportunity to live, Gisèla. Is that your final say?"

"Óc, Monsen."

"Step back."

Andreva moaned. She turned and buried her face in Jaques' shoulder.

The priest looked at the next name. "Jocelyne de Mauléon, stand forward."

Andreva looked up sharply, and held her breath while the Inquisitor asked the same questions.

Jocelyne replied, "I will not."

Each woman had her turn to renounce, and each refused. None would abjure. With each answer, Andreva grew more convinced that the list was authentic. She clung to Jaques, fearing she would collapse.

Father Stefe called Mémé's name last. Hearing it, Andreva lurched forward but a servant stopped her. Jaques took her back in his arms. She trembled uncontrollably.

Of course, Mémé could not step forth. Two servants dragged her limp body out of the cart, and held her up. Her head rolled forward. Andreva hid her face as Father Stefe asked, "Will you denounce the Cathar beliefs and your part in the consolamentum?"

Mémé could not respond.

"Take her to the pyre." Father Stefe waved his hand. "She must pay also for the murder of Gerrard de Fortaner."

Andreva gasped and shot a glance at Father Tomàs who did not remove his stare from the Inquisitor.

"Take them all." Father Stefe's order held disgust and a hint of boredom. "Let us get on with it."

Andreva still held to Jaques. "Father Tomàs, you said—"

"That I would discuss it with the council." He turned to her, his eyes glistening with tears. "I am sorry, Andreva."

"But, I trusted…"

Father Tomàs turned away.

The servants pushed the women toward the pyre. Gisèla walked without assistance, but the other three stumbled. Two men dragged Mémé by her arms.

Andreva pulled from Jaques' embrace to follow, halting when Father Stefe raised a hand. "Stay where you are."

Jaques gently took her again in his arms. Her head spun as she tried to think what to do.

A carriage approached. Andreva recognized it as the one outside the Fortaners' house. Three people sat on its seat: a priest, a woman, and a child.

"Dianne de Fortaner!" Adrenalin flowed through Andreva's veins and she escaped Jaques' arms.

Father Stefe grabbed the back of her dress as she pressed forward. "Stay out of this, Ma Soeur."

This? Andreva bit her lip as the meaning of his words sank in.

The newly-arrived priest dismounted the carriage and pulled Dianne down by the arm. Bruna climbed off without help, still hugging the doll, and ran to Andreva. She clung to her as the man brought Dianne to stand before Father Stefe. "This woman is Dianne de Fortaner." The man proudly held tight to her as if she were his prize. "Her name is on the list of those who have taken the consolamentum."

While Father Stefe glanced over the crumpled list, Dianne stared at Andreva, and a sense of alarm passed between them. Dianne mouthed the words, "Care for Bruna." Andreva pulled the girl closer.

Friar David stepped forward. "I will testify against this woman if there be a need, Your Reverence."

Andreva glared at the man. What could he possibly know

about Dianne?

"I rode with her and her husband from Montgiscard to Avignonet-Lauragais. I heard her speak in favor of the Good Men."

Andreva shook her head in shocked disbelief as she recalled Dianne's few words.

Father Stefe smiled. "Mercés, Friar David." He motioned toward the pyre. "Put her with the others. I think we have completed our list." He refolded it. "The rest of them died today at Montsegùr."

"Will you not give Dianne an opportunity to abjure?" Andreva asked. Surely Dianne would once again choose to live. "You offered such to the others."

Father Stefe rested a fist on his hip. "Every heretic receives an opportunity to abjure." He scrutinized Dianne for several moments, then asked her the same questions he had asked the others.

She glanced briefly at Andreva before she answered. "I will not abjure, Monsen."

"Dianne!" Andreva gasped.

"Idiots!" Father Stefe cursed under his breath. "Take Dòna de Fortaner to stand with the others. But remove her gown first. It is too valuable to burn in the fire."

Dianne's guard showed no respect. She gave a small cry when he dragged the elaborately-embroidered frock over her head. He shoved her along to stand near Mémé who lay unconscious across the logs. Dianne lowered her eyes and crossed her arms to cover her chest. Her face was as white as her thin, cotton chemise.

Andreva looked from Dianne to her grandmother. In her white nightgown, Mémé appeared as a sleeping angel.

The usually-full village square was hauntingly vacant. Only a few people had gathered to watch, and their faces were bleak as the executioner tied the condemned women to the posts.

Aware that Bruna stood beside her, Andreva turned the child away from the scene. A servant brought a burning torch to light the pyre, and within seconds flames rose to consume the women. They screamed as the blaze engulfed them. Andreva trembled violently and sank to her knees, holding the frightened little girl to her chest. Jaques knelt and held them both.

"Mémé! Dianne!" Tears flooded Andreva's eyes, blurring her vision of her friend, the widows, and her beloved grandmother. "May you all...come to a good end."

She covered her face and sobbed, no longer able to watch.

will take you home." Jaques pulled Bruna from Andreva's arms.

Andreva struggled to raise her eyes to his. He helped her stand, and she numbly permitted him to lead her away from her grandmother's funeral pyre. He lifted her onto the cart, and a moment later, Bruna nestled up to her on the bench.

No one spoke as they rode along. Andreva stared at nothing. She waited on the cart seat while Jaques took Bruna into Colet's house. She heard him ask the woman to keep the little girl. It barely registered in her mind when he requested that Elodie come stay with Andreva.

At Mémé's house, Jaques helped her from the cart and spoke about her to Elodie in quiet tones as they entered the house. Andreva stopped beside the table to pull off her wimple and veil, allowing them to slip from her fingers to the floor.

Elodie's voice sounded far away. "I will help you into bed."

Bed? No bed could offer what she needed.

Jaques' arms encircled her, strong and reassuring. "Hold me forever," Andreva said, and rested her head against his chest.

"I will return after I care for my livestock." He kissed her brow. "Will you be all right until then?"

"Please don't leave me!" She clung to him, breathing in his scent, never wanting to let go. He held her tighter. After several moments, she relented and lifted her face to his. "Please...please, *hurry*."

"Elodie is here." He kissed her, a gentle kiss of promise. "Try to rest."

As Jaques left the house, Elodie's arm slipped around her waist. She led her into the bedchamber.

Andreva removed her frock, reliving the memory of the ruthless servant yanking Dianne's elegant dress from her. Elodie slipped one of Mémé's clean nightgowns over Andreva's head, echoing the act Andreva had done many times for her grandmother. She watched Elodie smooth out the crumpled bed sheets. The feather pillow still held the indentation where Mémé had laid her head.

Mémé. Andreva sat on the bed. Jaques could not return soon enough. She tried to calculate how long his tasks might take, but her mind was too numb to think. She was too spent, too disillusioned. Just too—

She surrendered her head to the pillow.

The afternoon light cast a strange red hue across the room, intensifying her mind's replay of the day's horrid scenes. Andreva lay for what seemed like hours, willing sleep to come.

Questions whirled in and out of her consciousness. What could she have done to save her uncle and her grandmother? Why did the widows have to die? Why hadn't Dianne abjured after escaping death once before? Why was she at last willing to endure the excruciating pain of fire? Why, *why* had all those believers in the fortress sang as they went down the mountain to suffer a horrific death—*by choice*?

As hard as she tried, she could draw no logic from any of the tragedies.

"Andreva? What may I bring you?" Elodie set down the stool she had carried into the room.

"I need nothing. Only tell me how Raoul fares."

"He was resting when I left the house. Maire made a salve to pull the infection from his wounds." Elodie pulled the stool close to Andreva, and sat. "Pray he will live, if God wants it." She stroked Andreva's hair from her brow. "I am so sorry about your grandmother." Her halting voice softened to a whisper. *"Je suis vraiment désolée. Plus désolée."*

"Oh, Elodie. I wish I could awaken to find this whole tragedy only a nightmare." Andreva turned onto her back and stared at the cracks in the plastered ceiling. "If I could, I'd go back to the day I first arrived here, and it would be exactly as I used to imagine it when I lived in the abbey. Uncle Bostel would come to fetch me, wearing his finest clothes. I would enter Mémé's house to the smell of venison stew and find her and Marta kneading bread at the table, the same as they did when I was young." She paused to swallow the lump in her throat. "Mémé's jolly laughter would fill my soul with hope and joy. She—"

The lump returned and made it impossible to speak. She bit her knuckle as tears slipped onto the pillow.

"Dream of sweeter days." Elodie stroked Andreva's brow once more before she arose from the stool. "Try to sleep. Jaques will return soon. On the morn, the sun will shine and bring us hope."

Andreva frowned. "Do you believe that, Elodie?"

The girl fidgeted with her belt. "Well...no."

At her admission, Andreva smiled, her first since Jaques had come to Montsegùr to bring her home.

Andreva tried to rest, but horrid visions troubled her dozing. Involuntarily, she reached out to stop the torch from lighting the pyre on Montsegùr, or to pull Mémé and the dear widows from the ravenous flames.

Later, when Jaques returned, he sat on the bed in the candlelight and took Andreva in his arms. She relaxed, yet her grief overpowered what solace he could offer. She wept, and Jaques soothed her head and back, but made no attempt to hush her.

"Please stay," she pled. "Do not leave me again."

He stayed, propped against the wall at the bed's head, holding her. Elodie crawled up next to Andreva, and the three huddled together through the dark hours.

Before sunrise, at the rooster's first crow, Jaques awakened Andreva. All the horror of the previous day rushed back to her and she clung to him.

"I must go, Andreva, but as soon as my work is done, I will return." He pressed a kiss on her forehead before he rose.

"Please hurry," she begged as he disappeared into the darkness. She lay on the pillow next to Elodie and tried to sleep again, but was haunted by memories of Mémé and her last moments.

Sometime later, somebody pounded at the door. Andreva sat up. "Jaques!"

Elodie climbed off the bed. Andreva listened to her friend's footsteps cross the floor, and to the sound of the door opening.

Andreva heard a man's voice, but could not make out his words. She heard Elodie respond. "I am sorry, but she still sleeps."

"Awaken her."

Andreva jumped from the bed. Father Stefe? Who else would intrude at this early hour?

Elodie argued, "But, mon père, the sun has not yet risen."

Andreva quickly twisted her hair into a knot before approaching the chamber room door. When she saw the priest, she set her jaw. "So, you have come to apologize, to admit your mistake. Well, it is too late. Your devilish deed is done!"

Father Stefe's expression was impassive. "It is God who wills it. Our task is not finished until every heretic is penitent or dead." He stepped inside and waved his hand to indicate the room. "This house is now the property of the Church. I hate to be the bearer of bad news," he said with a pious sniff, "but because your family were heretics, by right the Church claims this house and the Lumbert family properties." A thin smile etched his face as he eyed the contents of her home.

Andreva's anger blazed. With fisted hands, she charged toward Father Stefe.

He caught her by the wrists. "Calm yourself, child."

She struggled, with no success, and screamed. "You

murderer! You have taken everything from me—my family, and now my home. You can rot in hell for all I care!"

Father Stefe released her and she sank to the floor, weeping. Never had she felt so purely helpless.

Elodie knelt at her side but looked up at the priest. "Mon père." Her arm tightened around Andreva. "Do you not see she is hysterical? Such cruelty to bring distressing news so soon after her grandmother's death."

The priest was unmoved. "Ma Soeur Andreva!"

Startled, she looked up. His eyes flashed. "I should have thrown you into the fire with your grandmother." He swore under his breath. "Such a disrespectful child! You cannot speak to a servant of God this way."

She leaned into Elodie for support. "If *you* represent God, I want nothing to do with Him!"

He grabbed Andreva by the arm and yanked her to her feet. "Enough nonsense, child. You will return to St. Sernin this very morning."

"I will not!"

He shook her and the knot fell from her hair. "Silence! I have arranged for a horseman to collect you in an hour. This is more mercy than an ingrate such as you deserves. You will wait at St. Sernin until I come to begin your interrogation."

Elodie gasped and Andreva gave her a hushing look.

"But first, my work here is not yet finished." He glanced toward Elodie. "I must cleanse Lavelanet from the wretched heresy that still lurks within its shadows."

Andreva avoided looking again in Elodie's direction. "Cleansing" meant punishing all sympathizers of the Good Men, and the punishment usually included pain. Would Colet and her family be questioned further? Would the Inquisitors learn that Raoul had gone to Montsegùr?

Father Stefe tightened his grip. "My dear Andreva, I have faith that with time and much discipline, you will outgrow your youthful disrespect." He let go of her with a shove, throwing her again to the floor. "The Church now claims the Lumbert properties, which means you are a ward of the Church and have no choice but to return to the abbey. And dismiss any thoughts of the young man I saw you clinging to. You will remain a nun the rest of your life, if I have my say."

Andreva tried to raise her fist one more time, but found she was too exhausted to fight. He was wrong. Wrong! *Evilly wrong.*

The room darkened when Father Stefe stepped into the doorway, filling the frame. "Be ready. One hour." His white skirt and black robe sailed behind him as he stomped away.

Andreva hung her head in surrender. "I do not want to go back to the abbey." *How can I leave Jaques?* Giving in to discouragement, she laid her cheek on the cold stone floor.

"Come." Elodie pulled on her arm with urgency. "My maire will hide you."

Andreva lifted her head and glanced at the open door. "And bring the wrath of the Inquisition upon your family? No. You are in danger enough as it is for helping Mémé and me."

"Do you not know what an interrogation means?" Elodie knelt beside her. "They will torture you." Her voice lowered. "I have heard they string women up by their elbows and leave them to hang—naked ofttimes—until they confess whatever the judges wish to hear."

Andreva shuddered. *Interrogation!* Was there a pyre waiting in her future? What did she have to live for now? Her family, and even Jaques, had been taken from her. "Then it is even more imperative that I not put your family in jeopardy."

"But...God is with us," Elodie said. "He will help."

Andreva gritted her teeth. "He is not with me!" She sat up defiantly and held Elodie's shocked gaze. Her anger boiled over. "He allowed my parents to die. Where was He then? And where was God when the Inquisitors murdered *your* father? Where was He when the Good Men, Mémé, Dianne, and the widows suffered in the fire? None of it makes sense. How can you, an innocent victim of this insanity, still claim God is with us?"

"But He is. Though the Inquisition is merciless, God is still good and loving. Have faith."

Andreva stood. "I will never again be able to believe as you do. I refuse to, after all that has happened."

"Give yourself time." Elodie squeezed Andreva's hand. "Faith is a choice. If you open your heart, God will fill it."

Andreva sighed. "You never cease to astonish me. In truth, I have no choice but to return to St. Sernin. I know no way out of it. But please, stay with me this hour. I think I should go mad alone."

"Óc. I shall stay. I do not want you to turn mad." She smiled.

Andreva tried to return her smile, but turned instead to look over the room. "I will remember these last days with sorrow all my life. They are memories I will tell my grandchildren." She froze. "But I shall never marry and have children, nor grandchildren. If I am not burned, I shall be condemned to a life in the abbey." She gripped Elodie's hand. "My friend, I think I cannot bear it."

"Do not dwell on it now." Elodie's eyes searched Andreva's. "Speak of it to the abbess. She will help you. You may be surprised what the saints have in store for you. They will bless you for your good heart."

Was the girl's faith without bounds? Andreva turned away and searched her soul for the smallest bit of hope. But instead, found only her stomach, growling. She went to the loaf of bread on the table and picked it up. "Let us eat. I am famished. Mémé would not want us to go hungry."

She broke off a piece and handed it to Elodie. As Andreva chewed her bread, she gazed around at Mémé's belongings. "I cannot bear to think that the priests will come to take possession of Mémé's house." So many decades of life had passed herein. "Her tapestries, her bed, her full cellar—" Her head jerked toward Elodie. "I have thought of something wickedly delightful." At last she smiled as she formulated the idea.

Elodie giggled. "Pray tell."

"There can be a touch of joy in my misfortune. Let us fill baskets with the foodstuffs in the cellar and take it to your house. It will feed your family at least until summer.

Shall we?" She looked toward the bedchamber. "And the sheets and the dresses. But we must hurry for we have so little time." She gathered the baskets and opened the cellar door. "Let the Inquisitors think robbers have cleared out the house in my absence."

Elodie agreed happily. The two girls filled baskets, gathered up sheets filled with food, and headed cautiously out into the foggy semi-darkness to Colet's house.

As the girls entered, Colet and Elodie's younger siblings, all dressed in nightshirts, sat up in the straw beds that circled the fire pit in the main room. Bruna sat up as well, rubbed her eyes, and ran over to Andreva to hug her.

Colet rose from her bed. Her eyes widened upon seeing the girls empty baskets of dried vegetables and herbs onto the table.

"This is all for you." Andreva took joy in Colet's expression. "We will explain when we return." She squatted beside Bruna and turned to the other three children. "Come help us—all of you. But we must be quick and quiet about it."

Bruna and the youngsters pulled on shoes and cloaks. Still looking bewildered, Colet followed them to the door and watched them silently hurry to Mémé's house with Elodie and Andreva.

The girls filled the baskets with dishes and handed them to the giggling children. Andreva scolded. "Hush now, and go with care. We do not want anyone to discover us." She handed the smallest child the pot from the hearth and watched him lug it out the door.

With the last of Mémé's food, wines, straw mattresses, tapestries, and other belongings safely in Colet's house, Andreva breathed easier, confident they had done the deed unseen.

She went to find Raoul. He lay alone in the elegantly carved chamber room bed that was clearly a remnant of better days. Her heart squeezed with sadness as she knelt beside the bed and gently took his hand. His eyes remained closed, but she hoped he listened. "This is my farewell,

Raoul." She moved a few locks of hair from his brow. "I am grateful for your friendship and all your help."

He opened his eyes. He gripped her hand although the slight effort caused him to wince in pain. In a moment, he whispered, "I am grateful...to you for bringing me home. You saved my life. May God ever be with you."

Andreva kissed his forehead. The fever had left him. She smiled. "Get well, my friend." Her voice caught in her throat. "You must live...live for your family. They need you. Remember, always choose life, Raoul." She stood and blinked away the moisture forming in her eyes. "And soon, I will hear jongleurs in Toulouse singing your song, and will think of you."

He gave her a nod and a weak smile. "May God go with you."

Andreva let his hand slip from hers as she stepped away.

Back in the larger room, Elodie waited, still wearing her cloak. "I will come with you to your house."

"Stay here." Andreva hugged Elodie. "Please understand, I know I said I would go mad, but knowing your family will benefit from Mémé's things has given me peace. I want to savor the last few minutes I have there alone. I will be fine. I hope you understand."

Elodie's eyes glistened. "I do understand."

Andreva looked to Colet who also stood close. "You have been the best of friends to me." She hugged the older woman. "Please make Bruna your own."

Colet nodded. "I will."

Andreva knelt beside Bruna. "Colet is your maire now." She brushed the little girl's curls from her eyes. "This is your family. I hope we meet again someday in happier times."

Bruna still held the doll. Her curls bounced as she agreed. Andreva gave them both a hug, and with heavy heart, left the house without looking back.

The door still stood open when she returned home. Cool morning air had filled the house. The only thing left to do was to wait for her escort to arrive.

She climbed the stairs to the upper chamber. The empty wardrobe's doors gaped open. Aunt Aimée's beautiful dresses now belonged to Elodie.

"I wish I had more to give," she said to the empty room. "I wish I could give the walls and floors and—" She listened to her voice echo against the stone walls now devoid of tapestries. Her lower lip quivered as she went to the stairs. "But giving what I could has been…" her voice broke, "such sweet revenge." She sank onto the top stair and wept—for Mémé and Bostel—and for Jaques.

Please, she prayed. *Send Jaques. I wish one more time to feel his arms around me, and to look in to his eyes before—*

"Andreva?"

She looked down at the open doorway. Colet's youngest daughter stood there with Bruna beside her. They now wore dresses instead of nightshirts. Bruna held up the little doll. Andreva swiped at her tears and descended the stairs. "Do you want me to hug the doll goodbye?"

Bruna's dark brown eyes smiled up at her, but it was Maria who spoke. "She is thankful to you for bringing her here and wants you to keep the doll to remember her by." She shoved the poupée into Andreva's hand.

Andreva protested, but the two little girls turned too quickly. Hand in hand, they ran back to Colet's house.

She smoothed the doll's coarse hair and gazed at its hand-sewn face. "Girls and their poupées." Repeating Raoul's chiding caused emotion to swell in her chest. She sank onto the bottom stair and held the doll close. This little thing was all she had left of her mother and Mémé.

At the sound of approaching horses' hooves, Andreva jumped to her feet and again wiped away her tears before she went outside. The face of the man who rode one horse and led another was familiar, but it was not Jaques'.

"Bonjorn, Pons." She greeted the man, trying to hide her disappointment. She looked past him, hoping to see another rider.

"Going back to Toulouse, I hear." Pons dismounted. "Well, we had best get started."

Andreva retrieved her few belongings from the house. She tucked the doll into the satchel and hesitated, looking longingly up the road. She hoped to see Jaques just one more time. He would steal her away and hide her in his father's castle, and they would never have to part again.

"Ma Soeur. We must depart if we are to reach Pamiers by sunset." Pons took her satchel and tied it to the saddle. No chiding now, only kindness.

She allowed him to help her onto the horse. Had he been told of the tragedy of the day before? Her body slumped as they rode through the village. The sun danced above the eastern hills as they passed the gate. Andreva kept watching, kept hoping, but no one else traveled the road. Before the trail rounded the hill, she turned to catch, through a blur of tears, one last glimpse of the rooftops of Lavelanet.

35

ndreva's heart wrung in her chest as she walked with the other novices in a single line toward the chapel. The abbey's musty odor reminded her still of a crypt, and mocked the freedom she'd had the last three months. Organ music played softly as they entered. Wordlessly, she slipped to her knees with the others. They bowed their heads in unison to begin their daily devotional.

Andreva's lips chanted the rote words of prayer, but her bitter heart owned none. She stole a peek at the priests who stood at the altar, and imagined Father Stefe and his council's judgmental eyes staring down at her. He would come one day soon to begin her interrogation. At least then the misery of awakening to each new day here would finally end.

She lowered her head again. The previous night, she had dreamed Jaques held her, enfolding her in his secure, warm love. Earlier, she had relived in sleep the joy of filling the emptiness of Colet's poverty with Mémé's abundance. Only in sleep did she find happiness. Reality returned in full force when she awakened, and the relentless depression returned.

Sister Rosalind, a prioress, fell into step with her as she left the chapel. "The abbess would like to speak with you."

Andreva pursed her lips. She was not yet ready to discuss her loss—of Mémé and Bostel, nor of Jaques. Would she ever know joy again? Could she ever devote her heart to the Church that had taken everything from her?

Sister Penelope met them in the corridor. "Sister Agnes is ready to see you now." She led the way down the hall to the abbess' office, and stopped outside a carved wooden door. Sister Penelope motioned for Andreva to knock. Lifting her hand, she hesitated and took a deep breath before tapping lightly.

"Come in."

Andreva entered. The sisters stayed in the hallway and she closed the door behind herself. An open window lit the room. Sister Agnes sat near the window, at a small desk surrounded by several chairs.

"Sit, please." The abbess gazed at her kindly. Her fair skin and green eyes contrasted with her dark eyebrows and the gray of her wimple. "I am sorry we have not been able to visit until now, but I am glad you have returned. You have been gone from us not yet four months."

"I...went to care for my grandmother." Andreva wrung her hands. Why tell Sister Agnes what she already knew? She tried to keep emotion from overcoming her voice. She sat taller.

"She is dead now."

Andreva gave a slight nod.

The woman picked up a parchment and studied it. "Father Stefe sent you back to us after your family died the heretics' death." She looked from the parchment to Andreva and their eyes locked. The abbess' face now held no emotion.

Andreva's jaw tightened. She crossed her arms and sat rigidly, determined to be strong. Her dry mouth did not allow her to swallow. She forced the reply. "Óc. It is true."

The woman folded her wrinkled hands before her on the desk. "Tell me what you have learned from this experience."

The request took Andreva by surprise. Why would the abbess ask such a question? She opened her mouth, but words came slowly. "Learned?" Her mind raced over the last weeks. "Mother, what I have learned is..." She hung her head and, responding from the depths of her battered heart, wept.

The abbess waited.

Andreva at last bit her lip and regained control, but could not look at the woman. She swallowed and started again. "I have learned that oppression, one man's power over another, is the worst form of cruelty. I have learned that families can be torn apart in the name of righteousness, and that no one is allowed original thought, nor to follow their own conscience."

Her courage increased. "The only peace to be found in the world is within the souls of those who truly follow Christ's teachings to love one another as He said." She had seen this for herself: Bertrand and Bostel standing with other brave Good Men and Women, waiting to die, with peace illuminating their countenances.

Expecting punishment for speaking her thoughts, Andreva lowered her head. "Forgive me. You requested my response, so I answered."

A long moment went by before the abbess spoke. "You have seen the sinister side of the Crusade."

Did the Mother Superior understand more than Andreva realized? "I have." She lifted her head. "I still see its horror every night in my dreams, and live it again every day in my thoughts. I hear the screams of those unfortunate people who dared to follow their beliefs. I see their tormented faces as flames leap up around them. I cannot force the smell of their burning flesh from my nostrils." She hid her mouth behind her hand as her lips trembled. "The memory of my grandmother lying unconscious on the pyre is more than I can bear."

The abbess rose and went to Andreva, placing a hand on her shoulder. "My dear. I see you are not ready to take the sacred vows of a nun. Your heart requires more time to heal and forgive."

"Forgive?" A surge of heated emotion propelled Andreva to her feet. "Forgive those who killed my family and sent me away from my home and the friends I love? I have no one left in the world."

"You have many: the sisters here at the abbey, God, all

the saints, and the Holy Mother. To say you have no one is to disregard your many blessings."

Andreva gnawed her lip. When at last she spoke, it was with forced composure. "I love the Holy Mother, but I *do not* revere the men who killed my uncle and grandmother. I saw evil in their eyes, and yet they called themselves servants of God." *There.* She had spoken the truth. She braced herself for whatever punishment would be pronounced.

The smile left the woman's face. She walked to the window and gazed out. "You speak your mind too freely, Sister Andreva. Pray, be more prudent." The abbess turned back to her. "We will meet again in a few weeks. You need time to calm your spirit before you take the vows."

"How can I calm my spirit when I know Father Stefe will soon arrive to question me? He threatened 'an interrogation' —and you know what that means!"

The abbess picked up the parchment and again consulted it. "He has said nothing about coming here. He requests only that we watch you closely. He is a very busy man. Perhaps he will not come."

Andreva stood. "Oh, yes, he will. He carries out his threats. I know."

"You cannot live each day in fear. If he comes, I will soften his heart and tell him his threat to you has been torture enough." Kindness returned to the abbess' eyes. "Return to your studies and your duties in the abbey. I have assigned you to work in the sickroom." She slid her hands into the wide sleeves of her habit. "Serving the less fortunate will help to heal your heart that you may again find gratitude therein. With time, you will forget your fears. Thank God for life and the divine blessings the saints have showered upon you. The key to happiness, Sister Andreva, is to maintain a grateful heart."

Forgiveness? Impossible. *Gratitude?* Hard to make her own.

After being excused, Andreva went alone to the dormitory. She gazed over the rows of beds. This would be her life—one woman among many—and she felt anything but grateful. She succumbed to the lure of her bed, but when she lay her head against the pillow, it hit an unexpected lump.

What is this? She pulled the object from beneath her head and sat up. Tears stung her eyes as she gazed upon the doll from her childhood, the one that had been stolen from beneath her bed over a year ago!

Andreva opened her satchel, pulled out her mother's poupée, and held the dolls side by side. She gratefully pressed both to her heart.

Had a repentant soul returned the doll? The compassionate gesture touched a chord deep in her heart, so deep she knew this was a sign—an assurance God loved her. He was with her, after all. Might He save her from Father Stefe's torture and an almost assured doom?

A bird began to sing outside her window. Andreva pulled aside the linen curtain and peeked out. The tree where the bird perched had leafed out in ardent green. The grass and flowers below and the deep blue of the sky above all made her heart swell with joy. Because she had wallowed in gloom for many days, she had not noticed that spring had overtaken the world!

With spring comes new hope. She reminded herself of her mother's words. *Always.*

She inspected the dolls. If the thief had experienced a change of heart significant enough to cause her to return the precious keepsake, then surely Andreva could heal her broken heart as well, as impossible as it seemed. *What did the abbess say? The key to being happy is to maintain a grateful heart.*

Each day that followed, Andreva searched for ways to feel grateful. Besides springtime and the dolls that linked her to her mother and grandmother, she gave thanks for the miracle of life, and the blessings of a peaceful place in which to live, food to eat, and clothes to wear.

But forgiving those who had killed her family still loomed beyond her ability.

The abbess' counsel proved right. Serving in the sickroom began to heal her broken heart, and she looked forward to time spent helping others. Ill sisters, and often, sick townsfolk, came to the infirmary for healing and rest. Andreva's compassion quickly made her the preferred assistant to Sister Angelica, the infirmarian, and Andreva spent many hours at her side.

Andreva found solace in the quiet moments in which she sat with ailing patients. She still grieved for her family, and she still missed Jaques—memories of his smile, his kind eyes, and gentle voice were her constant companions. Yet her daydreaming was no use. Her world was confined to these walls.

One day, she was fortunate to find parchment, a quill, and a quiet corner in which to sit down to write him a missive.

> *Jaques Montré, I regret that I could not say a proper farewell after all you did for Mémé and me. I am very grateful you stayed by my side through...*

A lump grew in her throat.

...her tragic death.

She signed her name. It was not enough. There was so much more she wished to say. She longed to beg him to come for her. She wished she dared express her deep love to this intended knight who had the heart of a farmer. But the authorities might intercept the letter before it left the abbey, or at any point along the way. No, she could not jeopardize Jaques' safety in any way. She folded the letter and scrawled on the outside:

> *Jaques Montré, the Ariège village of Lavelanet*

"Oh, Jaques," Andreva whispered as she held the parchment to her aching heart. "I will never see you again." *You, Jaques Montré are nobler than I ever will be. You are a good man. A very good man. The best I have ever known. But I have no family, no dowry, nothing of value to bring to a marriage. I am rich, but only in blessings.*

The letter went southward the next day with a priest on his way to visit parishes in the region.

Several days later, Sister Penelope found Andreva changing bed linens in the crowded infirmary. "Come quickly, Sister Andreva." Her hushed voice was urgent. "An injured man now lies in the sickroom. Sister Angelica calls for your assistance."

Andreva fell into step with the sister as they hurried down the hallway. She had not dealt with an injury before, but would do whatever she could to assist. "What happened?"

"Robbers attacked him on the highway. They stabbed him several times, and he is the only survivor of his traveling party. That is all I know."

They reached a private room where closed shutters blocked most of the sunlight. A single candle lit the dimness.

Andreva rushed to Sister Angelica's side. The older woman stood over a man who lay upon an elevated bed and carefully washed the wounds on his chest.

"I am here, Sister."

"Sister Penelope." Sister Angelica looked past Andreva to her escort. "Take these rags and wash them. Bring back a fresh batch. Quick, now! We have no time to lose."

Sister Angelica had routinely assigned such errands to Andreva. Curious, she stepped forward and glanced at the bloody man. His stab wounds were several and deep, but fortunately, each had missed his heart. She straightened her back and resolved to be strong in the face of such an awful sight.

"He faints from loss of blood, and has a slim chance at life." Sister Angelica handed Andreva a fresh rag. "Take this cloth and clean the gash on his head."

Andreva dampened the cloth in a bowl of water and moved to the other side of the bed. She held the cloth against the man's bloodied forehead and for the first time saw his face.

Her breathing stopped. Her hand froze. Her heart pounded as she felt the blood drain from her head. She took a step back into the shadows.

Sister Angelica worked a moment longer, then looked up. "Andreva? Is this task too much for you? I thought you had a strong constitution."

"I—" Andreva could not take her eyes off the hated man's face, nor could she speak above a whisper.

"Father Stefe!"

trenta-e-sìeis
36

"Do you know this injured priest?" Sister Angelica's face registered her surprise.

Andreva pursed her lips and gave a terse nod. Know him? She loathed him from the depths of her soul.

"Travelers found Father Stefe and his companions on the highway outside of Toulouse. They must have been set upon by robbers. He is the only survivor." Sister Angelica laid clean bandages across the priest's chest. "The bleeding has slowed, but I question if he can make it through the night. You will remain at his side." She disappeared into a dim corner and returned with a chair. "Here, sit, and keep a cool rag on his forehead to bring down the fever."

Sister Penelope returned with a stack of rags and set them on a small table. She left the room as quickly as she had entered.

"I must attend to others now." Sister Angelica sighed wearily and placed a hand on Andreva's arm. "So much sickness, and then to have this happen." She gazed at the dying man. "Thank the saints you are here to tend to him. He is a holy man. God expects us to do all we can to preserve His servant's life. But having little hope, I will send for a priest to give last rites."

Andreva stood in the shadows, unable to move, long after Sister Angelica left. She stared at the man who was once the hunter, now laboring for each breath as would a hunter's prey with an arrow piercing its chest. He had destroyed her family, threatened her with torture, and condemned her to a life in a convent. And now God expected her to help preserve his life? She would rather turn her back and leave him to die.

Andreva used her sleeve to mop the perspiration from her brow. She closed her eyes to pray, but no words came. She forced her feet to move toward the bed, and her hand to grasp the chair. Pulling it back, she commanded her knees to bend and her body to sit.

Andreva stared at the detested face, and then shifted her gaze to the bandages on the man's heaving torso. A sheet covered his naked lower body and legs. He lay gasping, clinging to life—life he had so cruelly denied others.

Father Stefe's long, limp fingers hung off the edge of the bed, and he lay with his mouth gaping open. A trail of drool trickled across his jaw and down his neck, creating a wet puddle on the sheet. His eyes, now closed and incapable of pious glances, jerked restlessly behind their lids, but he did not awaken.

Andreva lifted her hand, freshened the cloth, and placed it on his forehead. She would do as Sister Angelica asked, but it would be without compassion. Minutes passed. She repeated the motions while wondering why she, a victim of this man's heartless cruelty, had been called upon to give him comfort.

Her thoughts were like daggers. *He received his just reward on the highway. Let him die!* She wrung out the cloth. *Let him answer before God for his crimes.*

No, let God wait His turn. She laid the cloth back on his brow and addressed the unconscious man. "To bring true justice, you should be strung up by your elbows until you confess your murderous sins." She began to shake. "And then a fire should be built in the street and onto it thrown your broken body, so you might die the same agonizing death you forced upon so many others!"

She was too angry and restless to sit. She rose and paced the floor, but turned when she heard him stir. The stubby candle flickered and cast shadows over the grimace on his face. Andreva returned to the bed and put her hand to his forehead. He burned with fever.

Good. Let him suffer.

"Hell!" the priest cried out with eyes still closed.

Andreva jumped back in alarm. He thrashed and one knee flew up, exposing his naked body.

"Fire! I'm on fire!" His hand flew to his head, knocking away the cloth.

She retrieved the rag, refreshed it, and pulled his hand back to his side. She pressed the cloth to his forehead and forced her eyes away from his exposed body. With one hand on the wet cloth, she used the other to pull the sheet back into place.

Father Stefe moaned in distress. "No, not hell! Eternal Father, I did Your bidding. I acted in Your name!" Speaking sent him into a fit of coughing. Tears ran down his cheeks as he gasped for air.

"Your Reverence. Calm yourself. You are very ill. You must lie still." Why must she speak to him? "You are not dead. You are in the infirmary at St. Sernin."

He opened his eyes. In their depths she saw a haunted, tormented soul. "Sister Andreva?"

Startled that he recognized her, she did not respond.

He stared toward the ceiling. His wounded chest heaved. "I see flames!" He fumbled for her hand. "So many flames!"

She moved out of his reach. "There is no fire." Her voice held no emotion. "Please try to keep still. You are badly wounded. The fever makes you delirious."

Father Stefe's breathing grew rapid. "I remember now. The attackers! Where is my council?"

She thought of the men who had followed the priest around like ducklings. "They are dead, Your Reverence."

He winced. More tears hurried along the trail to the sheet. He grimaced in pain and reached for her, but she dodged his grasp. He stared at the ceiling and his eyes widened. "Hell's jaws are opening. Do you see? They beckon me, saying, 'Come. Your works have damned you!'" He sobbed.

"Forgive me of my sins! Oh, Christ Jesus, save me from my due reward!"

Andreva caught her breath.

"Ma Bonne Soeur Andreva, hold my hand." He blubbered as if drunken. "I am afraid. Do not let hell claim me!" Father Stefe reached out to her.

Take the hand of the man she loathed, the man who had killed her grandmother? She could not touch him. But a sudden, strange sensation caused her to place her hand over her chest. What was it? She pushed away the feeling. His shaking hand found hers. Her breathing stopped. She stared at the gnarled knuckles that gripped her fingers.

"I am sure, Sister Andreva, your purity and forgiveness will save me. Goodness emanates from you and God sees." He motioned upward, staring. "Even now, hell waits to know what you will choose."

Andreva looked toward the ceiling and saw only shadows from the flickering light that danced along the painted motif.

Father Stefe surrendered to another fit of coughing. Blood replaced the drool. He squeezed her hand and wheezed. "Ma Soeur, please pray that God will forgive my sins."

Andreva choked. She believed this man deserved death—a painful death. How could she pray in his behalf and be sincere? She searched her wounded heart and answered honestly. "I cannot, mon père."

He took another raspy breath and coughed, releasing her hand. Andreva fought the urge to gag as she used the rag to wipe away the blood that dripped from his chin.

"You must pray. *You* must forgive me...or hell will claim me." He turned his eyes toward the ceiling. "I see it there, waiting...hoping you will refuse."

"The priest will come soon. He will give you last rites." She looked toward the door. Why did the priest take so long to arrive?

Father Stefe wheezed and found her hand again. "But I will die," he breathed, "before he comes." Andreva attempted to free her hand, but he cried out. "Ma Soeur, do not leave me! Pray for me."

"I do not know the words, Your Reverence."

He gasped for air. "Oh, Eternal Father—" He waited. "Repeat what I say!"

Andreva bowed her head and listened to him sob. How could she say these words for a man who had caused her such anguish? She raised her eyes and saw Father Stefe's tears flowing freely. At last she found a small twinge of sympathy in her heart. She opened her mouth and began hesitantly, begrudging him every syllable. "Oh, Eternal Father."

"Forgive this sinner. Now repeat."

Tears stung her eyes. "For—forgive this sinner." Her cheeks dampened. Her chest burned within.

"Who has sent hundreds of innocent souls unto Thee."

She could not say the words. "Mon père. Forgive me. I cannot..."

Father Stefe's voice weakened. "And allow the saving blood of Christ to atone for him, the lowest of all."

"And allow—" a sob caught in her throat. She swallowed. "And allow the saving...blood of Christ...to atone for him..." She could not finish. The strange feeling had returned with overpowering strength. What was happening inside her— this swelling?

"Who is not worthy of Thy kingdom."

She dropped her head to the hand that held his. Whatever the sensation was, it eased her resentment, calmed her hatred. She said the last words in an earnest, tearful whisper.

He pulled her hand to his lips and kissed it. "Mercés... sweet Soeur Andreva. I...I can now die in peace, knowing I have your forgiveness." He sighed long and closed his eyes. His hand still gripped hers as it dropped beside him on the bed.

Andreva listened to his gurgling breaths for several moments before she lowered her head and sobbed with overwhelming pity for this dying man.

✵

At the touch of a gentle hand, Andreva awoke and looked up to see Sister Angelica standing at the bedside with a priest.

"Father Lucas came to pronounce Father Stefe's last rites, but I see we are too late."

Andreva stood and looked down into Father Stefe's open eyes. Her fingers, no longer trembling, touched his forehead. No fever.

"He is gone." Andreva smoothed her hand over Father Stefe's eyes, closing the lids for the last time.

trenta · e · set

37

The burden in Andreva's heart lightened the night she prayed for Father Stefe. Each day that followed, she contemplated the meaning of the experience. She had forgiven the man—not his actions, but the man himself—and found consolation in knowing he was now doing penance in purgatory for his atrocities, and would at last receive a just reward.

Despite their many weeks apart, Jaques was still a cherished memory. Andreva hungered to see him, to feel his reassuring arms around her, but they lived in separate worlds. The miles between them might as well have been oceans. She prayed for the desire to commit herself to vows that would be set in stone the remainder of her life, but every time she prayed, Jaques' radiant smile came to mind. It was hard to be sincere in her petitions, yet she dared not ask for the desire of her heart. Might God understand her true feelings, even if they were unexpressed?

The inevitable beckon from the abbess came too soon. Her message directed Andreva to go to the vestibule of the chapel instead of the abbess' office. Andreva formulated her words as her footsteps echoed down the empty hallway.

Though her heart could not fully commit, she would take the vows to show her gratitude. She had been given a great gift in the ability to forgive. Working in the sickroom had brought purpose to her life, and here in the abbey she had a place to live and food to eat. Its plastered walls were now her home, and the sisters her only family. She would go forward and live her life under God's watchful eye. In time, her deep-seated longing for a husband and children would be replaced by a love for service, more profound gratitude, and a stronger sense of purpose—at least she prayed it would be so.

Andreva opened the small door to the vestibule and stepped inside. Sister Agnes stood facing her. She spoke to a man whose exquisite surcoat and leather boots indicated his nobility and wealth. Andreva waited in the shadows behind the archway for the abbess to dismiss the visitor.

The woman saw Andreva and came toward her. Were those tears she saw in the abbess' smiling eyes?

"My dear." Sister Agnes took Andreva's hand. "The saints have looked upon you with favor. May God be with you always."

Andreva peered into the chapel lined with statues of several saints. She gathered courage to share her pending commitment. There could be no better place for it than here.

"Mother, I am ready to discuss taking the vows."

The woman glanced back over her shoulder. She unlatched the door to the hall through which Andreva had just passed, and ducked through the opening without a word, closing the door behind her.

Andreva stared at the latch and waited. Did the abbess want her to take solitude in the chapel? She had made her decision and was ready to commit. Why prolong it further?

"Andreva."

The voice sounded much like Jaques', but she must be mistaken. She turned to see the nobleman still standing where the abbess had left him. "Who is there?" She stepped from the shadows.

"It is I, Jaques. Have you forgotten your old friend?" Andreva took a step closer.

"Jaques?" It was he! His broad smile filled her heart almost to bursting.

He dropped his shoulder bag to the floor, and came to meet her. She fell into his embrace. His arms felt like home as they had before, yet she feared she would awaken to find his presence was only a dream. She closed her eyes and relished the moment, wanting to hold him forever, but how could she indulge in such joy when she knew he would leave and she would have to stay in the abbey?

Tears warmed her eyes. "I have so wanted to see you!" She stepped back and gazed over him. "And how handsomely you are dressed! Did you get my letter?"

He appeared baffled. "I received no letter, but I have come for you." Jaques took her hands, and his smile turned into a nervous grin, the most handsome she'd ever seen.

"Me?" His words confused her.

"Andreva..." His voice dropped. "when Raoul and Elodie told me what happened—"

"Raoul has recovered?"

"Yes, he does well. When they told me Father Stefe had condemned you to the abbey, I..."

"Father Stefe is dead."

"Óc." He studied her hands as if gathering his thoughts. "When I received word, I sold my chattels in haste and came here to find you, but was told you were under strict observation and not allowed visitors."

He had come for her! Her heart leapt to her throat and she fought tears. "My confinement is Father Stefe's orders. Oh, how I wish I could have caught even the slightest glimpse of you that day."

He put his arms around her, and placed his cheek against hers. "I then knew not what else to do but to return to my father."

"But you are now here."

"Óc." He stepped back and held her hands against his heart. "Distraught, I visited with my brother, who is a priest, hoping he would know of a way to override Father Stefe's edict and bring you back to me. But he had no solution. After days of pacing the floor and stewing, I resolved to storm into the convent, swoop you up onto my horse, and ride away." He chuckled and kissed her forehead.

"We both would be on the Inquisition's death list if you had." She smiled. "But I would have gladly escaped with you."

"Fortunately, before I could put both our lives in danger, I received word from my brother that Father Stefe was dead."

"Word travels even to Lanfoix. Did you hear that Father Stefe was killed on the road?"

He nodded. "That news renewed my courage to come again and claim you. This time, I insisted to speak personally with the abbess. I have asked her to release you, and for your hand in marriage."

"And she agreed?" Andreva now understood the meaning of the abbess' words.

He smiled. "Óc—to my surprise, and great joy. All I now need is for you to accept."

Elation rushed through her. She opened her mouth to answer, but he held his fingers to her lips to hush her. "But first, you should know that this bag belongs to you." He lifted the satchel at his feet. "Before Bostel left for what I then believed was Toulouse, he brought it to me. He asked that I give it to you if he did not return. It is his treasure. He wanted you to have it to assure that you are well cared for."

Uncle Bostel has not left me destitute! She lowered her head as the tears started again, and all the trust she had held in him through the years returned.

Jaques opened the bag. Coins and jewels glistened within, as glorious as the treasure they had seen buried at Montsegùr.

"What a beautiful sight," she breathed. "He did not bury it with the rest. He left it to *me*." She touched a gemstone to be certain she wasn't dreaming. "An unexpected blessing." She felt overwhelmed with gratitude and love for her uncle.

Jaques lowered the bag to the floor and pulled her close. "Take it and do with it what you will. It is yours even if you choose not to marry me."

"But Jaques." She looked up into his hopeful eyes. "I choose you. I dared not dream you would come for me, but here you are." She laughed through her tears.

"You accept?" he asked. "You will marry me?"

"Of course." She could scarcely believe it, but there he stood before her and she felt his strong hands holding her—this was no longer merely a dream. "You are the noblest man I know. You are...the man I love."

Jaques pulled her closer. "Then you shall come with me

to Lanfoix. I have reconciled with my father and will finish my training—"

"To become the knight you were meant to be." Of course. It was time.

"Óc. And we shall ask my brother to perform our wedding."

A wedding! Her dreams of marrying as her father always wanted would come true. She would even wed a knight, albeit one with the heart of a farmer.

"But, Jaques, will you be happy as a knight?"

He grew solemn. "It is my heritage. My father is thankful his heir has returned to take his rightful place, and I am grateful to please him." Jaques' face brightened. "And he has much land. I am sure he will grant me a small plot where I may garden to my heart's content." He brought her hand to his lips for a kiss. "I may never be a great knight as was your father, but I will be a faithful husband. I promise."

Andreva rose to her tiptoes and kissed his cheek.

Jaques' grin broadened. "That is not a sufficient kiss to seal a betrothal."

Her heartbeat quickened and she closed her eyes against the rush of joy that rolled through her senses. Andreva melted into Jaques' arms and accepted his warm kiss, not caring that Mother Mary and all the saints gazed down upon them.

At last, she was home.

The door to the vestibule creaked open. The abbess entered, bringing Andreva's satchel with the dolls peeking out. Behind her came Sister Rosalind carrying a satin coif, followed by Sister Penelope.

The abbess smiled. "You have accepted Monsen Montré's offer, I assume."

"Óc, Mother." Andreva curtsied. "But..." Was she released from Father Stefe's sentence?

"You are free to go." She lowered her eyes and her voice became a whisper. "I have burned Father Stefe's orders."

Relief washed over Andreva. She dropped to her knees, took the abbess' hand, and pressed it against her own damp cheek. "Mercés, Mother! I will always be indebted to you for your generosity and understanding."

                    J. Sowards

Sister Agnes gently pulled Andreva to her feet. Tears glistened in her eyes. "We will miss you. Go with God's blessing."

Andreva took the offered satchel. "Thank you for all your kindnesses." She hugged the abbess and the two sisters. Sister Penelope helped remove Andreva's headdress and Sister Rosalind replaced it with the coif.

Holding to Jaques' arm, Andreva walked out of the abbey. She shaded her eyes against the bright sunshine and breathed in the morning air. Jaques led her to his horse, attached Andreva's and Bostel's satchels to the saddle, and mounted. He then pulled her up to sit in front of him. The nuns working in the garden glanced up as the two rode past. The abundant scent of spring blossoms filled the air.

"The old saying is true, I believe." Andreva nestled closer to Jaques. "With spring comes new hope."

"Yes, and from this day on, we shall leave the past and Montsegùr behind, and hope for a kindlier world."

She looked back toward the abbey and waved to the sisters who still stood in the doorway.

With Jaques' arms around her, Andreva's joy was full. She looked forward to their new life together. But mixed with her happiness, she knew that no matter how far they traveled, or where they made their home, a part of her would always live in the shadows of Montsegùr.

author notes

On visiting Montsegùr~

I knew very little about the Cathars when I began writing Shadows of Montsegùr. I thought I could write a story, and then plug in a few facts. Research soon told me the story of Montsegùr was more complicated than that. Writing it took me on a grand adventure that included traveling to Château de Montsegùr and climbing the steep trail to the ruins.

The original walls have been gone for centuries, but the ruins standing in their place still hold the essence of the Good Men's experience. I felt the spirit of those who'd died there. They seemed to appreciate that I had come and had cared enough to write their story.

Inside the ruined castle are the boulders upon which, in my mind, Bertrand stood to rally the Good Men into taking the consolamentum. His voice is silent now. Looking up the now-hallowed stairwell, I imagined hearing Andreva's footsteps echo as they had when she climbed it in search of Bostel.

Stepping outside into a chilly but gentle wind, I looked out over the spectacular view. In the distance lay the village of Lavelanet, with the River Touyre winding through its valley, just as Andreva had described it.

With new respect, I left those walls, hiked down the pog, and descended the challenging trail. I imagined Raoul, dropping his pack and declaring that he could go no farther, for that is what I did. I thought of the two hundred plus people—some hobbling, some carried—making their way down those rocks on that mid-March morning, death awaiting them at the end of the trail.

A stone monument stands beside the meadow where the massacre took place. It greets each traveler before and after their pilgrimage to the top. In French it states:

En ce lieu le 16 Mars 1244
Plus de 200 pesones ont été brulées
Elles n'avaient pas voulu
renier leur foi

In this place on 16th March 1244
More than 200 people were burned
They chose not to
abjure their faith

I stopped beside the monument and listened, hoping to hear one last echo of the past. I heard only silence and the whispering of the wind. The Good Men are long gone into the arms of their Spiritual God.

On the history of the Good Men~

Some modern researchers claim the Albigensian Inquisition never happened despite ample evidence that it did. I cringe when I see "scholars" dismiss this people's suffering, saying their deaths are myths propagated through the centuries. To me, that is like denying the reality of the Holocaust, or insisting that the Twin Towers never fell.

We must be watchmen, lest history repeat itself in our generations.

Suggested Reading~

The Devil's World: Heresy and Society 1100-1300, by Andrew P. Roach, publisher Routledge, 2005

A Fool and His Money, Life in a Partitioned Town in Fourteenth Century France, by Ann Wroe, publisher Hill and Wang 1996

Chronicles by Jean Froissart and Geoffrey Brereton, publisher Penguin Classics, reprint 1978

Heresy and Authority in Medieval Europe, edited with an introduction by Edward Peters, University of Pennsylvania Press, 1980

Web pages of interest:

Russian Books
http://www.russianbooks.org/montsegur.htm

Cathar Castles
http://www.catharcastles.info/montsegur.php

Atlas Obscura
http://www.atlasobscura.com/places/chateau-de-montsegur

Acknowledgements~

My mother's gravestone reads "In Love With the World." Her life's goal was to visit every country she could during her lifetime. When she'd return home from one of her many adventures, I'd sit and listen to her narrate at least a hundred travel slides. She had a talent for remembering dates, histories, and pronouncing each foreign name correctly. I thank her for instilling in me a love for world history.

I also want to thank Kristy Stapley for suggesting I write about the Good Men, Genevieve Ficquet for her advice and translations, and my writers critique group for sticking with me through the development of Andreva's story.

And what would an author do without beta readers? I am so grateful for each honest feedback.

Thank you to my husband for trekking with me to the ruins of Montsegùr in southern France to experience Cathar country.

And last, but most importantly, thank you to Kerry Blair for believing in my story, for her friendship, and for excellent editing.

Shepherds, Bring Your Flocks In Tonight

Pastres, Rintratz Vòstrei Tropèus

Traditional Occitan

full of vim,___ Danc-ing five steps in front___ of Him!
ques - te pas___ frin - gar da - vant eu lei___ cinc pas.

Let's Sing Christmas Again

Cantem Nadal

Traditional Occitan

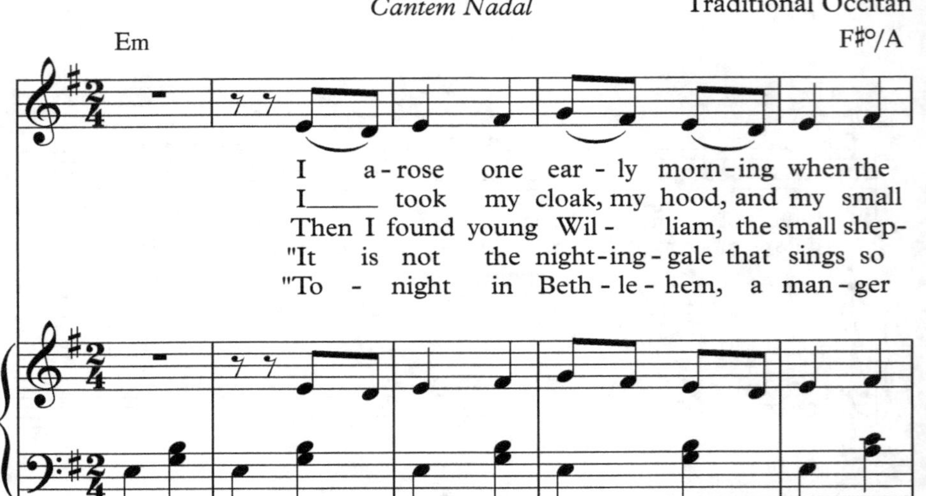

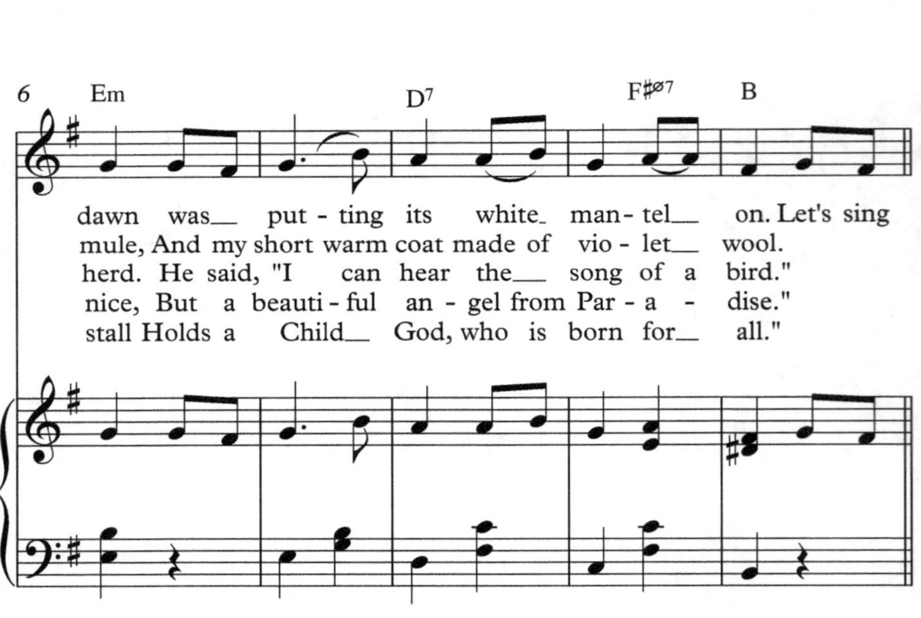

11
Em
D
Christ - mas, Christ - mas, Christ - mas. Let's sing Christ - mas a -
14
Em
gain.   Let's   sing   Christ   -   mas, Christ - mas,
16
D   Em
Christ - mas. Let's sing Christ - mas a - gain.

about the author

J. Sowards was the daughter of her high school's World History teacher, so the school counselor advised her to take Economics instead. Despite that, her inherited love for world history has persisted.

The things she enjoys most are her family, time to write and/or undertake family history research, and rocky road ice cream.

Though well-traveled, Sowards is truly a homebody who nevertheless craves opportunities to take her laptop to the mountains where she can write accompanied by nature.

The author enjoys hearing from readers. Contact her at summerhousebooks@gmail.com.